Sally McGrane is a Berlin-based writer and freelance journalist for *The New York Times*, *The New Yorker* magazine, and others. Originally from San Francisco, she has worked as a journalist in Russia and Ukraine. She wrote *Odesa at Dawn*, her second spy novel, in Odesa.

# Odesa at Dawn

Sally McGrane

V&Q Books, Berlin 2022
An imprint of Verlag Voland & Quist GmbH

Copyright © Sally McGrane
Editing: Katy Derbyshire
Copy editing: Angela Hirons
Author photo: © Gordon Welters
Cover photo: Unsplash
Cover design: pingundpong
Typesetting: Fred Uhde
Printing and binding: PBtisk, Příbram, Czech Republic

ISBN: 978-3-86391-338-0

www.vq-books.eu

# Prologue

'Well! I've often seen a cat without a grin,' thought Alice;
'but a grin without a cat!
It's the most curious thing I ever saw in my life!'

Lewis Carroll, *Alice's Adventures in Wonderland*

## 1

Mr Smiley was a fat, dirty cat, with ragged mouse-coloured fur, mottled with a darker shade of rat. His distinguishing mark, and the reason for his (wholly inappropriate) name was an ancient, jagged scar that ran from his left eye to his right jaw. His apparent indolence was, in fact, a highly-developed gift for intuition: Mr Smiley knew what was coming before it arrived, and made sure to be out of the way – or in the right place.

This talent was, in Mr Smiley's opinion, the key to his success. Of course, there were other important qualities as well. Brutality, the ability to walk away, a gift for the double cross, a keen understanding of the enemy, a keener understanding of your friends. The scar didn't hurt, either. As he said: 'You should have seen the other guy.' Followed by a long, low, rumbling purr.

Naturally, Mr Smiley understood, thanks to various insipid conversations he had overheard in his long life, that there was a general belief among the human set that cats could not speak. Pure stupidity! But then Mr Smiley had a generally low opinion of humans. There was a saying among cats: 'The bigger the brain, the less interesting it is to eat.' In all of Odesa, in fact, Mr Smiley knew of only one man, a poet, who truly understood that cats could talk.

This poet – his name was Fishman, *what a delicious idea* – lived in a small dacha at the edge of town and was, according to his nameplate, also some kind of doctor. Every afternoon, patients came to see him. Once inside, they immediately lay down on a red velvet sofa. There, under the dusky eyes of the icons peeping down from the walls of the poet's office – now and then, the odd ray of sun induced a quick gold wink – these humans behaved in a most astounding manner. Instead of curling up for an afternoon catnap, they lay rigid, arms at their sides, and affixed their eyes to the ceiling. And talked. They talked and talked and talked. The poet folded his hands across his stomach, tucked his chin to his chest, and listened. After fifty minutes, these humans stood up again. Then, smiling or weeping, they left.

Afterwards, the poet – a large calm man with a head of white hair, a white beard, very intelligent, with the exception of an inexplicable inclination to feed the trio of wild hedgehogs who waddled into his garden each evening – sat at his computer. There, he typed up a kind of diary, which was – Mr Smiley's spies assured him – read all over the city. The cats weren't certain how the diary was distributed. Not via paper and ink, like in the old days. Some sort of scent, was Mr Smiley's guess. Mysteriously out of the range of feline olfactory detection, emitted when the poet pressed the button on the right side of his keyboard.

Sometimes Mr Smiley read over the poet's shoulder as he typed. The diary described the goings-on in the city: boring (in Mr Smiley's opinion) fights over language; can a Ukrainian writer write in Russian? – *pah! Let's see him write in Cat!* – altercations at the Worldwide Club of the Odesites; the question of Ukrainian nationhood; ghostly visitations; what he ate for dinner. In this densely populated literary landscape, the only sane creature was the poet's own black puss, the desultory Miss Kitty, who ruled the dacha garden with an iron paw (when she could be bothered), and whose crackling, well-placed bon mots made even a scarred, old battle cat like Mr Smiley chuckle. Of course, there were plenty of human women who talked to cats – in every city, women talked to cats – but the poet did more than talk. He listened. And he understood.

*

It was a hot night, late summer, anxious. A thick darkness had descended to just above the streetlights, which were bright in a patchy way – how had Grisha, the new governor, put it? – 'Like downtown Tbilisi in 1995.' Of course, cats like shadows. Still, Mr Smiley agreed the city could use some serious spiffing up.

With a swish, Mr Smiley curled his tail. Pressed his body to a tattered brick façade. Listened. Felt. Became part of. The city had a single consciousness tonight. As if every building and every being breathed the violence in the air. Tourists in hot pants were jumpy. From car windows, the tinny beats were lower and louder than usual; from every corner came the sound of tyres screeching. The scent of burnt rubber. Soviet-made brakes wailing, heartbroken by their own demise. Boys were sensitive; of all the humans, they felt the energy first, and strongest. They revved their engines, sped through the cobblestone intersections, faster, more dangerous than usual.

Mr Smiley was among the few who knew exactly where the explosion the whole city felt coming was going to take place. Humans – the mafia, in particular – thought they knew everything. But who could know more, in this city, than the cats? The pretty orange ones who ingratiated themselves in exchange for fish; the louche white ones, sleeping all day on the sidewalks, the dark, ragged night-time spies who gathered in groups of six or seven, here on Gogol Street, eyes matted with gunk and bugs, awaiting instructions. The cats were everywhere, on every corner, under every café table, beside every terrace. No one knew more than the cats, and none of the cats knew more than Mr Smiley. For one simple reason: he was their boss.

Of course, he should have given this assignment to an underling, someone he could trust – like the muscular Tabby-kitty, or the clever, vicious Boots. But while all cats could talk, not all cats could make themselves understood to the average human. And this wasn't an average human! No, this was Sima.

Even her name! Ser-a-phi-ma. The fiery angel. Sima to her friends. Simochka to him. How long had he loved her? How could an old alley cat like him even think of love? But since the day Mr Smiley had first caught a glimpse of her long legs, her marmalade tresses, her innocent, yet not entirely innocent smile, Sima had been the one for him. If he were a man! Or she were a cat! She would live like a queen among felines with that golden fur, those shapely limbs. He would make sure of that – if she were his concubine.

He had often thought of just what he would do with – and to – her, but it was no use. As it was, Mr Smiley wasn't sure how she felt about him. Sometimes, it was true, Sima chucked him under the chin and gave him an anchovy if she saw him outside the restaurant. But a lot of women did that. And of course, she had no way of knowing how important he was. How many felines would be thrilled if he showed a tenth – a thousandth – of this interest in them! How they threw themselves, quite literally, at his feet, splayed their hindquarters. But, no. No, he was no fool. Mr Smiley understood that when Sima looked at him, there was no hint of desire – no, for her, he was just another grubby if somewhat endearing stray. Not even good enough to be a pet.

Mr Smiley buried his anger. It wasn't Sima's fault. None of it was. And he knew what was going to happen here, at her mother's restaurant. 'Angelina's.' Quite a cook, that Angelina! She made a wonderful *forshmak*, a perfect combination of herring filet and apples, sugar, vinegar and eggs, mushed to a pasty consistency, ideally spreadable by knife, or tongue of cat – and she wasn't stingy with the leftovers, either. A generous woman with the elegant proportions of old age – as wide as she was tall – oh, Angelina would have made a wonderful mother-in-law for an outlaw like Mr Smiley, who needed the comforts of family life all the more, given the blood he was obliged to spill … He swished his tail in anger. Pipe dreams, again! It didn't matter. What mattered – what really mattered – was Sima.

Sima was in danger, and Mr Smiley was going to save her.

When it was time, he jumped up with surprising grace, and ran to the restaurant's back door. It was open. He poked his scarred head inside.

He was rewarded with a sight of Sima, her marmalade hair pulled back, her skirt hiked up as she knelt to scrub the floor of the restaurant's dining room. What thighs! thought Mr Smiley, licking his lips. She turned her head, and in the darkness Mr Smiley saw the birthmark, shaped like a heart, just under her left eye – a marking that, in a cat, would indicate pure blue blood.

The plate-glass window reflected the night like a mirror. 'ASS-HOLE!' A loud squawk caught the cat off-guard for an instant. 'ASS-HOLE!'

Where was that horrible bird? That would be a silver lining! If Jacques the grey parrot, that large handsome creature, spoiled, taunting, sleek, healthy, his feathers shining like polished stone, happened to die – but the cage wasn't in the window where it usually was. The parrot's cry pierced the night again. 'ASSHOLE!' No time for settling old scores, thought Mr Smiley. The cat looked hard at Sima. And concentrated.

# 2

'ASSHOLE!'

Sima stood. Took off her plastic gloves, rested her hands on her hips. What had she just been thinking of?

'ASSHOLE!'

'Pretty bird,' she called softly, surveying the small, darkened dining room absent-mindedly. It was a hot night, very late – much later than she'd planned. She had turned off all the lights – her mother said she was crazy, but to Sima it always felt cooler that way. Looking around, Sima could make out the grey outlines of tables, with chairs stacked on top of them. For the 'Big Clean' – the first since they'd opened the restaurant a month ago. The heavy zinc bar glinted in a splash of light reflected from the plate-glass picture window. 'You're a pretty bird, Jacques.'

By now, of course, Sima could have found her way around the little dining room – only seven tables! – blindfolded. Sima lifted her arms above her head, up towards the restaurant's soaring ceiling, and stretched. She yawned, a long deep yawn, and dropped her arms. She was tired. In the best possible way, after a day of hard work: up at dawn to meet the fishmonger; pressing a delivery of farmers' tomatoes for homemade juice, dark red and thick like blood; chopping sorrel for the week's green *borscht*. She lifted her long fingers. They were stained just a little still. Dark green. A fresh, verdant smell. Sharp. Like Mother Nature rapping you on the knuckles. Telling you not to give up just yet.

She pushed her green fingertips through her long strawberry blonde hair. With one finger, she touched the black birthmark, shaped like a heart, beneath her left eye. It was one of her habits when she was deep in thought. She wondered if Grisha, the new governor, was really going to come for dinner one of these nights. That was the rumour. She'd heard it several times now.

'ASSHOLE!'

A lot of her friends were really excited about Grisha. Grisha (everyone called him Grisha) was young – not yet fifty – American-educated, forward-thinking. Not to mention the fact that in his native Georgia, he'd been president – twice! And Georgia and Ukraine, they weren't so very far apart. Kind of like first cousins, in the post-Soviet world. Anyway, from what you heard, his reforms had really succeeded back in his country. The traffic police stopped taking bribes, for example. Then he was ousted. And now he was here, in Odesa.

Grisha was a charmer, that was for sure. No Soviet-style politician, locked away in his office. On the contrary, Grisha was always on the go, a real man of the people with his boyish smile, his bowl-cut hair, his post-presidential pot-belly – the kind of man who would order third and fourth helpings of *forshmak* and pay for it too. He didn't go anywhere without a camera crew: On TV, he was always shaking hands with everyone he met – *babushkas*, beachgoers. A month into his tenure, Sima had the feeling that she knew Grisha's famous birthmark – a wine-coloured stain in the shape of the state of Florida that stretched from wrist to knuckles of the governor's right hand – as well as if it were her own.

Should she take the chairs down now? Sima inhaled. The lemon scent of cleaning fluid. Still wet. First thing in the morning, then.

'ASSHOLE!'

The strangest feeling had come over her. Like she'd forgotten something. She shook her head. It would be great publicity if Grisha really did come to dinner with his camera crews.

His political plans sounded good too. *Rout out corruption! Bring in transparency!* But Odesa wasn't Georgia. There, Grisha had been president of the whole country. Here, he was just the governor of a single region. And right here, in Odesa, the region's capital, he was up against powerful forces. Mephisto, for example. The city's mayor had already declared all-out war on the new governor. Sima shook her head in disgust. Mephisto! He'd earned his nickname, that was for sure. A former gunrunner and current Thai boxing champion, with a Russian passport and direct ties to the Kremlin – as Sima knew all too well, short, squat, bald Mephisto could make your life hell.

She sighed. The best approach was to wait and see. Not get your hopes up.

'ASSHOLE!'

Sima looked around again at the friendly grey shapes. What a strange feeling. What could she possibly be forgetting? After all, she'd worked at her mother's beach restaurant since she was six. Twenty years. A wonderful restaurant, everyone said so. Sometimes, they added: 'Why don't we take it off your hands?' Sima and her mother just smiled politely. Nothing ever happened. No one 'took it off their hands'. Until, one night, they did. A year ago, now. A warm summer night, dark and humid. Like tonight, actually.

A policeman had pulled up in a black BMW. Not a regular policeman – a regular policeman could never afford a car like that in his whole life. A crooked policeman, who sauntered over to the kitchen after closing time. He'd said the restaurant didn't belong to them. That they had to get out. Angelina stood in the door., blocking it with her broad frame. 'No,' she'd said. The fire came a few days later. They lost everything. All of it. Burnt to a crisp. Cooks understand: when that happens, you just have to start over again.

'ASSHOLE!'

For six months Sima didn't work. For six months, she got up in the morning and had nothing to do. She'd never experienced anything like it before. As if life was passing through her – she reached out, but she couldn't grasp it.

Finally, to have something to do, Sima signed up for a French pastry course online. She was a natural when it came to sugar sculpting; so good that she won a prize. Children's zombie parties were all the rage in Odesa. So Sima baked a cake in the shape of the undead. She invented an entirely new method to make the eyeballs – butter cream and a hard sugar glaze. The results were eerily lifelike – even the French said so. The judges had never seen anything like it, and Sima came away with a silver medal.

But baking wasn't enough to keep Sima and her mother going. When this space opened up in the city centre, they'd hesitated at first. What they knew was thirty tables, at the beach. But the city centre was an opportunity. So, they sold their family apartment in the centre, the one they'd had for generations.

They had just signed the new lease when Mephisto called. The mayor wanted to invest. Of course, Sima and her mother had known Mephisto – he got his name in a Soviet prison – for years. He had come to the beach restaurant, like everybody else. Sat in the corner with his thick neck and dull eyes.

Sure, they knew it was a risk to go into business with Mephisto. But they thought they could handle it. Until Mephisto stopped by. Sima offered him coffee. He didn't respond. Instead, the mayor of Odesa strode to the centre of her new restaurant. Held up a meaty fist. She'd never noticed just how thick Mephisto's neck was. How the veins bulged whenever he wanted to emphasise a point.

'If you or your mother STEAL...' he was saying, in a deep, angry voice. Sima was so surprised, it didn't even occur to her to be scared. '...ONE' (bulge) 'HYRVNIA...' (bulge). Sima shook herself, tried to pay attention to what he was saying. Something along the lines of, then he, Mephisto, was going to... (bulge) '...TAKE A SAUSAGE' (bulge, bulge) and 'STICK IT...' Here, Mephisto paused. Seemed to decide that further emphasis, in the form of pantomime, would be helpful. He clutched his meaty fist around an imaginary *kielbasa*, then brought it with some violence towards his shaved skull – '... in ONE EAR' (he paused and raised his other fist) 'UNTIL IT COMES OUT' (he clutched what appeared to be the other end of the invisible sausage) 'YOUR OTHER EAR!!!' Then he turned and walked out.

After that, Sima and her mother decided to give Mephisto his money back. If they were frightened, it was of what would happen if they kept working with him. So now they had no advertising budget. None at all.

A small price to pay, as it turned out. Word of mouth was enough, so far. And now? They were working again. People were coming. The new restaurant was different. But it was good. Sima smiled.

'ASSHOLE!'

Jacques the parrot, for one, loved the new location. The parrot always wanted to be at the centre of things. In the old restaurant on the beach, Jacques had lived in the busy throughway next to the big kitchen, surrounded by busboys. A rough, fearless bunch. Pretty free with the word 'asshole'. When the restaurant burned, one of them went back for Jacques. Brave, or foolhardy. Certainly, kind.

'ASSHOLE!'

In the new place, Sima hung Jacques' cage in the big picture window. From there, the parrot could keep an eye on everything that went on in the dining room. But he could also watch over the street – a responsibility he shared with no less a personage than Gogol, who, from a bronze plaque just across the way, looked out over passers-by with a mysterious half-smile.

'ASSHOLE!'

For the 'Big Clean', Sima moved the parrot's cage to the back. Of course, Jacques didn't like that.

'ASSHOLE!'

'Sausage in your ear,' Sima whispered, shaking her head. At least Jacques hadn't picked up on that. Thank goodness for small blessings.

'SQWAWK!'

Sima was tired, all of a sudden. So, so, tired. 'I'll put you back in the window tomorrow, Jacques,' she said. Something tugged at her. A thought, or a memory. 'Promise, pretty bird.'

'SQWAWK!'

Sima paused. She had a feeling it was behind the old zinc bar, whatever it was she'd forgotten. What on earth could it be? Had she dropped something? What was it?

\*

Ten. Nine. Eight. From the doorway, Mr Smiley's lips curved back over his incisors. 'Get down!' he said. 'Get down!'

Seven, six.

Only when he saw Sima bend to the floor behind the bar, in safety, did the cat run out the back way, as fast as his paws would take him.

Five, four.

In the distance, the caged parrot cried out faintly. 'Asshole!'

Three, two, one…

# 3

'With due respect, may I present my report on the bombing of 'Angelina's' restaurant?'

Inspector Krook sat at his desk on the second floor of Odesa's police headquarters. Studied the deep crack that ran like a miniature canyon through the dark brown veneer of his standard-issue desk.

'With due respect, just a few hours ago, "Angelina's" restaurant was bombed.'

With a deep sigh, Krook raised his eyes. Gazed not at the speaker waiting eagerly in front of him, but out the window. There, in the dusty courtyard below, an old striped, grey cat emerged from the shade of the grapevines. Turned his scarred face to the sun. The very image of peace and calm. But Krook knew better: just last week, a moneylender was shot to death right there. Beneath the grapevines. In broad daylight. Krook frowned. That was embarrassing, of course. Made the police look bad.

'Sir, I think with all due, due respect, we should really hurry ...'

With some effort, the policeman lifted his heavy lids. Took in the fresh-faced youngster with dark hair, pink lips, and dimples – *dimples!* – in the crisp, new black uniform. One of these 'New Ukrainians'. A degree in 'Business English', a co-dependent relationship with his new-fangled telephone, idealism out the wazoo. In short: someone with no business being a policeman. Why was Inspector Krook stuck with him? Simple! Grisha, the interloper from Georgia! As governor of Odesa, Grisha had first inspired and then hired this moron.

Not that the problem was that Grisha was from Georgia, Krook reflected. Odesa had always been a multicultural city. Its founding fathers had been French, Italian, Russian. Today, the Odesa region was home to no fewer than 136 ethnicities! No, the problem was that this Grisha was a grandstanding idiot who pretended that opening a Las

Vegas-style drive-through wedding chapel in front of the Regional Administration Office was a piece of meaningful reform. Meanwhile, as everyone knew, whenever there was a threat that corruption was going to be curtailed, it set off a flurry of larceny as everyone tried to get what he could. Who had to deal with that? With the missing guns and the sudden inexplicable lack of staples? Inspector Krook, of course.

Then there were the morons like Dimples. Instead of getting a job in advertising, the kid saw Grisha on TV and joined the police. Great! Now he was standing there in his uniform, demanding Inspector Krook's at least semi-valuable attention.

The uniform! It made Inspector Krook angry all over again. The snappy, black, collared shirt just like the one the California Highway Patrol wore. Like a goddamned TV show. With costuming! Already, Odesites were calling them 'the Instagram Police'. Apparently, this Dimples had even gone to the United States for two weeks, for training. Let's see how long you last, thought Krook. With your 'training'.

Krook sighed. He was no longer a young man, and just now, his belly was threatening to dislodge his own snappy new shirttails.

Sensing he had his superior's attention, the young man launched into his report with renewed vigour. 'Another bombing, with due respect,' said Dimples, who had accepted his colleagues' nickname and tried to make the best of it. 'Sima – Angelina's daughter – got a real scare. I was just there! I interviewed her. She had …' Dimples checked his iPhone, scrolling through his notes. '… extra clean-up to do. The bomb came right through the plate-glass and went off two feet away from her. Luckily, she was looking for something behind the bar. That was, with due respect, a real stroke of luck!'

Krook stared silently at Dimples. Then he let his gaze fall. It settled on the cracked brown desk, as his mind wandered. Did Krook take the occasional gift? Sure he did. How else would his daughter get a doctor's appointment for her diabetes? How was his granddaughter going to get a spot at a kindergarten? The new governor could talk about reforms all he wanted to. Where was the reform that was going to undo the routine hospital visit that had given Krook's no-good son-in-law hepatitis C?

Something was irritating Krook. He realised it was Dimples' voice. 'They'd just installed an old bar. Zinc, super solid. Parisian-made, 19th century. Saved her life! Sima's husband salvaged it from the old Mason's house – you know, the one that just collapsed into itself from neglect last week? What a shame, actually. The architectural heritage that's lost every time something like that happens. With due respect, I'll make a note to talk to Grisha about it when he holds his next "Town Hall Meeting" – you know it's an American thing, all televised! And citizens really get a chance to speak up, at these ...'

'Maybe you oughta work at UNESCO,' barked Krook.

Dimples looked up at him. Pleading.

'Go ahead,' said Krook.

Dimples went back to scrolling with his forefinger.

'"This is Odesa's thirteenth victimless bombing,"' read Dimples. '"All of the bombings have targeted pro-Ukrainian groups – people actively working to keep Odesa part of Ukraine, instead of breaking away to rejoin Russia."'

Krook rolled his eyes. Talk about stating the obvious! But Dimples was still staring at his telephone. '"... The private apartment of internationally acclaimed Odesa poet Yefim Fishman, who is also a practicing psychiatrist ... the Ukrainian secret service's Odesa headquarters ..."' The boy looked up. 'With due respect, last night's bombing fits the pattern – after all, it's well known that Angelina was taking *borscht* to the hospital to feed Ukrainian soldiers wounded fighting the Russians in the east. I suggest we investigate the possibility that the Russian secret services – the FSB ...'

'I know what they're called,' growled Krook.

Dimples paused. Then, breathless, said: 'So, sir, can I investigate the FSB? To see if they're behind this? With due ...'

Dimples broke off. Krook had buried his chin in his chest. The answer, of course, was no: political cases got bumped upstairs to the highest level. No plain Ukrainian copper was going to investigate the Russian secret services. What did they teach that little idiot in San Diego?

Just then, one of Krook's long-time colleagues wandered in. Paused to re-tuck his snappy new shirt into a waistband as generous as Krook's own. He looked at Dimples, then at Krook. His glance was withering. Krook grinned. At least someone understood him!

'Why doesn't Angelina just pay the protection money?' mused the colleague.

Krook shrugged. 'She still thinks her old friends will keep her safe.'

The colleague shook his head. 'Only a cretin could bomb "Angelina's", after they'd tasted her *forshmak*.'

'A good restaurant is a little gift from God,' agreed Krook.

The colleague raised his eyebrows philosophically. 'At least no one was hurt.'

'Oh!' said Dimples, looking up. 'With due respect – that – that's not quite true. Let me see …' He looked down, scrolled. Paused, fingertip hovering. 'You know they have a parrot – an African grey. Ah, yes! Here it is: "Since the explosion, Jacques the parrot has been afflicted … with a stutter."'

# Part One

I have not felt so much at home for a long time as I did when I
'raised the hill' and stood in Odessa for the first time.
It looked just like an American city; fine, broad streets,
and straight as well ...

Mark Twain, *Innocents Abroad*

## 4

Max Rushmore flew LOT from Warsaw. Like the train station, the
new Polish airport was a kind of wonder of modernity. A dream in
steel and electronics and granite; spacious, well-designed, fast, easy
to navigate – from the city centre it was an entirely smooth, seamless
ride, and you were checking in at your squeaky-clean gate practically
before you knew it.

Certainly, given the country's tack towards authoritarianism, its
refusal to take any of the EU's Syrian War refugees, and its generally retrograde politics, the slick lime green posters dangling from
the aviary-esque boughs of the new airport's ceilings struck Max as
a little ironic. 'POLAND: OPEN TO THE WORLD.' Yeah, right.

Still, security was a breeze – well organised, uncrowded. And the
Nordic countries had nothing on the understated decency of the
Poles' duty-free zone. Stocked with all the global musts: stale Swiss

chocolate, bottled French water, bottled local water, soccer championship-themed key chains.

The clientele wasn't quite what you'd find in Copenhagen though, thought Max, as a desiccated man in a suit like a time warp – brown polyester, thin silky shirt, brown narrow-brimmed hat – picked up an 'I Heart Warsaw' coffee mug. Max stopped in front of the key chains. The man stooped a little. His skin was drawn taut over his face and hands. As if he had been living in the desert for a long time and wasn't suited to it. Max turned a key chain over. Felt the sharp ridges and laminated valleys with his fingertips. Glanced down. Black. White. A soccer ball.

With a sudden surprising grace, the desiccated man held the mug up to the light. Studied it. Or rather, affected to: as Max watched, the man's free hand darted out. Fast, like the flash of a lizard's tongue. In a single smooth motion, he pocketed a tin of British breath mints. Impressive, thought Max. For such a casual act of malfeasance. Over the loudspeakers, a woman's voice announced that the flight to Odesa was boarding. The man turned, listened. His right eye was covered in a leather patch. 'Final call for boarding,' echoed the voice. 'Please proceed …' The man with the eye patch lost interest in the Warsaw mug, and Max lost interest in the man with the eye patch. Both men hurried towards the gate.

The national airline had come a long way too, thought Max as they boarded. He was too young to have flown LOT in the days when it was known to the Berliners as 'Landet Och Tempelhof', or, in the Berlin dialect, 'Sometimes Lands at Tempelhof', due to the frequency with which Polish planes were highjacked by passengers desperate to flee the constraints of the Iron Curtain. Still, the LOT of the 90s, with its peeling cabin wallpaper, homemade pastries and unsettling mechanical groans, couldn't have been much of an upgrade. Those planes had nothing in common with this slick new one, small but steady, blue upholstered, purring.

Now that Moscow had cut off flights to Ukraine, you had to go through Kyiv, Munich, Vienna. Minsk. Max chose Warsaw because LOT was having some sort of super sale – 1 euro for a flight to Odesa.

In the old days, of course, a secretary named Kenneth had taken care of conference flights. These days, it was up to the conference attendees. Paid out-of-pocket, with expenses reimbursed on presentation of receipts. 'Under the new policy, expenses will be paid once the report is filed and okayed at all levels,' said a temporary secretary, when Max asked when he could turn in his receipts.

'But that can take a year,' said Max. The decision, she replied, came from the very top.

Ah, well, thought Max, as an entirely sober-sounding pilot announced they were beginning their descent to Odesa, and thanked them for choosing LOT. The only constant is change. The landing would probably be smooth, and none of the passengers would applaud. He was right, on both counts.

*

The aeroplane's rounded door opened onto a hazy, brown sky. Tacked like a paperboard over the shimmering grey tarmac. When Max's turn came, he nodded at the stewardesses, then averted his eyes. He made it a rule not to flirt in English – out of respect for Rose, his wife – and only a fool would try to seduce a Polish woman in Russian. As he stepped across the threshold, the stewardesses smiled through their pink lipstick and sibilant Polish farewells. As if they appreciated his sensitivity.

In the noonday glare of the Black Sea sun, Max blinked. The heat hit like a body – heavy, encompassing. Thick. He shrugged his shoulders under his light wool suit – bought, in keeping with the straightened circumstances of his semi-employment, off the rack. A 'Big and Tall' store, with plastic tags scattered on the floor. In an act of solidarity, Rose had driven over with him. Waited on a plastic bench outside the dim dressing room. Smiled, her rosy cheeks dimpling, when he emerged. Pronounced it 'not bad at all'. The cheap suit pulled a little, in the wrong places. Belly, elbows. Max began to sweat.

A grandmotherly type in a synthetic leopard-print shift wobbled. Max reached out and steadied her. She turned around, nodded gratefully. Ahead of her, a line of passengers filed sluggishly down the steep steel steps. Limped across the tarmac. An accordion-style bus idled, distorted by plane exhaust, in the distance.

You'd never know it from here, thought Max. But somewhere beyond the broken-down Tupolevs, the thirsty grove of trees and the pale crowns of the suburbs, lay Odesa. 'Ah-dee-YES-a!' as the Russians said, eyes brightening. 'Ah-dee-YES-a!' – as if those four syllables held within them all the promise of summer, sunshine and the sea. 'Ah-dee-YES-a!' The wedding-cake opera house. The baroque facades. Built, all of it, according to the 'Golden Rule' – in this free city, went the idea, even the streets should give you room to breathe. 'Ah-dee-YES-a!' With its priests and flaneurs; striped-shirted sailors and tanned girls in short skirts. Everyone, all of them, ready for a holiday in the ruins of what was, once upon a time, the Russian Empire's glittering, glamorous third capital.

Max felt a tug on his elbow. He looked down. A pair of large green eyes were staring at him. A little girl. She was four, maybe five. But small. Elfin. Beneath the large green bow tied in her curly hair, she wore a deeply serious expression. 'Will you carry me?' she said in the sweet, slightly nasal sing-song of Odesan Russian. She looked down at her legs. They were too short for the steel stairway.

In the doorway, the girl's mother was struggling with an infant and a baby stroller. The girl followed Max's glance, then said, 'Mama, can the man carry me?'

'Alright!' she said.

Max bent and picked the little girl up. 'Thank you,' she said, now that they were face to face. 'My name is Cassie,' she said. 'My papa left us.'

'Oh,' said Max. 'I'm sorry to hear that, Cassie.'

She shrugged. 'I told her …' – she nodded towards her mother – '… that he would.'

What a strange little girl, he thought.

'I can see things,' she said, as Max hauled her up. 'My mama says I shouldn't tell people. She says they won't like me.'

'Is that right?' said Max. She nodded, seriously, with those green eyes. Then she lay her head against his shoulder in the warm, sticky way of small children.

Max leaned against the steel railing as the little girl's weight sunk into his left side. His shoulder began to ache. Just a little. He had long ago accepted that whatever magnetism it was that drew women to him also attracted children and dogs. Well, he thought. Everything has its price.

The little girl was wide awake again. Her little body alert in his arms. Those green eyes bored into him. 'Why are you here?' she said.

'Uh,' said Max. He was about to say he was there for work. But the little girl had relaxed again. She seemed to have fallen asleep. The line had not moved. The sun beat down. Max closed his eyes. Turned her question over in his mind. What *was* he doing here?

*

Like most disasters, it was simple. It had taken him a full eight months to tell his wife, Rose, that he had lost his job at the Agency and was now working, part-time, with no benefits, for a private contractor called Nightshade.

When Max did finally come clean, Rose reacted far better than he'd expected. She was more supportive than livid, when she learned just how long he had hidden his semi-unemployment from her. She hadn't even lost her temper when it became clear that Max's confession came about not due to a sense on Max's part that he should be honest with his wife, but rather because he couldn't afford to keep paying the rent on his Bethesda pied-à-terre, where he had been hiding out during the week while he pretended to go to the office.

No, Rose wasn't angry. In fact, to Max's surprise and relief, the news of his total career failure and the resultant end of their joint economic stability had, if anything, invigorated her.

In the weeks following his confession, however, Rose had begun to take active notice of his underemployment. This, Max had thought at the time, was bound to lead to no good.

He was correct. It was not long before Rose hit on an idea that was, ironically, not so unlike the one proposed by Nightshade's HR man, known affectionately as the HR-Prick. Like Max, the HR-Prick had been downsized by their former mutual employer, the CIA. Like Max, the HR-Prick (who had earned this nickname after leading a particularly painful, government-mandated three-day Agency seminar on sexual harassment) had been almost immediately reanimated, if only in a kind of sad, twilit way, by a new gig in his old capacity at the private contractor Nightshade. Like Max, the HR-Prick had jumped at the private contractor's offer, despite the not-insignificant drawbacks of less pay, minimal stability and no health insurance. 'Better than nothing,' could have been Nightshade's employee motto.

Anyway, this very same HR-Prick, calling on behalf of Nightshade, had once urged Max to 'opportunise' his unemployment in order to 'leverage his liquidity'. Which to Max sounded like an activity better suited to a hydraulic pump than a human being, but whatever. Rose's idea was similar. Similar, but more concrete.

In the relentless heat of the Black Sea sun, the line moved. One step down. Two. Balancing the green-eyed girl on one arm and wiping his brow with his free hand, Max slowly descended.

*

A Tuesday. Oh, about a month ago. Over coffee in the late morning sun, on the terrace of the split-level ranch house an hour outside of DC that they could no longer afford. Rose had looked up. Turned her full-wattage smile on him.

Her suggestion was delivered with a lowering of her eyelashes. Shyly. If Max were to take his name off the Nightshade go-to list, she began. Max felt himself brace. Well, she continued – then, he'd be free. Freer, anyway. He could even come to work – full-time, could he picture that? In the wonderful world of real estate. A wonderful world in which she was respected and well-established – or, on her way to being pretty well-established, you know.

Rose's pale blue satin robe slid open, just a little, as she leaned forward over the artificially distressed patio table. The glimpse of his wife's cream-coloured décolleté distracted Max for a brief, dizzying moment. 'Marty and Mike are doing it,' Rose was saying when he tuned back in. Max looked at her, astonished. He hadn't seen her so enthusiastic about anything since the doctor delivered the news that they weren't going to be able to have children.

'You know the Andersons?' Rose continued. 'Marty was just telling me about it at book club. Anyway, Marty says she knows several couples who are doing it. As a second career. Like us! Marty and her husband call themselves "Team Anderson". And it makes sense, you know? After all, a couple – a couple really knows how to work together, how to problem solve. You take advantage of all this "emotional capital" – that's the term Marty used, I know, it sounds a little cheesy, but I mean, it makes sense, "emotional capital" – that you've accumulated. And of course, you're in it together. You're not exactly going to cheat your spouse out of a commission!'

Max had been so glad to see her looking more like her old self, to see a sparkle in those blue eyes – even her loose blonde curls seeming to bounce a little more brightly when she talked about 'accumulating emotional capital' – that he had in all seriousness promised to 'seriously, seriously' consider the idea of taking his name off the Nightshade go-to list. At which point, yes, of course, he would be free to put his various foreign languages to use instead; peddling high-end greater Washington DC-area residences to well-heeled Russian and German and Chinese buyers, and maybe the odd francophone dictator in exile, as part of the duties naturally incumbent on fifty percent of 'Team Rushmore'.

Nightshade's call came the very next day. As far as Max was concerned, the timing couldn't have been better. One day! One day couldn't possibly be considered enough time to have given such a radical career shift adequate thought. One day! Max was free to agree to anything he wanted to. And indeed, the sound of the HR-Prick's squeaky voice on the line brought a stab of brief unadulterated joy to Max's slightly fatty heart. (In the last medical paid for by his Agency health coverage, he tested positive for cat hair allergies and, more troublingly, learned his cholesterol levels were sky high. When he finally came clean to Rose, he told her about that, too. A show of good faith. She immediately put him on a new diet that involved subsisting almost entirely on Greek yogurt).

'Hello, Max? Ahm – Max?' The HR Prick's slightly nasal voice sounded wonderfully familiar as it squeaked into a whine. 'Oh – ahm – good. I was afraid we might have an outdated phone number on file. Let's get down to – ahm – brass tacks, shall we?' The HR-Prick paused. Seemed to be shuffling papers.

Max waited, standing with the phone to his ear in the ruins of what had once been the kitchen – the tardy news of Max's unemployment had put an end to Rose's endless renovations, leaving the heart of the house in media res for the time being, with the half-torn-out kitchen island covered in plastic, and Ikea hook-rugs spread across the unfinished concrete floor. Max and Rose had both grown accustomed to regular minor bodily damage resulting from various stray nails, sharp corners and splinters.

'Verrrrry, ahm, good,' came the voice, finally. 'We'd like to know if you still feel comfortable with your Russian language skills, ahm, not too rusty, you know. We have a couple of leads, ahm, related to the region that the regular, ahm, staff can't handle right now.'

'Sure,' said Max, trying to make it sound as if it didn't matter much to him either way. He shifted his weight against the plywood breakfast bar, and a shot of pain ran up his thigh. Max swallowed a curse.

'Ahm – pardon?' said the HR-Prick.

'Nothing, nothing,' said Max, spotting the culprit: a rogue metal staple jutting out. 'Go ahead. Shoot.'

\*

The next day, Max made his way to a drab, deeply familiar conference room. Located not just in his old building – a 1950s confection known to Agency hands as 'the Flying Saucer' – but on his old floor. In fact, to reach this conference room, Max had to pass the door of his old office. As he made his way down the fluorescent-lit corridor with its linoleum floors, worn thin in patches, Max resisted the urge to pop his head in and see what they'd done to the room where he'd spent the last fifteen years of his life. Instead, Max straightened his shoulders, walked past his old door, and plunged into the meeting space.

Only one of the room's two overhead lights were on, which gave the windowless room the feeling of a cave. The brown office chairs still tilted at slightly odd angles. The blonde wood table was still scratched. Across the table, two men in grey suits rose to shake hands.

One had shaggy, very masculine-looking black eyebrows and high sculpted cheekbones. The other was overwhelmingly pale. His buzz cut caught the light from the single working bulb overhead. Both men wore their suits very narrow – chic – and shared that glossy look that comes from growing up in a country with a highly functional social welfare system. 'Emissaries from across the pond?' Max said as he leaned in. The dark-haired one smiled, showing slightly crooked front teeth that would signal strained circumstances in an American.

'Why, yes!' said the dark-haired man, with inexplicable delight. 'I am Belgian! My colleague …' He nodded at his companion, who registered the acknowledgement with stony silence, '… is a Dane. We are here …'

Overhead, the light flickered, beating like the wings of a moth. A bang sounded. Loud, like a shotgun. The Belgian jumped. Half an inch at least. Max grinned. Apologised and withdrew the flat of his palm from the wall. 'Force of habit,' Max said, glancing at the ceiling. Both bulbs had come back on. They hummed steadily, dousing the room in a restless yellow light. 'Didn't mean to startle you,' Max added, giving the wall a gentle pat. 'Needs rewiring.' Max turned back to the Belgian. 'So, what can I do you for?'

The Belgian frowned. Gathered his thoughts. Then he started over. He leaned in towards Max. 'We are here,' he said, drawing his shaggy eyebrows together, 'on behalf of a group of concerned EU parliamentarians. An informal group. Brought together by a common threat –'

Russia, thought Max.

'Russia,' said the Belgian, drawing his impressive brows together. 'It's right on our doorstep!'

Max nodded, responding to this stunning geographic revelation with as much sympathy as he could muster. He had never been able to take the idea of Russia as a nefarious, all-powerful bogeyman seriously. The country was too disorganised, too chaotic, in too much existential pain. The Belgian was still talking. '... We simply cannot ignore the Russians.'

Trolls, thought Max. With a silent groan.

'In St. Petersburg, entire "factories" of multilingual young people campaign against democratic, Western values,' said the Belgian. '"Trolls", they are called!'

In Max's memory, there surfaced a wan, pale girl in a woollen cap with bunny-ears. He had met her in a makeshift café on Bolshoi Prospekt. St Petersburg. Winter – the last winter of his employment. The girl had travelled an hour with her little boy to see him. The boy was sick, and no matter how many times the girl wiped his nose, it was always running. Max bought them each a piece of cake decorated with a lurid kiwi slice. A big plate-glass window. Outside it was pitch black, and the temperature was in free fall. A digital sign flashed Roman numerals, in red. Minus 25. Minus 29. Minus 30. The girl with the bunny-ears had worked in a new office building on the edge of the city. Twelve-hour shifts. The pay was good, enough to support herself and her little boy. But she'd felt bad after a while about all the terrible things she had to post, about Ukrainians. 'His father,' she said, glancing at the boy, 'he's Ukrainian.' So she went to the press. Now every journalist from New York to Taiwan had interviewed her. Max was supposed to see if there were any crumbs they had missed. There weren't. She was out of a job and aside from the lurid kiwi cakes, Max had nothing to offer. He'd felt sorry for her.

The Belgian was still talking. 'They wage Twitter wars. Yes! They are educated, and they write not only in Russian, but also in French, German, English, Italian and ...' The Belgian peeked at his silent colleague, '... even Danish.'

Max was about to comment that the Russian economy had recently shrunk from the size of Italy to the size of Spain. Instead he pinched himself. Whatever this job was, he wanted it. Max smiled more broadly, by stretching the left and right corners of his mouth towards his left and right ears. It seemed to work.

The Belgian was growing more impassioned, '... Today, the role played formerly by the Habsburg Empire – that is to say, a buffer between Europe and the East – is now being played, though it has gone largely unacknowledged, by Ukraine.'

Ukraine. The overhead light flickered once but decided to stay on. Ukraine caught Max's attention. He hadn't been there since the Maidan protests that had ousted the pro-Russian puppet president. A quick trip, just a couple of days. Max had caught a plane from Moscow to Kyiv. Winter. Cold. The central square – the Maidan – was at the height of its occupation; the smell of petrol hung in the air; a handful of students were decorating a Christmas tree at the square's centre.

For the next twenty minutes, the impassioned Belgian delivered the standard 'Ukraine for Dummies' lecture. In the great tug of war between Russia and the West, Ukraine was the rope. The Russians were pulling hard in the industrially rich, largely Russian-speaking east, sending in unmarked soldiers and weapons, waging an unofficial but de facto war. They had local support too: in the east, plenty of Ukrainians wanted to break away from Kyiv and go back to being part of Russia. The Ukrainian-speaking western part of the country, on the other hand, yearned for Europe. The tension between 'pro-Russians' and 'pro-Ukrainians' threatened to tear the fledgling Ukrainian democracy in two.

Max grunted. The Belgian shot him a glance. 'Fascinating,' said Max.

But that wasn't all! continued the Belgian. Part of the reason Russian-speaking Ukrainians wanted to break away from Kyiv was that Russia's ubiquitous state-run media had been broadcasting an all-out smear campaign against Ukraine; Russian news clips showed, for example, reports that Ukrainians captured, cooked and ate little Russian children. 'I have many friends in Ukraine,' said the Belgian, with a weird chuckle. 'And I can assure you, they do not cook and eat any children!'

'Yes, yes,' murmured Max. 'Quite outrageous, this propaganda.'

The Belgian glared at him from beneath his shaggy brows.

Oh, right, thought Max. It's not called propaganda any more. These days it's called 'Information Warfare'. Like regular war but sexier, and without such a preponderance of actual deaths. Waged not with guns and drones but through television, Facebook, Twitter. Much like its neologistic big sister, 'Hybrid Warfare', which called to mind an expensive environmentally-friendly car, 'Information Warfare' came across as young and fun. Easy to grasp, even for politicians. Easy to explain, even to journalists.

It was the kind of thing Max hated; the kind of coded talk he'd never been good at. If you wanted to talk about propaganda, why not call it propaganda? He just didn't see the point of making up new terms, as if civilisation were evolving, as if history were linear, instead of repeating itself over and over – and that inability to sell himself and his work as something splashy and new, it had held him back. He knew that. With a quick movement, Max rubbed his eyes against the conference room's non-flickering light.

The Dane was utterly still. The Belgian leaned in, so that his chin was almost touching the scratched blonde wood table. Max leaned in too. 'Russia is waging an information war,' the Belgian confided. He paused. 'And we are losing.'

Max nodded. On the phone, the HR-Prick had told Max to agree to whatever they proposed. (The HR-Prick had also alerted Max to the fact that, due to a merger, they were both now working for FORCE ONE. Nightshade no longer existed. Max said it was all the same to him and hung up).

Now, in the name of FORCE ONE, Max agreed to fly to Odesa in a week's time and attend a conference on this important topic of 'Information Warfare', etc., etc. The Belgian thanked him profusely for his time and interest and said some of the usual things about building bridges and strengthening the transatlantic relationship. Max nodded. He was just thinking about the best way to break it to Rose – somehow the image of a camel with a piece of straw on its back came to mind – when the Dane placed both palms on the table and unexpectedly availed himself of speech.

'In my country,' he said in a clipped, serious voice, 'we have forest trolls. We have trolls of the plains, the lakes, the rivers and the paths. In my country, we are not afraid of trolls.'

# 5

Max had sweat through his suit by the time he and his small charge finally reached the bottom of the aeroplane stairs. He deposited the girl gently on the ground. Cassie stood on her short little legs, looking in the direction of a shiny black van. In front of it there now stood a curvy, earnest girl dressed like a waitress and holding a sign: 'Trilby. Rusmoor. Albu.'

'That's you,' sighed the little girl.

Max nodded. *Rusmoor, Rushmore* – Max wasn't going to split hairs. Let them misspell his name if they wanted. What did he care? But *Trilby, Albu* – he groaned. Of course, he should have expected Alan Trilby to be here, and Vlad Albu. 'Tweedle Dum and Tweedle Dee' as the two elder statesmen were known among the younger, more waggish members of the post-Soviet conference circuit. Under normal circumstances, Max would be happy to see them. They had always treated him like an annoying little brother, but he didn't mind. Now, though – news travelled fast in these circles. Max was hot, tired, sweaty and in no mood to joke about his moribund career.

'You're lucky,' said the little green-eyed girl. She threw an accusatory look across the tarmac. 'You don't have to get on that stinky bus.'

'You're right,' said Max.

'I'm always right,' she said, sadly. Then her voice changed. Steadier, deeper. Adult. She straightened, seemed to grow taller. The green eyes were empty, as if the girl had absented herself. 'You'll find your love here,' she intoned. 'But you might lose her too.'

'Uh,' said Max. He was about to tell her he was married to his love, and that she was in Washington DC worrying about kitchen islands, when the little girl relaxed. Became a child again.

'Cassandra!' called the girl's mother. 'Don't scare the nice man!'

Cassie shrugged. Max set off in the other direction, towards the van. Years ago, on the Agency's 'intuition' test, he had scored an unheard-of 98 percent. They had wanted to run a whole battery of tests on him, after that but old Rex, his mentor, said no, it might interfere with Max's gifts. Now, he couldn't quite shake the feeling that the spooky little girl was right.

As he climbed into the black van's ice-cold interior, Max thanked the curvy, earnest girl dressed like a waitress, and she beamed back at him. Then, to be fair, Max gave a quiet nod of additional thanks to the foresight of the organisers of this particular boondoggle conference, 'Victory in a Time of Hybrid War: In the Black Sea Region', for the provision of air-conditioned transport. As his damp shirt turned cold and clammy underneath his jacket, Max sighed. He wondered, not for the first time, if there was some kind of rule that said you couldn't hold a conference unless you put a colon in the title. And if so, how hard could it be to use the colon right?

# 6

'It's like Siberia in winter in here!' said Alan Trilby in his old-Etonian accent as he stepped from the sweltering tarmac into the air-conditioned van. He was dressed, as always, as if he'd stepped off the set of a low-budget Cold War spy drama. Olive trench coat, belted. Narrow-brimmed felt hat, pulled low. Smudged coke-bottle spectacles.

'Don't exaggerate, please,' said Albu from the front. The Romanian had defected from Bucharest in 1980, been thoroughly cleaned out at Langley, then posted to Munich, where he was put in charge of internal reports on Black Sea politics at Radio Free Europe – a job that left him plenty of time to pursue his two passions: medieval churches and classic German children's literature.

Now, Albu inclined his large head, bald except for a black monk's fringe. Trilby took out a pipe. Without lighting it, he placed it between his lips. 'My dear Albu,' he said as the van pulled away. 'When did we last meet? Was it Budapest? "War, Peace, Economics: Development" …'

'I believe,' said the Romanian with great dignity, 'we last met in Prague. "Security Memorandum of Today's: Conflicts".'

Max looked out the van's tinted window as the two men fell into discussion about the current Ukrainian president – a pro-Western oligarch known as the 'Bonbon Baron', after his eponymous brand of sweets. The Bonbon Baron had made his fortune in the 90s, buying up defunct Soviet confectionary factories for pennies. Using the old Soviet recipes, he was able to turn a very tidy profit among denizens of the former Soviet Union who, though now divided into various distinct countries, were still united in their love of inexpensive childhood sweets. But the Bonbon Baron was pro-Ukrainian, someone who wanted to break away from Russia's sphere of influence and align with the West. This had already led to tension with the Kremlin: Russia's leaders had responded to his election by taking the immediate and unpopular measure of banning the sale of his candies within their country's borders.

'It's remarkable,' sniffed Albu, 'to think that low-cost sweets are a quite war-resistant income. If the Russians attack your coal mines or your steel factories, well. Everything grinds to a halt. But cheap chocolate? People always want that.'

'True,' said Trilby, with that impressive accent that, like so much else about him, was completely put on – Alan Trilby having spent the first two decades of his life in Eugene, Oregon. 'The Bonbon Baron has a good eye. We see that with Grisha.'

Ah, thought Max. Grisha, the former president of Georgia, whose last name was unpronounceable for anyone who didn't speak Georgian ('You can call me Ivan Ivanovitch, if you want,' he'd told a reporter, when asked about his preferred form of address. 'But my name is Grisha').

Of course, Grisha was the biggest news in the region, ever since the Bonbon Baron appointed him Odesa's governor. From what Max could tell, the thinking seemed to be that if Russian troops started annexing Ukraine piece by piece, most of the world would just shrug. But Grisha, whose gift of the gab had delighted journalists and George Bush alike, had an unusually high profile in the West. By placing Grisha in the east of Ukraine, where the Russians were likely to head next, the Bonbon Baron was betting that the Western world would pay some attention if the Russian military moved in. This in itself might work as a deterrent for the Kremlin.

Grisha, for his part, had jumped at the chance to escape his post-presidential retirement-slash-exile in Brooklyn. Where, Max had read in the 'Style' section of the paper of note, the former president had cultivated a hipster beard and engaged in a quixotic attempt to stave off death by boredom with the help of cocktails, bicycling, and an increasingly eccentric coterie that included a special 'bite' masseuse, who really used her teeth.

A showman who spoke perfect English, Grisha was the kind of man who attracted myths, reflected Max, as Trilby and Albu discussed whether the new governor could hold off the Russian military's 'little green men' through sheer force of personality. His appetite was so insatiable that aides worried he might die at the dinner table; he was a cocaine fiend; he held his press conferences at three in the morning because he'd sold his soul to the devil. Then there was his political chutzpa. Take, for example, the morning when then-President Grisha declared war on Russia. After the Russian president announced he was going to hang Grisha up by his balls, Grisha quipped: 'Why is the Russian president so interested in my genitals?'

From the front seat, Albu had begun describing a wonderful little church in downtown Cologne where the walls are decorated with the bones of 11,000 virgins. '... of course, the bones are men's,' came Albu's deep voice. 'Soldiers probably.'

Max shrugged. He knew Grisha, a little. Had shaken his hand a couple of times – the hand with the famous wine-coloured birthmark in the shape of the state of Florida that ran from his wrist to his knuckles.

Max stared out the van's tinted windows. There were weeds on the runways. '... and you know,' Albu was saying, 'this de-Sovietisation of public symbols that the Bonbon Baron has ordered – it's the kind of cheap populism that masks a lack of progress on a policy level ...'

'Yes,' murmured Trilby comfortingly, 'yes, that's right.'

'1,300,' said Max. The sound of his own voice surprised him a little. 'That's how many statues of Lenin they've taken down, already. A hermit – one of these holy types – has been wandering the countryside outside of Kyiv, with a nose ...'

No one said anything.

'... in a wheelbarrow,' Max added. 'It's a giant iron nose. Really heavy. So he has to use a wheelbarrow.'

Albu coughed. Silence filled the van. As if the two older men had only just realised Max was there.

*

The van parked in front of a one-storey airport building. Dull cinderblock façade. A single evergreen bush. The VIP arrivals lounge.

How the other half lives. Max thought of little Cassie and her family. They were probably still out on the tarmac, sweating.

Trilby and Max thoughtfully averted their eyes, as the Romanian manoeuvred his large, heavy frame towards the door of the van. First one leg, then the next.

'I believe I know which one the Hotel Gagarin is,' Trilby announced.

'You think it's that same one?' said Max, with a grin. 'What was it, '97?'

Trilby closed his eyes, like a Buddha, and smiled. '1999, I believe. Right out of Tarkovsky, even then. Hardly fit for a gathering – of this calibre. Ah, well.'

Max was still grinning at the memory – or what remained of it, anyway; a series of dystopian still frames tinged in dark green and black – when a sudden movement drew his attention back to the van. The Romanian had tentatively placed his weight on one foot shod in a plain black shoe. Apparently satisfied with the support it offered as better than none, Albu heaved himself all at once onto this shoe. He and his monk's fringe came to a halt upright, and with both feet on the ground. Ah, thought Max. He felt suddenly very sorry for the two old men. What kind of geriatric conference was this going to be? And how long before he'd be in the same boat? Fifteen years? Twenty, tops.

'Did you know,' said the Romanian, looking around, slowly, 'that the Soviet space program originated in the quest for, well – nothing short of human happiness?'

'Why, my dear man, I did not,' said Trilby.

'Yes, the first Russian space engineer was a devotee of a philosophy,' said the Romanian. 'Called Cosmism. In the 19th century they had already conceived of space travel ...'

With a first show of impatience, the curvy, earnest girl herded them towards the cinderblock building. 'What need was there for man to conquer space?' continued Albu, not at all perturbed. 'The answer was very practical: when we achieve perfect human happiness, the souls of the dead will be resurrected. And they will all need places to live.'

Inside, the airport's VIP lounge was tiled in slabs of shiny rose-coloured stone. Like a 3-star hotel's bathroom. The curvy, earnest girl ushered them to a row of giant, overstuffed armchairs, then collected their passports. No standing in line for VIPs, thought Max. Passport control was for the little people.

'I don't know if you've ever seen footage of Gagarin's life,' said Albu, after he'd half sunk, half fallen into his faux-leather seat. 'He grew up in a hut, literally a wooden hut. I think perhaps they had a goat.' The Romanian paused, shifted his large black shoes. 'Only a deep capacity for mystical belief could have taken that village boy and sent him to the heavens in a spaceship.'

The curvy, earnest girl reappeared carrying a tray. She set three thin white cups on a glass table. The tea was transparent, with a high sour taste, garnished with the East's eternal, heartbreakingly pale slice of lemon.

# 7

It all started with the eyeballs. That's what Luddy 'the Lion' Shturman thought, as he lay on the narrow fold-out bed in the lime green bedroom he had rented in a communal flat on Pushkin Street. He was feeling jumpy. He tried to remember his self-improvement mantra. From jail. He closed his eyes. Focused. 'I'm a rock star I'm a rock star I'm a rock star,' he muttered.

'Positive visualisation,' they'd called it. Supposed to keep him off the juice when he got out. Well that hadn't worked, had it? Still he had enjoyed those Thursday afternoons. Tearing photos out of magazines. Gluing them together. 'Feelings collage', that's what the touchy-feely chick with a man's haircut had called it. Tai Chi. Your own personal mantra. *I'marockstarI'marockstarI'mafuckingrockstar.*

The room shimmered a little with a rosy light reflected from the bright pink façade of Odesa's best hotel – the Bristol – directly across the street. When the cash started coming in – and now that 'the King' was on his way, that had to be pretty soon – Luddy was going to rent the penthouse over there. Pretty girls, pool parties, eight balls. *I'marockstarI'marockstarI'mafuckingrockstar.*

From his prone position on the fold-out bed – the heat was really getting to him – Luddy performed his signature move. Opened his mouth wide, shook his head from side to side, and exhaled a long, silent ROAR!

'Mr Shturman?' a woman's voice, from the kitchen. The matriarch. 'Everything ok in there?'

'Fine!' barked Luddy. Silence. Good. The little plastic fan ticked. Emitted a light breeze. Moved the hot air around. Maybe he'd buy this little family an AC unit once he came into some real money. And he was on the right path, he could feel it. In his fingertips. Taste it on his tongue. Oh yes. This was one of the great ideas. *I'magoddamnfuckingrockstar. I'marockstarI'marockstar.*

Luddy dozed. When he woke up again, he heard the sound of dishes, clank, clank, clank, and his mind began to wander over recent events ... A crash. Broken glass. The landlady cursed. Luddy felt a shooting pain in his head. He closed his eyes.

A month ago. Back in Miami. Luddy 'the Lion' Shturman had been out of the slammer for a whole week. He'd rented a shitty little room downtown, brown and green. Like a fucking stage set for a 70s movie, except it smelled worse.

It was the kind of situation that got a man thinking. Philosophic. So, sure. Luddy was a man of a certain age, and like other men of a certain age, he'd made a few fucking mistakes in his life. Who hadn't? The answer was: his brother Perfect Sergey. Perfect Sergey. He was a dentist. Had a nice practice in New York. Green Point. Good for fucking Perfect Sergey. *I'marockstarI'marockstar.*

Right before Luddy got out of the slammer, Perfect Sergey had flown down to Miami to see him. Offered him a job when he got out. 'Lyosha,' he'd said. 'Masha forgives you. You can work with us, train as a dental hygienist.' Luddy told him to fuck off, and not to call him Lyosha. He'd been Ludwig ever since his stint in West Berlin in the 80s. 'Mad King Ludwig', that's what they'd called him, and it stuck. Anyway, he was too old to start sticking his fingers down strangers' throats. No thank you.

The fact was, Luddy had never fit in with his family. 'The cuckoo's egg', his father used to call him. His mother had always shot his father an angry look, then. Well, Luddy's mother had loved him. She'd always loved him, even with his fiery temper. He was always getting into trouble, as a kid. 'You're just too clever for your own good,' she would say, proudly. 'Just too many ideas!'

He didn't even look like them, with his bright red hair. The birthmark, so dark it was almost black, in the shape of a heart, under his left eye. When his little brother was born, Perfect Sergey, he'd had chestnut-coloured hair like their parents. But Luddy's mom did always say there was a great aunt, on her father's side, who'd had red hair. Or, auburn anyway. And even the birthmark, she seemed to recall ...

The first thing Luddy did when he was old enough was get that awful birthmark removed. Now there was just a jagged white scar there. It looked good, he thought. Tough. *I'marockstarI'marockstar.*

A knock on the thin door. 'Mr Shturman? Tea?' Luddy held his breath. Pretended to be dead. She went away. He exhaled. Luddy was just a kid, really, when his family left Odesa for Netanya. Even so, he saw right away that it was no place for him. West Berlin was no picnic, either. But at least he could get a little action. A little nightlife, a little glamour. He started setting fires for the local Russian mobsters.

But 'Mad King Ludwig' went a little overboard in Berlin and had to get out, fast. The Wild West – that was the place for him. While Luddy was in Berlin, Perfect Sergey had moved to New York. Brighton Beach, a little one-bedroom. Got married. Luddy moved in, got his bearings, tried to put the moves on his brother's wife (it was an accident, really, he hadn't meant to). He moved out.

He'd started in on his arson-for-hire services in earnest, after that. Got in with the Italians. Started working the front rooms: crappy little Irish rope dealers, carpenters, whatever. Collecting the 'pizzo' that kept them from burning to the ground. He was young, he was handsome. Long hair, a real mane. They started calling him 'the Lion'. King of the jungle! He liked that. He started working out, pumping iron, getting bigger and bigger. Roaring, whenever he wanted to make a point.

Finally, Luddy got a tip. Why freeze your tuchas off in New York when you could be working with the Colombians in Miami? Cocaine hadn't gone out with the 80s. This was the 90s, and business was still good. So he'd headed south.

For respectability's sake, he started a strip club. Named it 'Weekend at Bernie's', after the movie. He'd really liked that movie. Witty, it was. The real America. The real American dream. Nice cars, good roads, plenty of shopping malls to set fire to.

*

'Mr Shturman?' floating through the room's rose and green light came a woman's voice. It was Ilona, the landlady. 'Mr Shturman? Would you like to join us for breakfast?'

'NO!' shouted Luddy. Then, just in case the landlady's buxom daughter was there, he added, 'thanks.' Luddy closed his eyes again, in the heat. Was that pounding the sound of his heart? Fuck!

He'd gotten along with the Colombians like a fish in water. They were creative like him. Together, they'd worked out a bunch of good plans. Shipping cocaine from Ecuador to Russia, hidden in cargoes of iced shrimp.

Then came the best idea of all. He was out one night with Alejandro, one of the Colombians. Luddy had had a bad day – one of the girls was threatening to walk, and there'd been a big scene. Sure, they'd worked things out, out in the parking lot. But the whole thing had depressed him. He wasn't a bad guy! He was a hardworking small businessman, trying to keep his club afloat.

So that night he went out with Alejandro the Colombian to blow off some steam. Alejandro started bellyaching. The coastguards were breathing down their necks, blah blah. At which point Luddy – the Lion – had a brainwave. He roared! At first, Alejandro laughed. But Luddy wasn't kidding. The next day, he called up a buddy in Kronstadt. There was a graveyard there full of old Soviet hardware, just waiting for a buyer. All kinds of nuclear subs. 'Whiskey, Tango, Foxtrot,' they were called. That made Luddy laugh. Army talk. What the fuck!

He found a 'Foxtrot'. Started bargaining. The Colombians ate it up. Of course! How better to transport drugs than underwater? The Foxtrot, plus crew, was going for 5.5 million USD. A bargain! The Colombians were all set to go.

Luddy was sitting at his kitchen table, drinking a cup of coffee, a papaya juice, and sweating when he heard a terrible ruckus. The DEA. They kicked down Luddy's front door. Before he knew it, he was on the floor. Boot in his neck. He watched blood – his blood – spread over the white linoleum floor. He didn't even feel his nose break.

After that it was prison. Prison. Prison. Now, in the present, Luddy heard the sound of dishes clanking in the communal kitchen outside his door. He cursed.

*I'marockstarI'marockstarI'mafuckingrockstar.* In the violently rosy, reflected light, Luddy looked down. He was losing weight like crazy in this heat. Like a popsicle. Fuck! His hands were shaking.

# 8

The Hotel Gagarin turned out to be brand new. A towering patch-work of silvery windows and slippery, cheap white stone accents. Twenty storeys high, it dwarfed the Soviet high-rises that used to ruin the shoreline.

The three men descended – Albu accepted the driver's arm, this time – and stood for a moment. Heads thrown back. Looking up.

Max heard his own voice. 'Did you know,' he was saying, before he had really thought about it, 'that this entire city is built on catacombs?'

Trilby placed his pipe, still unlit, between his lips. Albu rubbed his neck.

'Sandstone catacombs,' said Max. 'These new buildings are all completely illegal. Developers bribe a judge, get the permits.' Trilby was sweating beneath the felt band of his hat. Max looked back at the towering hotel. 'All these high-rises, they're much too heavy. One day, the entire city is going to fall in on itself.'

Albu broke the ensuing silence. 'Probably not today,' he said, and plunged ahead towards the lobby on his large black shoes.

*

Max's room was on the fifteenth floor. He opened the curtains. Looked out. Onto a ten-storey car park. Resigned to the view, Max turned his attention to the next order of business. Where was the minibar? He looked around. Opened one flimsy white cabinet after another. Nothing. No fridge. No drinks. Zero, zilch.

He sighed. Opened his laptop. Logged on to his email. This was one of the conditions Rose had laid out: if he was going to travel for work, he had to stay in regular touch. 'And I don't want to hear any more about "secret locations" and "keeping a low profile",' she'd said, hands on her wonderfully solid hips. 'You all say that, but your old colleague Marie – you know, the one who used to be in charge of organisation in Moscow; she just moved back for that adorable husband of hers? Well, we had a welcome lunch for her, just the ladies, and she told us that the other side, or sides, or *whatever* – that they know where you are anyway. Or they can find out if they want. And that, actually, the more normal your behaviour is – the more, that is, you communicate with, say, your wife – the less attention you're bound to attract. So, there.'

Even if he'd wanted to go into the two competing theories – the relative merits of 'High Contact' versus 'Silent Mode', which forbade everything from smartphones to Google searches – Max didn't have the heart. He made a mental note to have a word with Marie next time he saw her. Then he agreed, he agreed, he agreed. Capitulated. So, now, he hit 'compose' on his email account and watched as auto-fill turned his 'Ro' into 'Rose Rushmore'. An automated affirmation that they belonged together, that she belonged to him, that all was right in the world.

He typed:
*To: Rose Rushmore*
*Subject: Blue without you*
*Hot as Hades here. Miss you already. Have a cool drink for me.*

Almost instantly, Rose wrote back.
*Re: Blue without you*
*Don't forget I've confirmed with 'Team Anderson' for the 'Mixing business and pleasure' dinner party at their place Thursday. Try not to be a jetlagged disaster, ok?*

*Re: re: Blue without you*
*My one and only, I think of nothing but 'Team Anderson.' And you, of course. Will be fresh as a daisy. This looks to be quick and painless. Like a lobotomy. Luv ya.*

Max logged off before she could write again. Looked around. Everything was white – the faux-wood floors, the bed, the curtains. Max undressed, turned on the shower. The water was scalding hot. He turned the tap left, then right, then left it in the middle – no difference. He called reception. 'Oh yes,' said the girl who picked up, brightly. 'Try again in twenty minutes.'

Max lay down on the bed. In twenty minutes, he tried again. If anything, the water seemed hotter. Forget it, he thought, and headed downstairs.

\*

'Oh, there you are, Mr Rusmoor!' The lobby, too, was blindingly white. No socialist-realist sculptures. No massive wall art. Still the place retained a Soviet feel. As if the architects simply couldn't let go of their formative ideas of what a hotel should be.

Max looked down. The curvy, earnest girl from the van had taken his elbow. 'I'm so glad I found you. Cocktail hour begins in just a few minutes – right over there, see? By the … little, small tree?'

'Sure,' said Max, spotting a sad, green plant. 'What's that, a ficus?'

She beamed. 'Ah, the ficus. Yes. But I just received an urgent message – from your wife.'

Max took the piece of paper she held out to him, and then mumbled his thanks. She smiled earnestly, as if they had something in common. Respect for the importance of family, perhaps. Or maybe an interest in the happiness and well-being of women in general. And, at that moment, a dedication to the happiness of his treasured wife, Mrs Rusmoor, in particular.

# 9

Max folded the note and put it in his wallet. Then, following its instructions, he took the steps down to the hotel's massive restaurant. Wave-shaped windows. Through another room to a pair of tinted glass doors. Emerged into a shopping mall. Huh, he thought. So the hotel connects directly to the shopping mall. What an American idea.

The mall itself was an original: made entirely of black glass, and shiny with artificial light. Max stepped onto the inclined moving walkway that took the place of escalators. A flash of movement caught his eye. Was he being followed? He turned and looked. But the mall was deserted in its eternal night.

On the fifth floor, Max found the children's toy store. Just as the note, which had not, in fact, come from Rose, said he would. He did a quick double take at the collection of child-sized luxury cars in the display window: a real, drivable little Ferrari. A Porsche. A Range Rover. Max kept an eye out for the Barbie Dream House, as instructed. In the corner. Barbie and Ken were – barbequing? – on the front terrace. They looked happy. After all these years ... Huh, thought Max. Good for them. He made his way over, saw the unobtrusive door to the left, opened it and went inside. The door clicked shut behind him.

Looking around, Max found himself in a tidy little waiting room. There were no windows, but the lighting was good. Everything was tan. He took a seat on a tan sofa. Spotted a copy of the *Odesa Preview* – the local English-language magazine – on the tan table. Max picked it up. 'Special edition: BOATS!' read the cover. A photo showed a gold-leaf stairwell lit by a waterfall of a crystal chandelier, with a pretty girl in a sailor's cap, barefoot, wearing very short white shorts and a striped, boat-neck shirt. Her legs were incredibly long. She had red hair and was smiling. 'Take a tour inside the oh-so-intriguing *Inna*', read the sub-caption.

The girl looked every bit as intriguing as the ship, thought Max. Still it was the ship that caught his eye – something about the interior was familiar. As if Max had been there before. But surely he'd remember the gold leaf? Well, it was a far cry from the old Soviet tub he'd spent six weeks on back in the nineties, working undercover as a cabin boy. Max shrugged. Turned the magazine over. Read the label on the reverse. 'Special Delivery,' it read. 'Potomac, Maryland. Persimmon Tree Road. James and Suzanne Dunkirk.'

Max stared. Could Jim Dunkirk be here? It seemed unlikely. As head of the CIA's Moscow office, Jim Dunkirk had people to oversee, diplomats to entertain. There were dinners nearly every night in his spacious, if bugged, government-paid flat (Max had been among the guests on occasion). And, ever since the Ukrainians had stopped all direct flights to Russia, it was a real headache to get from there to here. Anyway, Odesa was a backwater – 'an open sewer and a criminal outlet,' as old Rex, Max's dear departed mentor had once put it, so corrupt that all reasonable countries (including Russia) had given up on trying to keep tabs on what happened there.

Max glanced at the 'BOATS!' issue, again. Could Jim Dunkirk, Max's senior by fifteen years and about a thousand successes at the Agency, possibly be here? And – might it mean something good? A promotion? A political assignment? Maybe –

Max was still musing when Jim Dunkirk himself entered the little tan room. Tall and silver-haired, Dunkirk walked in with his famous limp, begotten in the 80s while passing Russian secrets to Afghan rebels. Right hand out, ready to shake. Max only had time to half stand before the hand reached him. Obliged him to take it. He shook Dunkirk's hand with as much dignity as possible from his semi-crouched posture. Was it Max's imagination or did Dunkirk prolong the interaction just a little longer than absolutely necessary? Dunkirk finally let go of his hand and Max managed to achieve a fully upright position. 'Me and Sooz are thinking about redoing our boat,' said Dunkirk, nodding at the magazine in Max's hand. Dunkirk smiled. He looked younger than ever, as if success were ageing him backwards.

'Who's the girl?' said Max.

Dunkirk shrugged. 'Somebody's daughter, mistress. We could look it up.' Dunkirk's eyes rested on the magazine cover. 'Love what they've done with that gold leaf. Sooz would go crazy for something like that. On a smaller scale, of course. Boy I tell you, if you want any really good work done – bevelled glass, say ...'

Max wondered for a moment if Dunkirk really thought Max might be in need of yacht remodelling advice. Dunkirk's thin Boston Brahmin lips kept curling up, showing his small incisors.

'... We've got a friend, German surgeon – boob jobs, basically, he's got a string of clinics in the Black Forest – invited us out on his boat. Showed us his cabinets. Gorgeous stuff. Anyhow!' Dunkirk put an arm around Max's shoulder to guide him. Max was uncomfortably aware of the fact that he hadn't showered. Dunkirk frowned and continued. 'Good to see you, Rushmore. Sorry to spring this on you like this. Bet you weren't expecting to see me.'

By now Dunkirk had led Max back into another room. The single window was blacked out. Recessed bulbs shed a soft, bright light on a large rosewood desk and an orchid. Dunkirk motioned for Max to sit, and then made his way, with that famous limp, to the burgundy leather seat behind the desk. 'Nice digs, right?'

Max nodded. 'Puts the Moscow office to shame.'

'Hell, it puts HQ to shame,' said Dunkirk. 'I mean – orchids!'

Then Dunkirk shook his head, in a bygones-be-bygones kind of way. 'Max. I don't mind telling you, your work on the Ostranova case got a lot of attention.' Max tried not to feel good about the compliment. 'Complete waste of time and energy, of course,' Dunkirk added, breezily. Max felt himself deflate a little. Kicked himself for not having his emotions under control. Especially around Jim Dunkirk, who was not only not unemployed, but who had his own, albeit small-ish, yacht, plus bona fide captain's licence, and who had tried on at least one occasion to seduce Rose.

Dunkirk was still talking. '... You turned a couple of heads, Max, I don't mind telling you. Reason you're here is we asked for you over at – what the hell're they called now? – FORCE YOU?'

'FORCE ONE,' muttered Max.

'FORCE ONE. Right. Whatever. FORCE ONE. They had to invent a whole new protocol, actually.' Dunkirk chuckled. 'Turns out they work on a numbers-only basis. Bodies for jobs. Jobs for bodies. They didn't even know how to respond to a request for a particular agent – their computer system can't tell the difference between any of you.' He shook his head, as if to say, 'What's the world coming to out there?'

Max concentrated on keeping his face impassive. 'Team Rushmore.' How bad could it be? Sure, there were things about this life that he'd miss. He just couldn't think of any of them right now. 'Team Rushmore.' He and Rose would be together. Day and night. Night and day. Oh, God.

Max glanced at Dunkirk. As his mouth was moving, his lips worked their way slowly but steadily upwards until his sharp little incisors showed.

And Rex? What would Rex say about 'Team Rushmore'? Max pictured his old mentor, reeking of cigarettes in a crumpled suit. 'Don't do it, Max,' came Rex's voice, as if back from the dead. Gravelly, deep, sure. 'You'll kill each other.'

'You still with me, Max?' Dunkirk sounded annoyed. The old shark. Even Rose couldn't identify with such unerring accuracy the moment his thoughts began to wander.

'Where else would I be?' said Max. He was suddenly self-conscious. Sticky. He could feel the sweat, dried on him after the journey.

'Good question,' said Dunkirk, eyeing him. Only Dunkirk, thought Max queasily, could make the word 'good' sound so bad. Still, it's a good sign that Dunkirk is here. It must be a good sign.

'Sunflower oil,' said Dunkirk. And waited.

'Ukraine is the leading exporter,' said Max. '75 percent of the world's sunflower oil moves through Odesa's ports.'

'Been reading up, I see.'

Max bent his head and spread his hands, as if to say he couldn't help being prepared.

Dunkirk sighed. 'Right,' he said. 'That kind of – attention to detail – is just what we need. For this, hm, *assignment*.'

'Assignment?' said Max. Wondered if he'd imagined the air quotes in Dunkirk's voice. Persimmon Tree Drive, thought Max. One of the toniest addresses in Washington.

Dunkirk paged through the manila folder in front of him. Paused. Grimaced. Chuckled.

Was Sooz Dunkirk happy, Max wondered. Would Rose be happy, too, if she lived in a big brick Colonial in Persimmon Tree Drive? Or … The manila folder came flying at Max, jolting him from his thoughts.

'Get a load of this,' said Dunkirk.

Max caught the folder. Opened it. Inside was an old-fashioned glossy print, on thick contact paper. These days, it was accepted that anything digital was up for grabs. If you wanted to keep an image out of circulation, you kept it analogue. For as long as possible, anyway.

Max frowned. The picture showed a severed hand. Pudgy, white. Soft. Still, clearly the hand of a man. Glistening slightly. A large, wine-red birthmark ran from the wrist to the knuckles. Shaped distinctly like the state of Florida.

Max looked up at Dunkirk. 'What the …?'

'Weird as it looks,' said Dunkirk. He chuckled. 'Weirder. This fucking part of the world …'

'Grisha lost his hand?' said Max. 'That's … how? … why isn't the press …?'

Dunkirk shook his head. Sat back comfortably in the big chair. 'So, a big container of cheap cooking oil docks in Baltimore,' Dunkirk began. 'US inspections are still pretty good, all things considered. If it had been, hell, Bombay, they probably wouldn't have noticed. Would have just fished it out and forgotten about it. But in Baltimore the inspectors are on their game. Add to that, they've just gotten some new high-tech sensors – some kind of carbon analysers that use space tech or some crazy thing. You put in a little of the substance – olive oil, or honey, or chocolate – then burn it, and the machine can tell exactly what's in it on a molecular level. So, these guys are playing with their new toy, and they get a wonky reading on the sunflower oil. Human DNA.'

'Human DNA,' said Max.

Dunkirk shrugged. 'They go in, open up the barrel. And they fish out this – well, it looks a helluvalot like a human hand. One of the inspectors is a Georgian. Emigrated in the 90s. You know how Georgians are – you can take the man out of Tbilisi, but you can't take Tbilisi out of the man. He recognises the birthmark. Goes ballistic. Starts making calls, to the police, to his relatives back home. Our guys get wind of it, get a hold of the hand before there's some sort of international incident. Start running tests. The fingerprints are Grisha's all right. We don't even want to ask.'

Max nodded, remembering Grisha's penchant for practical jokes – like the time he tricked the whole sovereign nation of Georgia into thinking they were under attack, by broadcasting a made-up news report on state TV.

'But we do ask, of course,' said Dunkirk, throwing up his bulky but not inelegant hands. 'Ambassador McClellan's making his maiden voyage to Odesa. He's been Ambassador to the Ukraine for, what, three weeks. Anyway, McClellan's just arrived from Kyiv, checked into the Bristol downtown. Nice place, by the way. Stayed there myself, last night. Spiffy. So Grisha, he takes a tram over – you know that's his thing, public transportation – how he manages, I don't know. It's what, eight in the morning. But Grisha makes the receptionist march him right up to McClellan's suite. Practically bangs down the door. McClellan is in the middle of his sit-ups – do you know that man does fifty sit-ups every morning, no matter where in the world he is? Admirable. McClellan opens the door, and there's Grisha. Shirt soaked entirely through from the tram ride – there's no air conditioning on public transportation here, apparently – and thrusts that wine-red Florida birthmark right at him. "Sir," he says, "I'd like to shake your hand!"' Dunkirk shrugged. 'So, Grisha's got both his hands.'

'But the DNA was human?'

Again, Dunkirk shrugged. 'We're testing it, of course. But it seems to be some kind of hoax. Apparently, you can use pig flesh and get a similar reading.'

'Fingerprint tattoos have come a long way, too,' said Max.

'Johnson's on it, in DC,' Dunkirk added.

Max felt himself blush. Hoped Dunkirk hadn't noticed.

Dunkirk tensed his square jaw. 'Jesus Christ, Max,' he said. 'You didn't really think we'd put you on the case if the governor had lost his hand? I mean, we have staff for that. Don Johnson …'

Max couldn't help it – every time he heard Johnson's full name he laughed. Poor guy. 'Course not,' said Max. 'Johnson's a good man.'

Dunkirk exhaled. 'Right,' he said. 'What we want from you – special request – are some really good, detailed notes on this conference. Who's here, what are they saying. Stuff like the sunflower statistics. Those are terrific. I know it's not really up your alley. But I figured I owed you a favour after the last case. Anyway, you can handle it, right? Be here, write it up?'

'Yeah,' said Max.

'Great,' said Dunkirk. 'I've really gone out on a limb for you. But if you can pull this off, it could pay off for you. Big time.'

Max grunted. Persimmons. Homer. Lotus eaters. Content on their island, indifferent to the rest of the world. According to one theory – it came back to Max – it wasn't flowers but persimmons they were eating.

'See,' said Dunkirk. 'The official line is a little divided on Grisha: in Kyiv, the Embassy loves him. They want to embrace him. Hell, they want to hug him tight! But inside the Beltway – the administration isn't so sure. They haven't forgotten the little matter of Grisha's declaration of war on Russia, for one thing. They're worried he might do something stupid again. And then they don't want to be left holding the bag.' Max nodded. 'So, whatever there is to be said against conferences, this one's coming at a crucial time. People in Washington, they're looking for information. Content. And that's what we're going to provide. Write it all down. Hell, even Trilby's presentation.'

'Sure,' said Max.

'One other thing,' said Dunkirk. 'We've got an intern on the way. Mark Hope. Poli-sci, with a minor in biology. Spent a year working on some sort of crazy genetics project, revivifying a strain of dinosaur. Nutty. Anyhow …' Dunkirk put the manila file back in his desk. 'We're really trying to beef up our science recruiting, these days. So, I want you to show him the ropes. He'll be here Wednes-day. Nice kid. Lotta promise.'

'I'm not exactly a glowing example,' said Max.

'Exactly what I was thinking,' said Dunkirk. 'I want this kid to get a dose of reality. See if it's really for him.'

Max opened his mouth. Shut it again.

'The conference is what, three days? I want you to stay on for a couple of days after that. Play Baedeker for the intern. Think Rose'll let you do that?' Dunkirk spoke in a jarring, jokey way that made Max wince. In fact, Rose wasn't going to like it at all. He was cut-ting it close for dinner with Team Anderson, as it was. A few more days, and 'mixing business with pleasure' was out.

'I'll talk to Rose,' Max said.

Dunkirk grinned.

Dunkirk stood, and Max followed. 'Here, c'mon, use the back entrance.' Dunkirk pushed open a door to the left of the side table. It screeched, metallic, then opened onto a tar paper roof.

As it opened, a little yellow kitten darted inside. As if he had been waiting by the door, for just this moment. Max felt a tickle in his throat. Then a wave of fear. The little cat jumped up on the desk, sniffing the manila folder. 'Who's this?' said Dunkirk, softening. 'Hi, kitty, kitty.' He shook his head, once, turned back to Max. 'Can you get 'im outta here?'

Max hesitated. Considered telling Dunkirk he was allergic to cats. Couldn't. What did the doctor say? A one in – was it one hundred? Max decided to take his chances with anaphylactic shock. Held his breath as he scooped up the yellow kitten.

For some reason, Max had carried Dunkirk's yachting magazine into the office. Now, for no reason he could think of other than the quiet joy of purloining something Dunkirk might miss, it was still rolled up, stuck casually under his left arm. He held his hand out to Dunkirk, who stepped back, palms flat, as if to block Max. 'Ooh,' he said. 'Don't want to get worms. Or whatever it is these little critters carry.'

Max nodded. The tickle turned into a scratch. Oxygen. He was running out of oxygen. Max stepped out onto the brand-new tar paper roof. Like a frying pan. Dropped the kitten. Breathed deep.

'Straight across the roof, you'll see the fire escape,' said Dunkirk from the doorway. 'You'll get right down to the parking lot from there.'

Max nodded. The door shut with a clang behind him. Max breathed again. The tar paper didn't quite cover the surface of the hot roof – as if the builders had run out before they finished – and was already peeling up in little rolls at the edges. In the distance, the sea sparkled.

He set off across the baking tar paper. Then he spotted the little yellow kitty again. Moving stealthily along the far wall. He drew back. Then, against his instincts, moved towards it. The creature had something dead-looking in its mouth. 'Whatcha got there?' said Max, feeling the tickle again. 'Dinner?' The cat looked at Max with a flash of green. Dropped the thing in its mouth. Nudged it towards Max, once, with its pink nose. Ran away.

Max bent down. Felt his throat scratching. A brief wave of nausea. Could it be …? He decided it couldn't. Looked more closely. Got a whiff of something foul. The thing was dead. The thing was rotten. The thing was … human.

A toe. A man's toe. A big man. His big toe. Grey, with a splash of colour. Something that looked more like merlot than rosé.

Max worked quickly. Automatically. Felt in his pockets for his plastic hotel keycard. He looked around. Pulled up a section of tar paper. Folded it into a kind of sticky black shovel. He considered the magazine. Then he took out his keycard, used it to gingerly push the thing – the toe – onto the tar paper. The smell wafted up in waves. Rot. Rot and something else. Max held his breath. The scratching in his throat was gone. Old cheese. That was the smell. He slid the packet between the pages of the *Odesa Preview: BOATS!* edition.

*

Cradling the toe, Max made his way quickly down the fire escape. He felt his heart beating. Focus, he told himself. Focus.

Angling the plastic card key into the gap in one of the doors, he pried it open. He was back in the hotel. The Gagarin's laundry room. It smelled fresh here. Like detergent. He inhaled deeply. Then Max

54

grabbed a couple of extra towels and climbed the maid's staircase to the fifteenth floor.

Safely in his room, Max called the reception. Withdrew to the glossy white bathroom. He turned the shower on. The little room filled with steam – enough to fog a camera, if there'd been one. Carefully, Max set the tar paper on the plastic shelf below the mirror. He picked up a towel and held it under the shower. Wrung it out and used it to cover his nose and mouth. Breathing shallowly, Max turned on the shaving light. It was a sharp LED, round like an eyeball, at the end of an adjustable white tentacle. Max bent it over the tar paper.

Just then, a buzzer sounded. Max dropped the towel, turned off the shower. Opened the door. A slender young man, almost a boy, held a champagne bottle in one hand and a metal bucket in the other. 'Great,' said Max. 'Extra ice?'

'Lotta ice,' said the boy with a smile. He nodded at the steam pouring out of the bathroom. 'You wanna shower? You gotta let the water run full strength. Twenty, twenty-five minutes. After that, it cools down enough to use.'

'Ah,' said Max. 'The receptionist said to try again in twenty minutes.'

'Yeah, they always say that. But that's not how you get a shower around here. You gotta let the boiler cool down first. The plumbing in this place – it's through the ass.' Max grinned. 'Through the ass' was a Russian term that meant, essentially, 'to do something badly'. Max liked the phrase. He himself had completed many a task 'through the ass'.

He gave the boy a tip.

Back in the bathroom, Max turned the shower back on. Pulled the wet towel over his nose. Readjusted the shaving light. His heart was beating like a hummingbird. This could be it, he thought. His big break.

Max pulled the shaving light down to the toe. There was no question at all: illuminated there was, clearly, a right big toe that had once been attached to a man. Running along the digit's flat, dirty top, from the broad nail to just above the place where it was severed, was a dark-red marking. Wine-coloured. Shaped distinctly like the state of Florida.

Keep cool, Maxiboy, he told himself. Breathe. He breathed. Felt his heart slow, just a little. Still, with all his being, Max knew. He'd found something. Something important. He glanced back at the grey and red digit.

Now all he needed was a refrigerator.

\*

A couple of phone calls later, Max slipped back into the lobby. In the corner by the ficus, he found himself in the midst of a toast being led, slowly, by Trilby. 'One. Of. My,' Trilby said, leaving a gap between each accented word, as he always did when he wanted to command attention, 'Favourite. Toasts.'

Someone pressed an ice-cold tumbler of vodka into Max's hand. He looked up into a smile right out of a toothpaste commercial. Behind it was a bright-eyed, dark-haired boy in a cheap suit. Max grunted a thanks. The boy leaned in, whispered, 'Mark Hope,' and, nodding enthusiastically, produced a business card. Then he turned back to Trilby. Almost in spite of himself – Max knew the toast already from other conferences; other, more dilapidated hotels; other, more promising decades – Max turned his attention to Trilby, too.

'From,' trilled Trilby, still decked out in that ridiculous trench coat, 'the old days!' Trilby brandished his glass in his rather stubby fingers, and the little manly circle that had formed around him followed suit. The men held their sweaty glasses at chest height, waiting, the lead-crystal catching the lobby's aggressive light. Trilby's voice took on a deeper, appealingly mischievous tone. 'The Black Sea Fleet!' he cried. 'To the bottom!'

# Part 2

I'm a child of my age – and I love all its blemishes, all its venom.

Vladimir Jabotinsky, *The Five*

## 10

The beach was no place for a cat like Mr Smiley. It was for the losers, the loners, the cats who didn't belong. They roamed in the early hours, picking up the scraps left by the pigeons. A pathetic life. But they could be useful, too, these losers, these loners. One of them had made his way to Mr Smiley's den, in the courtyard next to the police station. A sad, wiry specimen, wild and dirty with camel-coloured hair clumped by the sea breeze. Cowering, neck bent, the beach cat scum had made his report. A strange object. 'Neither fish nor fowl,' the beach cat said.

Mr Smiley listened, kneading his paws. The beach cat scum quaked. He was hungry, Mr Smiley could tell. 'Which beach?' Mr Smiley wanted to know.

'Nemo,' replied the beach cat.

Mr Smiley's claws stopped mid-knead. Nemo Beach was the closest to the city, just a short walk from downtown. Packed in the summer. Tourists and rats. Fish tails, salted, fried. Nemo! Nemo was Sima's beach, the one where she went for midnight dips after she closed the restaurant. Of course, she hadn't been swimming since the bombing. She wasn't up for it just yet. The bomb had left her entirely unscathed, but a little shaken.

'When?' said Mr Smiley.

The beach cat quaked. 'The first one washed up a week ago,' the beach cat said. Then another 'thing' washed up. And another.

Mr Smiley finished his kneading. He thanked the beach cat, gave him a shiny raw sardine. Watched him devour it, silver scales catching in his bleeding gums.

Cats have a sense for things that are cursed, and something told Mr Smiley these 'things' the pathetic beach cat told him about were bad luck. Nothing he wanted his Simochka to accidentally discover. Of course, it might be too late to keep the news from getting out. The pathetic beach cat said one of the little golden house kitties – the cosseted youth from the villas along the shore – had been slumming it on the beach the night the thing that looked like a toe washed up. The golden kitten had been too fast for him, said the pathetic beach cat, dropping his head in shame. The rich kitty snatched it. Well, Mr Smiley would take care of that, if it became a problem. Those spoiled, bored children with their catnip overdoses … one bat to the neck and the kitten would crumble.

That night, Mr Smiley waited until the very early hours of the morning, just before the tide turned – a dangerous time, cats knew, when death and betrayal hung heavier than usual over the city. Then he made the dark, lonely underground trek to Nemo Beach.

Mr Smiley paced in the damp sand. Beyond the grating sounds of the sea, he could hear the plaintive calls of the dolphins. They were imprisoned in a miserable tank built inside a hideous-smelling new hotel, all woodchips and asbestos, and were trotted out every few hours to perform for tourists. The humans called this prison the 'Delfinarium'. Spelled out in big blue letters, in full view of the beach. A warning to the sea creatures who still swam free. The cat licked his lips. If he had more time – and a few helpers – he'd like to 'liberate' one or two of those poor dolphin prisoners. Heh heh.

Then Mr Smiley grew serious. Dolphin would make an excellent cat feast, the next time there was a meeting of the bosses. Periodically, the chief cats came to congregate from the neighbouring regions: Trans-nistria, Bessarabia. They always had to be fed, of course … the meal was a sign of power … Of course, there were the logistics to consider … how many cats would you need to transport a dolphin carcass …?

Mr Smiley froze. In the darkness, someone was approaching.

# 11

Over the Black Sea, dawn was just breaking. Green light cracked the horizon, drove a wedge between the dark sky and the murky sea.

Rodion strode towards the water, carrying his shoes. He felt the damp, cool sand between his toes. He had worked the entire night through. Again. Well, he liked the lab best at night. Silence. And he had made a breakthrough of sorts. Now, as a reward, he'd decided to come straight to the beach.

Rodion stripped. White T-shirt, black skinny jeans. No underwear – he hadn't had time to do the laundry. He was a good-looking young man. Twenty-five. Tall, with a swimmer's body. Strong, broad shoulders. A narrow waist. His back was covered, completely, in a tattoo. A green pond with pale pink flowers. Water lilies. His blond hair was pulled back in a rubber band. He let it down, and it flowed over his shoulders. Sure, girls hated it. But he didn't care. Rodion didn't have time for girls right now, anyway. Soon, of course, he would need to get married. Before he got too old. But not right now. Not today. Today was just beginning – he stretched his strong, pale arms to the heavens and yawned.

It wouldn't be the first time Rodion had gone without sleep. In fact, these days, ever since Felix had contacted him with the plans he'd found, sleeplessness was the rule, not the exception. Well, he couldn't give up the coffee shop job. After all, he still had to make money! With just a tiny stab of regret, he thought of his old Jupiter 5. He had loved that motorbike. But last year, when his family needed money – his young mother, who loved him to distraction, his ten-year-old brother – of course, Rodion had sold it.

Now, he looked out over the water, which was turning grey and then silver as the sun rose, a pale, rosy ball, above it. Reviewed his plans for the day. First, a swim. Then the exotic animal market. Then he would open the coffee shop.

Ah, the coffee shop. Café Delicious. Ever since Felix had made his amazing discovery and they'd set up their lab, Rodion's business partner had wanted him to give up the café job. Rodion said he'd think about it once they had some money coming in.

But the truth was, Rodion loved working in the café. It was what was missing from his biology studies. He liked the people at the café. He liked people, in general. Dead frogs and cows and corpses and computers – they were interesting. Rodion was good at them. But there was nothing quite like frothing a perfect cappuccino and delivering it to a pretty girl. He was just beginning to discover sex. Not that he hadn't had sex before. He had, of course. But it hadn't fascinated him. Since working in the café – where he had painted the walls a lush smoky lavender, and he changed the flowers on the tables each day, chosen to match the decor – sex had changed for him, too. Become more interesting. One of the 'tools of pleasure' as he called them. He found he was attractive to women. And they were attractive to him.

Now, he held up his black jeans and took a small, flat object shaped very much like a seashell from the pocket. He dropped the jeans with the rest of his clothes. Walked to the water. He glanced down, once, in the dawning light at the object in his hand. The wine-coloured mark irritated his artist's sensibility. There was something wrong. He had gone over all the instructions until it became clear to him that a crucial step was missing. There must be another page. Felix hadn't found everything.

He glanced down again. It was a shame, of course, to throw it away. But if Felix found out about his little experiments, he'd be furious. No, no. It was better to develop the technique, then present the results. Then Felix would see for himself. And Felix would know what to do next. How to market it. But first: first Felix had to go back to the state archives and search again. See if he could find the missing fifth page.

Rodion glanced at the soft seashell shape in his hand. Swung his long, strong arm backwards. And threw the thing way, way out. Into the water. Safer than in the trash. Some fish would eat it. He bent down and rinsed his hands in the gentle little waves.

Then he stood. Walked out into the grey water. When it reached his knees, he stopped. Dove in. It was grey now, absorbing. Cold. His whole body felt it at once: shock, joy. Rodion was alive! Alive, alive, alive! He was alive! He took long, sure strokes beneath the surface until his lungs were bursting. Then he erupted upwards. Gulped the air. Stared, transfixed, at the city, just beginning to sparkle like a giant sandcastle with the first light of day. He was alive, alive, alive! Rodion was naked, naked, naked and alive!

# 12

Max wondered if he had died. He could feel the white bed floating, swaying, high above the pale, early-morning waters of the Black Sea. Max was floating, too. Like some heavenly creature. An angel, maybe? Or something more organic – a bird, a seagull suspended mid-flight, frozen at full wingspan … Max shifted his head slightly on the pillow. A hammer fell. The pain seared. Shot through his skull. Pierced his Adam's apple, inducing a wave of nausea. Ran on at a dizzying speed, to land like a punch in his gut. Max groaned with his whole soul.

His gut. Someone had stripped his stomach with acid overnight. Who? He was sure he could remember. If he just concentrated. Another blow of the hammer. Concentrate. White lobby. Dark suits. Vodka. Trilby, toasting. Max cursed.

Trilby! Of course. Every time! This happened every time with Trilby. Max tried to open his eyes in the fragile dawn light. It hurt. He closed them again. Last night trickled back to him …

In the white lobby, Trilby was telling the old story. 'To outdrink a Russian,' he said in his put-on accent, 'you have to really – *feel* – your body.' At this point in the narrative, Trilby always shut his goggly eyes. Looked inward behind the coke-bottle glasses like some sort of vodka Buddha. 'Feel,' he intoned, 'your*self*.' All the men, but especially the younger ones, held their breath. Rapt. With a little shake of his head, Trilby resurfaced. Put the unlit pipe between his lips. Made eye contact, one by one, around the captivated circle. 'I'll tell you how I know,' Trilby confided, on cue. 'Once, many years ago, I was invited to a dinner. High-ranking KGB, all around the table. They poured out the vodka. Looked at me. Very sceptically. The colonel at the head of the table said, "Please. Be careful." I smiled, thanked him for his concern. And then I proceeded to outdrink them. To. A. Man.' Trilby paused, stared modestly at his unlit pipe. 'Afterwards,' he beamed, 'well! They were all convinced I was MI6. *Very* high up.'

Max winced. In no way did he doubt the veracity of this story of Trilby's. Maybe that was why it triggered his competitive instincts. Every. Single. Time.

What had happened next? Trilby had been talking about the Odesa bombings. Max had read the item, too: that restaurant – Angel's – Angelina's – was the thirteenth bombing in as many months; so far, no one had been hurt, though this time a young woman had come within an inch of her life.

The targets looked political: an office that collected winter coats for Ukrainian soldiers fighting in the east; the Ukrainian secret service's local office; the vociferously pro-Ukrainian poet Yefim Fishman's downtown apartment … that one had given Max a scare! He knew Fimka Fishman, liked him … Thank God no one had been hurt …

'Russians,' said Trilby, confidently. 'Russian secret service, written all over them. Really, the Russians – it's just like in Dostoevsky. They commit the perfect crime and can't resist going back to the scene.'

An ambassador from one of the EU's olive-oil countries, wearing a red silk bowtie, tried to object: didn't the Russians excel at chess?

'No, no, no,' said Trilby. 'Their fingerprints are all over this. If you just knew what to look for, you could catch them in twelve hours.'

The circle broke up. Mark Hope excused himself. It was an honour to meet Max. But he was going to hit the hay. Wanted to be fresh in the morning. 'Sure,' Max had said. 'Good thinking.'

One of the local expats, an Irishman, got a call. Went home to his Odesan wife. 'Former Soviet fencing champion,' he'd said, sadly. The bartender locked up. And then – oh no, thought Max. Oh no. He remembered a pound coin soaring up. A silver glint. It succumbed to gravity. Still tumbling, like a circus performer. Heads or tails. Tails or heads. Who won? Max couldn't remember. It didn't really matter: He and Trilby were equally capable of picking the lock on the lobby bar's liquor cabinet.

Now, in the present, Max became aware of a putrid, slightly cheesy smell. It crept through the room, had taken up residence in every corner, in every fold – blanket, curtain, skin. Another, weirder image surfaced on the turbulent river of Max's consciousness, along with a sickening feeling – that he had forgotten something. Something big. His big chance! And he'd missed it.

Of course! Max rolled over, spotted the metal champagne bucket. He lifted his head. Floating in a pool of ice water, between glassy slivers that had once been cubes, was the hotel's shower cap. It was knotted at the top. Waterlogged a little. Anchored, Max knew, by a greying, bloated, severed human toe. Marked by a small wine-red stain shaped like the state of Florida. Even in his current condition, Max's heart leapt a little at the thought of it.

Max heaved himself up. Checked the time. Ok. Ok. Ok. He wasn't at his best. But he wasn't too late. He gave himself five minutes. Five minutes, then he'd get up. In the meantime, he lay down. Closed his eyes. Last night unspooled in his mind's eye to its inevitable conclusion …

… The corner by the ficus. A fresh bottle sweating in the dark. A ring of perspiration on the low white table. And then?

… And then, fool that he was, Max had challenged Trilby to a drinking contest. To the bottom!

# 13

Luddy woke up again with a start. Dishes were clanking in the communal kitchen. Still? Again? He opened an eye. Peeked at his hands. Squinted. Not shaking. *Notshakingnotshaking. I'marockstarI'marockstarI'marockstar.*

Luddy looked around at the green room. The violent, pink reflected light. *Notinjailnotinjailnotinjail.* Luddy squeezed his eyes shut again.

Fifteen years in the slammer. Jesus fucking Christ! The only one who came to visit was Perfect Sergey. The meth started a few years in. When he could get it. He could usually get it. Now he was trying to break the habit. But he got the shakes. The willies. He'd lost weight. *I'marockstarI'marockstar.*

The day they let him out, back into the world, Luddy set up camp in a green and brown shithole of a room in South Beach. Every night, he pulled the green and brown curtains shut and surfed the Internet, like he'd learned in computer literacy class in jail. Some do-gooder type had donated a bunch of old black IBM laptops to the prisoner release programme. That meant Luddy could surf 24/7. None of these 40-minute limits, like he was used to in jail. Luddy had $10,000 in a bank account – honest earnings from 'Weekend at Bernie's' – and now, he needed a new plan.

At first, he researched. Between hits. Porn, mostly. He was still a businessman, after all. In fifteen years, the industry changes. He thought he might open another strip joint – it wasn't big money, but it was something – and he had to catch up on trends. What do men want? What do they expect?

To be honest, some of what he found shocked him. Really perverted stuff! What happened to a red-blooded man wanting the regular things in a woman? That night he blew a week's budget on a bottle of Johnny Walker Black label. He poured a nice, five-fingered drink. Turned the computer back on. Decided he wanted to hear some fucking Russian.

Luddy poked around on the Internet for a while. All kinds of things were happening in his homeland. Gene therapies. Foetal stem cell injections. They could cure spinal damage, liver disease, old age. No regulations, no problems. Those pussies in the US always had to test, get approval. The Ukrainians – they just did. They were doers. Like Luddy was a doer. A *macher. I'marockstarI'marockstar.*

And that was when it happened. A video popped up. Some sort of ad. Luddy watched as a strapping blond youth, tall with bright blue eyes – a real Cossack-of-the-steppes type, he thought – appeared onscreen. He was wearing a lab coat, like a costume. His long hair was pulled back in a ponytail, and you could see the tendrils of a couple of tattoo flowers just barely poking up at the base of his neck. A voiceover said, 'Ukraine is the WORLD LEADER in the legal production of body parts ...' The camera panned over a tray of eye-balls. 'Come and SEE for yourself. EASY ETERNITY.'

Another blond youngster joined the handsome Cossack type. This kid was portlier, with a snub nose. Piggy looking. Red necktie. He had one of those black plastic devices in his ear, what were they called, Bluetooths? That must be right, there it was, glowing with a little blue light – the kid looked like a fucking fool. 'Call us,' said the piggy fool.

There was a phone number at the bottom of the screen. Luddy poured himself another drink. He walked over to the brown and green curtains. Pulled them to one side, just a little. Sunrise. The sun was rising over Miami. Fine. He drank the whiskey. Then he dialled the number. The Cossack wasn't available, said a stern young man's voice. 'I'm the one you want to talk to,' said the voice. His name was Felix, he handled the business end of things, and he had a very interesting offer for a serious American investor.

# 14

Daybreak. Max stepped out of the hotel lobby. Once outside, the atmosphere rose up, embracing. Warm, gentle, humid.

Max made his way down a narrow set of rough concrete steps. Skirted the rickety foundation walls shoring up more new construction. Proceeded gingerly along the sidewalk.

At a traffic roundabout, a glistening grey stone obelisk pierced the overcast sky. FOURTEEN it read. As in April 14th, 1944: the day the Romanians occupying the city left. They had aligned with the Nazis, the Odesans were glad to see them go. Max bent, hands on knees. Caught his breath. Two huge ships' anchors leaned against the obelisk's stone base. Max stood. Held out a hand. There were anchors everywhere in this city. As if to keep it from floating away …

With a screech, a Lada pulled to a stop. Max took hold of the flimsy door handle. Bent. The driver was strong, squat. Crew cut, black eye, cheek still bleeding – a man whose last fight lay not days but hours in the past. Max did a quick calculation. 50-50, he decided. Either this guy was brutal, itching for a fight. Or he was a sweetheart.

Max glanced at the gym bag in his hand. The toe lay wrapped in a fresh shower cap, followed by several layers of towels, doused variously in hotel shampoo and Max's own cologne. Still, Max thought he caught a whiff of something rotten. He looked back at the boxer. His nose was crushed flat.

'Train station,' said Max.

The boxer grunted. They took the roundabout fast. Max's body pressed against the door. For one disorienting moment, his stomach seemed to stay behind near the obelisk. With a lurch, the car straightened. Max breathed deeply.

'Polish?' asked the boxer. His voice was low and rough. If Max had to guess, they were suffering about equally from their hangovers.

Max answered carefully. Tensed for a punch. 'American.'

The boxer brightened. 'Ah!' he said, a smile spreading across his battered face. Max relaxed. Sweetheart, then. The boxer winced – the smile had reached his bleeding cheek. 'Our city, you know, is a mini-America! It was always like this, from the very beginning. Greeks, French, Italians, Jews – everyone is welcome!'

There was a loud, terrible crunching sound. For a moment, Max thought they had crashed. But it was just a pothole. '... completely open!' the boxer was saying, as the car rattled and shook over the cobblestones of the French Boulevard. A half-built Orthodox Church rose, gutted, in the gloom. 'If you are Russian, you are welcome! Or you – American! Welcome!'

'Thanks,' said Max. They had reached the old sanatorium row; a dozen Brezhnev-era high-rises devoted to Soviet health and relaxation, perched at the edge of the Black Sea. A thick grove of acacias appeared at the side of the road. A tram stop, labelled 'Sanatorium Russia'. Beneath a single naked bulb, someone had crossed out 'Russia' with a sharpie pen. Max asked if any Russians were coming these days.

The boxer shook his head as he tilted the car into a curve like a rollercoaster. 'This war has been a disaster!' he said. 'Odesa is a tourist city! Russians, Europeans – they watch TV, see Ukraine, explosions, shooting, bombs, they think it's here. But actually, the fighting's way in the east. Here, it's perfectly safe.'

Max braced himself against the dashboard as the car swerved. Anyhow, said the driver, since the Russians stole Crimea, things had gotten better in Odesa. 'Now they can't go to Crimea, all of Ukraine comes here instead for vacation!'

Max nodded. 'What about these bombings?' he asked. 'Is that a problem?'

The boxer waved his meaty hand. 'No big deal! No one's hurt!'

They drove on, in silence. Overhead, rows of old maples bent over the French Boulevard. Leaves drooping. Like hands, reaching. Max thought of Fimka Fishman's surreal online diary, in which the news of the latest bombing had been framed poetically: an explosive struggle between the renowned cook, Angelina, and various devils.

'Purrrrradise lost,' in the words of Miss Kitty, the only reliable narrator in all of Odesa.

'What you have to understand is our history,' the boxer was saying. 'Odesa is not Ukraine. It's not Russia.' He swerved again, and a wave of nausea rose up in Max from the pit of his being. 'Odesa is a place where independence is born. The free Greek state, modern Bulgaria, Israel – they all began here!'

They hit another pothole, hard. Ahead, a cluster of onion domes reared up, black like a paper cut-out, against the morning sky. 'So it's a hotbed,' said Max, pushing the sick back down with a deep breath. 'Of revolution.'

The boxer liked this. 'A hotbed of revolution!' he grinned. His lip split and began to bleed again. He mopped the blood with a dirty tissue. 'And a nice place to spend the summer holiday, too.'

# 15

The King woke with tears flooding his good eye. He felt a rocking motion, back and forth and up and down, and in half-sleep felt as if he were deep, deep, deep underwater – but it wasn't water, it was memory; he was immersed in memory, the softly rocking motion of a time before consciousness ... rocking, rocking. Memories swirled in his head, his heart. Memories he didn't know he had, memories from before he could remember. Dry, kind hands. Dark, warm eyes. His mother. The fresh smell of laundry hanging in the courtyard between dusty clusters of grapevines. They lived in Moldavanka, back then, Odesa's poorest neighbourhood, with the criminals; it hadn't changed, not since the time of Babel ...

The old man woke, halfway, remembered his cackling old grandmother telling him the stories, over and over, about Benya Krik – Benya-the-King – the most famous Odesan mobster. With a heart of gold. As a boy, he couldn't get enough of those stories of Benya Krik and the tricks he played; it would never have occurred to him that Moldavanka's own Benya-the-King was a fictional character, sprung from the mind of Isaac Babel, and not a real person ...

The rocking motion continued, and the old man drifted back into a dreamy state. Sinking, sinking. A wave of sublime sadness that might have been joy overcame him, all at once. Her voice! His mother's voice. Soothing. Sparkling. A language he must have known once. 'Angelito,' she said, and the old man could feel her arms, encircling. 'Angelito mio!' The rocking motion continued, and the King fell gently back to sleep.

# 16

The train station was busy, despite the early hour. Beneath the soaring archways of a great empire, tourist families pulled small suitcases back and forth. Bare-limbed, healthy. Dressed for the beach. Bright colours, navy stripes. Pale or tanned – coming or going. In the main hall, pretty, young mothers and neat, sun-kissed children were fast asleep on the floor.

Max made his way to the station's café, with its high, pale green ceilings and gaudy, florescent-lit offerings – plastic-wrapped baked goods, packaged cookies, and pale-yellow salads. He ordered coffee. Carried the little paper cup to a table. Watched the sky changing outside the window. Red, tinged with deep yellow. The city a shadow. Onion domes and electric wires. The coffee tasted like the paper cup it came in. Max drank it anyway. He felt a little better.

The sky softened, losing colour: from red to pink, then pale pink, then white. When there was a hint of blue, he walked out to the platforms. He waited until the night train from Kyiv arrived, then walked out as if to meet it.

Gym bag under his arm, Max mingled with the passengers arriving from Kyiv. Flowers, balloons, embraces, well-wishers. New arrivals, laughing as if they were already digging their toes into the sand. Max hoisted the gym bag over his shoulder. Saw a girl in a pink dress. Waved.

The girl's dark eyes lit up. 'Natasha!' said Max, drawing closer. He grasped her shoulders, held her at arm's length. Limp blonde hair pulled back, as befits an academic. There was nothing academic about her legs: they were tanned and terrific.

'You look great!' Max said, as a faint smile played on the woman's lips. 'Much too attractive to be teaching business students.'

Natasha's smile faded. She sniffed. Made a face. 'Your NGO can't afford to send you from Kyiv by plane?' she said.

Max chuckled ruefully. He hadn't showered on purpose. He thought it might help mask the rotten smell. "Fraid not,' he said. 'You know how it is. "Mending is better than spending." Or whatever the organisation motto is.' He shrugged, gave his best lopsided, incompetent-but-endearing grin. 'Thanks so much for putting me up at your place – I couldn't believe it when I realised I'd booked a room in a brothel. I mean, it was listed on one of those hotel websites … I guess I should have known the price was too good to be true … and now everything in the city is booked out!'

Natasha giggled, briefly. 'A pair of Belgian journalists I know did the same thing,' she said.

'Oh, yeah?' said Max, who had come up with this particular fiction after stumbling across a vitriolic Francophone review of the 'Starlight Hotel' on TripAdvisor. ('Room had NO window! Ceiling so low we BUMPED our heads! Howling noise ALL NIGHT! TERRIBLE HOTEL!!!! No stars').

Max grinned. Said, after all, it was the perfect excuse to get in touch with her. After all these years.

Natasha lowered her eyelashes. They had met, oh, a decade ago. At a conference in DC, just off Dupont Circle. Max was posing as a mid-level employee of a post-Soviet mental health services NGO. Natasha was a young visiting scholar at Hopkins. Attractive, oh yes. The conference was a bust – they usually were – but Natasha was a bright point. Her talk was on 'the modern Ukrainian'. From the audience, Max asked a few pertinent questions about the hegemonic Soviet devaluation of Ukrainian as a language (Russian was the language of Pushkin, went the official line; Ukrainian, the language of peasants). What after-effects could be felt on the contemporary Ukrainian psyche? Afterwards, at the conference's pay-bar, Max bought her a drink. 'Were you for real, with that question?' was the first thing Natasha said, her dark eyes flashing. 'Or did you just want to be my friend?' Max didn't answer. 'Because,' she added, archly, her pink lips pursed above the narrow straw garnishing her vodka tonic, 'it's almost as if you read my PhD thesis. And nobody read my PhD thesis.' They never really got along. Like two birds of prey, circling.

Alighting, now and then, but never finding a foothold. When the semester ended, Natasha went back to Odesa. Where, last time Max heard from her, she was engaged to her department's dean.

Now, as a crowd of passengers jostled past, an unexpected lightness came over Max. Could he be genuinely glad to see this woman? Somehow – he felt hopeful. As if he had just received a postcard from a younger, stronger self. The sun was up, and already it beat a soft, steady tattoo over the station platform, the travellers, the old women with the bent cardboard signs ('Room to Rent, Best Price'), the taxi drivers' jowls, glistening beneath their stubble. 'It's good to see you,' Max said, gathering the gym bag with its precious cargo closer to him. 'I'll give you a proper hello later – after I've had a bath.'

Natasha crinkled her pert nose. 'I can wait,' she said.

# 17

In the early morning sunshine, Rodion passed beneath the horse-shoe-shaped archway and into Odesa's exotic animal market. He passed the parakeets, then the rodents, mice and hamsters stacked in homemade dwellings constructed from cardboard boxes. 'BON-BON BARON Watermelon Suckers' read one box. Rodion thought of Felix. Felix always saw all the angles! What had he said, about how nobody should eat Bonbon Baron sweets anymore? 'Who's gonna send inspectors to the president's factories?'

That hadn't occurred to Rodion, who liked watermelon suckers. But of course, Felix was right!

A big green parrot cocked its head at Rodion. Winked.

Now Rodion thought of Jacques, his friend Sima's foul-mouthed grey parrot, and stifled a giggle. Rodion shouldn't laugh. There was nothing funny, after all, about the bomb that went off in Angelina's restaurant. He worked just up the street, and had gone to see Sima the next day, before his shift started at Café Delicious. When he came in, she was kneeling on the ground among the shards of glass, with a dustpan and brush. Like a very brave Cinderella. There were violet rings beneath her eyes. And Rodion saw, for the very first time, that her eyes were the exact same shade of violet.

That violet colour did something to him. He felt a strange sensation in his chest. Quiet, irreversible. Like glass cracking. And for the first time, he realised what it was that the little black birthmark beneath her left eye was shaped like: a heart. Not a blob, as he'd thought before. No, it was clearly a heart, a little heart.

Rodion felt his own heart contract, thinking about it. He shook his head. Actually, the bombing made him angry. What did Angelina think would happen? After they gave the mayor back his investment, Angelina should have just kept quiet. Instead, Sima's mother posted an exposé detailing the mayor's long history of corruption on her Facebook page. Next thing you know: ka-boom! The mayor wasn't called Mephisto for nothing.

Angelina should stick to cooking, in Rodion's opinion. Stay out of politics. He himself was more interested in the results of Odesa's first-ever barista championship (Rodion hadn't slept for three nights, and he'd still taken second place!) than in the mayoral election. Politics was full of Mephistos. But a little business, making something beautiful – that was the future. Rodion dreamed of opening his own street-food stand. A hot-chocolate truck. Maybe with the money from this EASY ETERNITY project with Felix, if it ever got off the ground.

This American investor of Felix's, this 'the Lion', well, he sounded like a crook. An Odesite, just out of jail in Miami. Rodion had looked him up. Ran a strip club, some drugs, some arson ... but he'd got nabbed for trying to sell a Soviet nuclear submarine to Colombian cocaine dealers.

Of course, that kind of 'out-of-the-box thinking' was right up Felix's alley. So, fine. Let Felix handle it. Though, lately, Felix had been acting cagey. Edgy. Demanding. Scared, almost.

'HEYA!'

Rodion looked up at the green bird.

'HEYA!'

'Heya,' answered Rodion. The parrot nodded, and Rodion's thoughts wandered back to Sima. No, nothing about that bombing was funny. Except the parrot. He giggled, this time. That was a little bit funny. Sima's parrot used to curse like a sailor ('ASSHOLE!'). Now, he cursed like a sailor with a speech impediment ('A-A-A-A-ASSHOLE').

To be polite, Rodion said goodbye ('Seeya') to the parrot, then headed off. He walked past a bone-dry aquarium housing a litter of fluffy, white puppies. Past a sad, black dog. Entered a narrow, make-shift alley. Past the glistening eyes of a pair of Komodo dragons. The dank smell of snake. The alleyway ended in a wet wall of mossy aquariums. A corrugated plastic roof kept the sun out.

Rodion scanned the glass boxes. Some of the aquariums were empty. Others were mostly mud. Poison frogs, he guessed. Rodion spotted the sign he was looking for. 'Axolotl,' handwritten, on a notecard. 'Mexico.'

Rodion dropped to his haunches. Peered at the deep, slightly brown glass case. There were three of them. White, nearly translucent, with long, thick bodies and four pudgy, toddler's arms. The salamanders' eyes were small, goggly, and set very far apart on their flat, stubby snouts – which lent the ungainly little creatures a look of wise innocence, as if their eternal infancy gave them a special kind of knowing.

An old woman appeared from behind a curtain. She was breathing heavily and hobbling. A raven with one leg hopped along the ground behind her. Its wings were clipped, and it had a chain around his neck. 'You again?' she said. 'What, you boiling them?'

For a moment Rodion's voice stuck. Then he recovered himself. 'Salamander soup,' he said, with a smile. 'Speciality of the house.'

Five minutes later, he was back outside in the sunshine. In his hand he carried a large plastic bag, slowly leaking water. Inside, pawing now and then with their thick, immature legs, three axolotl salamanders took their first look at the city streets in this unfamiliar country. To judge by the wide-set expressions on their pale white snouts, they found what they saw somewhat surprising. But they were prepared to make the best of it.

# 18

'I want to change my life,' Natasha announced as she pulled her neat Japanese car into city centre traffic. Her pink skirt slid to one side as she shifted gears. Max averted his eyes. Out of the window, a man with no legs begged on the corner. His torso was set on a square platform, with little wheels. To move, he reached down and propelled himself with his hands. A young priest strode by. Thick black robes swaying around his ankles in the heat.

'Two revolutions,' Natasha said. 'It's enough for me. How was the train?'

Max shrugged, smiled lopsidedly. Said it was fine. Interesting.

'Yes, for you, I suppose it's interesting,' she said. 'Like when I was in Sudan, working as a business consultant. I thought, "Ah, how great, nothing works! Look, no electricity! No clean water! You can't shower! How wonderful! It's so interesting!"' She shook her head. 'That's probably what Ukraine is like, for you.'

Max shrugged. 'Non-committal.' That's what Natasha had said about him, all those years ago. Pushkin Street. Plane trees, leaves caked in exhaust. Crumbling facades. Tattered Greek columns. Urns.

'MEPHISTO IS A CRIMINAL,' read an advertising billboard. It showed a tough-looking, muscle-bound man. Shaved head, thick neck. Suit and tie.

'Mephisto?' said Max.

'Our new mayor.'

'I thought the new mayor was named Volodymyr something-or-other.'

'Yeah, Mephisto's just a nickname,' said Natasha. 'Like the shoes – you know Mephisto shoes? French, I think. Moccasins. Very popular in Soviet prisons in the 1980s.' She rolled her eyes. 'Typical dearth economy commodity fetishisation.'

'Ah-ha,' said Max.

At the old synagogue, Natasha turned left. Max's eye lingered on the building as they passed it. Dark grey. Haunting, Gothic. Lovely. Diamond-paned windows. Turrets.

Natasha parked up the street, in front of a dowdy wedding-dress shop. Cut the engine. Began listing instructions. Max should always lock the doors – had he heard about the new 'amnesty'? Natasha's door slammed shut. 'Our new president, the "Bonbon Baron" ...' – traffic surged, filling the air with fumes and dust – '... pardoned prisoners if they would go fight in the east. Against the Russians.'

They crossed the wide, tree-lined street. 'These are really bad guys! Thieves, murderers, rapists. They're wandering the streets, free – but they're heroes. No one will say anything! This army! It's not a real army.' Traffic welled just as they reached the safety of the opposite sidewalk. Natasha's tough, pretty face fell. 'I'm tired of it.'

*

Natasha stopped at a large, grey stone archway. Leaned all her weight against a black metal gate. They stepped into the sunny courtyard. Grapevines and laundry. Like a thousand others in this city. Max sneezed. Felt a squeeze of quick, existential fear. He'd forgotten to pick up the doctor's antihistamine prescription before the trip.

'Let me introduce you to Boris ...' Natasha was pointing at a dissipated orange cat, asleep in the sun. Beside him, already spoiling, was a feast: eggs doused in mayonnaise, an open tin of sardines. 'Here, in our building, he is a kind of inspector.' The orange cat opened an eye, looked up at her. 'You see? He understands when you talk to him.' Max's throat scratched, contracted. He coughed. '... He likes to go through each of the apartments, check what's happening. And inspectors, of course ...' Natasha gestured at the untouched feast, her eyes twinkling. '... You have to bribe them.'

Max held his breath as they continued across the courtyard. He would feel like a real idiot if he died in Odesa because he forgot to bring antihistamines. What a bullshit allergy to develop late in life ...

A strange smell suffused the air. Max cursed. The toe. The toe must be putrefying. Natasha was going to kick him out … But Natasha was walking towards a strange metal cylinder. Like a little turret, set into the ground. Max followed. He closed his eyes. Inhaled. Haight Street in the eighties. Every single college party he had ever attended. Max opened his eyes. 'Incense,' he said.

Natasha nodded. 'Our building had a special nuclear bomb shelter below it, and this, here, is the old airshaft. Now the New Age shop in the cellar uses it as storage …' At a metal door painted ox-blood red, she pressed a code into the corroded metal number pad. Max followed her inside, keeping his distance. The stairwell was concrete, its walls painted a bright institutional blue. 'Our nuclear bomb shelter wasn't just any shelter …' A good building, thought Max. The people who lived here had some money. '… ours was very high-tech, with its own a medical research facility. When I was a kid, a thousand people went to work there, in our shelter, every day.'

By the third floor, Max could hardly breathe. Cat hair? Was he just winded? A wilting jade plant languished on a windowsill, along with a bottle of stagnant water. '… actually, though, most of these Soviet shelters – they just built them right into the catacombs …' he heard Natasha's voice continuing from the stairs above.

Max stopped to catch his breath. 'Can you get to the catacombs from here?' he called up to her.

Her voice floated down. 'Every building in Odesa has an entrance to the catacombs,' she said.

Max felt his heart racing. Heard the blood in his ears. 'Actually,' Natasha was saying, from somewhere above him. 'I was down there, before I moved to the dacha for the summer …' *Click-click-click-click-click*. '… Boris likes to kill stray kittens. He had one down there, and it was making the most pathetic mewling noises …'

Max paused on the stairs. Bent. Hands on his knees. Caught his breath. Natasha's voice: 'I went down. To get him to knock it off …' How far up did Natasha live? '… turns out the esoteric shop's storage room isn't locked.'

Max eyed the next flight of stairs. It occurred to him that, as fifty percent of Team Rushmore, he would have a more regular routine. Plenty of gym-time. And working with Rose was bound to be healthier than his current job: unlike Alan Trilby, Max's wife never challenged him to drinking contests. Natasha's voice came floating down. 'I guess they don't know about the door. But you can still get down there ...'

'You've been in the catacombs?' Max called up.

He heard the click of her heels stop. Thank God. 'Of course! I grew up here,' said Natasha from somewhere high, high above. 'Every Odesan childhood has stories from the catacombs'.

Max bent, one more time. Tried to look forward to his new life. His impending healthfulness. He felt something hollow. Near his breastbone. Glanced at the gym bag. To think, he was doing all this because he needed a freezer! Max took one step, the next. Exposed pipes. Gas. Electricity. 'Once,' Natasha was saying, 'we made it all the way to the archives – in the old synagogue, across the street.'

Max reached the top. Natasha was fumbling in her purse. 'The Gothic building?' he said.

'That's the one,' said Natasha, brandishing a bundle of keys. 'There was a loose board. It led up into the basement. We wandered around a little in the dark. My brother said he saw a ghost, and we all screamed.'

Natasha pivoted on those legs of hers. Then she smiled. That wide, clear, fleeting smile. He'd forgotten. 'The tunnels can collapse at any moment, of course,' she said. 'But we thought it was great fun when we were kids.'

*

Natasha unlocked the door – one, two, three, four locks – and led Max through a large, handsome apartment. Bright colours: salmon, green. She delivered the rest of the instructions: 'The cleaning lady comes Tuesdays, wants to be locked in for safety. Odesa's very best writer, Isaac Babel, was born across the street – from the balcony, you can see his statue ...'

'What's his mobster character's name?'

'Benya Krik.'

'Right,' said Max. 'Benya-the-King. "The mobster with a heart of gold."'

Natasha tilted her head above her pretty shoulders, in affirmation. Max followed her into the bright orange kitchen, noted with some relief that a large beige refrigerator with a freezer door stood in the corner.

'... the sink has two taps; this one has filtered water.' Natasha shrugged. 'I drink it, and I'm still alive. When you leave, you can drop the keys off at the Bristol Hotel. Down the street. Bright pink, you can't miss it.'

'Sure,' said Max, following Natasha back to the airy, salmon-coloured hallway. In the doorway, Natasha turned back for a moment. Her dark eyes twinkled. 'It's nice to see you,' she said, softly. Max reached out. Laid a hand on her smooth, bare shoulder. For a moment, a warmth that had nothing to do with the Black Sea sun infused the entryway. Max was about to say that it was good to see her, too, when she crinkled her nose again and grinned. 'But you really need a shower.' With that, she spun around and disappeared down the stairwell, leaving a faint trace of incense in her wake.

Max locked the door behind her. One-two-three-four. Sat down right there in the salmon hallway. A line from his parochial school days floated back to him. *Oh Lord, give me chastity* ... Was he still drunk? *But not yet.* Oh, God. What if Natasha had? – what if Rose sensed? – Max pressed his eyes shut until the feeling passed.

Then, gingerly, he stood up. Carried his gym bag into the bright orange kitchen. Opened the beige refrigerator. He was in luck.

Like any good Odesite, Natasha kept her freezer stocked with ice cream. Packaged, according to local custom, in a plastic skin. Like a very large, shiny sausage. 'Eskimo' brand – the good kind. Max took the ice cream log out, let it sit for a few minutes on the kitchen's orange counter. In the sun.

Outside, the trees shook as a breeze puffed through the courtyard. The pre-school children began to cry out in the yard. Playtime. A loud techno beat joined their screams. Kids these days! Max tested the ice cream with his finger. Soft enough. Eskimo was the best. Nougat flavoured. A shame to ruin it. With a dull purple kitchen knife, he sliced the sausage longways. He scooped a few spoonfuls into the sink. Then he unwrapped the hotel towels. Held his breath. Fished out the toe. He found a cache of plastic grocery bags. Put the toe inside one. He tied the bag shut. Then he stuffed it, carefully, into the ice cream. He wiped the Eskimo casing clean and placed it back in the freezer.

# 19

Every morning, the Passage struck Rodion anew. The arcades were so beautiful! Pale pink corridors with their crumbling plaster nudes, arms raised towards the heavens. Breasts bared, cornucopias overflowing. The discoloured glass ceiling's patchwork of tiny rectangles. All of it, so early, suffused with a rose-coloured silence. The air still cool but already slightly stuffy, in happy anticipation of the day to come. He sighed, content.

His café was tucked away in the corner, behind the tourist shops stuffed with Russian porcelain; handmade wool socks; bright, embroidered Ukrainian costumes; striped Russian Navy shirts. There was a piano, too. At night, after the Passage gates were locked, he sat there and played. The empty corridors echoed with film scores (those were his favourite), the notes wafting up, up, up, to the glassed-in sky. Refracting the city light in the darkness.

He unlocked the café door and made his way to an old fish tank in the back. Maybe he should invite Sima, one night. He could play something for her. Rodion poured two new bottles of spring water into the aquarium. Originally, they'd used tap water, but the axolotls died. Rodion could have kicked himself – the city's water was full of lead. 'Live and learn,' Felix had said. But Rodion could have cried when he saw those helpless little creatures, white, transparent, floating on their backs.

Now, he released his new salamanders into their temporary home. Then, as he picked up an old washrag, ready to polish the tables to a high-shine worthy of the Passage, Rodion indulged in a little bit of daydreaming. Once the hot chocolate truck was up and running, if there was any more money left over ... well, he would buy another motorbike. Another Jupiter5 ... or maybe a Karpaty ... vroom, he thought, remembering the sound, the feel, vroom, vroom.

# 20

At a building like an Egyptian crypt, Max stopped. Looked up at the row of flat-faced sandstone goddesses. Wondered if their expressions had always been so sad. Or if they had seen too much, from up there. Then he pushed open a much-painted black metal gate. Crossed the barren courtyard. A wiry man in a tank top was curled up at the foot of an old-fashioned water cistern. Fast asleep.

Max rang a bell. Waited. Rang again.

Max heard a lock moving. Another. Then the door opened. A short man with a comfortable face, bushy eyebrows and a mop of salt-and-pepper hair stood blinking in the light. His pyjamas didn't match. The man rubbed his eyes. Gazed at Max, then past him into the dirt-packed courtyard. He considered the sleeping man in the tank top with something like yearning. His bleary gaze came to rest again on the man in front of him.

'Max-the-swimmer!' the man said, finally. He squinted, looking up at the clear, not-yet-blue sky. 'Do you know what time it is?'

'Six in the morning!' said Max, slapping the man on the back. 'Come on, Dr Natan. Let's have a cup of coffee.'

Dr Natan rubbed his eyes with both his fists, like a child. Rolled his eyes at the heavens. Grinned.

The ground-floor apartment was small and cosy. Wood floors, sepia wallpaper. A stand for ticket-taking stood in place of a coat rack. The living room sofa had long since been forfeited in favour of a series of glass cases. 'A museum of absence' was what Dr Natan called the project to which he'd dedicated his retired life – namely, turning his personal apartment into Odesa's only Jewish Museum.

'Our museum of absence has grown,' he said.

'The museum?' said Max. 'Or the absence?'

'Both,' said Dr Natan. The place had a wonderful hush. A kind of peace that had settled long ago over the modest dwelling.

Max followed Dr Natan through what had once been the living room, past precious objects: a single silver spoon from Odesa's best cafe. Carried halfway around the world in an emigrant's pocket. An official, state-issued electrical engineering textbook, in Yiddish. A bouquet of iron flowers plucked one by one from the graveyard just before Soviet bulldozers razed it. A list of statistics, painted on the wall, told the story of a city that, before WWII, was nearly half Jewish.

'... Almost everyone left in the nineties of course,' Dr Natan was saying. 'But now – with this instability, Russia, and the bombings – even more are going. "I emigrated without getting out of bed," as our mutual friend Fimka Fishman put it, in his brilliant diary-on-the-internet, what do you call it? – *blog*.' Natan yawned. 'But I can't complain. We have plenty of visitors.'

Natan opened the door to a small, cluttered room. Tiled floor to ceiling, like a public bath. The centrepiece was a dark green plastic table, piled high with papers. Max took a seat on a rickety wooden chair. Looked around. The kitchen counter was also covered in piles: books, fliers, papers. Notices were taped to the tiled walls. Calls for protests: 'Save the Mason's House.' 'Save the Odesa Archives.' A photocopy of a black cat: 'Have you seen our Regina?'

Amidst the papers, Natan located the tap. He filled a blue plastic canister. Next, he conjured from the mess of printed pages a spoon, two chipped cups, and after an extended hunt, instant coffee. The comfortable sound of water boiling filled the little room. Natan cleared a space on the table and set the cups down. He spooned the coffee crystals into the cups, poured the hot water, stirred once, twice, and carefully handed Max a cup decorated with little pink strawberries. Max held it in both hands.

'Max, my friend,' said Dr Natan, regarding him now with a steady gaze from under his bushy eyebrows. 'Tell me: what are you doing here?'

Max sipped the hot, bitter drink. For a moment, he felt like a sailor back on land. Listing.

'Another conference,' Max said, putting down his strawberry-printed cup. 'The usual people, talking about the usual things.' He shrugged. 'You? How's your grandson?'

'Steven!' said Dr Natan, with an eruptive smile. 'Since they emigrated, he is called Steven. He is well, very well! He has just received his American driving licence. Now he is able, legally, to drive – his mother crazy!'

Max laughed. Both men were silent, then. Lost for a moment in their own thoughts. When Max looked back up, Dr Natan had tears in his eyes.

'Come on, Dr Natan,' said Max, clapping the other man on the shoulder. 'It was a long time ago.'

'Max, my friend –' said Dr Natan.

'Hush,' Max said. He tried a new tack. 'If I hadn't been there, someone else would have ...' Even as Max said this, he realised it wasn't true – it was an early morning, April, before the summer season started, and the beach was deserted. One of Max's first trips – a conference? Probably – Alan Trilby's presence would explain the hangover that had driven Max down to the beach for a hair-of-the-dog swim. Max was just descending the last flight of uneven concrete steps to the water, when he caught sight of the little figure thrashing in the waves. Max ran. Out to the edge of the broken concrete quay. He dove. Hauled the child back to shore. In a moment, it all came back: the little body on the sand. The taste of salt. Overhead, a gull swooped and cried. Then the little figure jack-knifed. Coughed up half the Black Sea. Began to cry. Thank God. Max's neck had ached after that. For hours.

'Everything turned out fine, that's what matters,' said Max, blushing. 'Look at him, now! Sixteen. Stronger than you and me, I bet. Come on – tell me, what hopeless cultural conservation project are you championing, now?'

'Ah, Max,' said Dr Natan, sniffing once, then brightening. 'Since you ask!' He turned to the computer monitor on the table next to him. He picked up a pair of cloudy reading glasses and put them on. Then, slowly, peering through the half-moon lenses, he moved a mouse over the green plastic table. A newspaper article popped up onscreen. 'I begin it in the only way possible – as a fairy tale. "Once upon a time …" Well, I won't read it all. A new scandal. A true scandal, in our scandalous city. You are really interested?'

Max nodded, yes.

Dr Natan sighed. 'Well, then …' He turned back to the screen and began to read aloud. '… Once upon a time, there was a beautiful synagogue. Neo-Gothic architecture, built by Austrian Jews who came to Odesa for the lemon trade …'

'Oh!' said Max. 'I'm staying just across the street. It's a wonderful building.'

'The building is probably doomed,' said Dr Natan, holding up a finger to silence Max. 'Half the foundation collapsed fifteen years ago when part of the catacombs fell in. It would take an enormous amount of money to restore it – if it's even possible. Which we doubt.' He peered back at the screen. 'I'll summarise the next part: after the Nazis invaded, the city's Romanian occupiers turned the synagogue into a cinema. After the war, the Soviets made it the home to the city archives. A few months ago, in their infinite wisdom, the regional government decided to give the synagogue back to the Jews.'

Before Max could say anything, Dr Natan held up a finger to silence him.

'Good, you think!' said Dr Natan. 'But no! This is probably not a good thing. First – nobody asked for this building. And then there is the question – which Jewish community gets it? Here in Odesa there are four. The city government, in its infinite wisdom, gave the synagogue to the Hasidic community. But! It was a reform community that built this synagogue. They were very progressive, very engaged with European art, culture, philosophy, science. So our ultra-Orthodox community, they have nothing to do with the history of the building. No motivation to restore it, either. As a result … well.'

Dr Natan peered over his cloudy reading glasses. 'There are some who think this is just a way for one of our local developers to get his hands on the property, very cheaply. Mephisto – our mayor, perhaps you know him?' Max nodded. 'Mephisto has a lot of real-estate holdings in Odesa. He will wait for the synagogue to fall down. Two, three, five years. Then he will build a twenty-storey apartment house, or a casino.'

Max shook his head. He was about to say what a shame that was, when Dr Natan raised his finger. As if to say, 'don't cry over spilled milk'.

'We are concerned, now, about the archives! The regional government says, "Don't worry! We have found a wonderful new location. Former psychiatric hospital number 4, just outside of the city."' Here, Dr Natan peered at Max. 'Mostly used to incarcerate dissidents, during Soviet times. Perhaps you know that our mutual friend Fimka Fishman was a psychiatrist there?' Max shook his head, no.

'Yes!' said Dr Natan. 'Fishman took detailed notes about how many dissidents the regime incarcerated. Passed them to an underground group. It all went fine, until one of his friends was committed. She forgot she wasn't supposed to know him and greeted him in the hall! Well, after that he lost his job there.'

Dr Natan turned back to the screen, 'But that is ancient history. Let's return to the present. We do not trust the regional government, entirely. So we drive out to the former psychiatric hospital number 4 –' here, Dr Natan paused, scrolled down. 'And – look!' Max moved closer to the screen. Squinted at the black-and-white photo: four walls. No roof. Empty window frames stared blindly at the forest. Leaves covered the floor, in piles.

'It's a ruin,' said Max.

'Yes,' sighed Dr Natan.

'The regional government – does that mean Grisha?'

Dr Natan shook his head, no. 'Grisha would help us if he could. But Mephisto holds the real power in this city. No governor can accomplish anything without Mephisto's help. And Grisha has publicly declared war on Mephisto. Which one can understand, of course, but … just imagine! When it comes to saving the archives, the history of our city, every document, every record, everything that is left, from complete destruction – Ukrainian archives are not digitised, you know – Grisha's hands are tied!'

An image came to Max, involuntarily: a glossy photo sheet; white, pudgy fingers; a wine-red birthmark shaped like the state of Florida. A hand that was not tied – but severed. He shivered.

'... So, now we are protesting,' Dr Natan was saying. 'We are likely to fail. Memory, you know, is the enemy of every corrupt regime.'

'You're a wise man, Dr Natan,' said Max.

Dr Natan shrugged. A warm light was creeping in from the single window. Outside, the sun must be climbing. 'Let's see if I'm so wise,' he said. 'We'll make a little test. Am I correct, when I say: you have not come so very early in the morning to drink coffee and talk to me about memory?'

'Right again,' said Max, with a grin. 'Actually – I have a medical question.'

'High cholesterol?' said Dr Natan, raising a bushy eyebrow.

'Oh!' said Max. 'No – how did you know?'

Dr Natan shrugged. 'You are a little thick in the middle, you are the right age, you demonstrate many symptoms of a hangover. Alcohol, as we know, is not conducive to a healthy lifestyle.'

'I'm cutting down,' said Max. 'Anyway, that's not my question.'

'Alright,' said Natan. 'What is your question?'

Now it was Max's turn to clear a space on the table. He shuffled a few papers into a new pile, added them to a neighbouring tower. Then took out the ice cream and placed it carefully on the green plastic surface.

'Eskimo nougat!' said Natan. 'My favourite flavour! But really, if this is the kind of breakfast you are eating, it's no wonder –'

Max interrupted him. 'I found a toe.'

'A toe?'

Max felt for the slit in the log. Found the corner of the plastic bag. Pulled, slowly. Natan watched with a mixture of interest and horror. When the bag was removed, he put on his glasses. Fished a pair of pincers from a metal jar containing forks and knives. Then he took the toe from the nougat-covered plastic. He held it up to the bulb hanging from the ceiling. The lampshade, Max noticed, was pink plastic, covered with stickers. Butterflies and rainbows.

He stared for a long time at the flat surface where the digit once connected to a body. Natan turned it over. Saw the wine-coloured mark shaped like the state of Florida. Turned, took out a plate. Put the toe down on it. Natan looked up at Max with his deep brown eyes. Then he shook his head, sadly. 'Nougat,' said the doctor, 'my favourite flavour ...'

'Sorry about that,' said Max. Then: 'The birthmark. You recognise it?'

Natan peered at Max over his eyeglasses. Nodded. He struck a match, held the flame to the ruddy miniature Florida. 'In this state of decomposition, it's very hard to tell – this could be a stain, some kind of topical ink, or – even a tattoo. Applied before severance.' He looked up at Max again. 'To me, it looks like a threat. Typical mafia. You know in the 90s, what they used to do – the "security men" like our Mephisto? They would get a homeless man, pick him up off the street. Feed him, bathe him, clean him up. Put him in a business suit. Then they took him to the guys who owed them money. They said, "this businessman didn't pay us." Then, right there, they would –' Dr Natan made a motion of drawing a knife along his own throat.

Max's heart grew heavy. Mafia – that wasn't very interesting. Nothing Dunkirk would get excited about. Nothing that would eclipse Don Johnson (poor guy!) in DC. Nothing to count as a breakthrough in a failing career. Only when Max said this to himself did he realise that was what he'd been hoping. Maxiboy, he said to himself, you are an idiot. 'So not the Russians,' said Max.

Natan looked at him. Snorted. 'The Russians! Whenever something goes wrong these days, people say, "It was the Russians!" I'll tell you what, Max. We don't need the Russians to mess things up. We can do it all by ourselves.'

Max nodded. Said he guessed a DNA test was out of the question, for now. He would need a lab, and he wasn't sure he wanted anyone else to know about this. Natan nodded, sadly. Max asked if it was ok to keep the toe in the freezer. 'Not here – don't worry. I rented an apartment. With a freezer.'

Natan looked relieved. 'That's fine. As long as the temperature is minus four degrees, you can preserve DNA for quite some time. Of course, minus seventy degrees would keep it for years. But minus four is ok. The ice cream –' he shuddered a little. 'That's optional.'

'Great,' said Max. 'Anything else strike you about the toe? I'm no medical man. I don't know what to look for. What to make of it.'

Natan frowned. Using the pincers, he lifted the toe back up to the lamp with the butterfly sticker. Peered at the surface where it had been severed. 'See the ridges of the tissue?' he said. 'How they ruffle a little bit?' Max nodded. 'I don't know for certain,' said Natan. 'But it looks to me as if it's been frozen at a very low temperature. Cryogenically.'

He paused, looked again. Then, as Max watched, the retired medical doctor brought the digit towards himself. Stuck out his tongue. Touched it, for the briefest of moments, to the toe. 'Just what I thought,' he said. 'It also ... seems to have been exposed to salt water for some period of time. It's more or less brined.'

'Why would anyone do that?'

Dr Natan shook his head. Drew his bushy eyebrows together. 'Max, my friend,' he said. 'If you start asking these kinds of questions. Be careful.'

Max nodded.

'It's kosher.'

'Uh,' said Max. 'Ok.'

'Max,' said Natan, still looking at him. 'Have a I shown you my favourite anti-Semitic leaflet?'

Max shook his head, no.

In his mismatched pyjamas, Natan shuffled across a little wooden hallway into the next room. There on the wall was a glass case. A couple of pieces of paper were pinned up inside. He pointed at one of them. 'This was being handed out in an Odesa neighbourhood ... in front of a supermarket. Directly into people's hands!' Dr Natan leaned in. 'Can you imagine?' A headline ran across the top: 'BE CAREFUL – IT'S KOSHER.' Then below: 'Don't eat it, don't buy it. Because Jews use the blood of animals.'

Max said goodbye and had almost reached the courtyard's gate when he heard footsteps behind him. Natan, still in his pyjamas, was hurrying towards him. There was a magazine in his hand. 'This is a very long shot,' he said, breathing hard. 'Probably nothing – but it occurs to me –' he held out Odesa's only English-language magazine. Flipped through the pages. Pointed at an advertisement. *EASY ETERNITY*, read the ad. A blond man with a round face and a snub nose, porcine, in a red necktie. The blue glow of a Bluetooth device in his ear smiled up at Max. 'This young guy, there are … strange rumours about him,' Natan shrugged. 'Crazy things! He's bringing back the dead. Injecting foetal cells to cure tumours. Generating body parts. Obviously not true, but it just occurred to me. Not much, but I thought –'

'Thanks,' said Max.

As he was leaving, Max heard Dr Natan's voice once more, echoing from inside the courtyard.

'Be careful!' the other man called.

'It's kosher!' Max called back.

# 21

The old man with the eyepatch paused. Looked up: a traffic light swung overhead. Red. The cars rushed by on either side. A woman in cheap black high heels stopped. 'Can I help you, grandpa?' she said.

The old man took a long time answering. The woman shook her head, sadly. Why was this old man here, all alone? Where was his family? He was an emigrant – you could see that right away. Home for a last visit. You saw it all the time. Always alone, these old men. Why hadn't his children come with him? What was wrong in the West? What happened to families there?

'I'm looking for the Street of the Revolution,' the old man said, finally. His voice was gravelly, and the woman in cheap heels noticed a scent of mint as he spoke. 'That street doesn't exist any more,' she said, gently. 'Now it's called Cossack Street.' She patted his arm. 'That way.'

*

The King shuffled in the direction she had pointed. It was very hot already, and he reached up to wipe his brow with his long-sleeved dress shirt. His good eye welled. The lukewarm bath of the past: the electric power station. He stood, stared. As if it was a monument, a great token of mankind. He turned at this landmark. As he had done a thousand times in his childhood. Headed down the street – their street, his street – deeper into Moldavanka. Why had he never visited his childhood home, in all these years? It was all so long ago ... so long ...

He reached up, wiped his eye. How ironic, he thought, that it would be his enemy – that Georgian politician Grisha, the man who had single-handedly destroyed his second empire, the vast criminal

94

network he had built up with such care in Tiblisi, after he had to flee Odesa ... how ironic that Grisha, of all people, would be the reason for his return home.

The King stopped. On the sidewalk, in front of a low grey building, stood a husky middle-aged man in a flowered robe. His head was wrapped in a towel; he wore small pearl earrings and pale pink lipstick, and was smoking a cigarette. He narrowed his eyes at the old man with the eye patch.

The King ignored him. Instead, he turned to enter a grey plaster archway. Crumbling, exposing the bricks beneath. Inside, he paused. The courtyard was hung with grapes and laundry. Like a thousand others, all over the city. The King felt dizzy. He put his hand out, steadied himself on the wall.

The drag queen had followed him in. Now she stood looking at him.

'I used to live here,' said the old man. Even as he said it, he wondered why. It wasn't like him to confide in strangers. To confide in anyone. 'Seventy years ago.'

'Seventy years,' said the drag queen, drawing on his cigarette. 'That's a long time.'

\*

In her 55 years on this earth, Madame Tulip had seen everything. But last night was a wild one. Three fist fights at the club, two knives, one gun. One of the new girls had run screaming into the streets, and Madam Tulip had had to slap her, once, twice, to calm her down. Now she had a black eye. Madame Tulip sighed.

Time to get ready for a new day. She had washed her long hair, shaved her face, put on some light makeup, and was smoking a well-earned cigarette when the narrow old man with the eyepatch showed up. He caught her eye. Sure, just another emigrant, come back for one last look. They got them there sometimes. At the club, too. But there was something about him ... when he went inside to her courtyard, she followed. It was much too hot out for a long-sleeved dress shirt. But old people, sometimes they got a chill in their bones that no sunshine could bake out. Madame Tulip smoked and watched as the old man with the eyepatch looked up at the two-storey buildings, peered into the grapevines.

Then he faltered. Instinctively, Madame Tulip reached out. She was a big, barrel-chested person, strong. She took the old man by his narrow elbow and guided him to a plastic chair. As Madame Tulip helped him sit, the button at the wrist of the old man's long-sleeved dress shirt popped open. The sleeve pulled up a little, and Madame Tulip saw the tattoo. An eye. A grey eye. Gazing, unblinking, up from the back of his wrist. Made with needles and shoe polish – a prison tattoo, oh yes. Those she knew. She saw enough of them in the club; epaulettes drawn right into shoulders, cathedrals and skulls, stars and roses and women. One little old man's whole chest was covered in a portrait of Lenin, so the guards couldn't kill him in a firing squad: you can't shoot your idols, after all! These tattoos all meant something, said something: who'd been who in the Soviet Union's criminal hierarchy. The 'Vor', as they were called.

The old man was woozy, didn't seem to know where he was. Let alone that his tattoo was showing. Madame Tulip felt a wave of pure fear wash through her. Then she crushed her cigarette out beneath her plastic house shoe, went inside, and locked the door behind her. Once inside, she crossed herself. Once, twice. That tattoo! That staring, searching eye. She'd seen it only once in her life. And she never, ever, wanted to see it again. She crossed herself again and waited for the old man to leave.

*

Outside, the King leaned back. Gratefully. He didn't even notice that the drag queen had left. His head spun. His good eye trickled. He closed it. And saw … his father. Dressed in an overcoat. The scratch of papa's beard as he bent over his sleeping boy – to think that he had once been a boy! *Ingeleh.* And the words his father spoke came back to the old man, now. '*Ingeleh*,' said the bearded father, 'I have to go now. Your grandmother will take care if I …' The father's voice cracked, and the boy woke more fully from his deep childish sleep. The father reached into his coat pocket. Drew out five pieces of paper. 'My son,' he whispered, leaning in. 'These are very precious. They are powerful. They are power. Save them. If the soldiers come, hide them. Hide them safely. In the wrong hands, they can create an army that is unconquerable. Be careful, my son. Be careful.'

# 22

Max stopped at the corner. A woman with stringy hair pulled back in a red scarf looked up from her card table. Her teeth flashed, craggy with darkened gold.

She held up ten plastic-encased cards. Like she was going to read his Tarot. Her fingers were stiff. 'For luck,' she said, showing him the telephone numbers. Max felt his throat close, ever so slightly. He coughed. A fat orange cat jumped up on the card table, and Max stepped back. Felt his heart race.

With her arthritic hand, the woman petted the beast. 'Ah, Borechka,' she murmured. Max wondered if all the orange cats in Odesa were called Boris. He took the cards. Looked at the numbers. Couldn't remember which combinations were lucky. Picked five. Ukraine was one of the few places where you didn't need to provide any identification to buy a telephone SIM card. For law enforcement, this had disadvantages. But for everyone else it was a plus. Take the Bonbon Baron's pro-Kremlin predecessor: After he was deposed as president, angry citizens found 800 brand-new iPhones buried in his garden. Each had been used exactly once.

The woman grinned at Max, her face breaking into a web of wrinkles. Her teeth flashed again. Max paid and pocketed the SIM cards. He kept walking. Along the rolling sidewalk, sinking slowly into the catacombs. Corncobs for sale, piled as high as a man. A glimpse of white kernels, like strings of pearls.

On Preobrazhenska Street, Max ducked into a bus shelter. In the far corner, underneath the bench, lay an opal-grey cat. Fast asleep. Max sneezed. Dialled. The cat's sleek coat stretched over remarkably highly developed musculature, Max noticed. The phone rang until it went to voicemail. He called again. This time, it picked up. A sleepy voice said, 'Hello?'

'Marie! It's Max.'

'Max!' she sounded pleased. Max was glad. It was good to hear her voice. They'd worked together for years in Moscow, where she'd taken over and, despite a significant age difference, become friends. Born in Moscow, raised in Brighton Beach, Marie was a good girl, smart, oddball enough to get along with Max – take, for example, her peculiar fascination with the lives of early Christian saints. Marie's shriek interrupted his reminisces. 'Do you have any idea what time it is?'

'Um, let's see, nine a.m. minus seven hours –'

'Two in the morning, Max! It's two in the morning in DC. Where you are currently calling ...'

An East German convoy truck rumbled past. Like a time capsule. The sleek opal cat didn't stir a muscle.

Marie's voice, again. '... nine a.m. your time, aren't you supposed to be at a conference? It doesn't sound like you're at a conference. Don't tell me you're playing hooky already?'

'Just standing outside the hotel,' Max lied. He decided to change the subject. 'How's married life?'

'Oh,' Marie said, sounding pleased again. 'You know. So far, I can still stand him.' In the background, he heard sounds of a scuffle. Marie giggled. She had given up the Moscow office to marry a semi-famous computer hacker, the son of friends of her parents. A blind date, on one of her visits home. She liked him. He liked her. That was that. The agency, in *their* infinite wisdom, had let her exchange her full-time Moscow job for a part-time contractor position back home. 'Cut it out, Robby,' she said, still laughing. 'Go back to your programming, or whatever it is you do. This is business.'

'Speaking of which,' said Max. 'I hear you gave Rose and the girls a little tutorial in High Contact.'

'Oh,' said Marie. She sounded, Max thought, appropriately guilty. 'I might have mentioned it. And – they asked. So, I told them.' With a wave of self-justification. 'It's the new theory, after all. And anyway, you all use "Radio Silence" as such a prop, you know, to, like, not communicate.'

'Uh huh,' said Max. An old woman walked past, tapping the side-walk ahead of her with her stick. As she approached the bus shelter, her stick tapped centimetres away from the cat. The cat didn't move.

'Look, Max, I'm sorry. I owe you, ok?'

'Just what I was thinking,' said Max. A couple of crumpled cups lay on the sidewalk. Thin, plastic, the size of vodka-shots.

'Anytime you –'

'I need something now, actually.'

Marie groaned.

'You still have that special friend in forensics?'

'Max!' she said. 'I'm married. I don't have any special friends any more.'

'Not even me?'

'Except you.'

'Good, because I need you to get a copy of a report. When it's out. They're analysing a severed hand –'

'Ew,' said Marie.

'Completely ew,' agreed Max. 'The thing is, it might not be human flesh. Some sort of fake, apparently. Don't ask me, I'm not a biologist. Anyway, I just want to know what they find.'

'Severed hand – got it. Is that it?'

'For now, that's it,' said Max, ignoring the sarcasm in her voice. 'They picked it up in Baltimore. Couple of days ago. A week, maybe. In a vat of sunflower oil.'

'Grooooooossssss,' said Marie.

'I don't make the news, I just report it,' he said. 'By the way, Johnson's on it.'

Marie giggled. 'You mean Don Johnson?'

'Yep,' Max said. Serious. To set a good example. After all, it wasn't Johnson's fault.

'I know it's not his fault,' said Marie. 'But he doesn't have to dress like *Miami Vice*. Those white slacks!'

'Yeah, yeah,' said Max. 'Give Rose a hug for me, ok?'

'You'll see her before I do,' said Marie. 'Isn't that "Team Rushmore" real estate dinner she's been going on about this week?'

Max didn't say anything. He was watching the opal-coloured cat. Was its ribcage moving, ever so slightly? He didn't think so.

'Ooooh,' said Marie. 'I see. You aren't going to be back. Have you told Rose?'

'I gotta get going,' said Max. 'Let me know when you've got that report. And don't worry, I was just about to tell her.'

'Uh-huh,' said Marie. 'Good luck with that, Max-a-million.'

'Bye, Marie,' said Max. 'You're a queen among women.'

Max hung up. The opal-coloured cat was still lying in the corner of the bus shelter. Max shook the phone chips in his hand. Like dice. That cat was not asleep, thought Max. That cat was dead.

*

The tram ride back to the hotel was hot, sweaty, packed. The dented blue metal carriage heaved and tossed along the French Boulevard. Bodies pressed together, skin on skin, intermingling sweat. Blue and white stripes everywhere. Navy shirts. Men and women. The ticket taker – a short, nearly perfectly square woman with bright red lipstick – jabbed him in the side. He handed her two hryvnia. She nodded, once, and gave him his ticket.

They passed beach after beach, and the tram emptied. Max could breathe again. He took a seat and looked out the window. Sanatorium. Flesh-coloured apartment blocks. Sanatorium. Sanatorium. In front of the elegant yellow columns of the famous Odesa Eye Institute, men and women milled beneath the shady trees. They all wore eyepatches. Big fluffy balls of white cotton, taped left or right. 'In the land of the blind …' thought Max, glancing down at the magazine in his lap. *EASY ETERNITY*. Generating body parts. Trading in souls. Bringing back the dead. A feeling of unease came over him, as if he was holding something cursed. '… the one-eyed man is king.'

# Part 3

It happened,
It happened,
In Odesa.

('A Cloud in Trousers', Vladimir Mayakovsky)

## 23

The Gagarin's lobby was packed. Men in grey suits. Coffee-break snacks spread out on tables. Baked, twisting things. Flutes of orange juice and silver pots of coffee. White tablecloths. Max's head began to ache. As if returning to the scene of the crime reminded his body of what he'd done to it, the night before.

'Well, you're looking chipper, Rushmore!' Trilby's voice set off a chain of tinkling pain in Max's temples. 'So nice of you to join us. I was afraid you might be, ahem, indisposed.'

In his felt hat, Trilby looked truly chipper himself. Only if you looked very closely – and Max did – could you see the thin pink rim running along his lower eyelid. A sure sign that, if Max had suffered, Trilby had not fared much better. Max gave Trilby a weak, cotton-mouthed smile. 'You old bastard,' he said, affectionately. 'You still got it.'

Trilby smiled then, too. 'Fetch your caffeinated swill, Maxwell. Chop chop!'

'My name's not –' Max started to say as Trilby walked away. Then he stopped. Trilby knew, of course, that his name was Max. Not Maximilian, not Maxwell. Not Maximus. Max Skipovitch Rushmore. Of course, Skipovitch wasn't really his name, either – he had invented the patronymic for the Russians, who demanded it for various kinds of paperwork and, throughout the nineties and into the 'aughts, in order to get into nightclubs with doormen and metal detectors and names like Night Flight and The Number One Club. Skipovitch was as good as any other, he thought. Though to be honest, Max had always wondered how his mother could have married a man named 'Skip' and been surprised when he left her.

Max took a deep breath. Approached the silver pot labelled 'coffee'. Held out one of the dull white cups. Like an offering to the hangover gods.

Holding his caffeinated swill in his hands, Max looked around again. Saw the guy with the toothpaste-ad smile. Over in the corner, by the ficus. He seemed to have made friends with Trilby and Albu. The three men were gathered around a laptop. Max pulled up a chair. The toothpaste-ad guy turned. Flashed his bright smile. 'Good morning, Mr Rushmore!'

Max looked at the bright smile. The bright eyes. Oh, God, thought Max. The young man hanging on his reply was Mark Hope. The intern.

Max nodded. Albu pressed a button. Max joined the other three men, as they all turned their attention to the computer.

*

The screen showed a perfect beach day. Blue skies. Black Sea spray rising from the breakers. The camera panned away from the sea. A path leading to the beach. Grisha appeared. Dark bowl-cut hair. Chubby boyish cheeks. Polo shirt tucked into his shorts – he had gained weight since Max last saw him, at a three-a.m. conference in the middle of the Georgian war. The new governor was leading a small group of people, like a post-Soviet Pied Piper. They came to a stop in front of a wall. Tall, plaster, terracotta, the wall blocked the path. Grisha, animated. Gesticulating wildly.

'This is an illegal wall, built by an oligarch, blocking public access to the beach for his new villa,' interjected Albu. 'Oh, hello Maxime.'

Max nodded. Turned his attention back to the screen.

Grisha was waving over a bulldozer. The crowd applauded as the bulldozer attacked the terracotta wall. The video ended.

'Two million views,' said Trilby, triumphantly. 'And more than half of those are coming from Russia.'

'Russia is watching Odesa,' said Albu, nodding his monk's fringe.

Max glanced back at the screen. An ad was playing. Some sort of faux laboratory. Ukrainian production values. Suddenly, EASY ETERNITY flashed across the screen. Max watched. A strapping blond youth appeared onscreen. Tall, with bright blue eyes, wearing a lab coat like a costume. Hair pulled back in a ponytail, showing a green and pink tattoo peeking up along the back of his neck. Flowers? Max looked closer. Water lilies. A nice smile. Like he brought fresh air with him wherever he went. Looking at this kid, thought Max, made you think of Cossacks, galloping over the steppes. EASY ETERNITY flashed again.

'The Russian regime –' began Albu.

'Hang on a sec,' said Max. 'Can you turn the volume on?'

Trilby leaned over, looked. 'What nonsense is this, Maxwell?'

'My name isn't –' said Max.

Albu turned on the sound. They all listened for a moment, as the man in the lab coat said in broken English, 'Ukraine is the world leader in body parts production ...' The camera panned over a tray of eyeballs. 'Come and see for yourself!'

Trilby shook his head. 'What nonsense,' he said. Max muttered an assent.

'Cool idea, though, right?' said Mark Hope. 'I mean, whoah. Eyeballs.'

No one answered. Albu snapped his laptop shut. 'As I was saying,' Albu continued. 'If Grisha is successful in his reforms, it could have a very destabilising effect on the current regime to the north.'

'The Russian people are resigned, for now,' said Trilby. 'But if they see that it's possible, in Ukraine, to combat everyday corruption – !'

'They will demand change,' said Albu, his monk's fringe nodding up and down.

'Revolutions have been started for less,' agreed Trilby. 'Why do you think the Russians provoked the "Soccer Massacre" here, last month?'

Max looked at Mark Hope. Watching the conversation like a ping-pong match. His open face, wide eyes.

'… to make Odesa look like it was descending into chaos, under Grisha,' said Albu.

Mark Hope's eyes moved to Trilby: 'Where even a soccer match turns into a political bloodbath, with scores of dead.'

Max remembered, now, that he and the intern had been having a heart-to-heart last night. Mark Hope, it transpired, was pining for a Bosnian woman. 'We worked together in the dinosaur lab,' Mark Hope had said earnestly, in the white lobby last night. 'Of course, the cultural differences are immense. And she's completely traumatised by the war. But this girl …' Mark Hope sighed. Shook his well-formed head. He had the kind of plain good looks that young women liked. Soft, like a girl. '… she really got under my skin!' Max had grunted, sympathetically.

Now, everyone was standing. Heading, herd like, back to the conference. Trilby, Max, and Mark Hope joined them. Someone greeted Trilby – a tall, Brahmin-y American on the Jim Dunkirk model, who had kicked around the world as a journalist, then built shopping malls in the Russian provinces. Now, he was telling Trilby, he was back in news: launching an English-language rag in Kyiv. 'Ah,' said Trilby, 'And I thought newspapers were dead. Do, do tell.'

As the two men moved further ahead into the crowd, Mark Hope addressed Max, in a low voice. 'Mr Rushmore,' he said. 'By the way, thank you for your advice. I wrote her – you know the one – last night.' The toothpaste-ad smile lit up the whole hallway. It hurt Max's head. 'She wrote back right away,' Mark Hope said. 'We're going to meet. Next time I'm in DC.'

'Great,' said Max, who was surprised, and rather pleased to hear that this had been his advice. 'Glad I could help.'

*

Max woke up with a start. Grey room. Grey men. Conference. He glanced down at his phone. It was vibrating. He picked it up. Wrote back. Glanced at his laptop. Felt a terrible sinking feeling, as the chat box sprung up.

*Rosie Posie:*
*Anything you want to talk about?*

*Maxiboy:*
*Sweetpea! Why awake?*

*Rosie Posie:*
*Couldn't sleep.*

*Maxiboy:*
*sorry*

*Rosie Posie:*
*Sorry I can't sleep or sorry you're missing the Team Anderson dinner and didn't even bother to tell me?*

*Maxiboy:*
*Both*

*Rosie Posie:*
*…*

Oh, God. Would this be the chat that ended the marriage? Don't think about it, Maxiboy. Or, do think about it, but later. Max snapped his laptop shut. Looked around. A round table had begun.

Max looked for Mark Hope. Still sitting up front. Typing diligently. Good boy. He must be getting every single word down.

Max sidled past the pyramid of water bottles. Failed to distract Mark Hope. Reached into the conference packet. Tore off a piece of paper. Stuck it in his mouth. Chewed. Took a straw from the base of the pyramid. Positioned himself. Got his target in his sights.

Mark Hope started, slapping a hand to his neck. Max grinned. Mark Hope looked around. Max put on his most serious face. Beckoned.

'Mark,' he said, when the young man had ducked and threaded his way to the water bottle pyramid. 'Show me what you got, noteswise.'

Mark Hope handed Max his laptop. Max read the first two lines:

*International companies can and should serve as engines for growth.*

*Ukraine = the standard bearer of hope for developing democracy in the Black Sea region.*

'Great,' said Max. 'Hey, look. I want you to pretend I'm not here. That you're in charge of content delivery for Dunkirk.'

Mark Hope's clear, smooth face. Young, eager. Happy. There was tuft of fuzz where he'd missed a spot shaving. 'Sure thing, Mr Rushmore.'

The boy's sincerity hurt Max, somehow. 'Call me Max,' he said.

# 24

The Black Sea Shipping Company's main door was nailed shut. The building was black, faded. As if shadows had descended, and no amount of sun would ever burn them off. Even the pre-revolutionary workhouse next door – crude metal letters over the gate spelled 'Factory' – looked sunny, by comparison.

Max double-checked the address. EASY ETERNITY. He walked around to the courtyard in the back. In the far corner was a vegetable garden. An old woman was bent double, jabbing at the earth with a spade. She stood as Max walked over to her. Max showed her the advertisement. She studied him, from clouded eyes. She lifted a gnarled hand to touch the cross that hung from a chain around her short, plump neck. With her spade, she indicated the rickety metal stairway that led almost straight up to the third floor. 'Thanks,' said Max.

For a moment, the wind shifted. The sound of the docks. Hollow, crashing. Like waves, or distant thunder. Max made his way up the stairs. In places, they were rusted straight through. At the top was a metal door. A message, chalked across it: 'Devil's work!' Max wondered who had written it. Not the old lady, he thought. The stairs were much too steep.

At the rusted metal door, he knocked. Scuffed his knuckles. Nothing. Knocked again. Examined his hand. The door had drawn blood. Just a little. Max shook his head. Tried to remember when he'd last had a tetanus shot. Turned to leave. Just then he heard footsteps.

*

The door opened with a wrenching noise. In the shadows, Max recognised the well-fed, snub-nosed, somewhat porcine young man from the magazine advertisement. A red necktie. A black plastic device fit over his ear. Glowing blue light. Like a Cyborg. Max wondered if the Cossack of the steppes was really part of the EASY ETERNITY operation. Maybe he was just an actor.

The young man gave Max a hard, mistrusting look. He stepped out onto the narrow metal platform and, standing very close to Max, extended his hand coolly. It was bad luck to greet anyone over the threshold, and apparently, he hadn't decided yet whether to invite Max inside. Down below, Max saw the old lady shaking her spade at them.

Max spoke English. He held up the *Odesa Preview* apologetically, like a shield. Then he flipped to the advertisement. Standing on the narrow metal platform, he switched to Russian, employing, on instinct, a heavy American accent. He pointed at the advertisement. Expressed his interest in the EASY ETERNITY project.

The young man's round face softened. His expression grew oily. He grabbed Max's hand and shook it again, this time with feeling. 'You are an American investor! I am Felix. Call me Felix. Come in! Please!'

Leading Max inside, Felix repeated the words 'American investor' two or three times. Max didn't contradict him. In Odesa, a middle-aged Western man travelling alone was a sex tourist or a spy; it was always better to claim to be a spy – that way, everyone assumed you were a sex tourist. That Felix was calling Max an investor without trying to procure him a woman was, Max thought, a very good sign. Maybe things were changing here. Maybe Grisha was doing something right, after all.

With a wrenching sound, metal on metal, Felix pulled the door shut behind them. The space was large and dark, like a barn. Sunlight trickled in through narrow gaps in the walls and roof. Felix flipped a switch, and the large room became flooded with greenish light.

Felix swept an arm around the room, and Max followed with his gaze. The former shipping company's office seemed to be empty except for half a dozen cylindrical tin canisters, about waist-height, clustered like urns in the back. 'Grisha promised Western funding!' said Felix. 'Grisha said he'll make Odesa a second Batumi!' Felix shook his sturdy head. 'I admit! I was sceptical.' He trained his round, slightly piggy blue eyes on Max. 'But now! Here you are! An actual investor! In the flesh!'

Max smiled politely. Felix cast one more glance at the magazine advertisement, still visible, rolled up in Max's hand. 'We have an aggressive pre-payment plan for angel investors,' he said. Then he added, with a transparent, almost child-like craftiness: 'But only this week.'

Max summoned as much boredom as possible into his facial expression. Checked his watch. Sensed Felix getting nervous. Good. 'And what,' said Max, stifling a yawn, 'exactly, does EASY ETERNITY do?'

Felix inhaled deeply. Pulled himself together. Smiled. Oily, again. 'Here at EASY ETERNITY,' he began. 'We are in the process of trade-marking the brand, of course, though naturally in Ukraine there is no respect for intellectual property, which is why we have our eye on the world market –' He paused, flaring his nostrils as he breathed in again. The kid was worried about something, thought Max.

Felix went on: 'We have a very simple philosophy. It is: death is a 0% ROI – Return on Investment. Sunk costs far exceed any profits. It's the ultimate Ponzi scheme! No reasonable businessman would enter into a deal like this. Obviously, not all human beings on the planet are businessmen. My grandmother, for example, is a superstitious old woman! Even the best escalator – pardon me, I mean elevator – pitch in the world will have zero effect on her.' He shook his head, sadly.

'But let's talk about businessmen. With sense! Right now, even the best businessmen sign on to this very bad deal that is: death. With EASY ETERNITY, that's going to change. Why? Because we offer the world's first viable alternative.'

Max coughed. 'Very interesting,' he said.

'Of course it's interesting!' said Felix, irritated. 'That's why I founded this company. We're among the first to offer an alternative – if you don't count organised religion, which, no offense, is not a real business offer, but rather a bait-and-switch scheme. Now comes the gazillion dollar question.' Felix paused for effect. 'How do we do this?'

Max nodded. Went along for the ride. 'How?'

Felix smiled. Relaxed a little. 'People assume that because technology can't do something now, it won't be able to do it in the future. This is absolutely illogical, of course.'

Max acknowledged the truth of this.

'You may not realise, but thanks to the shipping industry, refrigeration technologies in Odesa were very advanced already, under the Soviets. In fact, we are in possession of some very unique technologies both in the cryogenic and – other – fields ...' Was that a crafty look that passed across Felix's face? Max thought it was. Wondered what that meant. '... that give us, we feel, several advantages over similar, more established firms in, say, your country. I will provide you with a fact sheet later.'

Max nodded gravely. Felix had led him slowly across the big, dusty room during the escalator pitch. They had reached the tin cylinders in the back. Waist-height. Most appeared to be empty.

Now, Felix walked over to a cylinder like the others. Unlike the others, it stood alone, and was covered with a lid. 'Here we keep our current clients,' he said. He lifted the top of the cylinder, and a dense fog poured out. 'That's the liquid nitrogen.'

'What do you mean, *clients*?' said Max.

'The recently dead,' said Felix. 'Who want to come back to life later.'

'Oh,' said Max.

'You are thinking, "there is not enough room in that canister for a body!"'

Max nodded, once: he had been thinking just that.

'... But let me explain,' Felix continued. 'We preserve only the seat of consciousness. Namely, the head.'

'Oh, I see,' said Max, who was beginning to feel a little ill. He peered into the canister, but the swirling fog made it impossible to tell if there was anything there. 'How many heads – I mean, clients – do you have down there?'

'Well,' said Felix, a little sadly. 'Only one, at the present. Actually, a pro bono case. We're a young company, of course. You cannot forget that! And people are dying every day, in most cases against their will. So our market is – well, almost all of humanity.' He smiled, as if in anticipation of great riches. 'Of course, we need to work on our marketing and communications strategies, to spread the word. But I think our ultimate goal – the revival of our patients through future science – will have a lot of resonance. Pay-to-play! Customers like that.'

'Sure, absolutely,' said Max. An anxious feeling came over him again. Like something was wrong. Like something bad was going to happen. He felt his throat closing, even though there were no cats in sight. 'So, this head is, um, cryogenically frozen?'

'That's right!' said Felix.

'Whose head – I mean, who is your first, um, client? If I may ask?'

'The pro bono client?' said Felix. He shrugged his round shoulders. Dropped his business speak. 'Actually, it's my grandpa. Well, you know, we Ukrainians – we're a naturally entrepreneurial people. Which is why the corruption in this country is so deadly. It just destroys everything! You build a good business and then thugs from the government come, thugs from the police come, regular thugs come. And they all want a piece of it. My grandfather, he saw his entrepreneurial nature thwarted under the Soviets. They put him in jail – for selling hats! Later, he saw how corruption continues to thwart us, under our so-called capitalism. I think that's part of why he wants to come back. To have another chance!

'Anyway, he was an enlightened man, very clever. He understood what we were doing with this business, right away. My grandmother, on the other hand – maybe you saw her, in the garden out back? We live there – she worked for the Black Sea Shipping Company. All her life.' He shook his head. 'But that grandmother of mine! She was completely against my grandfather becoming a client once she found out about the nature of the business.' Felix sighed. 'She's become very religious in the last few years. She says it's an affront to God. I tell her, Granny! God helps those who help themselves!'

'Human psychology,' said Max, sympathetically. 'When it comes to sales, it's the name of the game. Your Gran is giving you a good case study, at least. But, tell me, Felix. If – when – you succeed, um, well. What is your grandfather going to do with a head and no body?'

'Very good question!' said Felix happily. 'There are two possibilities. One is that biological sciences will have advanced to the extent that it will be possible to take the smallest piece of DNA and use it to generate not just, say, a tear duct or a nose, but entire bodies. Livers, hearts, hands. Lungs. In fact ...'

Here, Felix paused. Max thought he detected the same crafty look pass over Felix's round, open face again. Though it may have just been the flickering of the greenish industrial lights. Max's stomach somersaulted.

Felix was still talking: '... my preference, for such a time as I may become a client – is that we simply download our souls onto the Internet. No bodies at all.'

Max whistled. He felt slightly ill. 'Talk about eliminating sunk costs.'

Felix nodded happily. 'No haircuts, no meals, no doctors!'

'Absolutely, well done,' said Max. Then he went out on a limb. 'And – what about, say, a toe? Do you ever freeze toes?'

Felix looked at him blankly. 'Why would we freeze a toe? Do you have a brain in your toe? Is your soul in your pinkie finger?' He laughed, scornfully. 'I don't think so.'

'Of course, good point,' said Max. 'And what about these other technologies you mentioned? On the internet, I saw your ad with the, uh, eyeballs –'

Felix's piggy features contracted in anger. He clenched his jaw. 'That advertisement was supposed to come down. That technology is – not viable at the moment.'

'Maybe you could just tell me a little ...'

Felix interrupted him. 'No. We've got an NDA. That ad should never have still been running.' He looked up, forced a smile. 'I apologise for the inconvenience.'

'Hey no problem,' said Max, affably. 'When you've got a good thing, you gotta keep it under wraps.'

Felix's smile was half appeased. Half pleased. Still suspicious. Max decided to ask the most ridiculous thing he could think of. To ease the tension. 'Maybe you could just tell me, for example – is it possible, right now, to generate a human toe in a lab? Or even – say – a hand?'

The idea of generating a toe had no effect on Felix. But when Max said 'hand', a hard, dark look passed over his face. 'No,' said Felix. His voice was cold. Hostile. This was different to the eyeballs. There was something here. Something serious. It had the feel – it occurred to Max, somewhere in the pit of his gut – of life and death.

Max didn't know what to make of it: obviously the kid couldn't generate body parts. But maybe he was in on some sort of body parts trafficking scheme. Maybe he sold his grandpa's hand after he froze his head. Max felt a wave of nausea pass through him. Suddenly he just wanted to get out of there. 'Forgive me, it was a stupid question.' Tougher, Max thought to himself. Get tougher. 'Look, I'm no scientist. You know what they say: it's only by asking the stupid questions that you get the intelligent answers.' This sounded enough like a business school mantra to please Felix. His blue eyes grew placid.

'Thank you so much for your time,' said Max, heading for the door with perhaps just a little too much haste – the place made his skin crawl. 'It's an idea that'll turn …' Max winced as he held out his hand to Felix. '… some heads. I'll talk to some of my, uh, associates, and I'll be in touch.'

Felix nodded. He seemed preoccupied and didn't see his guest out.

# 25

The King woke from an uneasy nap, sitting on the plastic chair in his childhood courtyard. He looked down. The button had come off his dress shirt at the wrist. A tattooed blue-grey eye stared up at him. He pulled the sleeve down. Covered it.

Overhead, the grapes hung in fat bunches between the broad, dusty leaves. A yellow checked tablecloth flapped in the breeze. Just one more moment, he thought, and closed his one good eye.

After his father was shot, the boy was left alone with his grandmother. She had a head for crime, the old peasant lady who had somehow given birth to a scientist ('Look what good it did,' she used to say at night, when she had been drinking her cherry brandy. 'All his brains! Married a dirty foreigner, then got himself shot along with all his scientist friends by dirty Stalin'). She never called her grandson *Ingeleh*. She hardly called him anything, other than 'hey you!' or, when she was in a good mood, 'the boy'. Vanya missed his father sometimes, but he didn't dare tell his grandmother.

They were a good team, the old woman and the boy. The two of them made a lot of what she called 'business'. Bootlegging liquor. Dealing in smuggled cigarettes. 'It's the boy!' she would cackle when he came home at night, from the port or wherever he'd been practising one of their trades.

Then came the war. Far away, at first. Then closer. Then it was right at their door. The boy and Vanya's grandmother continued their trade throughout the siege. In times of desperation there was opportunity – that was something the boy learned at her knee.

The siege of Odesa lasted from August to October. Seventy-three days. Then the Romanians came. The first days were promising: the boy Vanya stole the soldiers' boots, then sold them back to them. Then, at 6:30 in the morning on 22 October, everything changed. A bomb went off in the Romanian commandant's office. A radio signal, sent from Crimea. 'Quick!' said his grandmother when she heard. 'Get down to the port.' The boy Vanya didn't know why, but before he left, he took those five pages his father had bequeathed him, out from under the mattress. He folded them under his shirt, next to his heart.

By 9:30, the first massacres had begun. By noon, 5,000 Jews had been hung in the city centre, in the streets and the squares. Vanya hid at the port. He knew all the smallest places, didn't he? Up in the stores of wheat. He was safe there: no army was going to burn their own dinner. It was warm and dry and smelled like the earth, and he fell into a torpor. A kind of waking death.

Later, much later, he learned that 19,000 Jews had been shot right there at the seaport. Over the next days, tens of thousands were taken outside the city. Lines and lines of people. His grandmother must have been among them, because he never saw her again.

After that, Vanya worked. Mostly at the port. He kept out of sight. When he had some money, he went to the movies. The Romanians had turned the synagogue downtown into a cinema. Vanya had never been inside before, but he liked it now. The old grey building with the soaring windows, like a castle out of King Arthur – his father read him knights' tales, before he went away forever. What did Vanya care if the movies were in German? He liked the way they looked up there, flickering on the screen. Black and white and full of romance.

Then one night, he watched a war film. Nazi propaganda. And for the first time, he understood what his father meant. About the soldiers. About an invincible army.

And afterwards, he hid behind the cinema's red curtains. When everyone had left, he walked around. Looking for a good place. He had had the strangest feeling – he remembered, now – like someone was helping him. Leading him. To a place in the wall where the wooden panelling came free. The boy Vanya put the papers safely away there. Replaced the wooden panel. Knew he'd done well. That his father would be proud.

Then Vanya stepped outside. Into the cold, dark world. All alone.

# 26

Max heard the metal door of the Black Sea Shipping Company slam behind him with a loud clang, and he inhaled with pleasure. He had never been so happy to be outside. He took another deep breath. And another: sea air. Clean, salty. Fresh. The stuff of life.

The vegetable garden was empty. He made his way towards it. A low wooden structure, with a sagging roof – probably the carriage house, once upon a time – bordered the garden. Through the ground-floor windows peeked gaudy red and yellow curtains. Felix and his grandmother lived there, he guessed. The upper floor windows had no glass at all.

There was a gap next to the carriage house. He walked towards it, careful not to step on the rusty nails and broken beer bottles littering the ground. From nowhere, a spotted kitten leaped out into his path. Yowled. Kept running.

On the other side of the carriage house, the earth extended, weedy, for several feet before falling off completely. From the street, you wouldn't have known it, but here, the city ended, abruptly. The Black Sea, straight ahead. Deep blue, passionate. The colour held in it every promise open waters could make: movement; distant shores; adventure; real, cold, deep, salty living.

Max skirted the edge of the cliff. Looked straight down into the port below. Like a toy landscape, visible in high relief: yellow cranes. White silos, black silos, blue silos. Containers in red, streaked with rust and oil.

A soft, sad whine of machinery. Like an old woman's weeping.

Max ambled across the weeds and drew up to Felix's grandmother. She wasn't weeping. No. She was sitting with her back to him in an old fold-out chair. Watching. The port, the sea.

Max sat on the dirt next to her.

'So, you're another one,' she said, finally, without taking her eyes off the horizon.

Max said nothing.

She laughed, bitterly. 'A so-called investor.' She shook her head. With shaking hands, she pulled a pack of cigarettes from her deep pink pocket. In the light, the white cardboard glistened, opalescent. Max leaned over. A flick of the thumb. A quick, rough, satisfying grate. The flame, nearly invisible in the morning sun. Never mind that Max didn't smoke: in this part of the world, a man was always ready with a lighter.

The old woman nodded. Inclined her head towards him. Inhaled. Expelled a thin grey mist. 'It's the devil's work, you know,' she said. She shook her head. 'Maybe he's seen too much darkness. My Felix, I mean.' She exhaled. 'His father was a good-for-nothing. His mother – my daughter – she was like me. She worked hard. When he lost his job, he just gave up. Stayed home all day and watched TV. She stayed with him, because of Felix. One night she came home, and he said to her, "Give me some money." She said, "I don't have any." He said, "Then go sell yourself on the street, I don't care." That's when she left him.' She was silent, remembering.

'The next one was even worse. When he lost his job, he started shooting heroin. He beat her. He went to jail. Then he died. After that it was just the three of us. And now my husband is gone, too. Or –' she snorted. 'Everything but his head. Sitting up there, pickled like one of my summer cabbages. Let me tell you – even when it was fresh, that man's brain was never his best attribute.'

'Pickled,' said Max. 'You mean, with salt?'

The old woman looked at him, like he was an idiot. 'With liquid nitrogen. Didn't he show you? He shows everyone.' She sighed. 'God only knows where he gets the stuff from. Though I guess, with our port, you can get anything. I should know.'

Max lit another cigarette for her. 'Felix said you worked for the shipping company all your life.'

She nodded. 'When I was hired, we loaded the bombs to send to Vietnam. Unloaded them, too. We sailed all the way there. And the Vietnamese, they came in their little bamboo rafts. Fine for fishing, but you can't keep a bomb steady. What could we do? We lowered the bombs down, and they tied them with reeds. From the deck we could see them, the whole way back to shore. A lot of them made it.' She closed her eyes, held her face up to the sun. 'I had a good job. It was a fine company. We had the biggest fleet in the world.'

'The Black Sea Shipping Company was a world-class institution,' said Max.

'We survived the nineties. If the company had failed, then I don't know how we would have eaten. But nothing lasts forever, I've learned that. Thank God Felix was old enough to work by the time those crooks closed everything down. *Privatising*,' she said, bitterly. 'That's what they called it.'

Max nodded.

'And now you people,' she said, her voice flat. 'The first one – with the ponytail. Stringy little thing. Always putting his head to the sky, like he's roaring,' She imitated the man, and something in her manner reminded Max of – something. Someone. 'Felix says to me, "*Babushka*, he wired $5,000 from the United States, before he came here." I say, "That man just got out of jail."'

'Huh,' said Max. Before he could add anything else, the old woman continued: 'What he needs, my Felix, is a good woman. Someone who can cook for him when I'm gone. Someone to knock some sense into his thick skull, before he's ready for pickling … when Angelina's daughter came by, I thought maybe –'

'Angelina's …' said Max. 'Like the restaurant?'

Felix grandmother was annoyed. 'Yes, like the restaurant. What does that have to do with anything?' Max apologised for interrupting. 'She's a good girl, that Sima. She has a good head on her shoulders, and if her cooking is anything like her mother's, it's good, too.'

She looked out again at the port. The cranes, the rusting, big-bellied ships. When she spoke again, there was anger in her voice. 'That soft-headed husband of mine. Do you know what he told Felix?'

Max shook his head, no.

'That brainless fool of a man. One day, after the pickling …' – she nodded towards Felix's offices – '… Felix came to me. He was trying to convince me, still. That he was going to make it as a business-man. He had a secret, he said. From his grandpa. His grandpa was descended – directly, mind you! – from Benya Krik. Benya Krik!'

'The mobster with a heart of gold,' said Max. 'Is it true?'

'Benya Krik doesn't exist! Invented by the mind of Isaac Babel, may he rest in peace. Benya Krik! How did the men in my family get such soft heads?'

'Babel modelled him on a real-life gangster,' said Max. 'Maybe that's what your husband meant.'

'Do you think such soft-boiled eggs would think of that? Things changed after that. Felix was so angry I didn't believe him. Didn't believe *dedushka*. He said he was going to prove it. Good, I said! Look in the archives! I will! he said. I'm sure he never did. We rarely seek to disprove our illusions, after all. But it was soon after that … something changed.'

She flung her cigarette butt out, this time. Down, into the abyss. 'The fool with the ponytail came, oh a few weeks later. Claims he's from Florida. But I tell you, that man is an Odesite. And a jail bird. And –' she paused, almost spitting, 'a drug addict.'

A fool with a ponytail, thought Max. Roaring? Something tugged at his memory. Florida. Odesa. Jail.

Felix's grandmother was still talking. '… "the Lion", that's what Felix calls him.'

The Lion! thought Max. Of course. One of the more colourful small-time criminals to emigrate from the former USSR in the late '90s. The Lion almost graduated to the semi-big time when he ar-ranged for the sale of a Soviet nuclear submarine to Colombian co-caine dealers. But before the deal went through, the DEA broke down his door in Miami. Sent him to jail. Could he be out, now? Fifteen, twenty years? Sure.

Max glanced around. From here, he saw, you could just make out the very top of a dilapidated set of stairs. They seemed to lead straight down. Felix's grandmother had stopped talking. Max had the feeling she wanted to say something more but didn't dare. He didn't push her. It didn't seem worth his while.

Instead, Max stood. Said goodbye. Walked away with a heavy tread. An ex-con from Miami was even less promising when it came to career-building than a local mafia plot.

*

From the window of the Black Sea Shipping Company, Felix gazed out, unhappily. Watched the American leaving. What had he been doing out there? Talking to his grandmother. Why?

Gordon Gekko. 'Greed is good.' *Wall Street. Wolf of Wall Street.* He had watched all those American movies as a kid, with his grandfather. On Ukrainian television. Dubbed, the English coming through. Round, confident, rich syllables. The language of money. While his grandfather told him all about the family hat company, about capitalism, the free market …

Felix had been a lonely kid. He'd always had a sweet tooth, and the other kids made fun of him. Called him Porky. Those evenings with his grandfather, their long talks, they were some of Felix's best memories. 'Dress for the job you want!' Well, Felix had started wearing that red necktie. 'You gotta spend money to make money,' that was another one of his grandfather's mantras. Even if they never had an extra cent in the house the whole time Felix was growing up …

Felix glanced over at the cylinder. The cryogenics company had been his grandpa's idea. Right before he died. Felix had gone along with it, hare-brained as it was. He had always had the feeling that there was something big out there for him. When his grandpa asked him to preserve his brain, well, Felix had had plenty of qualms. But he looked into his grandfather's milky eyes, saw how important it was to him. They set up the vat together. When the time came, Felix bribed the funeral home and got it done.

Had he believed in it? Not really. But now, looking at it all, it had set off a chain of events that had led to something big … After all, if his grandpa hadn't gotten himself 'pickled' – that was how Felix's grandmother referred to it, and Felix had got into the habit of calling it that, too – then Felix wouldn't have needed to come up with an advertising campaign to raise money for the electric bills. And when Rodion took him by Sima's new place to show him her award-winning buttercream eyeballs, Felix never would have seen their internet-advertising potential. And then, if his grandmother hadn't gotten so angry about the pickling, they wouldn't have had the fight about Benya Krik. Felix would never have gone to the archives to prove her wrong. Wouldn't have made his discovery ... Felix shivered in the dark warehouse.

And now? Why did he have such a sinking feeling in the pit of his stomach? Why couldn't he sleep? Ever since the bombing ... Felix pushed the thought away. He'd had no idea what 'Luddy the Lion', his investor, had meant to do with that list of materials he'd told Felix to get for him ... he couldn't have known ... in fact, even now, he didn't know what had happened. Maybe the Lion hadn't done anything at all with that all that fertilizer and hydrogen peroxide ...? Felix shivered again. He wasn't a criminal. He just wanted to be a businessman. It didn't matter that there was no money for business school. He read all the textbooks, everything he could get his hands on. *Show me the money!*

What if Sima had –?

Felix banished the thought. Money. That was the answer. 'Money makes the world go round.' That's what his grandfather had always said. Felix could fix this with more money. He caught a glimpse of himself, reflected in the window. The blue light in his ear. Like a businessman. As for the rest? As a businessman, you had to be realistic about what you had to offer. And sex appeal? He didn't have it. Rodion – that was another matter! Take Sima – Felix's stomach did a miserable little flip again out of guilt and fear – the way she looked at his friend! She had never and would never look at Felix that way. Felix wished she would, just once, so he'd know what it felt like. Sure, there was that Lilia from the archives. She'd taken a shine to Felix. But then, she probably didn't meet a lot of people, working there.

Money. Felix needed more money. He was going to get it! And Rodion was going to help him. Good things came so easily to Rodion! When Rodion first moved to Odesa, his aunt's mother's cousin called Felix's grandmother. Asked for Felix to give the small-town boy a hand. Show him the ropes here in the big city. Felix didn't mind. The fact was, he'd never really outgrown being a lonely kid.

When he met Rodion, it was like yin and yang. Rodion was handsome and optimistic, Felix was shrewd. They hit it off, became friends. And when Felix found those papers in the archive, Rodion knew just what to do with them. It was a lucky partnership, that was for sure.

Yes, Felix was lucky to have Rodion. And he knew how Rodion felt about Sima – even if Rodion didn't yet. So how could he, Felix, have –?

Money. The answer was always money. Felix looked back out the window. The American was gone now. Where was that grand-mother of his? She would lay down her life for him, Felix knew that. But right up until the point of sacrificing her life for his, she would do anything she could to ruin everything he undertook ... just like she had never supported his grandfather's ideas ...

What had the American been doing, talking to her? Had his grandmother told him about Benya Krik? She'd been doing that, lately. Telling people. Not that it mattered ... but he didn't like it. It made him nervous. Felix started to feel bad again.

Then he dialled a number. On the screen, a photo popped up. A bottle blonde with witchy eyebrows. 'Lilia.' Felix cocked his head a little, as the Bluetooth hummed. A young woman's voice, whisper-ing that she was at work, that her boss was due back any minute. 'She's down in the Trotsky archives ...'

'Hey,' said Felix, interrupting her. 'Do me a favour? If an Ameri-can comes by looking for Benya Krik ...'

# 27

That damned cat. That damned alley cat. Né Prince. But the name that stuck was Cheeky B (the 'B' stood for 'Bastard'). Mr Smiley had spotted him as a kitten. He was special. That beautiful glossy opal coat, despite his guttersnipe origins. The confidence in his paws. The way he knew instinctively how to use them. Mr Smiley had kept an eye on him. The first time he saw how Cheeky B used his little kitten paw to strangle the fluffy white kitty who was getting his cream – Mr Smiley's heart had almost burst with pride. He'd taken him under his wing. Treated him like a – like a son. After all, Cheeky B was everything that his real son, Vladislav – that coddled, spoiled, weak-tailed disappointment with the little white patch over his chest, as if he were a human wearing a pocket-square, the dandified little twerp – was not.

Mr Smiley had looked at Vladislav differently, though, when his son came to him and told him how Cheeky B was planning a break-away group to take over the port – *the port!* Admittedly, the fish leavings were scantier each year. In fact, Mr Smiley had read that these days, you were more likely to catch a refrigerator than a fish, in the Black Sea. But still! The port was crucial – in addition to the rotting gold mine of discarded fish, there was simply everything there. Everything that came into Ukraine. Which meant it was where you could scrounge – prawns, cocaine, gossip. A cat boss without control of the port couldn't call himself a cat boss at all.

Vladislav might not be good for anything that got his paws dirty. But it seemed he had other skills. Sneaking and betraying. That was good. That was very good. A tattle-tail wasn't the highest form of cat, of course. But it was useful. Mr Smiley had swished his tail, once, in thanks. Then he put out the word: he wanted a meeting with Cheeky B. At the regular place: Preobrazhenska Street. In front of the Train Cabin Bar. So named because it was the size of a train cabin. And decorated to look like one, too (Mr Smiley knew, because he had travelled to Kyiv on business, twice).

Cheeky B was there, of course. The bar was closing. The old drunks missing their teeth were stumbling out, holding vodka shots in thin plastic cups. Tilted their heads back, crumbled the cups like paper. Threw them on the ground. Pigs!

Cheeky B was as cheeky as ever, it turned out. The cat denied everything. Of course, he would. Then, when he saw that wasn't going to help him, Cheeky B had stood to fight. He was young, he was strong. But Mr Smiley was the better killing machine. It was that simple. It was a struggle, but in the end, he had Cheeky B by the throat. A brief application of claw to aorta finished the job. Mr Smiley had dragged the body out himself. Left it under the seats at the bus stop. A sign for any other cats who thought of betraying him. This is what happens. End of story.

But was it? For days, now, that last look in Cheeky B's eyes, before the life went out of them, had haunted Mr Smiley. Those eyes came to him in his sleep. Reproached him with their innocence. It distracted him. Was he losing his grip?

Mr Smiley swished his tail. In anger, now. Self-doubt was poison. Even a house cat knew that.

Anyway, right now he had something else to worry about. On Nemo Beach, in the darkness, Mr Smiley had crept up to the black jeans the boy with the green lizard back had left on the sand. He put his sensitive nose to the back pocket, where the thing had been. The smell of coffee grounds and cigarettes. And something else. A complex smell. The governor, Grisha. A whiff of black magic. And a hint of some delicacy. At first, Mr Smiley thought it might be caviar. But no, it wasn't caviar. It was something rarer. More delicious. Mr Smiley's stomach rumbled, and his mouth watered, as he remembered the scent. Salamander. It smelled like some kind of salamander.

# 28

Max was standing in a glinting canyon, white and grey and silver. Flashy edifices, filled with shops rose up around him. Sealed out the sunshine.

Max held his hand up. Shielded his eyes from the glare. Searched again. No, there was no delicate, old-fashioned ironwork arch. No ring of chestnut trees, leaning like elder statesmen, tall and top heavy, slightly diseased. No dirt path. No old women moving slowly from the city towards the soft blue sparkle of the sea.

This was the wrong place. Light flashed from the bright, glassy facades. It hurt his head. Max closed his eyes. Felt a meaty hand on his shoulder.

'Don't recognise it?' Josiah Homily's voice was raw and low. He was wider than the last time Max had seen him. More grizzled. Grey. Decked out in summer casual wear: a big, much-washed polo shirt, cargo shorts below the knees. Teva sandals. Socks. Homily threw his meaty hand out at the white soapstone walkway. The polished facades. 'Where are the trees, am I right?'

'Where are the trees! Where's the sea?' said Max, grasping his hand. 'What happened to Arcadia? Hey, what happened to your face?'

Homily's weak blue eyes were as faded as his polo shirt. But the left side of his face was vibrant: deep purple, scratched. 'Oh, the wife signed me up for one of these "Nazis versus Russians" battles, down in the catacombs.'

'What?' said Max.

'Oh, yeah,' said Homily, shaking his head. 'You know these role-playing fanatics. My wife's cousin is a history buff, can't get enough of it. They go down there, and it's all set up. Totally unofficial, of course. Could collapse any time, I guess. But that doesn't stop anybody. A couple of nutcases have made a kind of "living World War Two museum" down there. They got old army helmets, they got old hand grenades, they got old artillery guns. Then they've built a sort of re-enactment area. One cave for the Nazis – decorated with Bund Deutscher Mädel posters and everything – and another cave for the Russians. Then you battle it out in the passageways. Only problem is ...' Homily started walking, '... there are never enough Nazis. Uniforms are too expensive. So, the wife, she told me I had to help out.' Homily shrugged. 'We lost, of course. Russian uniforms are a dime a dozen.'

Overhead, LED lights flashed like a ticker tape, from a rectangular archway. ARCADIA-ARCADIA-ARCADIA. Max followed Homily through the archway. ARCADIA-ARCAD--

They emerged onto an open-air shopping strip. Shop windows, gleaming. Bathing suits, mobile telephones, ice cream.

'What the ...?' said Max.

'Coupla mobsters bought Arcadia, what, two years ago,' said Homily. 'Tore everything out. Built this. It's a real little cash machine.'

'Aesthetic appeal of an ATM, too,' said Max.

'Charming it is not,' agreed Homily. 'But you see how clean it is? S'basically a little police state. I thought we'd go here –' Homily indicated a café whose large black sign read, in English, Roast Darkly.

'Sure,' said Max. 'Lead the way.'

A large, dark, deeply-shadowed terrace. Low wooden ceiling. Painted black. Low black couches. Low black tables. An abundance of overhead fans.

'Joe,' said Max, as a cool mist fell from some mysterious overhead source. 'You're a sight for sore eyes.'

'You must have had a rotten day,' said Homily, lowering himself awkwardly onto one of the low couches. In the half-light his face looked less purple.

'Try a rotten year,' said Max. He saw an emotion flit, ghostly, across Homily's faded eyes, and felt a prick in his own heart. Sadness? Regret. Max was an idiot. Homily had had a rotten decade. And he, Max, should keep his mouth shut.

Poor Joe Homily. If Trilby and Albu were the winners in the stay-on-a-payroll game, Josiah Homily was the loser. In the end, it all came down to luck. Bad luck. The truth was, what happened to Homily could have happened to anybody. He'd been working in Moscow. Height of the oil boom, before the US economy went into freefall. An American environmental NGO wanted to launch a pilot water clean-up project in some rural wasteland, and Homily had been chosen to pitch it. Max could imagine how it was: standard-issue, smoky back room. Torn-out sections of a girlie calendar – some shiny woman in a thong – taped to the wall. A flat fold-out table with metal legs. The local government official wanted $50,000. To begin his review of the application.

Homily should have said no. Not because it was morally wrong, but because – as it turned out – the government official was on his way out. Homily, as was not unusual in those fatter days, borrowed the money from the Agency's office funds. The official pocketed it. Went missing the next day. The money was gone. The ascendant apparatchiks who took the missing man's position had managed to get the smoky back-room transaction on videotape. Took it to the local security forces. They picked up Homily at his cruddy hotel, stuck him in jail for a few days. To make a point. When Homily did get out, there was a big stink.

Back at Langley, old Rex – Homily, Max remembered now, had been another of Rex's protegees – was, in his own way, on the way out. More than a few people wanted to hurry Rex's exit along, and attacking a proxy was one way to do it. 'Thief,' cried one of the Agency's ascendant apparatchiks. Offended, Homily tendered his resignation. He never expected Dunkirk to accept it. Dunkirk did. The first round of agent buyouts came a month later. The Agency cut staff by half, that time. Homily was one cut they didn't have to pay for. (Rex's departure from the CIA took place shortly thereafter, when Max's mentor left an eight-hour meeting, went back to his computer, and died).

And Homily? He went home. To – was it Alabama? Tried to start over. Failed. Bought a car, drove through the south. But he couldn't rest. Max ran into him once in DC. At the movies. Homily was there alone. They were both waiting in line for popcorn. Rose was saving seats – they were newlyweds, and it was date night. As the popcorn line crept forward, Homily said he had the feeling he didn't belong anywhere, any more. Afterwards, Max wondered if it was an accident that Homily was there. They had never been close but maybe Homily thought Max was different from the others. Not as ruthless. Next thing Max heard, Homily had relocated. Odesa. It made sense, in a way – a sort of Stockholm syndrome, coupled with a willingness to accept the next-best thing.

'This place ok with you?'

Max nodded. 'Spinach wraps – very civilised.'

'Burgers're good, too,' said Homily. 'If you've been missing a burger.'

'Promised my wife to lay off the cholesterol,' said Max. 'Although it's tempting. I've got a hangover like a sailor – last night Trilby was telling his old joke and –'

'Trilby's here?' That ghostly emotion flickered across Homily's eyes again.

'Just for a day or two,' said Max. 'Conference. Dull as the dickens.'

Homily nodded. A giant hookah arrived. Green. A sickly-sweet smell rose up. Overhead, a hissing sound. Then a cool, damp mist. 'And Rose-by-any-other-name? All's well?'

Max smiled. He'd forgotten – but it was true, when he first wooed Rose, that was what he'd called her. 'Thriving,' he said. 'And you? You got married?'

'Local lady,' said Homily. His faded countenance brightened as he took a puff of the hookah. All he was missing, thought Max, was a mushroom to sit on. 'Light of my life.'

'Terrific,' said Max. 'You're keeping busy?'

'Yeah,' Homily said. There was pride in his voice. 'I've got a blog. Homily's Homilies. Dot net. "Policy-politics-plus".'

Max nodded. Homily wasn't clever, but he was smart. 'Guess Grisha's really put this place on the map.'

Homily nodded. Puffed. 'American senators, World Bank, international journalists – every weekend, they're crawling all over the place.' He exhaled. 'The new ambassador, McClellen, was just here. Pulled me aside at a party and said: "We're running full-scale amphibious exercises with the Ukrainian navy this weekend. Send a signal to the Russians. If they launch a marine attack, the Ukrainians can mobilise on a dime."' Homily took another puff. Glanced down modestly. 'Wanted me to write a blog about it.'

'Great,' said Max, wondering how Homily managed to live. There must be some money somewhere. A few scraps from McClellen wasn't going to pay the rent, let alone subsidise role-playing military uniforms. Maybe the wife had money. Max hoped so. 'And Grisha? He have a chance?'

Homily shrugged. 'I think so. But he's going to have a hard time instituting reforms. Mephisto – the mayor – runs a construction company. Makes most of his money that way. State wants to build a new road, Mephisto's company submits a tender. It's always four times anybody else's, they never do the work, and they always get the contract. There's a reason Odesa's got the worst roads in Ukraine.'

'Just what Grisha's campaigning against,' said Max.

Homily nodded. 'Mephisto owns two TV channels and has pretty much used them to declare war – the spinach wraps are good, actually.'

Max looked up. A teenage waitress with long straight hair the colour of mahogany, and a face that was absolutely blank, except for a pair of wide, black painted-on eyebrows – like a heroine from Lermontov – was standing silently over them. The two men ordered.

When she left, Max looked up. 'You remember Luddy the Lion?'

'The submarine guy?'

Max nodded. 'That's the one. DEA got him in Miami.'

'Didn't he kill one of his strippers?'

'Almost. Made her eat gravel, after he beat her half to death in the parking lot. She dropped the charges ...'

The sparkling lemonades arrived in giant blue glasses, with curling pink straws and yellow paper umbrellas. Max took a sip. 'Supposedly, he's been spotted in Odesa.'

Homily shrugged. 'Could be true. I mean, I haven't heard that, but Odesites are like homing pigeons. They always come back.' He took another long puff. Watermelon-flavoured smoke poured from his nostrils. 'That's another problem Grisha has. Not the Odesites, but the Georgians. See, when he was president in Georgia, the way he got rid of the mafia was to call them in for questioning. His police would say, "Are you part of the Vor?" I don't need to tell you this – but it's against criminal code to deny being part of the Vor. So they always said yes, and then Grisha deported them. A lot of them came to Odesa. So you can imagine … they all have it in for Grisha.'

'Sure,' said Max. 'Makes sense.'

Homily squinted. Puffed. 'Hang on a sec,' he said, pulling out his iPhone. 'It's the wife.' He smiled happily as he typed. Then he looked back up, with an air of contentment. 'Her uncle's one of the biggest Odesa mobsters there was. Retired, now. Lives in Beverly Hills. Refuses to learn English. A real character! "If Americans want to talk to me," he says, "they can fucking learn Russian!" If there's any Odesa mobster trivia you ever want to know, just ask. She's kind of the unofficial family historian. Oh – hang on –'

As Homily typed, Max took the yellow paper umbrella from his drink. Closed it and opened it again. Took a sip. So the wife had mobster money. Not the worst retirement plan. The blank-faced Lermontov heroine brought the spinach wraps. Set them down without emotion. Not even her dark brows moved.

Homily finished typing. The only sounds were the rise and fall of holiday voices and the spray of water from overhead. Then Max decided to go out on a limb. 'Severed toe say anything to you?'

Homily paused, mid-bite. His wrap dripped mayonnaise.

'Sorry, Joe,' said Max. 'Not really lunch time conversation. I was just wondering – any local mobsters known for cutting off …' Max hesitated. It sounded ridiculous, even to his ears. 'Well – toes?'

Homily finished chewing. Swallowed. Looked thoughtful. 'Fingers, yes,' he said. 'I mean, Grisha's been going around talking about Mephisto and his shears, trying to drum up opposition to the new roads tender.'

Overhead, there was a hissing sound. The other man continued: 'Of course Grisha's absolutely right. In the '90s, when Mephisto worked for a weapons dealer, that was one of the things he was famous for. Going around with a pair of shears and a finger, to collect money.'

'Sure,' said Max. The sound of holiday-making surged again, until the spray of cold water put it out.

'But a toe,' Homily mused. 'No, I don't think anyone makes threats with a toe. Not really big league, if you know what I mean.'

The girl brought the bill, without any expression. Homily reached for his wallet, but Max said no. Homily could take him out next time he was in DC. Homily grinned happily. Said 'Sure thing, Rushmore. You got it, buddy.' Max counted out the bills.

'Don't leave such a big tip,' said Homily, suddenly.

'Why not?'

'It's all mafia,' he said.

Max looked at the teenage waitress, shrugged. 'She's not mafia.'

'Oh, they're taken care of, all right,' said Homily, darkly. 'Last week there was a shooting here. Two a.m. No one saw anything.'

# Part 4

Every city has a sex and an age which have nothing to do with
demography. Rome is feminine.
So is Odesa.

John Berger, *Keeping a Rendezvous*

## 29

The screeching sound of a siren going off woke Max. SCREECH
SCREECH SCREECH SCREECH. He rolled over. Picked up
the phone. It was Marie. She was saying something. About …
something. Had the screeching stopped? Max checked. Yes. It had
stopped.

'Hang on, hang on,' said Max. 'It's Grisha's DNA?'

'I just told you that, like three times,' said Marie.

'Not quite awake yet,' said Max. 'Sorry.'

'Anyway, it's definitely going to get kicked up a level, classification-
wise. I just got this while it was in-between, if you know what I mean.'

Birthmark, fingerprints, DNA. Max groaned. Apologised for
groaning. Assured Marie he was not groaning about her. Assured
Marie he was listening. Listening to her, Marie. Thanked her. Assured Marie he understood that she wouldn't be able to get any more
information whatsoever on this disgusting hand. Thanked her again.

Assured Marie he was not hung over and that he was doing an entirely conscientious job taking notes on the conference and had not just given the job to Mark Hope because Mark Hope had an Ivy League degree and could probably do it better than he, Max, ever could, in a million years. Thanked her again.

'By the way,' said Marie. 'When's the last time you talked to your wife?'

'Rose?'

'Do you have another one?'

'No. No, I – I just talked to her – I don't know. I talk to her all the time. Why?'

'No reason,' said Marie, as if there was a reason, and then hung up. The truth was, Max had tried to call Rose last night. After a few vodkas. She didn't pick up. Nothing like that had ever happened before, and Max had been struck, suddenly, physically, by a new possibility. He could almost see it in front of him: the smooth surface of their marriage cracking open. A single tectonic shift, reshaping their emotional landscape forever. Max had had another vodka. Two. Tried again. Rose didn't answer. Max dialled a third time. It didn't work like a charm. Max shrugged. Went back down to the Gagarin's lobby. Mingled. Toasted. 'The Black Sea Fleet!' Tried not to think about Rose. The unanswered calls. 'To the bottom!'

Now, this morning, Max looked at the telephone. Decided to think about the Rose problem later. When his head stopped aching. He closed his eyes. Rolled over. Groaned. A memory surfaced. With a kind of painful, crunching feeling. Like a heavy tread on broken glass.

Last night: black. Sky. Balcony. Trilby and Albu. On the balcony, the two older men were – striking poses? Pipe-in-mouth (Trilby). Cigar poised (Albu). Trilby saw Max. Nodded towards the car park. Max followed his gaze. Sure enough, down below, the round black eye of a camera lens gaped up. 'KGB,' said Trilby, it being de rigueur among a certain generation to reject 'FSB', the post-Soviet era's new Russian secret service's appellation. ('You kin put lipstick on uh pig,' as one of Max's superiors had once explained. 'But it's still uh pig.')

KGB. Max remembered stepping back against the wall. Out of camera range. Force of habit. In his mind's eye, Max saw Albu lifting his large head. The Romanian blew a smoke ring at the hot, hazy heavens. 'The question, my dear Trilby,' said the Romanian, 'is: who are they here for? You? Or me?'

In the darkness, Trilby took the pipe from his mouth. 'It's not asking the questions that's dangerous,' he said, wryly. 'It's knowing the answers.'

# 30

Max let the shower run for twenty minutes. After, he felt better. Nearly human. Dressed and somewhat pressed, Max took the elevator downstairs.

In the hallway, in front of the conference room, Max passed Trilby and Albu. Heads together, deep in discussion. Surrounded by a circle of intent listeners. '... the Bonbon Baron is a classic Soviet politician.' '... shades of grey. Give a little, take a little ...' 'Whereas with Grisha, it's all devils and angels.' Max saw Trilby grin beneath his felt hat. Max turned away to avoid eye contact. Trilby didn't notice: he was focused on his captivated hallway audience. As Max pushed open the door to the conference room, he heard Trilby's plummy accent, carrying, in conclusion, down the length of the grey hall: 'And in the West, after all – we always want to be sure that we are – fighting on the side of the angels.'

Max closed the door softly behind him. Stepped into the grey room. Made his way through a crowd of some dozen badly-dressed men and women. Journalists. Sitting and standing, bored, in a miniature forest of tripods. Max almost tripped over a cameraman, a tough-looking guy with a face like an Easter Island stone statue. Max whispered an apology, and the cameraman slowly moved his giant head. There was murder in his eyes. Ahead, from the stage, the drone of words hummed on. *Despite challenges ... confident ... prevail ...* Max checked his watch. Skirted the snack tables. Pyramids of bottled water glinting in the artificial light. Max scanned the audience again. Grey men, grey suits. Staring at their laps, scribbling notes, sleeping.

Mark Hope was sitting in the front row. Excellent. An American stepped up to the podium. 'I'm Brent,' he said, taking the microphone, as if it was a religious revival. 'And, speaking personally, you haven't seen anything yet!' As Brent went on – something about freedom and democracy and 'this guhRATE Ukrainian people' – Max repeated yesterday's spitball action. Mark Hope slapped his neck. Looked up. Saw Max. Grinned.

Then Mark Hope ducked, with a look of relief, through the rows again. Almost tripped over a sleeper. Reached the snack tables. Smiled that toothpaste-ad smile at Max. Hopefully. Like something interesting might happen now. 'Heya Mark,' said Max. 'Grisha's talk get postponed?'

'How did you know?' said Mark Hope.

Max shrugged. 'Grisha's always late.'

Mark Hope beamed with a kind of pride in his choice of boss. Max coughed. Pressed a piece of paper into Mark Hope's hand. 'If you need to reach me, use this number. I won't have the SIM card in all the time. But I'll check regularly. You'll cover the notes for another day, right?' Mark Hope brightened at this. Nodded with great energy as Max turned away.

A flurry of activity. Break time. Max's throat hurt. Parched. He heard Rose's voice: 'Hydrate, hydrate, hydrate!' On his way out, he stopped at the table with the glinting pyramid of water bottles. Took one. A hefty man in a grey suit appeared beside him. Max passed him the flimsy metal opener. It almost disappeared in the other man's enormous hand. A popping sound. The two men drank in silence. 'Sasha,' said the man, whose huge head was perched on a thick, American football player's neck.

'Max.'

The other man nodded. 'I work at the port,' he said, in that sweet, slightly nasal sing-song with the long, drawn-out 'r's.

Max nodded.

'In administration,' the other man continued. 'Under Grisha, now.'

Max nodded, again. Encouragingly.

'It's not so easy these days,' said the big man, taking another bottle of water in his enormous hands. 'I'm from Odesa, so of course I speak Russian.' Another popping sound. 'I'm Ukrainian. But Russian is my mother tongue.' He offered the open bottle to Max.

With a shake of his head, Max deferred.

The other man shrugged, drank it in a single draught. 'But these days,' he said, 'you have to speak Ukrainian. So I learned Ukrainian! Now Ukrainians say, how do you speak such good Ukrainian? You must be a Russian spy!' The man lifted his eyes, without moving his strongman's head. Gazed over the crowd. 'The thing is, of course, we were brothers for so long.'

As Max joined the slipstream of departing journalists, the conference started up again. Onstage, a Brit took the microphone. 'If you want to talk propaganda,' he said with a twinkle, 'there are some simply outlandish stories. For example, there's one eastern Ukrainian town, all Russian state television, all the time, and they were convinced, absolutely convinced, of the imminent arrival of a fascist gay brigade coming from Holland to rape all the men in town. Then of course there was the poisoned *borscht* scare ...'

Max didn't hear any more: the door had swung shut behind him.

# 31

The Volga Max hailed drove like a hearse. Groaning, slow and steady, under the blue summer skies. The memento mori of taxis. A dented black reminder ... Get a grip, Maxiboy. It's just the hangover talking.

'You Russian?' said the driver. Grey as an undertaker.

'Yeah,' said Max. For the hell of it.

'It's good you're here,' said the undertaker, wiping the sweat from his brow. 'A lot of Russians, they're afraid.'

Max grunted. A single summer cloud flitted in reflection across the broad black hood of the Volga. The undertaker gave him a crafty, intimate look. 'You know the soccer massacre?'

Max grunted, again. Who didn't? Just after Grisha took office, a pro-Russian soccer team played a pro-Ukrainian soccer team in Odesa. The regular street fighting turned political. Ended in bloodshed. Unprecedented. Everyone wondered: had the Russians provoked the fighting? Would the Russian army use this as an excuse to march in? After all, claiming that ethnic Russians were in danger – and needed military protection – would be one way for Moscow to justify annexing Odesa.

They were hurtling down the French Boulevard now. The undertaker was rattling on, along with his engine, as Max half-listened: '... fifty pro-Russians died, they say ...' Max looked out the dusty window. In the afternoon sunlight, everything was green, lush. Jungles that had grown up behind the gates of abandoned villas.

The undertaker was growing more animated: 'Fifty dead, they say? Try 500!' A few afternoon beachgoers, moving slowly. '... Lies, all lies, and propaganda ...' They passed the Eye Institute. A handful of patients were braving the heat. '... In Odesa,' the driver was saying now, 'we are Russian ...' Max thought he recognised one of the patients. A desiccated old man with a hat. The shoplifter from the airport Duty-Free.

The taxi driver was still talking. '… signs of the end, the apocalypse – every day! There's a new crack in the catacombs. Nobody talks about it …!'

For some reason, it struck Max as odd to see the old man again. What could it mean? He craned his neck to get another glimpse. But the man was gone.

# 32

The Volga let Max out on Pushkin Street. In front of the violent pink Bristol Hotel with its white foam gods, its cotton-candy sconces. Like a nightmare sunset.

Max walked. Overhead, the leaves of the plane trees rustled in the breeze. Max stopped at a tall black gate. Gothic, spiked with tridents.

At a little green hut like a telephone booth, he showed his papers. The guard nodded him through.

In the yard, the sun spilled through the trees, and the sounds of traffic were mysteriously absent. The whole place seemed enchanted. The shady courtyard ended in a pair of turrets, with tall, diamond-paned windows. In the corner, a thickly flowering vine smothered the large wooden beams leaning against the building's stone wall.

A woman stepped out to meet him. She wore a blue silk suit and was shaped like a *matryoshka* doll, with a pretty face framed by curly, dyed-black hair. A profusion of black mascara and sparkling cobalt pencil set off her piercing blue eyes.

She held out a tiny, dimpled hand to Max, and smiled. She had a very nice smile.

'Thanks so much for meeting me,' said Max, gently shaking the little hand, which was warm and dry. 'Dr Natan said you're just the person to talk to.' He glanced down. Bashful. 'The thing is,' he said, 'I want to look into my family history a bit.'

She smiled, encouragingly. 'You see,' said Max. Charming, bumbling. 'I know it's unlikely, but – well there was a story, passed down, that we were related to Benya Krik. You know him?'

A laughing kind of smile played on her perfectly pink lips. The archivist nodded. Max went on. 'You probably hear this all the time, but – I think it could be true. In my case.'

She laughed then. A clear, tinkling laugh. 'I hear it less often than you would think,' she said. 'Come on, I'll give you a tour, and then leave you with the Yaponsky files.'

'No,' said Max. Deliberately dense. 'Not Yaponsky. Krik. K-R-I-K. Benya Krik.'

She smiled again. 'Benya Krik was not a real person,' she said, very gently. 'But it is possible that you could be related to Mishka Yaponsky, who is thought to be the inspiration for Benya Krik.'

'Ah,' said Max. Trumpet creepers, he thought. That's what those vines were. The archivist followed his glance. 'That section of the building broke – oh, fifteen years ago. See how it leans?' Max looked. Nodded. She said: 'A section of the catacombs collapsed, underneath that part of the building. So, we propped it up. And here –' she pointed at a section where there were no flowers. Several pieces of new plywood had been nailed to the scaffolding. 'Here, the earth shifted again. A few weeks ago. So we propped it up again.'

'It's a lovely building,' said Max.

'Yes,' agreed his hostess. 'This synagogue was the first with its own organ in the entire Russian empire.' She looked around sadly.

The metal door's frame was so low Max had to duck a little. Inside, what had once been a lobby was now a small, dark, cramped space. A metal construction climbed the walls and met in odd places overhead. Like a polio brace. The archivist followed his gaze. 'This section of the building – it's not really safe, any more. Although …' She lifted her gaze to the metallic patchwork overhead, '… we do our best. Come.'

Through another door, they arrived in a turret. Large, diamond-shaped panes rose the length of the tower, flooding the stairwell with a soft pink light.

'Here, come to my office for a moment,' said the archivist, taking hold of the wrought-iron stairway's railing. Edelweiss, thought Max, looking at the stairway's bars. A tiny iron souvenir from the Alps, a reminder of home. On the landing, the archivist paused. Asked Max if he wanted a cup of tea. Please, he said. She led him, then, down a narrow green hall. Plastic Soviet floors. Into a remarkable room – with its high ceilings, medieval windows, plastic-covered walls and spider plants, it was half fairy-tale castle, half citadel of Soviet bureaucracy. Three girls looked up from three laminated desks. One of them – a bottle blonde with witchy eyebrows painted in two large half-moons over her beady eyes – stood, to make tea.

Max followed the *matryoshka* doll to her private office in the back. A big wooden desk piled with papers took up most of the room. With practised grace, the archivist slid behind her desk, while Max took the chair wedged behind the door. The archivist pointed at a large, dog-eared book in front of her. Explained she was writing a mono-graph on Trotsky in Odesa. The bottle blonde brought tea. It was the colour of mahogany, strong enough to revive the dead. As she set it down, Max thought he detected her witchy eyebrows raise a little. As if she was studying him.

'Trotsky and his future first wife were both imprisoned in Odesa,' said the archivist. Would Max like to see the love letter he wrote to her from his cell?

'Sure', said Max, and she handed the book over.

'A complete egomaniac,' said the archivist, as Max studied the yellowing papers, the inky handwriting. These dark scratches that still remained … 'His feelings, his desires, his dreams – in all the letters, there is not one line about her.'

As she spoke, the archivist stood. Max followed her out, nodding to the girls behind the desks as they passed. The witchy one gave him a hard look. Then she reached into her purse. 'No texting dur-ing work hours, Lilia!' said the archivist, shaking her plump finger.

In the narrow brown hallway, the archivist turned to Max. 'Our staff is a fraction of what it was twenty years ago,' she said.

Max nodded. The ceiling was falling down in chunks. Pipes were taped to the walls.

She went on: 'It's very hard, the work here, of course. Very dusty. These days, only women work here.' She smiled at Max. 'Our work is simply too hard for men!'

They emerged into another, broader hallway. Cracks the size of Max's thumb zig-zagged up the plaster walls, bit into the ceiling. 'There is one exception, of course,' she said, with an infectious smile.

'Oh?' said Max.

'Our ghost.' She nodded confirmation, black curls bouncing. 'An old rabbi. Very kind. There's a good atmosphere here, I don't know if you can feel it. We think he has something to do with it.'

'You don't say,' said Max.

'Oh yes,' said the archivist. 'Our ghost, he comes at night, and helps us with our work.'

They entered a dark room, with a very low ceiling. A bent old woman shuffled out from among the labyrinthine stacks of boxes. 'Misha Yaponksy,' said the archivist. The old woman nodded matter-of-factly.

The old woman showed Max how to work the shoebox files. She pulled one out, lifted the front piece of cardboard and undid the front. Max tried to do the same. It was heavy, dusty, and not easy to do at all. She hovered. He walked over to a table piled high with maps. Nineteenth-century French geological surveys. She followed. He walked back to the Mishka Yaponsky files. She followed. Max began to think he would need to come back after hours if he was going to be able to really look around. Just as he had resolved to do this, the old woman spoke. Her voice was very low, and she looked at him quizzically. Suspiciously, even, thought Max.

'You're the second person who's claimed to be related to Yaponsky,' she said, craning her head up from her bent neck. 'Six months ago, I think. A local man came in. Young – he had one of those funny phones in his ear – flashing blue.' She paused again. 'He was quite excited when he left.'

'Maybe he stole something,' said Max. Jocular. A frown stole across the old woman's face. Apparently, theft was no joking matter here.

'I certainly hope not,' she said.

*

From behind one of the turrets, a man watched Max exit the archives. He had hurried here, in the heat, and he was out of breath. He bent, and an unnatural blue light glowed in the man's ear.

Max waited for a break in traffic. Then he crossed the wide, tree-lined street. At a distance, the other man followed. Saw which tall, stony archway Max entered. Kept closer now. Watched from the shadowed archway as Max crossed the courtyard. The man ducked into the dappled light of the courtyard, which was hung with grapevines and laundry. It smelled weird back here. Like ... church at Easter?

The man's eyes were sharp. He took note of the position of Max's fingers as Max pressed the combination that unlocked the stairwell's oxblood red metal door.

When Max was inside, Felix walked up to the oxblood door. Punched in the code. The door opened with a metallic clang. Then Felix stood at the bottom of the stairwell and listened for Max's footsteps to stop. They did, finally. On the fifth floor. From his spot in the sun, a dissipated orange cat raised his head.

Felix slipped back out. He had a lot to do before tonight.

# 33

The King made his way, slowly, by foot. From Privos market, past the junk dealers who lined the patch of earthen ground on the other side of the tram tracks with their wares: tin cup-holders, dented enamelled cooking pots, a knife. Old shoes. A vase shaped like a dragon. The narrow, dirty, spangled dress of a dead prostitute. He couldn't bear to even enter the new hall they had built. No, only these destitutes who camped out outside the market, only they had anything like the old feeling.

Crushed, half-rotted watermelons spilled out of the overflowing garbage bins. He inhaled: no tears. Thank goodness. He thought, again, of his grandmother. She was always pitting cherries, in his memory. He could hear her voice. 'It's the boy!' she cackled. 'How much did you get?'

The King walked on. Enough with the past! This crazy adventure, this scheme for revenge, had brought him unexpectedly to the future. Fate had a strange way of working. It was only thanks to the King's hatred for Grisha – that bastard who had destroyed his operations in Georgia – that he had discovered the existence of his only living child. A grown-up daughter …

It was dusty, and the King coughed. When the King heard about Grisha's hand showing up in a vat of sunflower oil … well, of course, he hadn't quite believed it. But it was Gigi who told him. Gigi was trustworthy; for years he'd headed the Baltimore port's liquor smuggling operation … that was an elegant one! It was the King's idea; it had come to him one night on his yacht, one night when he docked off the South Carolina coast, on a trip, oh, years ago. It started with a single image, like all his best ideas did, as he drifted off to sleep. The King saw it: a bottle of blue vodka … When he woke up, the plan was complete. It worked like this: In the US, a handful of em-

148

ployees collected grain alcohol from creatively-minded American distilleries. They brought the big plastic barrels to Gigi, in Baltimore. Gigi poured blue dye in the liquor. Labelled it cleaning fluid. Then shipped it off – without paying a single liquor tax. In Georgia, they poured it back into vodka bottles. Sold it in Russia, Ukraine, Kazakhstan. As top shelf. At top price, of course.

After Grisha broke up everything, that scam ended, along with countless others. But Gigi was a sly fox. He was never caught; he kept working at the port. Sometimes he passed a nugget along to the King, and the King made sure Gigi was compensated for these titbits.

It was Gigi, too, who put the King in touch with Luddy the Lion. A two-bit loser who'd had a minor role in the blue vodka ring.

As Gigi explained when he called the King about the hand, it was this Lion who started the whole thing. Called Gigi up, out of the blue. After, what, fifteen years. Said he was on to a big thing, out of Odesa. But this Lion couldn't travel – he'd just gotten out of the slammer, and his passport was no good. And he wanted to check out the goods in person before he committed.

Gigi had said sure, sure. After all – Gigi said to the King – the Lion was a little bit out there, but he had good ideas now and then. Take sending cocaine to Russia in frozen shrimp shipments. Creative, you know? The King had said nothing: he knew types like the Lion. He didn't like them.

Gigi asked the Lion if his contacts had access to the Odesa port. Yes, the Lion came back with. Then tell 'em to stick the goods in the next sunflower oil shipment. Biggest export out of Ukraine, Gigi explained, sunflower oil comes in all the time. In fact, Gigi said, he had used the sunflower oil shipments before – it was a fast, efficient means of transportation. Well, Gigi hadn't meant that they should dump this thing right *in* the sunflower oil, he told the King. But apparently, that's what these fools did. Didn't even put it in a plastic bag. Which, by the way, might have made a difference.

Regardless – Gigi had continued – even dumping it straight into the sunflower oil, well, that still shouldn't have been a problem. After all, Gigi was no shrinking violet; he could've just fished it out. But unfortunately, the very day the shipment was due to arrive, Gigi's car crashed on the Maryland expressway.

So there Gigi was, leg broken in the hospital. Still, everything should have worked out ok. The chances of someone finding something like that was about nil – a real needle in a haystack. But as chance would have it ('fate,' the King had thought), Gigi's department had just gotten some brand-new carbon-testing technology. This was the technology's test run – and Gigi's inspections partner found the hand with it. The kid was a Georgian – Gigi's wife's cousin's cousin's nephew. The kid was on the straight and narrow, wanted to go to college, become an American engineer. He didn't know anything about the plan.

Anyway, said Gigi, as it turned out the kid's American veneer was only passport-thick. As soon he saw his beloved Grisha's right hand floating in a vat of sunflower oil, he was a 100% Georgian, all over again. Raised hell. The police came, then some men in dark suits. By the time Gigi was up and about again, the hand had been spirited away.

*

The King turned down the broad, uneven street with the small, old-fashioned houses. Brown like dirt. Built on sandstone. A soft material. After two hundred years, it couldn't hold them all up. So they sunk, and rose, and rose, and sunk. In long, undulating waves. Still, they were standing. For now.

The King's thoughts went back to the twists and turns ('fate,' he thought, again) that had led him back here ... While Gigi was talking to him, another image had come to mind. Of Grisha's hand, flying in a long, slow arc through the air. Yes, he'd thought. Yes. And he had let the new plan form, as he thanked Gigi. Noted down the Lion's contact information. Yes, thought the King, as he phoned that two-bit poser and listened to his story, yes. Yes, he had thought, as he watched the ridiculous video with the eyeballs. Yes. His new plan with the hand was complete, set, formed – oh, he was finally going to get his revenge – when he started to wonder about those incredibly lifelike eyeballs in the video.

Who had made them? he wondered. A real artist. He asked Inna – he called all his girlfriends Inna – to look into it. She was always staring into that flat phone of hers, and he'd seen in the past how she could come up with all kinds of useful information on it. A few hours later, she brought him her findings. Flicking her long red fingernail over the screen's surface, she showed him the French Patisserie Guild's silver medal. Given to a Ukrainian confectioner. For her stunning *gateau de zombie*. There was a photo of the zombie cake, with its remarkably lifelike eyeballs. And next to it, the baker herself.

She was familiar at once: tall and red-headed, with long, loose limbs. High cheekbones, and – as the King looked more closely, he felt his heart jump. All the way up into his throat. He looked more closely. Yes. Unmistakably. A black birthmark in the shape of a heart, nestled just below the eye, on her left cheek.

*

At Cossack Street, the King turned right. He shuffled along, his head bent. His trouser cuffs were worn and caked with dust. He needed to sleep on dry land. The rocking of the boat was having a strange effect on him. With the tears, and the memories. That morning he had woken up in a puddle of his own urine. No, no. One night, maybe two, on dry land. That would do it.

The King looked up. In the distance, he saw the changed skyline, like alien spaceships had landed on the city. He shook his head. It was wrong what they were doing here. That Syrian developer bastard, with his chintzy towering 'Pearls'. 'Why settle for diamonds, when you can own a Black Sea Pearl?' Ten, twenty storeys high, brassy towers, like backdrops for low-rent productions of *The Thousand and One Nights*. The King had heard that the Syrian got tax breaks on them, from the Ukrainian government. 'Foreign Direct Investment'. And that they were empty, most of them. Money laundering.

The Ukrainian developer bastard was just as bad, of course. His rustic Tuscan farmhouse high-rises were an insult to the eyes …

A cat appeared from out of nowhere. A fine-looking animal – white with black feet like boots. The King let him get within an inch of him. Then, with all his might, he kicked. The animal shrieked: the King's sharp-toed dress shoe had landed square in its belly. It scampered off. Hm, thought the King, surprised the cat hadn't died on the spot.

In the middle of the block, the King turned into a courtyard. Narrow, like a railway graveyard. Glass and broken tiles, weeds and bricks were the only decoration. To the right, a single-storey building extended down the length of the yard. Every three feet was a front door. He took out his key, unlocked the third door. Now it was an apartment of sorts – two very small rooms, front and back. In the back, a window looked out over the sink and table. In the front room was a dirty, low couch.

He walked inside, locked the door. Sat. Relaxed. Up until the Revolution in 1917, this place had been a brothel. The girls lived in the small apartments. In his favourite Benya Krik story, Benya and the gang came here. To celebrate after a raid. The place had an air of good luck, for him. And right now, he had the feeling he needed all the good luck he could get.

# 34

The poet Fimka Fishman said Gogol Street was the nicest in all of Odesa, and Max agreed. When Max reached it, he began to stroll. Slowly, enjoying himself. Past the giant plaster Atlases carrying the heavens on their shoulders. Past a lofty, red-brick apartment house. Ornate metalwork. Mermaids, anchors, seashells. More anchors. Past the Gogol house, whose elegant windows and doors were boarded up; the roof sagged; a tree grew from the second floor. The writer had lived here for two years, writing the second half of *Dead Souls*. When he got back to Moscow, he burned it all. Everything he had written in Odesa.

Max was just beginning to feel relaxed – in the heat, a strange anxiety had settled over him, tickling his throat like he had swallowed something, a fishbone, and it was stuck – when the air was rent by a sudden, existential shriek.

'A-A-A-A-A-ASSHOLE!'

Max jumped. The cry repeated itself again and again. Max headed towards it without quite knowing why.

On a plain plate-glass window, a workman was painting 'Angelina's' in white letters. Three of his colleagues sat in the shade of a creaking acacia.

Through the window, Max saw a metal birdcage. It swung gently, as a big grey bird paced back and forth. Like an overseer. The painter paused, and the bird erupted.

Max patted a little reporter's notebook in his pocket. Then he pushed the door open. Inside, the restaurant was small and simple. A big zinc bar was the main attraction. Even in the afternoon heat, it was cool, shady. A thin dark line, skittering just beneath the ceiling, was the only sign of the bombing.

A girl emerged. Tall and pretty, her pale red hair pulled back in a knot. Long limbs. Flip-flops. An apron tied neatly around a trim waist. A Marilyn Monroe beauty mark under her left eye. What did they say? A beauty mark by the mouth signals sensuality. By the eye, it means she likes to flirt. The girl smiled. A lovely smile. 'I'm sorry,' she said. 'We're not open for dinner, yet.'

'Actually,' said Max, in his most mediocre Russian. 'I work for *Gourmeterie Magazine*. We're doing a, uh, special report. It's called "Pastry and politics". Our last feature was "The Napoleon" – very popular in Russia after the defeat of the French.' Max made a show of checking the notebook. Read, in an official voice: '"The pastry crumbs sprinkled on top represented the mighty Russian snow, which had defeated the French emperor and his army."'

Max took a breath. Said a silent thanks to Rose for dragging him to that pastry museum in Paris. 'Anyway, I was just doing a little research and I saw that your pâtissier won the Medaille d'Argent from the Pâtisserie de France – very impressive if I may say so. I came down here hoping I could interview the pâtissier.'

The girl laughed. Held her hand out. 'Sima,' she said. 'Pastry and politics – I guess you want to talk about the sugar cookies?'

Max frowned. 'Sugar cookies?'

'Our Right Sector cookies,' said Sima. She cast her eyes down modestly and added: 'We're a little bit famous for them.'

Max had no idea what she was talking about. It showed on his face. She indicated a table, and they sat down across from each other. 'The Right Sector,' she said. 'You know, the Ukrainian nationalist paramilitary group?'

'It's a little outside my field,' said Max. 'But yes, I've heard of them.'

Sima smiled. 'Well, I made sugar cookies that looked just like the leader's business card. His real telephone number, email, address – all in blue frosting.'

Max took notes as fast as he could. Then he couldn't help it; he laughed. He looked up into the girl's violet eyes. They were laughing too. 'Misha, the head, he was just so annoying,' said Sima, sitting back in her chair. 'We worked with him for a little while. Doing clothing drives for the Ukrainian soldiers fighting in the east. But then – the Right Sector – they're so aggressive. And Misha – after a while, he was coming in here like he owned the place. Always handing out his business card.' She rolled her violet eyes. 'Like it's soooo special to get one of Misha's business cards. And I mean, after a while, the Right Sector, they're just too extreme. Sure, my mom and me, we want an independent country. But the Right Sector, the way they talk about Russians – I mean, half my family is Russian. I don't really think it's a good idea to "hang all the Russians up by their tongues."'

'Weren't you scared?' asked Max. 'The Right Sector doesn't strike me as an organisation with a great sense of humour.'

The girl shrugged. 'I didn't think about it too much, I guess. And customers ...' she grinned, '... loved them.'

Max nodded. Looked up at the jagged line left by the bombing. 'So, did the Right Sector bomb your place?'

The girl smiled. Rueful. Shook her head. 'If it comes to that, the pro-Russians have just as much reason to bomb us.'

'What, you baked cookies with the Kremlin's phone number?' said Max.

'Not a bad idea,' she laughed. 'But no. I mean, basically, the way we got involved with the Right Sector in the first place, was that my mom felt sorry for the Ukrainian soldiers wounded fighting the Russians in the east. A bunch of them were brought to hospitals in Odesa to recover. They're just boys, you know. Mostly from very poor families, otherwise they wouldn't go and fight. When they get wounded, their mothers can't afford to come here to take care of them. So my mom ...' – Sima indicated the plate-glass window, where the painters had stopped for the day at 'ANGEL' – '... Angelina, she started cooking *borscht* and taking it to the boys in the hospital.' She paused. 'People have been bombed for less.'

'So, it could be the Russians or the Ukrainians who bombed you?'

Sima nodded her head. 'Honestly, it's just as likely to be one as the other. Then again, these bombings – they're supposedly geopolitical. But really, we have enough infighting right here in Odesa. Mephisto for example – the mayor – he hates us.'

'Why?' said Max.

'Oh, we decided not to let him invest in this place.' She shrugged. 'Of course, it didn't help that my mom also wrote an exposé of his life's history of corruption. You know he used to go around, in the 90s, collecting protection money with a pair of shears and a finger … Well, my mom posted it on her Facebook page …' Sima brought those violet eyes back to bear on Max. 'So, really … it could be anybody.'

Outside, the painter was packing up his paints for the day. The lettering was only half finished. 'Tell me, ah, a little bit about the cake you won the prize for,' said Max, who had discovered a photo of Sima with a very lifelike confectionary corpse online, the night before.

Sima smiled and took out her phone. Began tapping her finger on it. She held it out to Max. The picture was a still frame from a video. For the second time that day, Max found himself looking at a young, good-looking man with long blond hair, like a Cossack. Wearing a big grin and a lab coat. Standing in front of a tray of eyeballs.

'Wow,' said Max. 'They're amazing. Very lifelike.'

'Buttercream,' she said, proudly. 'With a hard sugar glaze.'

'That your sous-chef?' said Max, pointing at the screen.

'Oh, no,' she said. 'That's my friend Rodion. He manages Café Delicious. Just up the street, in the Passage.' She turned the phone, looked into it. 'They're really into third-wave coffee.'

'So he sells coffee and – eyeballs?'

She laughed. 'No,' she said. 'They sell macarons – it's his boss's big money-making scheme. Macarons for all of Ukraine. Why not? Anyway, Rodion's actually a biologist, that's what he studied. He and his friend, Felix, they have some crazy scheme …' She smiled indulgently. A pretty, young woman who had heard a lot of things in her short life from men trying to impress her. Learned not to take all the information presented to her too seriously.

For no reason at all, Max's anxiety came back. The stuck fishbone – it seemed to get bigger. Thicker, fatter. Max tried to clear his throat. The girl was still talking. '… claim they can generate body parts.' Max's pen hesitated, suspended over the notepad. 'They needed investments, of course,' Sima added, rolling her eyes affectionately as if to say that, in her experience, a lot of men need investments. 'So they made some crazy internet video. EASY ETERNITY, I think they call it.'

'Boys will be boys,' said Max. Like a man of the world. Then, carefully: 'Are you still making a lot of eyeballs?'

She shook her head. 'For now, no. Before we opened, I bought a wonderful, refrigerated dessert case. I was going to display them, there, right there.' She indicated an empty spot at the end of the zinc bar. 'But somebody destroyed the mechanism. It was weird. The day of the bombing, I had just gotten it repaired. Of course – it was completely destroyed. It will be a while before we can afford a new one.'

'A-A-A-ASSHOLE!' interjected the parrot.

'Pretty bird,' said Sima, glancing over at the cage. 'You know,' she said, 'we're lucky. You know Tavernetta? The Italian place? Well, they're right across from the Ukrainian secret service's headquarters. When the secret services office got bombed, all the glass shattered at Tavernetta. $30,000 worth.' She shook her head. 'We've just got this one window.'

Max nodded. 'Don't you want to know who it was?' he said.

Sima shrugged. 'I never knew my father, you know. He was lost at sea before I was born.' She paused, thoughtfully. Pulled on a pair of plastic gloves. 'The question of who did the bombing – it's a little bit like the question of my father's death, for me. It's something unfortunate. But it happened. You can't undo it. You don't need to understand it. You simply have to live with it. The important thing is to keep working.'

She twisted her pale neck, and looked around the tall, elegant room. 'It reminds me of a game we used to play as children. Girls, actually. A Soviet game – all Soviet girls played it, I guess. And we did, too. It was called "Making Secrets". You found some treasure – a beautiful pebble or a shiny piece of glass from the beach. Then you buried it. You marked the spot. With some flowers, say, or a cross in the dirt. And you never, ever dug it up.'

*

As Max left, a new feeling of unease came over him. High-pitched. It started at the back of his head where his skull met his neck. Radiated forward. Down to his lungs, where it gripped. He was being watched. He looked up the street. The painters were gone. The acacias sighed in the breeze. He looked down the street. A little electric bus, open-air, decorated with anchors shaped like hearts ('I anchor Odesa') had pulled up in front of the Gogol house. Tourists in sun visors lined up in front of the plaque. Smiled. Took pictures. Fanned themselves. Drove off. Max looked again, scanning …

But he didn't look down. Fool, thought Mr Smiley. He swished his tail. Once. Twice. And waited.

For cats like Mr Smiley, individuals fell into one of five categories: cats, local humans, foreign humans, dogs, and rats. Then there were two larger categories: Odesites and non-Odesites. Even Mr Smiley had to admit that, say, Jacques the parrot was an Odesite. On the other hand, many of the local humans were not real Odesites. No, no. Most of the real Odesites had left. The people and dogs who came in to take their places were mostly red-necked hicks. No sophistication. No sense of humour, no flair. No taste (just look at those new apartment buildings! With their sad, shiny faces and faux Tuscan balconies. What was the Syrian developer calling them? Pearl Number One, Pearl Number Two, Pearl Number Three. 'Pearls of the Black Sea?' Pah! 'Monstrosities for Peasants' would have been a better slogan). It took at least ten years for the city to really start to work on you. Ten years to even begin to become a real Odesite. Some individuals, and almost all dogs, could never become Odesites, no matter how long they lived here.

Now, the cat watched the Foreign Human pause outside of 'Angelina's'. Stop. Search. See nothing. Set off again, up the street. The Foreign Human passed right by him. Didn't so much as glance at the cat. Pah! In just a few moments, Mr Smiley had all the information he needed: the Foreign Human's slightly fermented smell, his somewhat virile pheromones. Weight, height. The sound of his tread.

Then, as the cat watched, the Foreign Human did something odd. Instead of continuing up the street, he doubled back. Towards the famous Atlas statue – those strong shoulders carrying the heavens for all eternity, except for right now, when the round plaster heavens had collapsed, falling in at the top like a broken eggshell.

When he reached it, the Foreign Human stopped. Construction scaffolding obscured the landmark. The Foreign Human jumped up, disappeared into the wooden scaffolding. The workmen were gone for the day. When the Foreign Human climbed back down, he was holding a mouldy old hard hat. He tucked it under his armpit and retraced his steps. Heading, with a sense of surety, in the direction of the city centre.

Mr Smiley filed all this away in his prodigious feline brain. After all: anyone who took an interest in Sima was of interest to Mr Smiley as well.

# 35

Noon. Luddy the Lion Shturman woke up with a hell of a hangover. His head felt about ten sizes too big. His biceps felt ten sizes too small. Luddy pounded his now slightly concave chest, as he lay on the fold-out bed with the little plastic fan ticking at him.

Panic rose up, engulfed him. He gasped. Was he still in jail? No. *Nononono*. He wasn't in jail. Was he still in Miami? No. *Nono*. So, what the hell? Then he remembered. Yesterday. A message. 'The King' was in Odesa and he wanted to meet. That was good. That was positive. The King wanted to check in on his investment. Any businessman would do the same. Luddy was, so to speak, his man on the ground. The King had invested not just in the product, but in Luddy too. It only made sense that the King would want to meet. *I'marockstarI'marockstarI'marockstar*. Luddy inhaled.

Through the paper-thin door of the communal apartment, Luddy heard the kid's voice. He was yammering at his indulgent mother. 'Mama, listen to this, what I did yesterday …' Luddy mouthed a silent roar. Willed them to leave the kitchen and go out into the hallway, where a piano covered in spider plants, and a bookshelf formed a kind of lean-to living room.

But no, the handsome kid's voice continued. Luddy listened in spite of himself. A long, rambling story about how the kid had decided to test Grisha's new police force. So, he'd brewed some tea, poured it into the family's empty bottle of Jack Daniels (how often Luddy had wished there was something in that bottle, displayed proudly in the front hallway!) and walked through the city, swigging it. 'Mama!' The kid's voice hurt Luddy's ears. Little runt was twelve years old, never shut up about it, like being twelve was an accomplishment!

The mother murmured something over the clank of dishes. Luddy groaned. The boy was still talking: Apparently, he'd walked by a policeman, then past the police station, swigging from the whiskey bottle. The policemen looked at him. Didn't say anything. He walked for three hours, through the city centre. 'Finally, Mama!' came the thin, boyish voice, 'a new recruit for the army stopped me. He said, "Young man, do you know that in our country, it is forbidden to drink alcohol on the street?"' Luddy found himself straining to hear the ending of the story. '… I said to him, "Thank you! You are the only person in this city who cares about the law."'

Silence descended, finally. The plastic fan was still ticking. Luddy had broken out in a sweat. Luddy was going to write a bad review of the flat on the internet. He started composing it in his head: GET SOME AIR CONDITIONING ALREADY. Ha, ha, that would show them.

So: Luddy hadn't swindled the King. No: the hand was real. As far as he could tell. Luddy's stomach turned over. He couldn't even think about what would happen if Felix had swindled him on that – if – I'marockstarI'marockstarI'ma …

Luddy opened his mouth in a silent roar. Had he spent some of the King's seed money on booze and meth? Ok, sure, but those were normal expenses. And anyway, it was Luddy's baby. Luddy's discovery. Did he need the King's backing? Sure. He needed an angel investor, so to speak. That just happened to be the King.

Through the paper-thin door, he heard the pipsqueak's voice again: 'So now I've tested it. I didn't trust the police before, and I don't trust them now!'

Luddy buried his head in the pillow. But it was too hot, he couldn't breathe. And the King – he'd be nowhere without Luddy. Without Luddy's instinct, intuition, nose, eye … The panic rose up again. Spilled out from his lungs, swamped every corner of Luddy's concave chest. Luddy had almost had a heart attack when he walked by that restaurant downtown. Looked in the window, saw the glass case full of eyeballs. What a mess! He'd gone to see Felix right away, roared at him. 'THE EYEBALLS ARE FAKE? YOU CHEATED ME!? ROAR!!'

Felix had practically started crying. Said it was just a marketing tool. A stop-gap. Something about spending money to make money. Swore on his life that the hand was real. Well it must have been, otherwise there wouldn't have been that uproar at the port. The King wouldn't have gotten Luddy a fake passport, helped him travel. Everything was fine – *rockstarrockstar* – and Luddy had handled the eyeball problem. *Handledithandledithandledit.* It'd all come out in the wash, he thought. All in the wash …

The King's message came back to Luddy now. He wanted to meet. Tomorrow. At the Odesa Eye Institute. The King was a legend. The King was a killer. The King wanted to meet at the Odesa Eye Institute. And the King, as everyone knew, had only one good eye.

# 36

Rodion took up position behind the Italian espresso maker. It was ok, but he dreamed of working a Slayer one day. The Slayer was made in Seattle: the true home of third-wave coffee. The Odesites still wanted full-bodied Italian roasts; you had to teach them to appreciate a different flavour. Well, it was like whiskey: an acquired taste. He grimaced, thinking of the first time he drank whiskey. In Kremenchuk, in the nightclub. He'd worked as a bartender. He never did learn to like whiskey. But he'd learned he was tough: he could break up a fight or throw someone out if they were bothering the girls.

If only he had some Geisha beans! But these were good, too. Rodion placed the two cups of coffee just so, on a tray, and carried them into the glass-ceilinged Passage. Here, the footsteps and conversations of the tourists echoed as they wandered around in a heat-induced daze. It was nice, and you could smoke here. He set the coffees down on one of the café's wooden tables. Two girls. They looked up at him. Smiled. He smiled back. They were pretty, both of them. Then he thought of Sima ... When he saw her last, he'd told her how he'd only just noticed that her beauty mark was shaped like a heart. 'You didn't look closely enough before,' she'd said.

Indeed, thought Rodion, as he sat down at the free table and lit a cigarette. The girls at the next table were talking about the Orange Revolution. 'What was so amazing about Maidan, for me,' one was saying, 'was that you saw there that Ukraine can function like a normal society. We can follow rules! I mean, for example, you couldn't come to Maidan drunk. That was a rule, and people followed it.' The other girl, it seemed, worked at the Green Theatre. That was a cool project, thought Rodion. A group of friends had gotten together and renovated an abandoned Soviet outdoor theatre. They'd put in a new stage, a couple of food trucks, organic tomato plants, wifi, bean bags, activities for children … Tomorrow the lead singer of his Rodion's favourite Soviet oldies band, The Time Travelers was speaking there.

The girl who worked at the Green Theatre was gossiping. Rodion couldn't help listening in; he liked gossip. 'So anyway,' she said, 'you know the Syrian developer?'

The other nodded.

'The one who builds the Pearls. They're all empty you know.' Rodion's attention was pricked. He did indeed know the Pearls were mostly empty. 'Investments.'

Rodion took a drag of his cigarette – it had been a stroke of genius on Felix's part to set up their lab in one of the abandoned Pearls … perfect air conditioning, total silence, absolute privacy, rent-free …

The girl was still talking: 'So his wife is Ukrainian, you know. She comes to the children's playground, like every day. With her kids and like, five bodyguards.' The two girls rolled their eyes. Rodion saw they had finished their coffee. Good. Very good. 'Anyway, the kids love to play in the sandpit. What we always say is: "Keep an eye on those kids! You look away, next thing you know – they'll build a fifteen-foot sandcastle!"'

The other girl laughed, and so did Rodion. 'Did you know,' he said to the girls, 'that this Syrian developer gets tax breaks on all his buildings?'

They shook their heads, no.

'That's right,' said Rodion, with a little giggle. 'They're "Foreign Direct Investments".'

As the girls shook their heads, Rodion spotted a man coming deliberately towards the café. He was carrying something under his arm. A hard hat? Rodion stubbed out his cigarette. The girls started talking about the new crack that had appeared along Pushkin Street, as Rodion watched the man approach. He didn't walk like a Ukrainian. German maybe? Alone, middle-aged. Sex tourist. Rodion sighed. Went back inside. Took up position behind the espresso machine. Waited.

Sure enough, the man came in. Put the hard hat down on the table by the window. Ordered coffee, in decent but clearly non-native Russian.

Rodion made it, albeit with less pleasure than he'd got out of making coffee for the girls. But the man seemed ok. Rodion got a good vibe from him. Could he possibly not be a sex tourist? Maybe he worked with Grisha? There were a few new types circulating in the city these days. Though to be honest, most western men were sex tourists when it came down to it. Even the ones who weren't. Show them a pretty Ukrainian girl, and they lost all control.

The man asked where the toilet was. Rodion nodded towards the back room. A real-estate investor, maybe? Rodion shook his head and started thinking about what he still needed to do today. He wanted to move the axolotls to the lab tonight.

The man's voice interrupted Rodion's thoughts. 'Hey,' he said. 'What are those guppy things you've got back there?'

'Axolotls,' said Rodion, reassessing this man. Anyone who was interested in animals had a heart, after all. 'A special kind of salamander.'

'Cute little guys,' said the man. With a slightly heavy tread, he walked through the little café to the plate-glass window that looked out into the arcades. 'Wow,' he said. 'It's beautiful here.'

Rodion walked over, joined him. He got a good vibe from this man. He didn't know why. But Rodion trusted his gut. Back in Kremenchuk, in the club, his gut always told him which guy he was going to end up punching out before the night was over.

'What's your name?' the man said.

'Rodion.'

'Max,' said the man.

The two of them were silent. Through the café window's slight ripple, you could see the surreal spill of the pink arcades, the crumbling nudes, the slow-moving visitors in blue and white striped shirts.

The man named Max interrupted Rodion's reverie: 'It's like being in that aquarium,' he said. 'Like we're those little salamanders, looking out at the world.'

Rodion grinned. 'You know *Alice in Wonderland*?' he said.

The man named Max nodded.

Rodion lifted his hand and gestured at the view through the plate-glass window. 'Sometimes, standing here, I feel just like Alice,' he said. 'Before she goes through the mirror. Because in here, in the café, everything makes sense.'

The older man grinned. 'But out there –'

'Yeah,' said Rodion. 'Out there, everything is backwards.'

# 37

Cocktail hour at the Gagarin, again. Max moved through the crowd, keeping an eye out for Mark Hope. Max overheard Trilby holding court somewhere near the bar. 'The thing is,' he was saying, in his impressive accent, 'we are not the same as the Russians. We do not want the same things. We do not have the same reality. Why should we?'

He found Mark Hope, finally. In the corner by the ficus. 'Max!' said Mark Hope, flashing that toothpaste-ad smile. He looked down at the hard hat in Max's hand. It was old, battered, a little mouldy. It stank. 'What's with the –?'

Max glanced at the hard hat, too. Shrugged. 'Oh, well, I've got a little, uh, research trip to go on ...'

Mark Hope's face lit up like a thousand light bulbs.

'... alone,' Max added.

Mark Hope's face fell.

'But I wanted to tell you, I gave my wife your number. In case she can't reach me.'

Mark Hope brightened at this. Like it was a promotion. Max slapped him on the back. He was about to walk away when something occurred to him. 'Look, Mark,' said Max. 'You worked on gene research, right?'

Mark Hope nodded.

Max went on, 'Is there any such thing as, I don't know, body part generation? You know, weird science? But maybe ... for real?'

Mark Hope nodded eagerly. Max felt a thrill of excitement. He was on to something!

'I'll look into it!' said Mark Hope. 'Right away!'

'Oh,' said Max. Disappointed and not bothering to hide it. 'You do that.'

# 38

Rodion was just locking up the café when his business partner arrived. Felix took a seat inside at one of the wooden tables set with fresh daisies. For a moment, Rodion paused to admire his own handiwork: he'd bought the flowers from a little old, white-haired woman from the countryside. She'd sat on a folding chair with an old plastic paint bucket full of these happy, yellow and white blossoms. She'd reminded him of his *babushka*. Rodion had brought them to the café, put them in little white vases.

'How's the,' Felix lowered his voice, looked around, 'new hand coming along?'

'Good,' said Rodion. 'Good. Should be ready soon.'

'We need it by the 24th of August.'

'I can't promise.'

Felix clenched his jaw, as he always did when he was worried. Rodion knew this look: he'd seen it after Felix's grandfather died; when Felix realized how much electricity his cryogenic tank was going to need; and whenever Felix's grandmother asked him about girls. 'We *must* have it ready then,' said Felix.

'Why?' said Rodion.

'That's when the new investor needs it.'

'What, for the soccer game?' Rodion joked.

But Felix didn't laugh. 'What's the soccer game got to do with it?'

'Nothing,' said Rodion. Then he hesitated. On the 25th, the Lugansk team – 'Dawn' – was coming back to Odesa to play the local 'Black Sea' team. It would be the first time the two teams were to meet since the 'Soccer Massacre'. The city was on edge, of course: last time, the game had somehow turned political; the regular hooligans transformed into pro-Russians (Dawn) against pro-Ukrainians (Black Sea). And fifty people – all pro-Russians – died. That was the story, anyway. It seemed no one really knew what had happened, or how.

Rodion had been at work that day – where else? And when he heard about the commotion, he ventured out of the Passage to Deribasivka Street. He couldn't believe his eyes! Instead of strolling couples with their little dogs, balloon sellers, and sleepy book stands, the street was packed with rowdies wielding broken-off beer bottles. Two feet in front of him, Rodion saw a man swinging a chain mace. As if it was medsieval times! Had Rodion been afraid? Yes, of course. But he knew what his duty was: he had to get back to his post at Café Delicious. Keep it safe.

Now, he looked at Felix. His friend was sweating; his usually open features looked pinched. This was new, there was something new. Felix had been acting strange ever since … ever since Rodion had realised he had feelings for Sima. Since the bombing. Maybe Felix was worried Rodion would fall in love, and he'd lose his friend?

Rodion said: 'It's a little weird that they want it before the soccer game. I wonder …'

'Let me do the wondering. I'm the businessman, remember? You're the scientist.'

'Sure, Felix,' Rodion said, slowly.

So far, there was nothing between him and Sima. And if there was, one day – then Rodion would reassure his friend. Felix was his first friend here, and Rodion wouldn't just abandon him as soon as he got a girlfriend! Having resolved that in his mind, Rodion turned back to business: 'Speaking of which: d'you get the missing document yet?'

'Not yet. Soon.'

Rodion nodded. 'I really need that,' he said.

'Fine,' said Felix. 'I'll go back tonight to look for it.'

After Felix left, Rodion stood in the café's window, rag in hand, looking out into the magnificent Passage. Something was still bothering him. What was it? The hand … Dawn … He wondered, not for the first time, who this mysterious new investor was. And whether his friend Felix had gotten in over his head again.

# 39

Dusk fell fast in this latitude. Upstairs, at Natasha's place, Max let himself out onto the little balcony. Looked out at the statue of Babel. In the hot, leaden twilight, Max could just make out the writer's kindly, myopic expression behind the wire-rimmed glasses. Someone had left red carnations on his lap. Like bullet holes.

Down below, the roar of motors grew louder. More aggressive. Revving and accelerating. Stopping and going. A tangle of loose wires flapped against the building's dark façade. Gusts of air wafted the smell of exhaust mixed with incense, a hint of curry. Max checked his watch. Glanced back, once, across the square. Poor Babel. He'd been having an affair with the wife of the head of the secret services. Stalin had him shot.

Max turned away from Babel and towards the old synagogue. The view was nearly perfect. He waited until all the lights in the Gothic building went out. One, two, three. When everything was dark, and the guard had locked the entrance and left, Max stepped through the plastic French balcony doors.

Inside, he put on the hard hat. Slipped a flashlight into his pocket. Locked the front door's four locks behind him and felt his way in the half-light down the stairwell.

Instead of turning to go out to the courtyard, he continued down the stairwell below ground. Here the darkness was almost complete. He felt something soft beneath his foot. A blood-curdling screech. Sharp pain. Max's shin smarted. An orange blur, up the steps. Damn! The cat – Boris – had bitten him. Max reached down and turned on his flashlight. His khakis had blood on them. Not much. He began to sneeze. The strange thing was, before the allergy test, he'd never noticed a problem with cats.

At the metal door at the base of the stairs, Max felt around the frame. Then he took the hammer and brought it down, hard, on the chain lock.

The noise was terrible. He tried again. Listened. In the stairwell, he heard nothing. A solid building. Well built. The third hit did it.

Max pushed the door open and found himself in a storage room. The smell was almost overpowering: there must be a ton of incense in here. He walked to the back. Another door. An easy lock. He listened first. Finally, he decided to take the risk and slid one of Natasha's hairpins into the lock. Then: SCREECH SCREECH SCREECH! An alarm! SCREECH! Close! SCREECH! Loud! Max swore, reached down, picked up the telephone. The ringing stopped.

'Jeez, Mark, I nearly jumped out of my skin,' he said. 'I hope this is important.'

'Yes, so sorry –'

'If it has anything to do with Jim Dunkirk, I'm hanging up.'

'No, it's, it's the topic we were talking about.'

'You're calling about the notes? I'm really in the middle of something. I'll have to call you back –'

But Mark Hope was already telling him: '… There's one very unique salamander.'

'Hang on,' said Max. 'A salamander?'

'Yes! Found in the wild only in one lake outside of Mexico City. Endangered. Cute little guys. They're white or black, with big goggly eyes and little paws. They mature without ever growing out of the tadpole phase. And because of this …' Max's thoughts were drifting back to the stairwell behind him, listening for footsteps. '… they've got the ability to seamlessly regenerate their body parts. One of the holy grails of genetics research.'

'Yeah?' said Max, wondering when Mark Hope was going to get to the point.

'They can grow new limbs. Arms, fingers, toes. Even tails. You can graft a head of an axolotl onto another axolotl, and it'll live with two heads for like, two weeks.'

'Wait,' said Max, thinking back to the coffee shop. The aquarium. *Through the Looking Glass*. 'Did you say "axolotl"?'

'Yeah,' said Mark Hope. 'The Aztecs believed this salamander was the god of the dead.'

'Huh,' said Max. 'But nobody's figured out how to –?'

'Harness the axolotl gene?' said Mark Hope. 'No way.'

'Ok,' said Max, disappointed again. 'Thanks, Mark. Food for thought.'

'You got it,' said Mark Hope. 'Sure are cute little guys.'

Natasha's hairpin did the trick. The door opened, right into the catacombs. He stepped across the threshold. Inside, it smelled not of human abandonment, but of burnt incense. Well, thought Max. Since the city's founding, the catacombs had been used to smuggle goods to and from the sea. Maybe good luck charms weren't the esoteric shop's only stock-in-trade; maybe they were making their money selling something else, entirely. Well, whatever contraband it might be, it was none of Max's business.

He shut the door behind him. Stairs. Broad, concrete, with a high reinforced ceiling – Soviet build. He flashed his light at the sandstone walls. They were damp. In places they were dripping. He liked the smell, here. Damp and clean, a whiff of stone – like a French chateau's wine cellar.

At the bottom, he turned right. Here, the passage was narrow, with a long bench-like concrete step running along each side. When the nuclear holocaust came, the Odesites would sleep here. Head to foot, like sailors. Overhead, industrial-style lights marked the way. To prevent hallucinations brought on by even a few days of daylight deprivation.

Counting his paces, Max kept a close watch. From Natasha's place, he must have travelled nearly the length of the block. He should turn soon. A gap opened in the concrete reinforcements. He pointed his flashlight at it. It was barely wide enough for him, and it twisted so he couldn't see where it led. Max stepped down, hit his head. He was glad he had his hard hat. Carefully, he eased through the passageway. Ahead and to the right, he saw how the wall bulged. 'A pregnant wall' – he'd learned that when Rose made him go caving. It was dangerous. Max turned sideways, bent his body around the bulge. It would give way one day, that bulge. With or without warning.

Somewhere in the distance, Max heard a sound. Low, rumbling. He strained to locate the source ... Max swore. He had put his foot in a puddle. The water filled his leather shoe. Great. With his other foot, he found a perch on the ledge of the sandstone wall. Climbed over the pool.

Suddenly, the passage opened up. A real little room, with a rough-hewn table and a couple of broken chairs. A bandit's hideout? The old synagogue's underground chamber? Max breathed with relief. He held the flashlight up, lit the walls of the little room. In one corner, the ceiling had fallen in. Opposite, there was a ladder. Max climbed it. Up and up and up and up. Then he felt the hard hat hit something. He shone the flashlight overhead. A round wooden door, like the top of a barrel. Max pushed, and it gave. He climbed up. Found himself in the basement of the archives.

He picked his way through towers of boxes. Sneezed. It was dusty down there. He came to a heavy metal door. Cursed. Then he tried pushing it. It opened slowly, creaking on its hinges. The sound must have resonated throughout the whole building. But Max heard nothing in response. No alarm bells. No footsteps.

At night, the streetlights illuminated the turret's stairway, casting latticework shadows through the Gothic windows. Max understood, now, what the archive directress had meant about the place having a good feeling. There was something peaceful here. He took the wrought iron stairs slowly, enjoying the stillness. He felt something under his hand, looked down. An edelweiss flower. A little wrought-iron remembrance of home ...

He found his way to the heart of the archives with relative ease, without the flashlight. He closed the door behind him. A deep, almost perfect stillness descended on the room. Max had a strange feeling, then. The sepia-coloured shadows darkened. As if someone, or something, had come in. Almost of its own accord – or as if someone was helping him? – Max's hand reached down. Into a pile of maps. As if his hand was being guided, Max pulled out a leather-bound book. 'EL DIARIO' it read on the cover. Max opened it. A single sheet of white paper fell to the ground. Max picked it up.

*Odesa 1932 Institute of Refrigeration Technology. Self-generating body parts. Page 5.*

Just then, Max heard a loud crash. A guard? Someone working late? Max still had the diary in his hand. He quickly slipped the piece of paper back inside. Then he put the diary in his back pocket.

Swiftly, Max retraced his steps. Down in the catacomb chamber, he turned on his flashlight. Breathed a sigh of relief. The strangest feeling came over him, then. That, contrary to all rules of archiving and basic thou-shalt-not-steal morality, he had done the right thing.

Out of the corner of his eye, Max caught sight of a little blue light. Flashing, like a dragonfly. Ah ha. So it was Felix, roaming around in the archives. Had Felix been watching him? There was only one way to find out. He'd wait for the little stalker and confront him. Find out what the hell was going on.

Just then, Max heard that low rumbling sound again. Deeper, closer. Then came a loud, terrible crack. Like bones breaking. Dust. Pain. Something heavy. Then nothing. Nothing at all.

# 40

Midnight. Inky: the sky, the sea. Nemo Beach, just on the edge of the city centre, was deserted this time of night. Sima smiled. Stripped off her work clothes: her skirt, her shirt, her tennis shoes. In the dark, she didn't bother with a bathing suit. In the dark, she felt free. She stood for a moment, on the sand still warm from the day. The evening was warm, too. She breathed, deep. The governor's dinner visit was a surprise, but it had gone well. Grisha had appeared with a camera crew, and he'd pledged support. He said the city of Odesa was behind them. He said the entire Ukrainian nation stood with their restaurant. Then he gave a little speech about nationhood, the kind of thing the poet Fimka Fishman was always writing about in his blog: that the New Ukrainian was a Ukrainian by volition, not by birth. Like Americans! Gone were the days of the Soviet Union, where your ethnicity was listed irrevocably in your passport: Russian, Ukrainian, Uzbek, Georgian, Jew. 'We are all Ukrainians!' Grisha proclaimed, in his deep Georgian-inflected Russian. 'Because we want to be!'

Sure, it was politics. But somehow, listening to Grisha, Sima felt her heart soar a little. Could it be hope? That they could make a better country? Freer, more equal? Sima sighed. Time would tell.

Grisha knew his audience, that was for sure. He had even told an Odesan joke: 'Rabbinovitch comes home. "Sarah!" he says to his wife. "You finally get your wish! We're getting a more expensive apartment!" "Oh, darling," says his wife. "We're moving?" "No!" says Rabbinovitch. "The landlord raised the rent."'

Sima walked towards the water. Cool dampness beneath her toes. Waves, small, gentle, reached her ankles, her calves, her thighs. Her waist. She ducked, and the cool water closed over her head.

Then she felt something else. Sima reached out. A fish? A dead fish? If there was a dead fish, she should show it to her mother. If the fish were dying, it might not impact the restaurant. But they needed to know. The fish slipped through her fingers. She tried to catch it again but couldn't in the dark. Then she shivered with a sudden, inexplicable disgust. Sima wasn't squeamish. Not at all. But now, she had the feeling she had to get out. Almost like a voice in her head. *Get out. Get out. The faster the better.* She swam, fast, until she reached shallow water. Then she stood and ran back to the shore. Only when she had towelled off did she start to feel better.

Maybe, she thought as she headed home, she really was overtired.

\*

Once Sima had stridden off on those long, strong legs, Mr Smiley carefully approached the edge of the water. He liked the feel of the sand between his claws. But water – no cat likes water! Still, he braced himself against the gentle roll of the waves. And when the moment was right, he reached a powerful paw out, batted. Batted again. Captured the object. Dragged it up into the light of the streetlamp.

The pathetic beach cat had said the thing would wash up tonight. The pathetic beach cat was right. The pathetic beach cat deserved a treat. Mr Smiley would get Tabby Kitty to take care of a reward.

Now, Mr Smiley carried the thing over to a lone streetlamp. Dropped it on the asphalt, in the circle cast by the bulb. Slowly, carefully, he began his examination.

It was an ear. A human ear. With a strange, wine-coloured mark. Long and bent, like a fisherman's hook. Hm. For a moment, Mr Smiley wondered if there might be a market in this: human extremities, ground up and tinned for cat food. He wondered how it would taste. Not bad, probably. Ground up fine, with a little day-old, Odesa-style fried gobbie fish? Then he dismissed this thought. Humans would never be creative enough to come up with it. No, no. The answer to the mystery lay somewhere else. And Mr Smiley was going to leave no stone unturned to get to the bottom of it.

In the meantime, it appeared the Foreign Human who had taken such an interest in Sima had got himself into trouble.

# 41

The smell was what Max noticed first. Iron and water. Then the cold. It was cold. Iron and water and cold. Max was shivering. He opened his eyes. His head hurt. His chest hurt. Everything hurt. He was covered in dust. He was buried alive.

He rolled over. So he wasn't buried alive. How could that be?

A focused pain in the back of his neck. Where the lizard brain makes its decisions. Had someone knocked out his lizard brain? Max needed his lizard brain. What would he do without his lizard brain?

Max concentrated. Iron. That would be blood. He remembered the crack. The rumbling sound. The 'pregnant wall'. The catacombs! The catacombs had caved in. On him. Crack!

Max sat up. Carefully. Saw the wall of rubble blocking his path. Ok. Someone had pulled him out. Ok. Lizard brain or no, he could get that far in his deduction. A blue light. Felix. Max felt his head. It hurt. He looked around. No hard hat. He reached into his coat pocket. The paper was gone. He reached back into his khakis. The small flashlight was still there. Better than nothing. His wallet was gone. And – damn! – the keys to Natasha's apartment. They were gone, too.

Max's watch was smashed. The little hands stuck, paralysed behind the shattered glass of the face. But his phone was still there. No signal. He shone the phone's little penlight in a circle. The diary was there. He picked it up. There was no sign of the piece of paper. He slipped the diary into his pocket again anyway. He pointed the little beam of light towards Natasha's apartment. No, there was no way through. Maybe he should go back to the archives. But no. That way seemed to be blocked, too. One little tunnel led into the darkness. So Max set off, following an entirely unknown route. He didn't have any other option.

# 42

The regular sound of the train, the feel of the wheels and the tracks beneath her – the traveller found all of this comforting. Like a second, more reliable pulse to reinforce her own sometimes faulty one. The woman pulled her hair back. Felt a blonde curl escape. Tucked it behind her ear. Then she stepped into the Czech train's long corridor. Through the large windows, the view was breathtaking. A long, slow sunset cast a warm light over the cool, dramatic stone cliffs between Dresden and Prague. A long, flat, snaking river. Toy villas crouched in the shadows. On a ridge, a castle.

How long had it been since she had taken a trip like this? The rhythm of the train. The simple beauty of the landscape. Why didn't she do this more often? Why had she waited until her marriage was – what was her marriage? On the surface, nothing had changed. She loved Max and he loved her. But she felt it. Slowly – or was it all at once? – they had come to the brink of an abyss.

The summer sun sank an inch or two. Cast a new, stronger light. Ochre. Over the woods, the shimmering water the colour of coal. The train rumbled on, lulling, and Rose thought back to their first date. She'd been an art student. Living in Baltimore, in a linoleum-floored studio on Mt. Vernon. Max drove up from DC; it was late winter, a huge snowstorm was pending, and when Rose took the elevator down, he was already waiting in the lobby. A tall, strong, handsome man – that's what she'd thought when they met. But now, as he looked at her, she saw something else entirely. A boy. Adrift. And in that moment, Rose knew exactly what role she would play in this story, saw it unfold in front of her. A lifetime of being the calm one. The sure one. The ship's figurehead. Wooden, bare-breasted, guiding this wayward ship of a man impassively through the storm.

And somehow, at that moment, in the linoleum lobby whose dirty windows softened the raw winter light, Rose knew she would do it. Take the part. And – she had never told Max, and she never would – but in that moment, the first of their first date, she watched his eyes light up with a painful kind of happiness at the sight of her. When Rose smiled back, amid her feelings of excitement, of anticipation – somewhere, among all these feelings, adventure and lust and love, there was also a distinct sense of resignation.

The train jolted. The sun sank. The woods grew dark in a single stroke. Nearly black. Overhead, the sky was pale. Below, the river inky. Rose pushed another rogue curl behind her ear. Now, it was eight years later. The abyss had loomed out of nowhere. Or had it been their destination all along? Regardless: if one or the other of them went over, there would be no going back.

Who would it be? Max was the obvious candidate, always thrusting and parrying with life, with her. But Rose had a feeling that it might be her. That she might be the one who went over the edge. Who couldn't come back. And so she'd booked a flight to Copenhagen. Then Dresden, and now the train. She had never done anything like this, not once in her well-planned life. On the flights, she felt numb. Only on the train did she feel like she was really moving. Not just physically, but emotionally. Into the hinterlands of her own experience.

'Rose?' The traveller looked up. It was her cabin mate, a woman named Rita. After squandering a lifetime serving beer in her family's pub, Rita had painted all the walls in her apartment yellow, and retired. These days, she boarded a train whenever she needed to outrun the past. 'You're going to see your husband, right?'

Rose nodded. Felt suddenly like she might weep.

'I've got a little love potion,' said Rita, and handed her a tiny glass bottle with a miniature cork in it. It smelled like lavender. 'Take it with you, hon.'

# 43

Max guessed he had been walking for a couple of hours. But it felt like days. It wasn't easy going. The paths were completely unpredictable – wide and high for a couple of hundred feet. Then a collapsed wall. A pile of rocks and sand. Max shone his light, found a round, narrow gap at the top. Crawled through. Found himself in a long gallery. Pictures on the walls. Scratched in a kind of dark blue. Ships. Ships of all kinds. A captain in the Czar's fleet. Graffiti of another era.

Max was feeling sleepy. He was hungry. He was thirsty. He heard dripping. He hoped he wasn't hallucinating. He shone his light and saw it reflect in a pool of water. Something came back to him: Catherine the Great's stonecutters lived down here for years at a time, never coming up for light or fresh air. Still, they were the only Odesites with a clean water supply. Max looked at the pool again. Potable in the nineteenth century? Good enough for him. Max lay down on his belly, formed his hands into a bowl. Drank long and deep. Rolled over. Mildly hopeless. Very cold.

He felt better once he had drunk. Revived. He heard Rose's voice… 'Hydrate, hydrate, hydrate.' Well, maybe she was right. Max sat, his back against the cold sandstone wall. Something was uncomfortable. Jutting. The diary. He reached back, took it out of his pocket. He would rest a little. Just a little. He leaned his head back, closed his eyes. He didn't want to fall asleep. He opened the diary. It was written in Spanish. A woman's hand. Max flipped through it a little. Then he turned back to the first page. And read with great attention from the beginning. 3 January 1931:

Dear Diary,

I am writing this, my first entry, to remember everything that happens. Why? Before, my life was very ordinary and I did not need a diary. But now I have been greatly honoured. I will be the translator for the first delegation of scientists from the Soviet Union to visit my country. I will do everything I can to make sure they are happy, and that they see the most beautiful side of Mexico. In fact today, I bought not only you - my first diary! - but also my very first lipstick.

Dear Diary,

The scientists are very young (not much older than me) and very nice. Especially one named Yakov. He is a biologist. We get along wonderfully. They were all happy to hear that my name is Maria. 'Maria!' they said. 'That is a Russian name!' Today we will go to the magical lake. We have seen the technological wonders of the city, and now we will see how backwards our country people are.

Dear Diary,

We travelled for a day and arrived at night. We are staying in a pueblo convent on an island in the middle of the lake. It is very dark here at night and sometimes I am afraid. The nuns are very small, all of them. The old ones reach only to my waist. Even the younger ones are not very big. Under Communism, says Yakov, there will be no religion and all people will be well fed. It sounds wonderful.

Dear Diary,

Today a peasant came to the pueblo. He was in great pain. He had lost three fingers and his thumb - a tragedy for his family, of course. Who can hold a hoe with a pinkie finger? He was very pale. 'Please,' was all that he said. I wonder why he came here - maybe the nuns are known for their healing? Still, it does not seem worth it to me to travel for days, as he said he did. The nuns conferred with each other.

*Dear Diary,*
*Some farmers said the nuns have found a way to make*
*fingers grow back. This is the kind of story I know from my own*
*grandmother. A good woman, if very superstitious.*

*Dear Diary,*
*I stayed up late and watched the Mother Superior. If I was*
*a religious person, I would think she had made a deal with the*
*devil! She took a strange little creature, very cute, translucent*
*white, with big, curious eyes and short, baby-ish legs. While it*
*looked on with those curious eyes, she pulled out a knife and cut*
*off three of its fingers and one of its toes. The poor creature! But*
*he didn't seem to mind at all. Then the little nun boiled the ani-*
*mal's white body parts. She stirred and stirred. As I watched,*
*she drew from the pot a yellow substance, like marmalade, and*
*painted it on the farmer's hand. Then she left. When he fell asleep,*
*I looked at his hand more closely. What hell are we in? Or is it*
*heaven? There were little bumps where his fingers had come off.*
*Like budding horns.*

*Dear Diary,*
*I had to confide in Yakov. He wants to see for himself. Tonight,*
*I will take him with me on the same nocturnal adventure. 'The*
*axolotl,' he whispered when he saw the strange little beast. 'The*
*Aztecs believed these salamanders were the emissaries of the god*
*of the dead.' Hush, I told him. We don't want the Mother*
*Superior to hear us. 'Clever little Masha,' he said (that is what*
*they call me) and there was such warmth in his eyes.*

*Dear Diary,*
*The Mother Superior agreed to speak to Yakov, who says I must*
*call him Yashenka, now that we are engaged to be married. Dear,*
*dear Diary, I have never been so happy in my whole life!*

*Dear Diary,*
*Yashenka says that the nuns here have made an amazing*
*discovery. He says that it will change the world. He says that*
*he will bring it back with us, and that the Soviet Union will be*
*a place of peace and prosperity and health for all times. When he*
*speaks like this, I believe him. But we must be careful, he said.*
*Knowledge is powerful, and power is dangerous. When he speaks*
*like this, I am afraid. But when he puts his arms around me,*
*I know that I am safer than I could be anywhere else in the entire*
*world.*

*Dear Diary*
*This is my last entry! Why? Because I am a married woman.*
*Tomorrow we will start on our journey into my new life, and I*
*will have no more time, as the wife of an important scientist, to*
*write to you. Mother and father wept, of course. Yashenka tried*
*to reassure them: Masha will live in a new world where humanity*
*will be better off, thanks in no small part to her cleverness. 'She*
*is clever,' said my dear mother (of course she had no idea what he*
*was talking about, with the new science he has written down, from*
*the nuns). I told my father, 'Papa, I will have your name, too.'*
*And I will! In my new country, Fimka told me, I will be called*
*Maria Jesusovna Lerner. I am so happy! A dios!*

Max felt the cold stone beneath him. The next page was blank. And
the next. Then he saw, on the last page, there was one more entry.

*Dear Diary,*
*I have been here in Odesa for three months now. Sometimes I am*
*very lonely. Yahsenka's mother does not like me.*
*My Russian improves every day. Thanks to Yashenka's mother,*
*now I even know some Yiddish curses. 'May you be like a chan-*
*delier! Hang during the day, and at night - burn.' Sometimes when*
*I look at her, I think she would like to poison my food. But of*
*course, no one would do that. And I will try hard, I will be a*

183

good daughter to her yet. Yashenka and I are as much in love as ever. More, I think. And, dear diary, I confide to you, first of all, that something wonderful and new awaits us. Yes, diary dear. I am sure now. There will be a child.

# Part 5

And if they ever in this, our country,
Consider erecting to me a monument,
I give my whole-hearted consent,
But with one condition – do not
Put it by the sea where I was born …

Anna Akhmatova, 'A Word about Pushkin'

## 44

High-pitched voices woke him in the dark. Oh no, thought Max. Hallucinating already. 'Come, come Sasha, we'll hide over here.' It was too soon to hallucinate. During training in Langley, he had held out a long time in the sensory deprivation chamber. But training was never the same as the real thing, was it? 'Shhh, let's scare them,' a small voice whispered. 'Of course, we'll scare them!' came the reply.

The figments of Max's imagination took on form. Two miniature little beings, flitting through the darkness. Glowing in the dark. An outline of green … skeletons? A flash of light. Two faces. Completely white. Another flash of light. Black eyes. Tiny zombies. Jesus, thought Max, this is really weird. The light came on, again.

'Sh!' one of the zombies squealed. She had blood oozing out of her mouth.

'Hey,' said Max.

The zombies started in fright. 'Hey Sasha! Look!'

The one called Sasha crawled closer to Max. Sasha had a death wound festering on his innocent little forehead. He looked at Max. 'Are you a zombie?' he asked.

'Yes,' said Max.

'A real one?'

Max nodded. Sasha's companion squealed again.

'Are you invited to the birthday party?'

'I'm not invited to the birthday party,' said Max. 'I'm hungry.'

'What do you eat?'

'Children,' said Max. He turned on the flashlight and held it under his chin. The kids gasped, clutched each other. 'But I also like birthday cake,' Max said. 'If you bring me a plate of food and a bottle of water, I won't eat you.'

Sasha and his companion looked slightly relieved.

'Don't tell ANYONE,' said Max, switching on the flashlight again. 'Bring a big bottle of water. And a beer.'

They nodded, very seriously. He heard the patter of their feet as they ran off. Max got ready to head down a narrow tunnel if he heard an adult approach with the children. Soon, the pitter-patter of small feet sounded again. They had kept their word: a big bottle of water, a paper plate piled high with something delicious-smelling, and a can of rum and coke.

'Do you eat lamb kebabs?' asked Sasha, eyes wide.

'If I can't eat children, I do eat kebabs,' said Max.

Sasha smiled happily. 'That's what I thought!'

'Thanks,' said Max. He held the flashlight under his chin. 'Now – SCRAM!'

The children shrieked and ran off. Max ate with his fingers, tearing into the oily meat as if he really were back from the undead. He drank the water and kept the bottle. Decided against the rum and coke.

Revived, Max kept walking. It was slow going, with just his little light. Every few feet, he bumped his head. It hurt. It really hurt, without a hard hat. The hard hat was a loss. Using his hands and feet to navigate, he crouched and slithered. He wondered if he would ever get out. He wondered if he should have asked the kids to take him to the adults. No, he thought. For one thing, he didn't want a whole group of people to know he was down here. For another ... it was just a hunch. A feeling. There was something too uncertain about the catacombs. The rich parents. The zombie costumes. Like carnival, where the rules no longer apply. But underground. Un-mapped. Unmarked. Uncertain. Where no one will ever know. It invited violence. No, thought Max. He would find his own way out.

# 45

An odd lunchtime customer, thought Sima. The workmen had installed the new plate-glass window that morning, and she and her mother decided they might as well open for business. A limited menu, of course.

The old man with the eye patch had walked in right as she unlocked the door. 'A-A-A-ASSHOLE!' screeched Jacques. The man looked askance at the bird. Jacques repeated himself. Poor Jacques, thought Sima.

The man took a table in the far corner. Furthest from the window. Asked if Angelina's *forshmak* was as delicious as ever. Of course, said Sima. Now, thinking it over, she tried to understand what it was about him that gave her the creeps. Not the eye patch, certainly. Odesa was famous for its eye clinic up on French Boulevard. When Sima was a girl, she loved the Greek myths. Every time she and her mother passed by the eye clinic, she imagined all the patients were undergoing surgery to become cyclops. After all, cyclops were much more powerful than regular people.

She shook her head at her childhood imagination. Maybe it was the man's subsequent questions that had unsettled her? He had eaten the *forshmak* with gusto. Then he called her over. 'Everything all right?' she asked.

'How old are you?' he said.

'Twenty-six,' she said.

The man's face was almost immobile. The skin of it stretched over his bones. But it wasn't just physiognomy. No, he was the kind of man, she thought, who keeps control of his emotions. Someone who starves his feelings. Keeps them weak. Still there was something – she couldn't put her finger on it, exactly – that flickered across those emaciated features when she told him her age. It was none of his business, of course. But lonely old men often wanted attention.

'You play chess?' he asked.

'A little,' she said.

'You know check mate? When the game's over and you lost?'

Yes, she said, she knew check mate.

'You should have two children, by now,' said the odd man. He frowned, above the eye patch. 'Twenty-six, no husband, no kids, check mate!'

For some reason, she found herself thinking of the parrot they'd had before Jacques. Rogér was a sensitive bird. When Sima's mother broke off her relationship with Sima's stepfather, he moved out. He was the only father she had ever known, and she'd felt a terrible, aching loss when he left. Rogér did, too. First, all his feathers fell out. Then the parrot died. His heart had broken. Maybe Sima had learned from Rogér not to give her heart. Maybe that's why she'd had no real loves, to speak of, in her life …

Sima had smiled politely at the one-eyed man. Asked if she could bring him anything else. They had a lovely fish soup. So fresh, the fishmonger was still drunk, she said – trying an old Odesan joke on the man. He didn't laugh. No he said, he had come for the *forshmak*. It was still wonderful, she could tell her mother. As he said that, he had looked her straight in the eye. A strange sensation had come over Sima. Her own eyes were a particular shade of violet that she'd never seen anywhere but in the mirror. As the old man looked at her, unblinking, she saw his eye – faded and watery as it was – was the same colour as hers. It gave her a bad feeling, and she crossed the room. Began arranging flowers for the tables.

The old man left very quietly. One minute he was there, sitting in the corner farthest from the window. When Sima turned around, he was gone. On the table, he had left a generous tip and a large red pomegranate.

Sima walked over, picked it up. A strange coincidence – pomegranates were her favourite fruit. This one was good. Deep red, the rough skin just beginning to pucker. Sima's mouth watered. Then she thought of Persephone. What was it again? Hades kidnapped her. Took her to his kingdom, underground. Her mother Demeter,

Goddess of the Harvest, petitioned Zeus to set Persephone free. Zeus said no, it was Hades' right to marry her. But Demeter was so distraught that nothing grew, and the people and animals began to die of hunger. Finally, Zeus relented. Persephone could go back to earth. But there was a catch: anyone who has eaten the food of the dead cannot leave again. Hades had tricked Persephone. During her long captivity, no morsel had passed her lips. Except for the pomegranate: when the God of the Dead offered her that, she couldn't resist. For each of the six seeds she ate, Persephone had to spend one month in the underworld, each year, for all eternity.

Despite the heat of the day, a chill ran through Sima. She threw the old man's gift in the trash, untouched. Just in case.

*

Mr Smiley watched the Odesite with one eye step out of 'Angelina's'. He was very old, even for a human. Bloodless. The restaurant's heavy, ornamental door swung shut behind him. He took out a telephone, dialled. Mr Smiley focused his attention. 'It's a good thing you told me the truth about the eyeballs, Felix …' Mr Smiley caught. '… The Lion will pay for thinking he could fool me with the bombing …'

Just then the wind shifted. Mr Smiley inhaled, deeply. Once, twice. Was that a whiff of black magic that Mr Smiley caught? Or just garden-variety evil? The cat wasn't sure. About one thing, though, there could be no doubt: Boots was right. This one-eyed man was Sima's father.

# 46

Hours later, Max wasn't so sure he'd made the right decision. How frightening could the zombie children's party parents be? He stopped. Shone his flashlight ahead. The catacombs branched off in two directions. He could take the tunnel to the left, or the tunnel to the right. Which one? He stood. Unable to make any decisions. Just then he thought he saw the flash of a fluffy white tail. A pink nose. A warm, living creature from the world above. The fluffy white tail flashed again. A little like a bunny. But more like a cat. Disappearing down the corridor to the left. Max sneezed. Then he followed it.

# 47

Luddy hadn't gone anywhere all day. Hadn't slept. Hadn't left. He felt like his brain was melting. Now, he was still sitting in the hallway in his underwear. Boxer shorts and a polo shirt. It was just so hot.

He looked around. A piano, covered in spider plants. No walls: the living room stretched the length of half a block. Was he hallucinating? Luddy took a deep breath. No. Now he remembered. The apartment was in some kind of former palace or administrative building and had a strange, dream-like layout, even if you were totally sober. All the apartments opened onto an enormous indoor hallway, with pleasant arched windows. As a result, each of the neighbours had staked out a living-room area, in this wide-open space in front of their doors. That's where Luddy was right now. Other families were sitting in front of their front doors, in their own lean-to living rooms. Sofas blocked off with sheets, bookshelves, a hamster's cage. Alone together. Together alone.

Ilona, the mother of the family, shook his shoulder gently. 'Mr Shturman?' she said, timidly. 'I'm doing laundry, so I took everything from your basket …' Luddy grunted a kind of thanks. Cursed inwardly that she knew his real name. The thing was, he had almost no cash. Especially once you subtracted the money he needed for drugs. And you could book an Airbnb with a credit card. Pay for it too. So he had. It seemed like a good idea at the time …

'Would you like to join us for a small snack?' Ilona asked, patting his shoulder now. Luddy grunted. He really wasn't feeling like himself … *I'maI'maI'ma* …

He must have said yes, because she smiled. Disappeared behind the beaded curtain hanging over the front door. Returned a few minutes later with a tray laden with glasses, ice cream, cookies, sliced melon and sweet Odesan champagne. She scooped ice cream from a plastic casing into a crystal cup. 'Nougat,' she said. Luddy smiled. He had loved nougat ice cream ever since he was a kid. Here, in Odesa.

The annoying son took a seat, smiled up at Luddy. Started telling the Jack Daniels story all over again. Luddy reached out with his little metal spoon. Scooped up a bite. Felt a drop on his bare leg. Melted nougat ice cream. Shit. His hand was shaking. He worried, all over again. The matriarch was leaning over him, with a big paper map. 'Here,' she pointed, 'Here we are on Pushkin Street, the Eye Clinic is here –' Luddy felt a splat. The entire spoonful of nougat ice cream had landed on his inner thigh.

'Let me help!' said the chestnut-haired boy, grabbing a paper napkin.

Luddy was about to smack the boy, when the matriarch put her hand on his shoulder again. 'You seem very tired, Mr. Shturman,' she said. He growled a response. *Don'tsmacktheboydon'tsmacktheboy.* 'What a strange place to meet, in fact,' she was saying, looking back at the map. 'I'll check the tram schedule. What time did you say you need to be there?' Luddy heard himself mumbling, five thirty … Wished he hadn't. Why did she need to know, anyway?

Just then the family patriarch came home. A gruff, salty-looking musician with long grey hair. The head of the family gazed abstractedly at Luddy, then took his seat in front of the piano. 'Dearest!' his wife called out in greeting.

Their buxom daughter appeared from the apartment. She was seventeen – if Luddy opened a new strip joint, she'd be perfect … The girl brought her father his guitar, and in front of the spider plants that clambered up and down the old wood piano, he began to sing. 'He wrote it himself,' whispered the girl proudly, as the mother perched on the arm of her husband's chair and sang along. The song was about Death, who hates her job. So, she goes to the bar to drown her sorrows. The refrain seemed to play over and over in Luddy's head. 'She can't go on like this/No more, no more, no more …'

# 48

Max had lost track of how many times he had hit his head. He had seen the cat tail three or four times now. Each time he was about to give up, he followed it. After all, cats didn't live underground. Sooner or later the cat would find a way out. The fact that this way out was likely to be cat-sized, not human-sized, was something Max chose not to dwell on.

Max sneezed. The cat yowled. Max shook himself. Followed the swishing white tail. The cat had four black feet and limped a little. Like it was wearing four black boots, one of which pinched. Max started calling the cat Boots, in his mind. Wondered what the hell it was doing down there. Wondered if Boots really existed or was a figment of his imagination.

Max walked and walked. Had Boots abandoned him? Et tu, Boots … a light. A light! Ahead, Max saw a light. His heart soared: a man. A man! Max saw a man. Sitting. At… a desk. Sounds echoed lightly as Max drew closer. Tiptiptiptiptap. Tiptiptiptiptap. Tiptip-tiptiptap. The man was thin, tall, hunched. A glowing light. Blue-ish. A laptop. A laptop?

'Excuse me,' said Max. 'I'm a little lost.'

'Oh!' said the man, sitting up with a start. 'You surprised me.'

Max gazed down at him. He was about twenty, with thinning hair. Gentle. The desk was bare, except for the slightly battered black computer. Stay focused, Maxiboy. Still he couldn't help himself. 'What are you doing?' Max asked.

'Me?' said the man, running his long fingers through his thin brown hair. 'Writing my dissertation. Particle physics. I just couldn't concentrate –' he motioned upwards with his eyes. 'Up there. Always checking Facebook, you know. A professor of mine said he knew a few people who had come down here to write their theses.'

Max felt a little dizzy. Get it together, Maxiboy. Focus. 'Is it working?'

The man smiled absently, staring into the darkness. 'Works great,' he said. 'Just great.'

'Hey,' said Max. The physicist looked up. 'Do you know how to get out of here?'

'Sure, of course,' he said. His eyes flicked back to the screen. 'To be honest, though, I'm right in the middle of a tricky passage. But the professor's down here, today. Organising a historical battle.' The man pointed his long finger into the darkness. Max swung his pen-light. 'Just walk straight down that tunnel, you can't miss him. He can lead you out.'

Max nodded, thanked him. Wished him well. Walked. Into a new tunnel. Hit his head. Turned a corner. Light. Light. Ahead, there was light. A tall, reinforced hallway. Lit every few feet by a bulb behind a small, corroded metal cage. Max wanted to kiss the bulbs. He had never been so happy to see electric light in his life.

A human figure. Max coughed. The man turned, stood. He was grey-haired, athletic. Wearing cargo pants and a long-sleeved T-shirt.

'This is really embarrassing,' Max said in Russian, with a heavy Bavarian accent. He wasn't sure why; maybe the war games had inspired him. 'You see, I'm visiting, and, well back home, I'm a member of the caving club. And well, I thought I could explore the catacombs on my own.' The other man was nodding. 'I got lost, and I've been trying to get back out, and …'

The professor clapped his hand on Max's shoulder. 'German?' he asked.

'Uh, yeah,' said Max.

The other man nodded. 'West or East?'

'Uh,' said Max. 'West.'

The other man nodded. 'I've been in Germany.'

'Oh yeah?' said Max.

'Rostock. With the Soviet Army.' He gazed for a moment down the long corridor. '153 Tuesdays.'

With that, the professor gestured for Max to follow him. 'You're lucky you found me,' he said. 'I've spent years down here. Even I only know a little.' He led the way further down the hall into a little sandstone room with a gate. 'This was the prison. For when nuclear war broke out. The people would live here.' He indicated the long concrete bench. 'And if they broke the law, they would be locked up here.'

He ducked, disappeared into a hole in one of the walls. Max followed through another very narrow opening. Along wooden planks set above a tiny underground river. The professor patted the sandstone wall where it bulged out at them. 'One day it'll burst,' said the professor.

Max thought back to right before everything went black, under the synagogue. '… Part of the catacombs just fell in downtown,' the other man was saying. 'Pushkin Street. A small section. But if you get stuck under it … you're a goner.' Felix, thought Max. Felix must have saved my life. A shiver went through his body.

He heard himself ask the other man what he was a professor of. Urbanism. This was just a hobby. 'Ok!' said the professor, stopping short at a long cave-like hallway. 'I've got to get back. I'm organising a WWII re-enactment. The soldiers used to fight in the catacombs, you know. Of course,' the urbanist sighed, 'these days, the Russians win every time.'

'Nazi uniforms are expensive,' said Max. 'Or so I hear.'

'You've heard about us?' the professor replied, looking pleased. 'We've been doing a lot of advertising, actually,' he said. 'I wasn't sure it was paying off. Anyway, just follow this path, straight out. And – Achtung! You should be more careful next time. Odesa's catacombs are not for beginners.'

# 49

Mr Smiley jumped up on the tool shed. Peered through the dacha's little window. With his two forefingers, the white-haired poet, Fimka Fishman, slowly, steadily chicken-pecked at his keyboard. On the screen over the poet's shoulder, Mr Smiley could just make out the latest diary entry.

> *Here in dusty Odesa, on Pushkin's street*
> *A crack in the pavement yawned*
> *Perhaps it hadn't gotten enough sleep …*

A doorbell rang. The poet looked up absent-mindedly. He rose and shuffled out to the gate.

Then, as Mr Smiley continued watching, the Odesite with one eye – Sima's no-good father – appeared in the little room. Tall, thin. Bone-dry. He looked around at the host of dusky-eyed saints on the wall. With slow, calm movements, Fishman indicated the low red-velvet couch, and took his own place in the deep chair by the desk.

The Odesite with one eye lay down on the velvet couch (like a sensible being). Stretched out his long, frail legs. Then he began to speak (like the other human fools). *Blah–blah–blah–blah*. Fishman's chin sank deeper and deeper into his chest as he watched the old man, thoughtfully. So as not to miss a word, Mr Smiley crept out along the very edge of the tool shed, which was painted like a Chinese pagoda. It was no use! Not for the first time, Mr. Smiley found that when it came to this particular kind of lying-down human talk, he simply could not make head nor tail of it! *Blah–blah–blah. Blah–blah*.

No matter. Fifty minutes later, when the Odesite with one eye stood up again, Mr. Smiley knew just what to do. The cat jumped down from the pagoda. Slipped through the rose garden beneath the grapevines. Picked up the scent of hedgehogs. Grimaced. Then he left through the wooden gate and made his way, as quickly as his four legs would carry him, towards the port.

# 50

The daylight was blinding as Max emerged from the mouth of a small cave. His retinas burned and he covered his eyes with his hands.

After a few minutes, he opened his eyes again. Looked out. At first, he couldn't believe it. But sure enough, he was standing partway down the cliff that led to the Black Sea. He looked up, winced. There it was! The Black Sea itself. Sparkling like ten thousand daggers.

As Max watched, a line of sun-baked beachgoers – men and women and children in various states of undress, carrying plastic chairs and rubber ducks – made their somnolent way down a path. There was something special about the way people moved along these cliffs, to and from the beach. A certain lack of will, meshed with imperative; like souls heading towards the light.

Max joined the descent. At the bottom, he looked up: a monstrous half-constructed twenty-storey building rose, blocking the view. Through the raw concrete floors, you could see the sky. At the bottom was a giant placard. ALEPPO CONSTRUCTION. It showed the ocean, and a flock of seagulls. PEARL #9: COMING SOON.

At this placard, the vacationers paused. They looked left, they looked right. Some went one way; others chose the opposite direction. Max couldn't begin to make a decision. Left or right? He followed the young family in front of him. Under the acacias. Here it was cooler, smelled greener. As if the trees were oozing ozone. Down another set of rickety wooden steps built Swiss Family Robinson-style into the cliff. Past concrete ruins – a narrow, three-storey lookout; a crumbling Soviet-era zig-zag structure. Whitewashed, abandoned.

Then he was at the beach. Swimmers and fishermen. Girls, boys, bright colours and beach umbrellas. Happy screams. The water was bright and cool. Max stumbled onto the sand, walked for a bit. He felt shaky. Unsteady on his feet.

There was nowhere to lie down. Beach towels lay end to end. Here and there where the sand showed through, pigeons flocked. They landed, picked up bits and pieces of fried fish. Fried dough. Women in bikinis chewed corn on the cob. Smoked. Babies crawled, fat, white. Men holding beers. The little waves crashed softly behind them. 'NEMO BEACH' read a bright blue sign. 'DELPHIN-ARIUM.' Max imagined he could hear the poor beasts calling in the distance.

Keep walking, Maxiboy. You'll think of something. He had no money. He had no ID. He didn't want to pass out and end up in a hospital. Dunkirk would never, ever let him forget that. Max felt light-headed. Faint. He looked up. Ahead, an apparition in teal green. TABOO. Teal green walls. Teal green umbrellas. Like the tops of pyramids. A green Egyptian dream. TABOO. Feeling like an apparition himself, Max slipped through a gap in the fabric barrier.

He found himself in a landscape of manicured sand, and olive-green loungers. He looked around. Chubby girls in bikinis were eating oysters. A small phalanx of waitresses was creating red crepe-paper flowers the size of human heads. Waiters used them to decorate a gazebo. Max spotted an empty lounge bed. He glanced at the half dozen boys in beige polo shirts running back and forth. TABOO read their uniforms. None of them glanced back. Max lay down on the bed. He looked up at the enormous teal umbrella. Then he fell asleep.

\*

'So, there's a doctor's convention, in, oh let's say Germany.' The sound of deep Ukrainian voices penetrated Max's consciousness. And in the background, waves. Gentle. The voice continued: 'Some-where nice. Bavaria, I love Bavaria. So organised!' Max listened as he slowly woke.

'Anyway,' continued the voice from somewhere nearby, 'this doc-tor's convention, it's international. Each doctor gets up, reports on the progress that's been made that year in his country.' Max opened his eyes. Saw teal. Heard waves. Closed his eyes again.

The voice continued: 'Finally it's the Russian doctor's turn. He stands up and says, "We've developed a new way to remove the tonsils. Instead of the traditional method, through the mouth, we developed a very high-tech method. Now, we sent a probe up through the rectum." Everyone applauds. Very high-tech, they say. Very advanced! Then one doctor, he raises his hand and says, "This is very impressive! But I have just one question. Why remove tonsils through the ass?" And the Russian says, "Because that's the way we do things in Russia!"'

Max finally looked over. The next bed along. Four glossy men. From Kyiv, Max guessed. Laughing. 'That's a good one, Volodya!'

Max sat up. Checked his pockets again. Still no wallet. He took a deep breath and checked in all over his body. He felt better. Sore, but not terrible. Like Lazarus, back from the dead. The next bed over seemed to have been abandoned. Max reached over and picked up a half-eaten plate of fish. Fried, salty. Odesa-style gobbie fish. Little black eyes looked up at him from the plate. Max helped himself to the remnants of a bottle of sulphurous Georgian mineral water.

A luminous blue-grey settled over everything. The glossy Ukrainian men from the next lounger got up to go swimming. Max watched them dive in and swim out. Ten metres, twenty metres, thirty. There, they miraculously stood. Walked on water. Max knew from experience that twenty feet from the shore was a concrete retaining wall, covered in barnacles. Still it always looked religious, from the beach, like some kind of miracle. Waves, water, swimmers and then, way out, men and women and children walking on water. The glossy Ukrainians had left their iPhones on the teal bed. Max laughed again at their doctor joke.

Then he stopped laughing. If you're going to do a thing, thought Max, why not do it 'through the ass'? He looked out. The glossy guys were still standing out in the glowing sea. They had turned their faces to the sky as dusk fell. Now was the time of day when colours – the bathing trunks, bikinis, beach balls – turned phosphorescent. Sublime against the deepening blue-grey glow of the Black

Sea. They were good fifty metres away. And they weren't heading back yet. Max closed his eyes. Picked up one of the neighbouring lounger's phones. Dunkirk's DC assistant answered.

'Charlene,' said Max, in a voice he knew almost as well as his own. He felt his left hip grow heavy with the weight of an old injury. Incurred in the 1980s while passing Soviet secrets to the Afghans. His upper lip curled back over his incisors.

'Mr Dunkirk,' she said. Clipped, polite, professional. Competent. 'I wasn't expecting to hear from you.'

'Yeah,' said Max. No, he thought. Too nice. 'Look Charlene,' he said. Impatient. Irritated. 'I need you to look something up for me. We got any labs working on limb regeneration? There's some kind of gecko involved. An *axy-lottle*.'

'Of course, Mr Dunkirk,' came the competent voice at the end of the line. 'I'll check ...' Max heard the sound of typing. The competent voice was back. 'There's a lab in Nashville. Salamander Regenerome Project. Specialising in axolotl research. Sandy Jones is the head.'

'Tell 'em, I'll call him. Tell him to pick up. National security. Code blue.'

'I'll make sure he knows.'

'Oh, and Charlene. Check the records. What have you got on Luddy Shturman, aka "the Lion"?'

'Can I put you on hold for a minute?' said Charlene.

Max rolled his eyes. Like Dunkirk would. People can hear it through the phone – just like they used to tell you to smile, in the old days, when a phone interview meant your potential employer couldn't see you. A few moments later, the voice came back. Much softer, less professional. Slightly husky. 'Shturman, Alexey, alias Ludwig, alias "the Lion",' cooed Charlene.

'Is he out?' Max said, impatient.

'Yes,' said Charlene. 'Three months ago. Current whereabouts unknown.'

'Good,' said Max, in a way that made the word sound bad. He was about to hang up when the woman said, 'I'm alone now, Jim. We can talk if you want. I've missed you.'

Jeez, thought Max. The old cad. Quick, thought Max. What's romance look like, to a guy like Dunkirk?

'Jesus Christ, Charlene,' he barked. And hung up.

Max looked up. The men dove back into the water. They were swimming slowly back in. Then they changed their minds. The men were racing. Back out towards the open sea. Max opened a browser. Typed in 'Fimka Fishman'. Decided to see what Miss Kitty was up to. He read his friend's latest diary entries. Sneezed. Grew thoughtful. Then, working quickly, Max took the iPhone apart and extracted the SIM card. Dumped it in the rest of the Georgian mineral water. Reassembled the iPhone without the card. Replaced the little machine on the teal lounge.

Max relaxed, then. Lay back one more time. Gazed out. There were a handful of swimmers in the dusk. As he watched, a woman in a cherry-coloured one-piece walked slowly into the water. In this light, the red pulsed, alive. Glowing like the tip of a match in the huge expanse of Black Sea.

# 51

Oh! thought the King, picking his way in the dusky light, through the port. Oh, that Lion! Felix had told him everything! How the Lion had gotten scared. Insisted that they bomb 'Angelina's' when he heard the King was on his way. Felix was a weak specimen, of course. He had cringed and grovelled as he told the story. But he had taken his share of the blame: 'After all,' he whined, 'we never should have tried to fool you. And before it went so far, it was up to me to stop him.'

Felix sensed the King's anger. The depth of his hatred for the man who had bombed the restaurant. Of course, Felix could have no idea why – where this feeling came from.

A fat, grey cat appeared in front of the King. The King kicked out at it. But this cat was too fast: in an instant, it was out of range of the King's sharp-toed dress shoe. The cat didn't lunge. No, it simply turned for a moment and looked at the King. Intelligent eyes in a scarred grey face. A sovereign kind of beast, thought the King. Then the cat set off, in the direction from which the King had just come.

# 52

Cocktail hour at the Gagarin. Yet again. Max stumbled into the white lobby. The bar. The corner with the ficus. The grey men milled in their grey suits. A few cast wondering glances in his direction. He looked down at his khaki pants. They were covered in brown sandstone dust. His hands were caked with blood and dirt. He would get this over with quickly. Where was Mark Hope?

Max took a breath, plunged into the crowd. Grey shoulders. Grey hair. Dandruff. '... you know the crops change at the border,' Max overheard. Was that Mark Hope's youthful dark hair? 'Ukrainian cornfields are neat and tidy.' Max changed direction, towards the low white chairs in the corner. '... can tell you've crossed into Russia right away. Just from the messiness of the fields ...' Max felt a tap on his shoulder.

'Maxwell!' said Trilby. 'You're just in time for the group photo –' he broke off, his bright eyes goggling behind the coke-bottle glasses. He was still wearing that hat, pulled down over his forehead. Max saw the tiniest evidence of pink outlining Trilby's lids. So he'd had a long night, too. 'You look a fright!' Trilby said, staring. 'What's happened to you?' Behind the bar was a mirror. Max checked. It was worse than he expected. Blood caked his hair. His face was scratched. His shirt was filthy.

'Ah, it's nothing,' said Max. 'A hit on the head – lot of blood. No big deal. Ah, just what I need –' Trilby was handing him a cold shot of vodka. It burned. It felt good. After the Chernobyl disaster, Moscow gave the clean-up crews rations of vodka, to protect them from radiation poisoning. That hadn't worked, of course. But maybe vodka could counteract cat allergies.

'Come along, hurry,' said Trilby. Max was about to protest that he was in no shape for a group photo, when he realised just how bad it would look if Dunkirk saw the picture and he was missing. As if he was thinking the same thing, Trilby nodded. Then he reached up and took off his felt hat. Placed it firmly over Max's head.

In the lobby, the grey suits had aligned themselves into rows, and before Max could thank Trilby, the two of them had been pulled into place. 'Cheese!' said the photographer, in Russian. Then it was over, and the group broke up. Max handed Trilby back his hat.

'Alan –'

'Oh, hush,' said Trilby. 'We've heard about your – employment situation. If there's anything I can do to help …'

'You seen Mark Hope?'

Trilby laughed. 'Maybe he's playing truant. You did leave him on his own for two whole days, after all!'

'Two days?' said Max.

'We haven't seen hide nor hair of you since, I believe Tuesday morning. You missed quite an interesting field trip to the law school …' Somehow they were both holding fresh glasses of vodka. 'Do you know, the director has his own private gun collection in the basement? Completely illegal of course … there was a lovely little specimen, a miniature Colt built in 1873, supposedly a gift for Wyatt Earp, not more than two inches long. I could hardly keep my hands off it –' A clutch of younger men interrupted him, demanding a toast.

'And did you know, Maxwell,' said Albu as they all finished their drinks, 'that law schools are a prospering business in Ukraine? Every year, 40,000 lawyers graduate.'

'40,000 lawyers!' said Trilby, opening his goggly eyes wide. 'Can you imagine? Every year! In a country with absolutely no laws.'

'Today's Wednesday,' said Max.

Trilby clucked. Albu frowned. Both of them nodded at the ticker above the reception desk. Thursday, it read, in Russian.

'Should we be worried about you, Maxwell?' said Trilby.

Just then Mark Hope appeared. He was breathing hard, looked worried. 'Max!' he said 'Where have you been? Never mind – Dunkirk has been calling for two days! He wants to talk to you.'

'Oh, shit,' said Max.

'I said you weren't feeling well. Food poisoning; it was the best I could come up with.'

'Give me your phone,' said Max. On Mark Hope's phone, Max dialled Dunkirk in Moscow.

'You find him?' came Dunkirk's voice.

'Jim, it's me,' said Max. 'You're not going to believe this, but I've been out flat. Worst case of food poisoning in my life.'

'You're right,' said Dunkirk. 'I don't believe you.'

The phone went dead. Jim Dunkirk had hung up.

Max waited. One minute. Two. The phone rang. Jim Dunkirk, calling back. 'By the way, Max, I don't know what you've been up to, but those notes had better be excellent. And if they are, I'll know who to thank for them. As for you –' Dunkirk let the threat hang in the air. Then he hung up.

Max hung his head. Walked back to the bar, handed Mark Hope back his phone. 'Thanks,' he said. 'You did your best. Appreciate it. Notes going ok?'

Mark Hope nodded. 'Don't worry about that. I went to Harvard. But, uh –' Mark Hope looked pained. 'Your wife called, too.' He paused. 'A couple of times.'

Max groaned. If there was one thing Rose hated, it was not being able to reach him when he said she would be able to. Maybe it wasn't too late. 'When?' he asked.

Mark Hope winced. 'Two days ago.'

'Since then?'

Mark Hope shook his head, no.

Oh no, thought Max. That was not good. That was not good at all.

*

When Max came back downstairs after a shave and a shower, Trilby was talking about the post-Soviet parallel court system. Basically, if two parties had a dispute, they could either go to the courts, or go to the gangsters. Most people went to the gangsters. They were quick; it took a fraction of the time to get a hearing as it did at the regular court. They were cheap; it cost about a third to have your case heard by the gangsters. And their decisions were binding.

'Fascinating stuff,' Mark Hope whispered to Max.

'Yeah,' said Max.

Mark Hope was holding out his telephone. The screen showed a photo: a tiny Colt, and Mark Hope's smooth palm lying the length of it. 'Take a look at this crazy gun! It's part of the law school president's collection.'

'Cool,' said Max. 'Did Trilby nick it?'

'You mean steal?' Mark Hope looked shocked. 'Of course not!'

Max shrugged. 'Wouldn't be so sure. Alan's got sticky fingers.'

'Huh,' said Mark Hope. Then he brightened: 'You know what else they told us at the law school?'

Max shook his head, no.

'Well,' said Mark Hope. 'In Odesa, in the 90s, the gangsters' court also had something called the "Vodka Option". If both parties chose the "Vodka Option", then they didn't have to present any evidence, they just sat down together and saw who could drink more.'

Max looked at Mark Hope with new appreciation. 'Is that right?' he said. 'I never heard that before.'

Max slapped the younger man's back and was just turning to head out towards the hotel's front door, the parking lot, the city, Natasha's – he didn't even want to think about what might be waiting for him there – when an ice-cold glass was pressed into his hand. Max looked up. Saw he was once again part of the circle. Trilby raised his cut-glass tumbler.

'The Black Sea fleet,' Trilby said, and grinned.

Max's voice joined the others: 'To the bottom!'

# 53

On the fifth floor of Pearl Number 5, Rodion looked out of what would have been the living-room window if anyone had ever lived there. Out at the darkness over the city. The bright lights. So much brighter than Kremenchuk! Rodion sighed. Usually the night-time view from his lab made him feel great. It was so beautiful! So cosmopolitan! So romantic.

But tonight, it left him cold. He reached up. Felt his left eye gingerly with his fingertips. Ooh, that would be a real shiner tomorrow. Rodion sighed again. Then he stood, smoothed out the torn pieces of paper. Laid them on the built-in bar. They fit together fine, still. Totally legible. Thank goodness.

Then he walked over to the corner, where the wires for an oven that would never be installed stuck out from the concrete wall like some sort of sea creature. He bent, picked up the short, stubby object that Felix had flung there in a fit of rage twenty minutes earlier. The toe had shrunk a little bit. Probably it had dried out, Rodion thought. He turned it over in his fingers. There was the faulty element: the wine-red birthmark shaped like the state of Florida, which showed up on every body part he'd generated so far. Clearly an error: the birthmark should only appear on the hand! He glanced back at the built-in bar, couldn't help feeling a little bit happy. Now that he had the final page of the instructions, he could perfect the technology. No more rogue birthmarks!

Then he remembered Felix's rage. Felt a little depressed. He looked back at his handiwork, the toe in his grasp. It was sticky. Rodion held it up to the light – there were little patches of some sort of beige substance. Almost like … nougat ice cream? No, thought Rodion, that can't be. Yuck! Nougat was his favourite flavour … He put the toe away in the refrigerator. He never should have thrown it away … but who knew? Maybe this was all for the best. Maybe this imperfect example would come in handy, later. Like, to compare 'before' and 'after.'

Rodion walked back to the uninhabited penthouse's giant bay window. But he hardly registered the spectacular view. He still didn't quite understand how Felix had found the toe, although that was neither here nor there at this point. The fact was, Felix had found it. And an hour ago, Rodion's business partner burst into their secret lab, brandishing the little digit.

Rodion had never seen Felix so upset: His round face was completely red. 'You've been making body parts on the sly!' he thundered, the blue light in his ear glowing. 'How could you?!'

Rodion tried to explain what he had been thinking, why he thought it would be a good idea to experiment a little. After all, if he hadn't, he wouldn't have realised they were missing some crucial instructions, that their formula was missing a page.

When Rodion said that, Felix lunged at him! Then Felix was shaking a piece of paper right in front of Rodion's face. *Page 5*, saw Rodion, to his delight. Then, to Rodion's horror, Felix ripped it in half! 'YOUR MISSING PAGE!! I'LL GIVE YOU YOUR MISSING PAGE!'

Rodion dived for the paper, picked it up. What a relief! The instructions were ok; he could tape them back together. That was when Felix punched him.

Sure, Rodion could have stopped him. All he had to do was raise an arm to block his business partner. Maybe put him in a chokehold until he calmed down.

But to be honest, Rodion thought maybe he deserved it. And even if he didn't, well, Felix was under a lot of pressure. He needed an outlet. And Rodion figured – if he could help, he would. So as Felix swung, Rodion stood still. Took the punch. Like a man.

Felix stormed out after that. He started sucking on his knuckles – could they have been bleeding? Well, thought Rodion, his friend was no tough guy, that was for sure. But he was a real business genius! As the door slammed behind him, some of the anger seemed to have gone out of Felix. Rodion heard one last barb, something like, 'How do you like that, you stupid piece of paper!' Then silence settled once more over the lab.

Rodion sighed. Later, maybe, when he was feeling calmer, he would listen to some Time Travelers. They always calmed him down. Deep, philosophical. *Time is a Field You Can Walk Across* – he might play that album. It always helped.

For now, though, he needed silence. Rodion turned to his axolotls. He had placed the aquarium right next to the bay window, so that the little guys could enjoy the view too. There were five of them now. Paddling slowly, imperturbably, with their stubby limbs. One of them had nearly grown his hand back. Another had a gash instead of an ear; a third had just a little stump on its hind paw where a big toe would be. Rodion looked more closely at the axolotl whose hand he had most recently severed. Was he moving more slowly than the others? Rodion knocked on the glass wall. The little animal looked up at him with those innocent, goggly eyes. Without remonstrance. Ok, thought Rodion. Ok.

He pulled up a plastic folding chair and set it next to the aquarium. Looking out at the city lights. He sighed. Then he and the axolotls watched as all the lights in the city flickered, once, then went out.

# 54

A power outage. A regular occurrence in this part of the world. Nothing to worry about. But it did mean that the night was as dark as the catacombs, when, a few Black Sea Fleets later, a taxi driver dropped Max in front of the Opera – a billowing dark shadow against the dark summer sky – and he made his way on foot back to Natasha's. Headlights were the only source of illumination. They flashed and disappeared. Rounding a corner, Max came upon tourists sitting in the dark. The white stripes of their nautical shirts glared.

Then he was alone again. The sound of falling water. Steady, disconcerting. Max looked up: an air conditioner was broken, haemorrhaging. Cars growled impatiently at the pedestrian crossing. Hungry.

As he neared the apartment, Max saw that the road in front of the wedding-dress shop had been blocked off. In the darkness, workmen were funnelling sand into the ground. Some of it had escaped. The grains crunched under Max's shoes.

He turned into Natasha's stony archway. The smell of incense hung in the air.

The lights went back on when he was mid-way up the stairwell. Bright. Crackling across his retinas. Painful.

Somehow Max knew what he would find. Natasha's front door swung on its hinges. Max heard a neighbour crack their door open, watching. He went in. Shut the doors from the inside. The television was still there. That was something. In the orange kitchen, Max flipped on the lights. They were bright in here. On the table, to his great surprise, lay the keys to the apartment. And his wallet. Minus the cash. A log of ice cream lay in the sink. Nougat flavoured. Eskimo brand. The plastic casing hung deflated in a thick beige pool. There was no sign of the toe.

Max pocketed his wallet, having put the money he'd borrowed from Mark Hope in it. He took the keys and locked the doors behind him. Outside, in the light of a single naked bulb, the metal mailboxes hung half open, lolling like the tongues of dogs that had been shot.

# 55

The power was back on completely by the time Luddy ventured out of the apartment. Ducked under the laundry line strung up in the hallway. Underpants, jeans, two of Luddy's matching polos. He needed to get a breath of fresh air. Maybe a hit. So he would be on his game for this meeting with the King tomorrow. He was shaking again as he made his way down the cracked marble stairway. Ducked beneath the hanging wires. Inhaled the smell of cat piss. He pushed open the metal front door. Marvelled again at how familiar it was from his childhood. Then, covered in oily sweat, he stepped outside into the night.

*I'marockstarI'marockstar*. Across the street, lit up like Las Vegas, was the bright pink Bristol hotel. Like a three-star brothel. Well, if they could afford it. They should knock themselves out.

Luddy nodded to the two tenants standing in the archway smoking. Plastic sandals. Shorts. Watching the Bristol. 'Dawn is due any minute,' said one of them. 'Dawn?' said the other. 'Soccer team. Always stay at the Bristol.' 'Come on a big bus… Russian thugs.' 'Drive like a bat outta hell.'

Luddy looked out over Pushkin Street. His landlady said part of the street had fallen in a few days ago. They must have patched it up already: In the dark, traffic was heavy. He didn't pay much attention. He was making plans. After he made some serious money with the eyeballs … Maybe he'd even stick around in Odesa. Start 'Weekend at Bernie's II'. Or maybe he'd call it 'Another Weekend at Bernie's'. Or … he had time to think it over.

*I'marockstarI'marockstarI'ma*. Luddy smelled mint. Looked up. A little old man was shuffling towards him in the darkness. Skinny. Dried out. A pathetic specimen. Luddy thought about sticking his foot out. Tripping him up. It'd be funny to see a brittle old guy like that go down. Ha! Luddy's brain must have wired directly to his foot while he was sleeping. Because before he knew it, that very foot was carrying out what had just been a casual thought … Oh no! thought Luddy. That old man is going down!

But the old man didn't go down. With an astonishing speed, he dodged the kick. Then the man looked up. Luddy saw a leather eye patch. The other eye bore right into Luddy's soul. In that moment, Luddy understood exactly how big a mistake he had made.

In a split-second, everything registered in the brain of Luddy the Lion. The eye patch; The King. With his one good eye, the King told Luddy that he had understood exactly what Luddy's imbecile brain had told his imbecile foot ('Kick the old guy! Ha!'). And the King's good eye told Luddy he was not going to forgive the trespass. REVENGE, it blinked. REVENGE.

The old man's arm flicked out. An astonishing amount of strength. Before Luddy knew it, he was falling. Into the street. He looked up. The front of a giant bus was bearing down on him. The last thing Ludwig Shturman, aka the Lion, saw in this life was the word DAWN.

# 56

Max headed towards the Bristol to drop off Natasha's keys – that's what she'd said to do when he left, and he thought he should cut his losses. Through a cluster of giggling couples – the girls all wore short shorts – a skinny old man walked past. Leather eye patch. The shoplifter. He looked again. Huh, thought Max. The old man seemed to be in a hurry. He passed right by Max, heading up the street.

Pushkin Street was jammed. Traffic had come to a halt, people were swarming. Talking. Craning their necks at a big bus. DAWN it read. There had been an accident. Max stood across the street from the bright pink hotel, next to two old men in plastic sandals. 'Accident,' said one of the men.

'Oh yeah?' said Max.

'Yep,' said the other. 'Soccer team's bus.' 'All the Russian fans are coming in tomorrow. Hope there's not another bloodbath like last time.'

As Max watched, the driver stepped down. He was yelling. 'The old man pushed him! The man with the eye patch! He pushed him!'

Max slipped through the crowd. Rubbernecking? Professional curiosity. Under the front tyres of the bus lay a man. What had once been a thick mane of red hair was now a stringy ponytail, entirely grey. A pool of blood was working its way through the roots, as if belatedly restoring his youth. The shrunken torso of a former body builder. Under – was that the exact same polo shirt Max was wearing? It was: 'Big and Tall', a three-pack. Max had the other two back in his hotel room. The dead man probably did, too.

Max shivered. Continued his assessment: staring eyes. Blue-violet. Time had not been kind to this man. But Max recognised him. Ludwig Shturman. Aka Luddy the Lion. Purveyor of strippers, cocaine and Soviet nuclear submarines, complete with crew. Dead.

216

As Max looked around, he had the strangest sensation. Namely, that the smell of breath mints hung heavy here, very heavy, in the air.

# 57

The Black Sea Shipping Company's former headquarters looked even darker at night. There were no lights on in the carriage house. Max turned on his penlight. Tried to avoid stepping on the vegetables in the garden. Felt something beneath his shoe – a corn cob? Garden hose? A hideous yowl pierced the night. Max jumped. At his feet, a dark shadow sprang. He flashed his light in its direction and, for an instant, saw a black cat's eyes. Glinting. Matted with gunk and bugs.

Max shook himself. Knocked at the carriage house. There was no answer. He lifted the door in its frame, jiggled the lock. Then he stepped inside.

Felix's grandmother was in the kitchen in the back. She was sitting in the dark. Through the window came an unhealthy yellow glow. From the port.

Max drew up a chair. Slowly, his eyes adapted. There was a bottle of vodka on the table. Empty. Max drew out another bottle, placed it next to the empty one. Even in the dark he could tell she'd been crying.

'Where is he?' said Max.

Felix's grandmother said nothing. Max unscrewed the bottle's cap, poured a drink for her. On the wooden shelf, he found another glass. Poured himself a drink.

'What happened to your nose?' she said, finally.

'Nothing,' said Max. 'Nothing important.'

She sniffled. Touched the cross around her neck. Pushed her glass towards Max. He filled it. And his. Finally, she began to speak. 'The first one, this "the Lion", he wasn't so bad. A buffoon, yes. But no one my Felix couldn't handle.'

Another silence. Something told Max not to break it. Instead, he refilled both glasses. The vodka was as warm as the night. When the old woman spoke again, her voice was dark. 'Then came the other one. With the eye patch.' An eye patch, thought Max.

'Felix won't listen to me. He says I'm old, that I don't see well any more. And it's true; the first time he came around, the man in the eye patch with his old man's gait, I wasn't sure. After all, they said he'd died. The night of the port raid. Twenty-seven years ago. But the next time I saw him, I knew. I had enough to do with him and his gang down at the port, didn't I.' She shook her head again. '"The King", they used to call him. Oh, he was a cruel man.' She stubbed her cigarette out in anger.

The King, thought Max. It didn't ring a bell. Or it rang too many. Every two-bit criminal called himself the King as some point in his career – usually right before they got caught or killed.

Felix's grandmother had grown thoughtful again. 'Maybe it's the darkness – up there.' She jerked her head in the direction of the pickled head. 'It goes against God. Begets more darkness.' She stared out to sea. Wooden. Regal.

'Felix didn't listen,' she said, sure in her anger. 'But I know Vanya Lerner when I see him.'

Vanya Lerner, thought Max. Even he had heard of Vanya Lerner! One of the most infamous Odesa mafia bosses of all time, Vanya Lerner had ruled the port for decades before he was killed in a Soviet raid. Could he really be alive? It seemed extremely unlikely.

'Where's Felix?' Max repeated. Low and dangerous, now.

'He left,' said the old woman, quietly. 'The King took him away.' She paused. 'Felix's knuckles were bleeding. Maybe it was your nose.'

Max shook his head, no. 'I got this in the catacombs.' He didn't add that, far from hurting him, Felix had saved his life. 'Where did they go?'

She said nothing. Then she turned her head towards the window. Towards the port. After a little while, she stood. Shuffled out of the room. Max waited. He wasn't sure why. Or for what. He poured another drink. Looked out the window. The glow of sulphurous yellow lights. The port. A place where no one – not the Soviets, not the Americans, not the Ukrainians, not the Russians – knew what really went on, and never would.

Max heard the shuffling steps return. She lowered herself slowly back into the chair and handed him a piece of paper. With a phone number. 'You can call her,' she said. Her voice was shaking. 'Marina. She used to be one of his girls. Years and years and years ago ...' she hesitated, lost in the past. 'The last I heard, she was running a Ukrainian bride company. Marina might know where they are.'

'Ok,' said Max. 'I'll ask her.'

'There's a golden yacht in the harbour,' said Felix's grandmother, sharply. 'It's called the *Inna*.'

The headline from Jim Dunkirk's yachting issue came back to Max. 'The Intriguing Inna.' Max waited.

'Inna was the King's great love. After his first wife died, he married her. She bore him a son. And then – the King went to prison. And she went crazy. They locked her up. What else could they do? When they let her out, she killed herself.'

'And the son?' said Max.

'A delicate baby,' she said. 'He died.' The old woman looked out at the port. 'If Felix is out there ...' Her lip began to tremble. 'I don't know if I'll ever get him back.' She grabbed Max's hand. Her grip was strong. 'Help him,' she said. 'Promise me that if you can, you will help him.'

Max looked down at the scrap of paper on the table. Marina, and a telephone number. He nodded. 'I promise,' he said. 'If I can help him, I will. I promise.'

The old woman cast a last glance at the scrap of paper too. 'She was a redhead,' she said. 'The King liked redheads.'

# 58

Dawn was breaking as Max reached downtown. He watched the rose-tinted opera house billowing in the sunrise. Against the white sky, a pretty facade blushed pink. Tin roofs. Gleaming like aquarium castles.

Max looked down at the text message from Joe Homily. Old Joe, you could always count on him, even in the middle of the night. As he left Felix's grandmother, he called Joe. Woke him up. Asked about Vanya Lerner. 'Max, I gotta wake up the wife. She'll know everything there is to know.'

> *Vanya Lerner, aka the King. Born Odesa 1935 (approx.). Died Odesa 1990. Story (likely apocryphal): his first wife waited for him to fall asleep, then gouged out his left eye. Started calling himself 'the King': 'in the land of the blind the one-eyed man is king.' Rumours: he didn't die but moved to Georgia. Unlikely says the wife.*

Max skipped to the end of the note, for the tenth time:

> *Known for cruelty. Legend has it (the wife swears this is true) his murders were always marked by the scent of breath mints.*

At the end Homily wrote:

> *A crazy fuckin town my friend. Come back soon! Bring Rose.*

On the corner, an ATM was set into a light green wall. Max took out as many hryvnias as he could before the ATM's limits kicked in. $150 worth. Ok.

Then he ducked into the building's light green archway. Pressed the code at the metal door. Nodded at the sleeping grandmother in a glass booth. Found himself in a large, perfectly square, high interior hall. Spacious. Airy. Dusty. Silent. He walked up the stairs to a wooden landing. Knocked. A hollow sound, echoing down to the elderly concierge's dreams.

The woman who opened the door was draped in a bright red faux-silk kimono. Her hair matched the dressing gown. Her lips matched her hair. Her face was wrinkled, powdered. She held a pudgy hand out to him. Palm down. Max bent and kissed it. She emitted a sour smell. Her slippers were high-heeled, with red feathered pom-poms. 'Marina?' he said. She nodded, turned her back to him. The kimono made a swishing sound.

Max followed her into the apartment. Past an open door, into the kitchen. Pots crowded the small stovetop. Crusted. Foodstuffs burst from the shelves: packages, cans. A dirty table with six – seven – used teacups. Cookies, crackers, crumbs. Max started: something that looked like a feathered pom-pom darted between his feet. Disappeared into the bathroom. Grey. A chinchilla. Max hated chinchillas.

A front room: high ceilings. Blue walls. An enormous oil portrait: a lady in a long dress. 1920s, guessed Max. Ships' masts rose behind her against a flat, grey sea. Max glanced down at the fishbone parquet. Chinchillas defecate every two seconds. Sure enough, the animal left a little trail of dark pellets behind it.

A set of French doors opened onto a second room. Mattresses covered every inch of floor. Half a dozen teenage girls were asleep on them. Cheeks pink in the heat. Long bare legs. Twisted sheets.

'No peeking!' remonstrated Marina, as she pulled the doors shut. 'First I must interview you. About what you are seeking in a wife.' She smiled a big lipsticked smile. 'Normally prospective husbands do not see – the girls asleep. But since you are in such a hurry, and willing to spare no expense in your search for happiness – that was a small glimpse. Behind the curtain, so to say.'

Max nodded. It was a scam, of course. College boys wrote the emails back and forth. Then, for the Western men who actually made the journey all the way here, the wholesome girls from the countryside were trotted out. The men were a pathetic lot: they talked about themselves in the greatest, crudest, dullest detail. They got nervous. They got diarrhoea. They took the girls shopping.

Now, he walked over to the tall, graceful windows. 'Nice place,' he said.

She nodded. Smug, thought Max. Her red hair was white at the roots. 'This apartment house was built by my grandfather. He was one of the original heads of the Black Sea Shipping Company. Naturally, he took the best flat for his family,' she said. 'They lost everything in the Revolution. He owned several ships, buildings. But he was allowed to keep one room, here – and to keep working.'

Max nodded.

'In 1936 the Soviets shot him. Right here, just around the corner. On Hevraisky Street.' She paused, then walked on her pompommed feet over to a dark wooden side table. A sashay that must have had great effect, once.

She drew a black disc from a simple cardboard sleeve. Max watched as the player's arm lifted mechanically and fell again. 'Rossini,' said Marina. 'He was Pushkin's favourite, you know. I left Moldova and came to Europe. Italian opera and French restaurants renew my soul! Pushkin preferred to eat oysters and white wine. Although he had very little money and could not afford it.'

'I'm married already,' said Max.

Marina narrowed her eyes. 'Well, if you're unhappy, you deserve a wonderful Ukrainian girl. Perhaps your wife is too Western. Doesn't listen to you. Doesn't cook? Doesn't take care of herself? Wears un-flattering T-shirts?'

'I'm not looking for a wife,' he said.

Marina stiffened. She laughed, a strange tinkling sound. 'I should throw you out,' she said.

'He's back,' said Max. 'The King.'

Marina flung her too-bright red hair over her shoulder. She's afraid, thought Max. Good. He could use that.

Max handed her the *Odesa Preview* boating issue. Opened to the photo of the pretty redhead in a boating shirt, with the short shorts and the long, long legs. Marina looked at the photo. She started. Then she shook her head. 'This woman is much too young.'

'Too young for what?' asked Max.

The woman studied the picture, again. Softened. Max wondered why. 'She looks just like Inna,' said Marina, tenderly.

'Inna?' he said. 'Like the yacht?'

That was a mistake. A crafty look came into the old woman's eye. She saw that he knew less than she did.

Just then, a tall blonde girl in a short sleeping shirt came in. SO YOU THINK YOU CAN TELL read the shirt. She rubbed her eyes. 'Marinka, I'm so sorry,' she said. 'I didn't hear you come in. Shall I make you some tea?' she asked.

The older woman shook her head. 'Go back to bed, Valya.' Valya nodded. Turned. HEAVEN FROM HELL read the back. The girl wandered back to the room with the mattresses. Shut the door.

Max laid nearly all his hryvnias on the low coffee table, next to a Russian-language copy of *All Quiet on the Western Front*. The crafty glance settled on them. Max waited. Finally, she reached for them. Counted. Slid the bills into her large bosom. The old woman studied the magazine cover again. 'It's only a superficial resemblance. Men like that – once they find what they like, every few years they just get a new model.' She reached out without looking and drew a pair of reading glasses from a mother-of-pearl bowl. 'Yes,' she said. 'You see? This girl's hair – it's dyed red. She's really a blonde, this girl.'

'Ah,' said Max. Glad for the insight.

'... I didn't believe it for a moment,' Marina was saying. 'That he died. Men like that don't die. It's the people around them you have to worry about.'

'Inna?'

'He killed her,' she said. Bitter, suddenly. 'Not literally. But spiritually. She was an innocent, you know. With him, she saw too much. Even if he tried to hide it from her. There was too much … His first wife. Do you think she died without any help?' The old woman laughed, a mirthless laugh. 'When he was arrested, put in prison … For Inna, it was a relief. But the damage was done. She started seeing little green demons. They came at night to torture her. Of course, the doctors had to send her to Psychiatric Hospital Number 4.'

Max looked up, sharply. Marina went on. 'What else could they do?'

Max nodded. 'What about her son?'

The woman laughed again, that tinkling laugh. 'You know, I'm not sure that baby died. I saw her once when she was released. Before she hung herself. And she told me – there was a doctor there. A man with a funny name. Dr Bunnyrabbit, something like that. She told me he took the child. Put him somewhere safe. She told me she wanted me to know, so that someone could tell him. Tell him his mother loved him more than anything in the world. One day. When she wasn't here any more. At the time, I thought she was raving. But since – I've seen a lot. A lot of women, a lot of grief. Madness, too. And I'm not sure, any more.'

'Why are you telling me this?' said Max.

The old madam looked up at him, then. Her eyes were muddy. Like a rough sea. Finally, they wandered down, those unhappy orbs, rested on the cover of the magazine. 'Inna was my sister.'

# 59

The King woke up feeling good. Back on the boat. He patted the sheets. He hadn't wet himself. He hadn't drifted into the past. One night on land, and he was cured.

Plus, he had always liked to see justice prevail. When that drugged-up idiot tried to trip him yesterday! The King understood, of course. It was the law of the jungle. That druggie saw an old man, thought he smelled weakness. Acted without thinking. But the druggie was wrong. The King was not weak. The King was strong. The King still had his whole life ahead of him. His whole family life ahead of him! And the druggie was weak. The druggie was wrong. The druggie was dead. Or if not dead, close to it. The King hadn't stuck around to find out.

Something was bothering him, though. As the ship rocked back and forth, he tried to think of what it was. Ah ha! The session with the psychiatrist. Fishman. It left him with a bad feeling; he hadn't gotten the answers he wanted. Well, he had been foolish. Remember how little they had helped his Inna, at Psychiatric Hospital Number 4! He had missed it all, in prison. But if they had been able to help her, everything would have been different. The boy wouldn't have died and ... the King stopped. His eyes were full of tears. The boat rocked back and forth like a cradle.

Fine, he'd given it a try. He wanted to talk about Sima. This was all new territory. How do you tell a daughter you've never met that you're her father? And that from now on, she'll be living with you, and with you only! That finally, the two of you will be a real family! And he had been trying to find a way to do it, a sure-fire way. His girlfriend, Inna, had been nagging him about going to couples therapy. And when he read the news item to her, about this Fishman's apartment being bombed, in downtown Odesa, she said, 'a poet and a psychiatrist! Let's go see him, next time we're in port.' Of course he had pooh-poohed her. He was the King! He wasn't going to couples therapy. But then, when he learned about Sima, he thought of Dr Fishman again.

That Fishman, though, he wasn't helpful at all. Just wanted to talk about the King's relationship with his own mother. What did that have to do with anything? The King didn't even know his mother! He clenched his fist. He would know what to do when the time came. And the time was nigh!

In the next room, the King heard Inna talking – he called all his girlfriends Inna. He'd keep her around for a while. Although it was true, she was almost twenty-five … a bit old, for a woman. But, she could be a friend for Sima! Yes, now that was a good idea. He wondered what Dr Fishman would say about that …

In the next room, the King heard a man's voice. Felix. Felix would need to help organise things for the big reunion. Soon, now, very soon – the King would get everything. All at once. His precious child, his revenge. The boat rocked. Back and forth. As the King was falling asleep again, he thought he heard something else. A pitter-patter, like cat's paws. Pitter-patter-PITTER-patter. Like a limping cat's paws. But there couldn't be a cat on the yacht. No … The old man nodded off.

# 60

Max stood in a dusty alley in front of a wooden gate. Through a flowering vine, he could just make out the dacha's garden. Small, packed with roses. The tool shed was painted red and yellow, like a Chinese pagoda.

'Dr Fishman', read a shiny bronze plaque. Max rang.

He heard Luba's voice, on the other side of the tall wooden door. Max identified himself, and with a sound of delight, Luba opened the gate and threw herself in his arms. 'Max!' she said. 'Where have you been? We've missed you!'

It was breakfast time. Luba, Fishman's sultry second wife, was also a poet. Now, she pushed back her long dark hair and led him through the lipstick-coloured roses. At a table shaded by grapevines, Fishman himself was sitting, stroking a slightly naughty-looking black cat. He was large man, solid, with white hair and a white beard. He exuded, Max thought not for the first time, an air of calm.

'Don't get up, please,' said Max. 'I was so worried when I read about the bombing.'

'Oh Max,' said Luba, as her husband nodded. 'We're all fine, no one was hurt.'

'I'm so glad,' said Max. Then: 'Hello, Miss Kitty.'

Fishman looked down at the black cat, lovingly. 'She can speak, you know.'

'Yes, I know,' said Max, as he took a seat on the bench. As far away from Miss Kitty as possible. 'I've been reading your blog.'

'Ah!' said Fishman, brightening. 'Then you are aware of the fact that, in this whole city, Miss Kitty is the only one with any sense.'

'I'm also aware of that,' said Max. The table was covered in a bright plastic cloth with large red flowers. Behind him, the scent of honeysuckle floated in the humid air. The roses bent in the midmorning heat. Overhead, the grapevines had been struck with some kind of disease – the leaves were green, but the grapes were brown, shrunken.

Luba emerged from the kitchen with a feast. A plate of sliced tomatoes, running red, clotting thickly; another plate of cheeses, a cucumber salad, a bowl of raspberries, a platter of corn on the cob with great gobs of butter. Bread, and black tea, and sugar.

'Luba,' said Max. 'How do you do it?'

'Oh, it's nothing,' she said. 'Eat, eat! You look hungry. So tell us, what are you doing here? Another conference?'

Max filled his plate and nodded.

'"Capitalism in the crime-based economy"?' said Fishman with a giggle. '"Criminal Capitalism and its Discontents"?' Miss Kitty meowed appreciatively.

'Oh God, don't even ask,' said Max. '"Hybrid War," they're calling it.'

'Ah,' said Fishman. 'Almost horticultural.'

There was a silence, and Max asked if they had any idea who was behind the bombing. Luba lit a thin white cigarette and shrugged. 'You know,' she said, 'the apartment that they bombed. Well, it is registered to Fishman, officially. But he hasn't lived there in years. And why would anyone bomb his ex-wife? So it must be someone who isn't from here. Everyone in Odesa, who knows Odesa, who knows Fishman, knows he doesn't live there.'

'Of course it was frightening,' said Fishman, stroking Miss Kitty absent-mindedly. 'It happened very early in the morning, and my ex-wife was asleep. Luckily the apartment has a very heavy metal door. It made a terrible sound, but no one was hurt.'

Max shook his head. 'What's the temperature in the city? How are things here?'

Luba exhaled a stream of smoke. 'Have you heard about our Green Theatre?'

Max shook his head, no.

'An old Soviet outdoor stage, a ruin. Then some young people, this year, they rebuilt it. You know the artist, Pavlensky?'

Max nodded. 'The one who nailed his private parts to Red Square?'

'Yes, exactly,' said Luba. 'Well! Last week he was here. Giving a lecture in Odesa. It was supposed to be outdoors, at the Green Theatre, but the weather was bad, so they moved it inside. The house was packed! Bloggers, painters – as Fishman put it, "all the usual psychopaths".' Luba glanced at her white-haired husband, who lowered his eyes.

'A very serious talk,' he said, with a giggle.

'They really are mad,' said Luba. 'You know, Pavlensky's wife, she gave an interview where she said she'd been unfaithful to her husband. And, afterwards, she realised what she'd done was absolutely terrible. So she cut off a finger. To remind herself she shouldn't do it again.'

'Not too often, anyway,' said Max.

Fishman giggled.

'So, Pavlensky had just come from Kyiv,' said Luba. 'And of course, Russian television said he was meeting with Ukrainian neo-Nazis there.' She rolled her eyes. 'So then, in Odesa, a very famous blogger came to the presentation – a complete maniac! He dressed his little boy up as an SS man a few years ago, took pictures and posted them on the Internet. And he's Jewish! Anyway, this blogger was drunk. He started making Nazi salutes from the back. He was sitting in front of the projector, so every time he said "Sieg Heil," the shadow showed on Pavlensky's genitals. There were two guards there, and they tried to subdue him. But he pulled out a knife! Finally, some police came, and sent everyone home. No one was stabbed. We all went home. But the guards weren't young; really, they were just two old men. And we found out later that one of them died on the way home. Of a heart attack.'

Fishman shook his head mournfully. 'Frightened to death.'

'Just a simple man, working to feed his family.' Luba raised her hands. 'That's about all you need to know to know how things are here in Odesa right now. Things are very bad, but not in the obvious way.'

'And Grisha?' said Max, after a moment of silence. 'Think he'll change anything?'

Luba said: 'Small things he's done are good. For example, Grisha was taking a tram somewhere, and one of these "Majors" – that's what they're called …' Fishman nodded, lowering his eyelids and ducking his chin deeper into his chest. '… had parked a brand-new Mercedes right on the tram tracks – they were having a drink nearby and didn't want to search for a parking space. So Grisha jumped out, called the police, had the car towed.'

'A good piece of theatre,' said Fishman. His eyes twinkled. 'Maybe too good.'

Luba laughed. 'Still,' she said, 'he's very humble, very nice. At the film festival, for example. He was very charming; he said he'd gained so much weight when he wasn't in politics and had taken the job so fast that he hadn't had any time to get new suits. So he pointed at his belly, and said he apologised, but he couldn't button his jacket, that's why it was open.'

'I'm friends with many poets in Georgia,' said Fishman. 'We used to travel there every summer for a wonderful poetry festival. And they say he enacted quite a lot of reform. That the police really stopped taking bribes. For the little people at least, it was an improvement. If he could do that here, well –'

'It would be wonderful.'

'It would be not bad at all.'

'Oh Fishman, you are so calm, always.'

'It is necessary for my work,' he said. 'Although I believe I am naturally a calm person. For example – when Luba and I heard about the so-called Soccer Massacre. We were in a taxi. And we decided to go and see what was really happening. Well – I wanted to go, and with my eyesight deteriorating so much, Luba had to come as well.'

'I was afraid,' said Luba. 'I didn't want to go. But I couldn't let him go alone.'

'We went to Deribasivka Street. The soccer game had finished – the local team against "Dawn" from Lugansk. Of course, the "Dawn" are pro-Russian. Supposedly, there were "ultras" among the locals – very pro-Ukrainian soccer fans.' Fishman shrugged. 'That kind of thing, it is difficult to tell. To us, they looked like young, drunk soccer fans. Marching through the street.'

'Regular young men,' said Luba. 'Drunk, but normal.'

'Maybe they would have broken the necks of beer bottles, got into fistfights. But what we saw on the roofs were snipers. Dressed in black, with no markings. One of them shot into the crowd.'

'That's when everything changed. It became a bloodbath.'

'Fifty people died,' said Fishman, sadly.

'In Odesa!' said Luba. 'In Odesa, to have this kind of death. We couldn't believe it.'

'A tragedy,' said Fishman.

'But you know, the next day, there were no riots. The city was completely quiet – even if 50 % of the population feels more Russian than Ukrainian, supposedly.' Luba paused. 'In my opinion, this is how the city said, "we do not want war."'

Fishman tickled Miss Kitty's throat. The cat stretched her black head luxuriously. Purred. 'War is bad for business,' he said, with a shrug. 'This has always been a mercantile city. Ever since the days of Catherine the Great. And imagine if it was like Donetsk, with soldiers, and shooting and bombs –' he shrugged. 'The middle class would lose everything.'

'If the Russians do come, we'll leave,' said Luba. 'We're not going to stay here under siege.'

'You think that could happen?' said Max.

Luba lit another needle-thin, white cigarette. 'There's always talk. Yesterday there were reports that Russian warships were gathering outside the city.' She inhaled. 'But I think the Russians have waited too long. A year ago, no one here could imagine a man in a Russian uniform as an enemy. Now, that's changed. Now, people would fight.'

Miss Kitty jumped down, approached Max. His throat contracted. Just a little. He inched away from her. 'You worked at the Psychiatric Hospital number 4, right?' he said.

'Yes,' said Fishman. 'I was a psychiatrist there. It was my first job, after medical school.'

'Did you know a Dr Bunny? Or a Dr Rabbit?'

'Oh yes!' said Fishman. 'Artyom. Yes, we were friends for a long time. Right, Luba?'

'Unfortunately, he has Alzheimer's,' said Luba.

'Well, not entirely unfortunately, actually,' said Fishman. 'You see, after the Soviet Union collapsed, anti-Semitism changed. It went from unofficially official to rabid and populist. And Artyom – everyone called him Dr Rabbit, because he has very prominent front teeth – he showed me the ropes when I first came to Psychiatric Hospital Number 4. After I was fired, we stayed close. Until one day, oh, a decade ago, well, he became completely anti-Semitic.'

'Yes, it was just untenable after a while,' said Luba, lighting another cigarette. 'Anyway, with Artyom, we broke the friendship.'

'Until he got Alzheimer's. Then he forgot he was an anti-Semite.' Fishman giggled. 'After that, it was quite nice to spend time with him again.'

Luba nodded wryly.

'Although,' Fishman continued. 'Sometimes, Artyom, he really forgot everything. One time, after we were friends again, he came to our house. I had *The Gulag Archipelago* sitting on the table. Artyom saw the book and he said, "Aren't you afraid? To have this book out, in full view?" He had completely forgotten the Soviet Union didn't exist anymore.'

Miss Kitty yowled, for no apparent reason. Jumped down. Began pacing the edge of the rose garden.

'The hedgehogs are coming,' said Luba. 'Fishman loves hedgehogs.'

'I love hedgehogs,' said Fishman, as Miss Kitty's wet black nose drew surreptitiously closer to the bowl of roe, glistening orange in the sunlight.

'No, Miss Kitty, you can't have any dessert,' said Luba. 'Max, don't give her anything. Do you know, Fishman, what I heard? I heard that Artyom is working again! I could hardly believe it. At the White Dove Sanatorium.'

Fishman shook his head. 'Well, of course he is a trained medical doctor, like me. But well, I wouldn't say he was in a state to work. Then again, our pensions being what they are ...'

Max checked his watch.

'By the way,' said Max. 'Do you know Vanya Lerner? Also known as "the King"?'

'Yes of course,' said Fishman. 'He was a famous mobster. In charge of the port, even when he was in Soviet prison. He was killed, in a raid. Oh, thirty years ago.'

'Did you know him?'

'A little,' said Fishman. 'After all, Odesa is not so very big, and we have always paid attention to our celebrities. And – well, supposedly, our families were very distantly related. At least, that's what a cousin of my mother, who was the family historian, always claimed.'

'Do you know anything about a son?' said Max.

'That was a sad story,' said Fishman. 'Vanya Lerner was said to be very much in love with his second wife. When he was sent to prison, she went mad, apparently. They put her in Psychiatric Hospital Number 4 – sometimes they did put mental patients in the hospital; it wasn't only for dissidents. But that was before my time. The child died, and she hung herself.'

The doctor gazed into space. 'You know it's funny you ask, actually. I was thinking of Vanya just the other day. A sad story, really. His father, Yakov, was a brilliant scientist. Vanya's mother was Mexican – they met and fell in love while Yakov was in Mexico, part of a Soviet delegation. Yakov's mother was a terrible person, supposedly. She hated the wife – Maria, I think, was her name. Made her life hell. There was even some rumour – that she poisoned her. Anyway, Maria died when Vanya was very small. Then his father was shot, part of one of Stalin's purges.' Fishman paused.

'In Ukraine, we have a tragic history,' said Luba, lighting another white-needle cigarette.

Fishman nodded. Miss Kitty jumped back up on his lap. Purred. 'After that, from what I know, Vanya lived with his grandmother. She was a natural criminal – that's what my mother's cousin used to say. But she died when the Romanians occupied the city.'

'You know, here, the Jews hadn't heard about the Holocaust,' said Luba. 'They didn't know what was coming. When the Romanians said to gather in the city centre, they went. Most of them never came back.'

'That's right,' said Fishman. 'Vanya was out that morning when they took his grandmother, with the other Jews. After that, he was alone. He worked as he could, at the port, in the city's darkest corners. It was the beginning of his criminal career, I suppose. He knew the port better than anybody – it was mother and father to him.' Fishman paused again. 'You know, he joined the Soviet Navy when he turned sixteen. Stationed on the *Maxim Gorky*, that was the story.'

'Wait,' said Max. 'The *Maxim Gorky*?'

'Yes,' said Fishman, gazing shrewdly at Max, before continuing. 'As I said, that was the story. But in the end – the criminal life was the only one for him.' Fishman sunk his white beard into his chest. 'As a matter of fact, I was just thinking of Vanya. A new patient came in the other day. Reminded me of him.'

'The cyclops who calls himself "nobody"?' said Max.

'Well!' said Fishman, with a laugh. 'You really have been reading my blog! Yes, now that you mention it – I suppose he must have inspired that figure, in the diary. Funny, I hadn't even thought of it ...'

\*

Before Max left, he asked if he could use the bathroom. Inside the dacha, Max turned left, not right. Stepped into a wonderful little room, dark and peaceful, lined in dusky icons. A large desk and a narrow red-velvet sofa. Books in a glass case. Max glanced around: Fishman's whole world. Here, he met his patients, wrote his poems, published his online diary – the one that set the tone for so much of the city's intellectual debate. The diary entry about the cyclops was posted two days ago.

Now, Max worked quickly. He pulled open the filing cabinet under the wooden table. Extracted a handful of manila envelopes. One, towards the top, had no name. Instead, it was marked with an X. Max opened it. *Patient refuses to give his name. Blind in one eye.*

Max read through the rest of the hand-written notes quickly. *Patient X recently learned about the existence of an adult daughter. Wants advice for how best to make contact. Feels it must require a good deal of*

*psychological acuity to win her over. Winning/losing. Dichotomy think-*
*ing. Patient resists discussion of own relationship with parents. Oral fixa-*
*tion (mint imperials).*

*Sociopathic traits: Lack of empathy, overdeveloped Id. Regressive in-*
*terest in birthday cakes.* Max was about to replace the papers when he
scanned to the bottom. *No follow-up session scheduled.*

From every inch of wall space, the watchful dark eyes of saints
looked down, their burnished halos glinting as he folded the sheets
of yellow paper and slipped them into his back pocket.

# 61

'Grisha!' said the taxi driver, a solid family man in a sleeveless shirt that read GETTING WARMER. 'What he does! I call it "Facebook governance". It looks good on Facebook. But it's not real. For example: he just set up a wedding chapel. Have you seen it? Yellow number in front of the administration building. You can apply for a marriage licence and get married within, I don't know, three hours. Ok. It opened last week, all over the news. But who really needs a fast wedding? Like my wife says, everybody plans a wedding. She would know!' he shook his head. 'It's an improvement nobody needs improved.' He shrugged. 'Like I said, "Facebook governance". Not to say I don't like him. He's a drug addict! But he's not so bad.'

Then he hit the brakes, throwing everything in the car forward: the seat backs, Max, a cloying scent of air freshener.

'You like swimming?' asked the driver.

'Yeah,' said Max.

'Me too!' said the family man. 'But not this year. Last winter, during the big storms, the rain carried all the dirt from the city streets, right down to the beach. That's why I'm not going swimming this year.'

*

Max made his way to the White Dove, avoiding a child-sized hole in the sidewalk . It was deep, round, treacherous. A little tree was growing out of it.

Spotting a drinks kiosk, Max ducked in. Bought the most expensive box of chocolates they had. They weren't very expensive. Added a packet of breath mints.

Through a white gate, past a billboard describing the White Dove's specialities: Circulatory problems. Lungs and eyes and nerves. Quite a smorgasbord, he thought.

The lobby was large, antiseptic, remodelled in the 'European style'. White, shiny stone. A German coffee vending machine in the corner.

An enclosed booth by the door was hung with keys and manned by a round little woman who seemed to crawl behind the curtain to sleep on a cot at night.

Max walked past her and made his way to the receptionist. A single round clock in a shiny brass frame showed the time. Below it, behind glass, sat a vital-looking woman with a dark beehive hairdo and a white nurse's uniform.

'I've been looking for a room all morning,' said Max. 'I don't suppose anything here is free?'

She shook her head. 'We're fully booked until September.'

'Is there any other place I could go?' Max asked, knowing full well there wasn't. Since the fighting began in the east, the old sanatoriums had filled with war refugees.

She shook her head.

'Ah-ha,' said Max. 'As a matter of fact, I really wanted to come for the medical aspect, more than anything else. Your high-pressure hose treatments are famous.'

The receptionist cast her eyes down in acknowledgement. 'Unfortunately,' she said, 'only guests can receive medical treatment.'

Max winked. Pushed the box of chocolates under the glass. She eyed them warily. Then she saw the bills Max had slipped into the cheap burgundy ribbon. She took the box gingerly. 'Your circulation is bad?'

Max nodded. 'My lung capacity is also poor,' he said. Max coughed for good measure. 'And I'm allergic to cats.'

The woman raised an eyebrow. Told him to wait. Max took a seat on a white leather sofa.

Twenty minutes later, the receptionist gestured to him from beneath her beehive. He rose. Approached. 'The doctor can see you now,' she said. 'But you'll have to pay for a room. For a week.'

'Lady luck is on my side,' said Max, with a wink. The woman with the beehive blushed. Then she smiled. He did, too.

*

Max walked the long hallway. The whole place smelled mildly of disinfectant, along with the mustier scent of ageing bodies and poor health.

When he reached the waiting room, he paused. He hadn't ever been to the White Dove. But every Brezhnev-era sanatorium was organised according to the same principles. The waiting room, for example, was painted dark green, with the requisite oil painting of the Carpathians. He walked through it, upstairs, and back to what had to be the doctor's offices. He knocked, and a voice inside told him to come in.

The door was brown, new, laminated in plastic. The room was large and airy, with two big rectangular windows. Venetian blinds, closed. The deep plastic sills were crowded with pale green spider plants.

From a plastic desk, a little white-haired man looked up. The lenses of his large, brown-rimmed glasses were dirty, smudged with fingerprints, flecks of dust and skin. He smiled tentatively, revealing two very large front teeth. Like a rabbit. Then fear crept into his eyes. As if he had forgotten who this patient was and was trying to remember. 'High cholesterol!' said the doctor, suddenly. A look of relief. 'Diet number 5. I'll tell the dining room. High-pressure hose therapy. Thirty-minute sports massage. Electric shocks – for your lower back. And you need to relax.'

Dr Rabbit was lucid. Max eased into his questions. 'Tell me, at Psychiatric Hospital Number 4. Not all your patients were dissidents – enemies of the state.'

'Of course not,' said the doctor. 'We had schizophrenics as well. Paranoid schizophrenics, mostly.'

He fell into a brooding state. The spider plants had been overwatered, Max noticed. Their little plates were overflowing, water spilled onto the plastic sill.

'Visits from the Angel Gabriel, and so forth?' said Max.

'No,' said the doctor. 'No. Most schizophrenics were convinced they were being followed by the KBG.' He brooded again, rubbing his hands over his stubble. He looked as if he hadn't showered in days. 'The number two persecutor was aliens. Number three was the American secret services.' He paused. 'We had no angels in our psychosis.'

Something rippled through the doctor's gaze. Something painful, unpleasant. He stood, picked up a plastic watering can. 'There were devils,' he said as he began to water the plants. 'Little green devils who tormented alcoholics. This was well documented. The delirium tremors were often accompanied by tortures enacted by small green devils.' As he moved from one plant to next, Max saw there was no water in the can. 'These green devils appear in folkloric tales, as well.' The doctor sat back down. Peered at Max through those dirty lenses.

'And what about the children?'

The doctor looked at him blankly.

'The children of the alcoholics, the schizophrenics, the dissidents who ended up in Psychiatric Hospital Number 4. What happened to them?'

'They went to the orphanage,' said the doctor, impatiently. 'Out in the countryside. Very close to the sea.'

Max struck. 'Inna Lerner. What happened to her son?'

The doctor froze. 'I can't discuss my patients,' he said. 'That's not ethical.'

'What about her husband?' said Max.

A pitiful look crossed the doctor's face. Searching and not finding.

'"The King,"' Max said. He was losing the doctor. He needed to bring him back, bring his memory back. Surreptitiously, Max popped three mints in his mouth. Chewed.

'Lerner, Vanya,' said the doctor. 'He's dead.'

'He's alive,' said Max. Exhaling. 'In Odesa.'

Suddenly the doctor clapped his jaw shut. 'No!' he said, a shudder passing through his body. 'No, no, no.'

He looked up at Max, his eyes wild with fear. He picked up the empty watering can and went back to the spider plants. Watered them one by one, until he was calmer. Without looking at Max, he said: 'Inna wasn't crazy. The world was crazy, her husband was crazy. Her response, to become crazy, was the only sane thing to do. She told me … terrible stories. And she begged me to take her son away. So that 'the King' would never find out. We came up with the plan – together. I sent him to the orphanage. For Inna, I created a death certificate. To show the King. I never realised at the time that by saving her child, I was signing Inna's death sentence.'

The doctor turned and looked at Max. The empty can shook in his hand. A look a fear crept into his eyes. Searching and not finding. Then a look of relief. 'Diet Number 5!' he almost shouted. 'I'll tell the dining room. And you need to relax.'

Then he turned back and began watering the spider plants, from the beginning.

# Part 6

We're painting our nails now
Get out of here – before it's too late

Ludmila Khersonsky, untitled poem

## 62

On the sidewalk, Max looked up to see a blue tram bearing directly towards him. He felt his muscles clench. Terror. Then his body was a foot away. The whoosh of hot air as the tram barrelled past. Max grimaced. He had forgotten that the tram tracks ran right along the walkways, here on the French Boulevard.

Heart pounding, he looked up at the blue metal tram. A pair of green eyes caught his attention: a little girl pressing her face to the window. With a start, Max recognised her: Cassie, from the plane. Strange. He shook his head. It gave him a spooky feeling.

His heart was just beginning to calm when he heard his name being called. An American voice. Upbeat. Happy. He looked up and down the street, then across the way. There, detached from a group of foreign men in suits, stood Mark Hope. Waving. 'Max! Thank God.'

'What's wrong?'

'You have a visitor,' said Mark Hope.

'Oh, shit,' said Max. 'Dunkirk's back?'

'No, no,' said Mark. 'It's just – that, uh, your wife, Rose ...'

'Did something happen to Rose?' Max heard the panic in his own voice.

'Uh, no. No, Rose is – here. In Odesa. She got to the Gagarin this morning. Really early, actually – but you weren't there.'

'Oh, shit,' said Max. 'She still at the hotel?'

'No,' said Mark Hope. 'Rose – she's inside. On the tour. You know, the champagne factory tour? Scheduled today –' he held out a pamphlet. 'Part of the conference?'

Max looked up. Overhead, a cluster of iron grapes hung from a gate. To the left and right, two-tone murals – institutional blue and oxblood red – showed a geometric woman and a geometric man in lab coats, holding geometric beakers. A big dusty truck rolled across the courtyard. Ahead, a few straggling men in dark suits were filing into a narrow door.

'She's in there?'

Mark Hope nodded. Absent-mindedly, Max took the pamphlet the intern proffered. Max glanced down. The conference schedule. His eyes alighted on the 'Farewell Dinner Dance' (who on earth were they going to dance with?) Then he forgot Rose entirely: the Farewell Dinner Dance was going to take place 'on board the "Intriguing Inna!" (as seen in the *Odesa Preview's* recent BOATING! issue).'

Max looked up and noticed that a deeply pained look had appeared on Mark Hope's handsome face. 'What's up?' he said.

'Uh,' said Mark Hope, in a small voice. 'Well, um. Rose wasn't alone, waiting for you. A, uh, Ukrainian bride was there, too. She said Marina sent her. She gave me this –' Mark Hope handed Max a little piece of paper, folded. 'For you.'

Max sighed. He took the paper. Unfolded it. A grocery receipt. Then a bolt of recognition: on the back, it read: 'He's on the *Inna*.'

Max put the paper in his pocket. Looked at Mark Hope.

'C'mon,' said Max. 'Let's face the music.'

*

The room was large and dark. All around rose enormous metal cylinders, dented and green, like old-fashioned submarines. Something out of *Ten Thousand Leagues Under the Sea*. The men filed through the empty spaces, looking up at the mighty casks. In their dark suits, they looked like shadows. 'In 1951,' a woman's voice floated through the room, 'Stalin issued an order: now, champagne will be the workers' drink.' Max didn't see Rose. The men ahead of him were filing up a rickety wooden stairway. Max followed. 'And so,' came the woman's voice from above, 'we built these tanks and started mass-producing.' At the top of the stairs, Max stepped onto a platform. The platform had been fitted over the rounded tops of the tanks. They emerged like inverse craters on the surface of the moon.

BANG. Shattering glass. Panic ricocheted through Max's being. A bomb! Where was Rose? Was she ok? There was no screaming. No one had reacted. Another crashing sound. BOOM! The sound of broken glass. '... Here, we test the bottles to make sure they are sound ...' Another explosion. 'They must be able to withstand very high pressure. As you can see, not all bottles are perfect ...' Max pushed his way past the men in suits, to the head of the line.

Max stepped into the filling room. Green champagne bottles marched by on an old-fashioned mechanical assembly line. He looked around, and then – there she was: standing at the front of the group, next to a handsome white-haired woman in a lab coat, listening attentively. Rose. His Rose. The sunlight coming through the windows caught her hair, turned her blonde curls into a sort of halo, more light than substance. Her shoulders were bare. He couldn't see it from here, but he knew the starburst-shaped scar on her left upper arm was showing. She had gotten it falling from a tree as a child ... and suddenly Max had the feeling he was seeing her, really seeing her, for the first time. That he'd gotten used to not looking. There was a sharp, shooting feeling in his heart, coupled with a sort of tenderness that made him feel like he was drowning. 'Excuse me,' said Max. 'Excuse me.' The explosions were louder, in here. The sound of shattering glass more violent.

The group began to move on. Rose at the front, then out of Max's sight. 'Good God!' From somewhere up ahead, Max heard Trilby's voice. 'Do you remember those Cold War New Year's parties? Salad Olivier and Soviet champagne ...'

'Sovietsky champagnski ...!' came another voice.

'... gave you a hangover before you were tipsy ...'

'... well, for old times' sake ...'

Back outside in the sunshine, champagne flutes were being distributed. Max spotted Rose again. She was standing next to the woman in the lab coat. Rose was listening, fascinated. Max made his way through the crowd.

'At first,' he heard the scientist saying, 'we could only mass produce sweet champagne. But in the seventies, we decided we were going to make dry champagne as well. They said it couldn't be done – they called us "the brutalists" – but we did it!' She held up her flute of sparkling, golden liquid just as Max reached Rose. 'Do you want to know,' the woman asked Rose, conspiratorially, 'the secret to staying beautiful?'

'Rose!' said Max.

Rose turned towards him, her blue eyes flashing.

'I – can't believe you're here!'

She frowned. Then she turned back to the chemist. 'Yes!' she said. 'Please, I do.'

The pretty chemist leaned back and drained the glass in one go. 'Drink champagne! Every day!'

Just then, a movement outside the gates caught Max's eye. A tram, lumbering down the French Boulevard. Max glanced up at it, then froze. Staring out of the tram window was a one-eyed man. The shoplifter from the plane, lover of breath mints. Killer of Luddy 'the Lion' Shturman. A man whose name, if Max was not entirely mistaken, was Vanya 'the King' Lerner. The tram was passing, passing, passing right in front of the champagne factory. Then it was gone. 'Rosie-Posie,' whispered Max. 'I've got to – I'll be right back.'

Before she could say anything, Max was pushing his way back through the crowd. 'Mark!' he said, keeping an eye on the tram bearing that narrow, desiccated figure slowly into the distance. 'Stay with Rose. Don't let her drink too much of that Soviet champagne.'

'Ok,' said Mark Hope. 'You got it! See you later, downtown?'

'What?' said Max. He stopped, halfway to the gate.

'Drinks in the City Garden? In an hour –' Mark checked his pamphlet. 'At six!'

'Got it,' said Max. And then he was gone. Running, after the tram.

# 63

Inspector Krook was dozing in the late afternoon heat, in the shade of the dacha's sun umbrella. The scent of Mrs Krook's shashlik grew stronger and stronger. Krook's mouth began to water in half-sleep. He reached up, scratched his prodigious bare belly. Inhaled. He could hardly wait ...

Just then something began to irritate him. He slapped at the sticky air around his head. No. It didn't stop. A kind of buzzing. He woke more fully. Right, of course. As soon as you try to get some rest, someone from the office has to call ... He reached over and picked up the phone. Dimples. Of course, it would be Dimples.

The connection was bad. 'What?' said Krook. Dimples was in a state, as usual. His normally irritating voice raised another pitch or two. Like someone playing a saw. 'A *lion*?' said Krook. 'What?'

Through the scratchy line he heard: 'I've been using a new ... check online rentals! And Ludwig Shturman ...' scratch scratch '... aka 'the Lion,' rated a room, on Pushkin Street ...' A few feet away, he heard Mrs Krook: 'SHASHLIK'S READY!'

'Wait,' said Krook. 'What is Air Pee Pee?'

'SHASHLIK'S READY!' Krook had to hurry! Otherwise his no-good son-in-law would eat everything. Well, all the best parts, anyway: 'For his health.' From the phone, there came more sounds of scratching, along with an extra layer of buzzing. Then Dimple's high-pitched voice: '... interviewed the landlady ... Ludwig 'the Lion' Shturman has a meeting ... in twenty minutes ... Eye Institute ... No, eye, like you see with ...'

A wasp landed on Krook's head. He jumped up. Shook it off. Dropped the phone on the dirt floor. Picked it up again. The Lion! Sure, it rang a bell. Something about a nuclear submarine and co-caine ... but the guy was probably just on vacation. A feat Inspector

Krook himself was attempting. With limited success! Still, better safe than sorry. And then there was Dimples. The phrase 'enough rope to hang himself' came to mind.

'SHASHLIK'S READY!'

'Sure,' said Krook, into the phone. 'Do what you want, Dimples. Send a man out there if it makes you feel better.'

# 64

Max hurried across the street. Saw the lumbering back of the blue tram. There was only one thing for it: Max started to run.

Before he had a chance to groan about the stitch in his side, the tram began to slow. In front of the Eye Institute, it stopped. Max hung back, now. As he watched, a line of old people slowly descended. Last of all came a desiccated old man with a leather eye patch. He hopped from the bottom step down to the ground. Spritely. He looked left, right, and ahead. Then he walked up a set of shallow steps. Past a set of pale-yellow columns. And disappeared.

For his part, Max cut away from the street, towards the beach. At the end of the walkway, the Black Sea hung, blue and inviting. Max spotted a set of stairs, heading down. A wrinkled old woman was selling tiny pink shrimp from a plastic bucket. He turned. Struck his way through the undergrowth. Reached the next set of stairs – vertiginous, concrete. Made his way back up to street level.

A park. A line of chestnut trees. An ornamental gate, reduced to rust and paint. Between them stretched a narrow alley. Lined in weeds. Old men and old women walked slowly up and down. Everyone had one eye covered. On a bench, in front of a worn, lichen-covered statue of a virginal Soviet girl, sat the one-eyed man Max had been looking for.

To his right rose the yellow building with smooth classical columns. Max ducked inside. The famous Odesa Eye Institute. Where better for a one-eyed man to blend in? Max opened the first door he came to. An examination room. Empty. Max rummaged through the cabinets. Fit a soft cotton pad over his left eye socket. Taped it, once, twice, trying to remember just how the patients outside looked.

In the mirror, Max caught a glimpse of himself. He looked good. Like all the other patients. Max left the yellow building with the smooth classical columns, through the metal door he had come in by. He wandered at a distance from the lichen-covered statue. The man was still there. But now, he was no longer alone.

*

The young man in a red necktie leaned in close to the old man with the eye patch. A blue light glowed from his left ear. Max recognised him right away, of course: Felix.

'Should we wait for the Lion?' said Felix. He looked, Max thought, very nervous.

The old man shook his head. 'Late!' he said. 'We will begin without him.'

'Whatever you say, Mr King,' said Felix. Even from here, Max could see he was sweating.

'And the new hand?'

'That's coming along nicely. It's got the birthmark in the right spot, and everything.'

'I need it ready by 25 August,' said the old man.

'Day after tomorrow,' said Felix. 'No problem. None at all.'

'Good,' said the old man. 'Bring it to the yacht tomorrow night. Be on the dock at …'

Felix stood. Max stepped back behind the yellow column. He wondered what it meant. The 24th – tomorrow – was Ukrainian Independence Day. Everyone dressed up in traditional shirts, thronged the main streets. What was so special about the day after?

Max would find out. He decided to let Felix go. The King was the prize. He was the one to follow. Max was just about to step out again, when he felt a sudden, sharp pain at the back of his head. A good-looking young man, smiling. Two prominent dimples … After that, everything went black.

# 65

Max came to in a dark, airless cell. Was he back in the catacombs?

It stank. Vomit and urine and iron. Blood, that must be blood. He was lying on a damp concrete shelf. His head hurt more than it had all week. That wasn't good. The sound of snoring. Max rolled to one side. The pain in his head increased. Sharp, shooting. Not so much his lizard brain as his human one. A wiry man with a shaved head was asleep at his feet. He reeked of alcohol.

'Wanna cigarette?' asked a jumpy voice in the darkness.

Max was about to say he didn't smoke. Then he thought better of it. 'Sure,' he said.

Out of the darkness, a hand appeared. The hand was pale, shaking like a leaf. It held a bent, dirty cigarette. Ukrainian brand. No filter. A lighter with a naked woman on it. Max put the dirty cigarette in his mouth. Lit it. Glanced up as the flame caught.

The man was skinny, young, blond hair. Bloodshot eyes. Glue sniffer. A typical informant: the kind of recidivist druggie the police used to spy on people in jail. The druggie gets arrested, then makes a deal: for a lighter sentence, he goes in, talks to the other guys they've arrested and want information from. Tells his story, wheedles stories out of the other guy. Ok, thought Max. Let's see where this is going.

'You ever pulled a big fish?' asked the informant. 'I gotta tell you, I was about to hook a big one, just the other day. Then my old lady comes home, sees I've been huffing again. Locks me in. I missed the shipment.' He hung his head. It twitched.

'Tough break,' said Max. He pulled on the cigarette. The tip glowed in the jail cell. It was definitely a jail cell. Max coughed. Like smoking a truck tyre. He handed the lighter back.

'Hey, you talk like a fuckin' Muscovite. What happened to your Odesa accent? Too long in New York? Hey,' said the informant, conversationally. Then: 'You really almost sell a submarine, one time?'

'Uh,' said Max. Interesting. So, they thought he was the Lion. Interesting. At least it would be easy to clear that up when he got out. If he got out: Max looked back at the informant. The pale blond was shaking harder now. He looked desperate: his eyes, his teeth.

'That's what I heard on the street. 'Bout you. You got your hands on a submarine, nuclear powered and everything, and you sold it. To some fuckin' Colombians. Right?'

Max said nothing. Took another poisonous drag. The cigarette woke him up, but also made him feel like vomiting. Well, nothing in life is perfect. He took another drag. In the red glow, something flashed. The informant moved quickly. In a moment, he had Max's head pulled back, was reaching with trembling fingers for his throat. 'Now you listen to me,' he muttered, getting a none-too-good grip. 'You better give me the goods or you're never getting out of here. You got that –?'

The wrenching sound of metal on metal interrupted his soliloquy. The lights went on. Max blinked, blinded. When he could see again, the informant was back in a corner, twitchily feigning sleep. And a big-bellied Ukrainian in a brand-new black police uniform walked in. He stopped, legs akimbo. Looked down at Max from over his belly. 'Rushmore,' he said. 'You stupid son of a bitch.'

*

Upstairs, the morning light was already shining through Inspector Krook's windows. Casting a honeyed glow on his brown office furniture. Max felt a little faint as he sat down across from the police inspector. Years ago, they had worked together. A chequered collaboration, which ended in the semi-successful busting of a money-laundering scheme that had reached from San Francisco to Bessarabia.

Except for the California-style uniform, Krook looked the same as ever, as he stood over Max. Peered down at him. Then he sighed. Walked over to a rusty grey medicine cabinet. Came back with a bottle of green iodine. 'Here,' he said, thrusting it at Max. 'Clean yourself up. The bathroom's down the corridor.'

Max walked to the bathroom. Saw a gash on his forehead, crusted with dirt and blood. He ran the tap. Stuck his head under it. It burned. He took a paper towel, dabbed it in iodine. Lurid green. Fine. He swabbed the cut. Fine.

Max washed his hands. Walked back to Krook's office. Sat down. 'Better,' said Krook, taking the iodine bottle. With a grunt, the inspector reached under his desk, took out two shot glasses, a bottle of vodka and a loaf of brown bread. As he poured, Max looked out the window. In the courtyard below, a tough-looking tabby cat strode into the sun. Stood to attention. Like a sentinel. On the second floor, Max sneezed. It hurt.

'To Lady Luck,' said Krook. 'That bitch.'

'To her,' said Max.

Max ate a piece of bread. It was dense, moist, a little sour. It tasted good. Krook poured him another vodka, and another. Max started to feel better. Stronger, more solid.

'So, what the hell?' said Krook. Max was silent. 'What the hell were you doing, putting cotton on your eye and skulking around the Odesa Eye Clinic?'

'Same thing you should be doing,' said Max. 'Watching the King.'

'The King?' Krook looked puzzled. 'The King's been dead for thirty years.'

'I wouldn't be too sure about that,' said Max. 'What's with the glue sniffer's questions for the Lion?"

'That's for me to know and you – not to know,' Krook said.

'Don't you know that Ludwig Shturman was hit by a bus and died yesterday? Right in front of the Bristol hotel. I saw him myself. Wasn't it all over the police reports?'

Krook had been looking at Max with a disconcerting interest. 'Shturman was probably using a fake passport,' added Max. Then he made a guess: 'But then, your guy should have known that.'

Now, Krook cursed. Muttering something about 'dimples' and 'air peepee'. Krook pounded his fist on the table. He shuffled through a stack of papers. Sat back in his chair as if all the weight of the world was pressing down on him. '... spend one extra day at the dacha,' he muttered. 'Same shirt, through the ass …' Krook sighed heavily. Poured two more shots. 'You have no idea,' he said, 'how hard it is to get good men these days. The pay is shit, and this – Grisha!' Inspector Krook said the name like it tasted bad in his mouth. 'This Grisha is running around making noise about getting rid of bribes. That scares off the new recruits. They know how it is – no bribes? You don't eat. Why should you be the one who doesn't eat? My neighbour's eating. I want to eat, too!'

'Yeah,' said Max. He rubbed the back of his head. 'No hard feelings.'

They toasted to no hard feelings.

Max was just wondering how he was going to explain his absence to Rose, when the solid, Soviet-issue telephone on Krook's desk rang. Krook picked up the receiver. Cradled it against his shoulder as he poured out two more shots. 'Mm-hm,' he said. 'Mm-hm. Now, calm down, Madame Tulip. Don't worry, we'll try to catch him. Skipping out on your girls!' Krook clucked sympathetically. 'We have some standards in this city, after all,' he said, looking up at Max and winking. 'Yes, of course we have a good relationship, Madame Tulip. You're one of my best sources! Now, calm down. I can't understand you when you're weeping like this.'

Then Inspector Krook frowned. 'What's that you say? A one-eyed man. With a tattoo … And you think he's –' Krook was silent. Finally, he said, 'Thank you for calling, Madame Tulip. This is very, uh, helpful information. I'll do everything I can.'

The frown didn't leave Krook's face as he put the receiver down. It was still there when he looked up at Max. 'Where you staying?' said Krook. 'How about I drive you home?'

\*

Max waited on the sidewalk while Krook pulled around with the car. The sun was beating down strongly now. The sky was a clear deep blue, and the footpaths were already crowded with holiday-makers. Girls and boys with deep tans and white teeth and bright smiles and happy colours. All the T-shirts had messages. LOVE. LIFE. NOT YOUR GIRLFRIEND!

Krook's white police Lada pulled up. Max got in. Pulled the door shut. The car felt like it was made out of tinfoil.

'We'll take the scenic route,' said Krook, heading out of town. 'Give us a chance to catch up.'

'Sure,' said Max.

Krook's little Lada turned onto the two-lane road that led to the city's main 'sleeping district' – what they called the suburbs, in these parts. Max looked out the window. Low, old-fashioned buildings, sagging. Soviet cars. A row of plane trees choking in dust. To the right, behind the houses, loomed a row of silos. Part of the port. To the left, factories. Also choking in dust. Krook made a U-turn. Headed back towards the city.

'It hasn't been easy, you know,' Krook said. 'After the regime change, they fired all the top-level guys. We coppers, we were afraid we'd be next. For six months, a year, everything was frozen. Paralysed. Then the new guys came in; they're all pro-Ukrainian. They gave us our new orders. I'm an ethnic Russian, I speak Russian, but ok. I'm still on the job. Investigating. Fine. A crime is a crime, right? Guy shows up on my patch saying he's seen Vanya Lerner with his own eyes, I've got to look into it, no matter who my boss is. So...' Krook turned his large body as well as he could, pinned beneath the steering wheel. 'How about you tell me what you know?'

Max shrugged. 'I heard it from a little old lady. Used to work with the Black Sea Shipping Company. She hadn't seen him, not up close. Her eyesight's not too good, either, I'd say.'

The traffic had started to move now. Crawling along. Despite the heat, Krook kept the windows rolled all the way up. The motor rattled around beneath them. It would be foolhardy to try to bug a car like this. Max went on. 'Her grandson's got some kind of "eternal life" scheme. Spooky kid. Keeps his *dedushka's* head frozen in his offices, in the old Shipping Company's offices. Waiting for technology to evolve so his grandpa can come back to life and finally live his dreams of selling hats on the free market.'

Krook's mouth twisted in a grimace. 'Gruesome,' said Max. 'It absolutely is. But somehow ... optimistic. Anyway, the old lady, she said her grandson had a new business partner. Vanya Lerner. That she knew him from way back when. Said he was a bad guy. Asked me to help.'

'That kid's in a world of trouble,' said Krook. 'What's-his-name. Felix. He's our number-one suspect for the bombing at Angelina's restaurant.'

Max frowned. 'Really?'

'Yep,' said Krook. 'There's not much doubt, actually. We've got the kid buying fertilizer and hydrogen peroxide the day before. Didn't even try to cover his tracks.'

They were turning up a large, sloped highway. To the left and right rose big Soviet apartment blocks. Dusty, dilapidated. Right now, thought Max, he and Krook could be driving through any mid-sized suburb, anywhere in the post-Communist world. They slowed. Out the window, Max saw an artificial lake. Brown, with a brown hut next to it. Set into a run-down park of dusty anaemic pines. 'Most dangerous park in the city,' said Krook, following Max's glance.

'So,' Max continued. 'Let me float this by you. The King isn't dead. No, he's very much alive. He's been hiding out all these years. Maybe still operating. From Brighton Beach. Tbilisi, maybe.'

Krook had begun to nod. Barely perceptibly.

Max went on: 'If he's been in Tbilisi, there's a good chance he's got a beef with Grisha. Grisha did a pretty good job getting rid of the mafiosos there.'

Krook said nothing.

'A lot of them came to Odesa,' said Max.

Krook grunted. In the affirmative.

Max continued: 'So maybe that's why the King is back. Maybe Grisha broke up his mafia ring. Maybe the King is angry about it.'

Instead of replying, Krook bent a little over the steering wheel. Pointed. A low-slung mottled building, old-fashioned, with a plaster horse's head. 'Here, old Odesa starts again. That's where horse thieves would stable their goods, in Babel's time.'

'Huh,' said Max. 'I've got horse thieves in my family.'

'Oh yeah?' said Krook.

Max nodded. 'Mother's side. Run out of Montana, way back when. For stealing horses.' The traffic moved forward. Max shrugged. 'That's the story, anyway. Maybe it's not true.'

They turned left and drove on in the sunshine. Narrower streets. Two-storey buildings, clay-coloured, with ornamental moulding. Rising and falling in gentle waves as the earth beneath settled slowly into the catacombs. Every other door was marked by a heart-shaped sign. Moldavanka. The criminals' district in Babel's time. The criminals' district, now.

Krook pulled onto the pavement. Parked. The two men stepped out of the car. Across the street was a tall, tiled apartment house. A man without a shirt stood on the top-floor balcony, smoking. Krook led the way into a courtyard. Long and narrow, weeds and glass. An old washing machine. All along the yard stretched a short building.

'Built as a brothel,' said Krook. 'You can see, right?' Max looked: every three feet there was a door, with a tiny window. 'It's in one of the Benya Krik stories, even,' Krook continued. 'After a raid, he and his gang come came here to celebrate.' Max nodded.

As he spoke, Krook walked to the fourth door. He took out a pin, jiggled the lock. Held open the door. Max stepped inside. Krook followed, closing the door behind him with surprising quickness, quietness and grace. The two men were standing in a small room. Just large enough for a flat blue sofa, with a broken back. The whole place was damp, cramped, unclean. More than that: an unhappiness clung to it. Infected the corners, the nooks and crannies. 'He stayed here,' said Krook.

'That what Madame Tulip told you?'

Krook nodded. 'She owns the place.' He shook his head. 'Apparently, when she was still a little boy – she's a, what's the term? Man who dresses up like a woman?' Max shrugged. The only Russian words he knew were derogatory.

Krook went on: '… well, back then, she had an encounter with the King down at the port. Scared her to death. That's how she knows what his tattoo looks like. An evil eye. On the back of his wrist.'

'He's cleared out now,' said Max, looking around.

Krook nodded. 'As of last night. Stiffed the girls, too.' He paused. 'That's what upset Madame Tulip so much that she called me.' Krook sighed. 'She's a little hysterical. But very reliable. A real businesswoman.'

Then Krook slapped Max on the back. Told him not to worry; he, Inspector Krook, was on the case now. Max could relax. Go to the beach.

Max nodded as they filed out of the room. He was thinking about Rose. How they could take a day or two. Just the two of them. Rent lounge chairs on the private beach. Hold hands under a red umbrella while the waves lapped. Order *borscht* and champagne …

Something caught Max's eye. On the ground next to the sad blue sofa. A shallow rectangular container. Open. Traces of white powder. Max froze for a moment. It was an empty tin. Of British breath mints.

# 66

Max reached the Gagarin just in time for the coffee break. He searched the white lobby. Found Mark Hope. Waved him over.

'You ok?' asked Mark Hope. 'You look kind of ... wasted?'

'Feel like I've been hit by a truck,' said Max. 'But actually, it's all my fault. Walked into a tram. Never mind – you get Rose home ok last night?'

Mark Hope smiled. Max wasn't sure he entirely liked that smile. For a moment, he considered punching Mark Hope. Just to make a point. '... she's a really sweet lady,' Mark Hope was saying.

'She upstairs?' Max said.

Mark Hope looked at him. 'No,' he said. 'She went on the tour. Of the orphanage. They left an hour ago.' Mark Hope hesitated.

'What?' said Max.

'She did, um, mention that ...' Mark Hope's eyes had found the ground. Stayed there. As if whatever he saw on that shiny white surface was so compelling, he couldn't possibly look back up. 'Uh,' he said, 'she said ... if you didn't join them, she was, um, going to, um, file for divorce.'

Max swore. He grabbed the conference packet out of Mark Hope's hand. Walked outside. Hailed a private car. Beat-up Nissan, black windows, cracked. Showed the driver the orphanage's address. The guy whistled. 'That's way out in the countryside. Very close to the sea. I gotta be home in an hour, otherwise I'd take you. My kid's birthday.' He smiled. 'Best thing is, you take a bus. I'll drop you.'

At the bus depot, Max made his way through grandmotherly flower-er sellers. Plastic buckets full of bright, spiked gladiolas. He boarded a yellow marshrutka. Inside, blue velveteen curtains with pompoms revealed a host of holy icons. Which, since the marshrutka listed distinctly to one side, was probably all that kept it from falling over.

## 67

'Ariadne, how old are you?' a young, bespectacled female volunteer asked.

The little girl's bashful grin lit up not only her face but her entire being, her whole small body. If she'd been a diva, she would have electrified a stage. As it was, the dark little room brightened. It was her moment, and she was thrilled. She held up her fingers. Two.

What a firecracker that little girl was! thought Max, as Rose squeezed his hand and smiled up at him. The caretaker moved on, introducing a dark-haired boy, smaller than Ariadne, with an enormous ball-shaped lump at the back of his neck. 'God!' said the little boy in a rasping voice. 'Damn!'

Max and Rose walked out into the hallway with the rest of the group. There were no lights on here, and no windows. The hallway was unusually tall and narrow – or maybe it just seemed tall because it was narrow. Painted blue, peeling.

Their group, like the others, was led by a volunteer psychologist. Among Grisha's new ideas to get the populace involved in governance were volunteer programs like this one, Max had read on the bumpy drive over. They passed another cluster of grey-suited conference attendees. 'We're just fifteen minutes from the beach,' said their volunteer. 'But we've been talking to these kids, and they've never seen the sea.'

They had never seen the sea ... Max thought of Dr Rabbit. An orphanage by the sea ... It was a long shot. Max squeezed Rose's hand. Inhaled the floral smell of her shampoo. Whispered, 'Be right back.'

Upstairs, Max found his way to the orphanage's offices. In the hallway outside, the orphanage matrons were milling around, obviously put-out. Usurped. Inside, a handful of serious, young volunteers were going through the place's papers. Doing impromptu due diligence. From their dark looks and muttered comments, it seemed they were finding a pretty impressive amount of graft. 'They collect money from the state each month for 500 children,' Max heard, as he strolled into the room. 'But when we counted, there were only fifty kids living here ...'

'The matron said she thought she could find some more children if she looked ...'

'What's that supposed to mean?'

'Who knows ...'

'And they're collecting salaries for 35 full-time employees ...'

'I counted five here today ...' The volunteers shook their heads in disgust.

Max opened the filing cabinet as if that was what God had put him on this earth to do. He always found this approach surprisingly effective: with the right attitude, almost anything was possible.

He flipped through the files. Papers and papers and papers. Children and children and more children. All these little lives, these tiny fates. '... So what I think,' an older, slightly cracked-looking male volunteer said while sidling up to Max, 'is that Grisha had better make it mandatory for every man, and woman, too, to take a class in how to be happy. That's the only way we're going to make our country strong ...'

'Uh-huh,' said Max, as his eye was arrested by the paper he held in his hand. *1962, January. Alexei Ivanovitch Lerner.* Max read further. *Adoptive family: Shturman.*

'... I think Grisha should be deposed if he won't help happiness!' concluded the volunteer.

'Yeah,' said Max. 'Absolutely.' The dates fit, thought Max. It all fit. He slipped the paper into his coat pocket. He would have to tell Rose about this later. What a stroke of luck it was that she made him come here. Max patted the paper. He wasn't sure what it meant, or how it would come in handy. But he had just learned something. Namely, that Ludwig Shturman, aka the Lion, was the biological son of Vanya Lerner, aka the King.

\*

When Max came back downstairs, he couldn't find Rose. The psychologists were smoking out front, talking to the bus driver. A frog had been flattened by a passing car. It lay covered in dust.

Max followed the labyrinth hallways to the back. Finally, through an open door, he saw Rose. In the dimly-lit toddlers' room, kneeling by a little bedside. Tucking in Ariadne.

The road seemed worse on that way back. Riddled with potholes. He remembered what Homily said about Mephisto's tenders. The hired van had no suspension. Every jolt ran from the pelvis to the teeth. Max took Rose's hand. There were tears in her eyes.

# 68

The weather had turned. The sky was overcast, the colour of mother of pearl. Then the sun burst out, before disappearing, again, behind the glowing haze. Maybe it was just the shirts, with their harvest flair, but the feel of autumn hung in the air. As if they could feel it, the metallic helium balloon clusters sagged a little.

Max was supposed to meet Rose in twenty minutes. At the Potemkin Steps. The only way he had got her to stop crying long enough to take her sleeping pills last night was by promising they would meet for lunch today. Talk over everything. Children, adoption – he'd been about to say getting a dog, but last time that had set her off all over again, which Max didn't understand, since she loved dogs. But ok.

Later, as Rose slept her artificial sleep, Max lay beside her. Staring up at the Gagarin's white ceiling in the dark. He was going to do everything differently from now on. He listened to her familiar, slightly ragged breathing, and made his plans: He was going to tell Dunkirk he was done. Or, well … He was going to take his name off the FORCE ONE list, then tell Dunkirk to go to hell. The idea filled him with delight. Followed by a dizzy, sickening fear. Max closed his eyes in the dark. Decided not to think about it.

*

In the morning, Rose left early: she was going to the Gagarin's spa. Then she said casually, her eyes still puffy with crying, that she thought she might sunbathe a little. At the beach. Or find a nice massage spot. Regardless, she said, she had to calm down before they could talk. Come back to herself. Max agreed. Wholeheartedly. When she left the little white room, he was relieved to have the morning to himself. He could get some work done … then he remembered his resolution of the night before. Take his name off the list. Buckle down. Get ready to be fifty percent of Team Rushmore. There was no work to do.

Fine, thought Max. He'd go downtown. Find something nice for Rose. A scarf, maybe. A hand-embroidered tablecloth. With a spring in his step, Max left the hotel and caught a taxi to the city centre.

The French Boulevard again. Overcast, now. The kid driving the car turned the music up loud. 'You hear about Darth Vader?' he asked.

'Uh,' said Max. 'What are you talking about?'

'The statue!' said the kid. 'They installed it last night. City centre. It was so cool! I filmed it with my buddies. They put it in the back of a truck, drove it around the city.'

'A statue of Darth Vader?' said Max.

'Yeah!' said the kid. 'I AM YOUR FATHER, and all that. Anyhow, on the truck, they had speakers. They played 'The Imperial March'. Super loud! Awesome.'

The car bucked as it hit a pothole. Whiplashed.

'Was that pothole there before?' Max asked.

The kid shrugged. 'Might be new. Anyway, the statue, it's got the safest wi-fi in the city. Password protected, dark-net safe, the whole works.'

\*

The streets here in the centre were crowded with men and women in traditional dress – white cotton *vyshyvanka* shirts. Embroidered at the neck and wrists to keep the devil out. Max remembered a young Russian politician he'd met one night in Ibiza. At a dinner party. She was swaying – the effects of Spanish white wine – and suddenly grabbed him by the lapel. 'Do you know,' she slurred, 'thadda eye've memorised every region in Ukraine?' He shook his head. 'Yesssir,' she said, 'show me a *vyshyvanka*, and I will tell you exactly which village it comes from.'

Max shook his head at the memory. He would make new memories now. Girls in old-fashioned hoop skirts strolled back and forth, selling candy. A young blonde woman with hollow cheeks rocked a baby, begging. Woman after woman passed in high heels and nothing but a thigh-high peasant shirt. That was when he had his brainwave. Not a scarf! Not a tablecloth. No, Max would get matching *vyshyvankas* for him and Rose. A sign of solidarity. To keep the devil out.

Twenty minutes later, shirts in hand, Max made his way to meet Rose. He would tell her about the Potemkin Steps: how they were built as a metaphor for life. They were built using a combination of steps and landings so that, when you stood at the bottom, it looked like a hundred small steps, one after another, that you would have to climb. But when you reached the top, and looked back, the steps disappeared. All you saw were a handful of broad landings. The big events. Rose would like that.

*

Primorsky Boulevard. The main pedestrian walk, with a stunning, almost unobstructed view. It ran out over the port, shaded by chestnut trees. Leaves were turning orange already. Everything was glowing: the sea, the sky, the families. A rainbow struck up, almost horizontally, next to the Hotel Odesa – an eyesore built right at the port in the late nineties. A huge, reflective-blue tower the locals had learned to ignore. When the elevators filled with water five years ago, the building was abandoned.

Max walked by a serious-looking boy. He was looking out at the sea. He lifted a bottle of Jack Daniels to his lips and drank deeply. Max looked again. He was no older than twelve. 'Aren't you a little young for that?' said Max. 'It's not good for your brain.'

Instead of staggering, the boy winked: 'Don't worry, it's just tea. However …' – his face clouded – '… you, sir, are the only person who has said something.' He glanced at a pair of police officers strolling past. 'Yet again, the conclusions I am forced to draw about the rule of law in my city are very negative.'

'Ok, then,' said Max, and kept walking.

Nearing the top of the Potemkin Steps, Max searched the crowd. There she was! Looking relaxed, her shoulders glowing. She was laughing at something. Mark Hope! Max frowned. Mark Hope was telling her a joke. Look at him! The way his face lit up when she laughed. Max felt something in the pit of his stomach. Get a grip, Maxiboy, he told himself. You're the one who asked Mark Hope to help Rose find a good spot to get to her massage. You're the one who asked him to help her find her way to the Potemkin Steps, afterwards.

'Rose-by-any-other-name!' Max said, stepping behind his wife. He took her shoulders in his hands. Inhaled the scent of coconut oil. Laundry detergent, hair shampoo and something tangy that belonged to her alone. He leaned in, kissed her cheek. He nodded at Mark Hope. 'Thanks for playing tour guide,' he said. Gruff. Cool.

'Mark is so great,' said Rose. 'He was just telling me that these stairs – we just walked up, and I see exactly what he means – were built as a metaphor for life! With the combination of steps and landings. When you're walking up, you just see each small step! But from the top, when you look back, all you see are the landings. Life's big events.'

Mark Hope blushed. 'I read it in the guidebook,' he said.

Max felt a twisting pain in his stomach, something like anger or regret. He was just on the brink of identifying the feeling more precisely when, out of nowhere, he heard a voice he recognised. '… you're on the dock now, right?' the voice carried on the breeze. From somewhere in the crowd. 'The skiff, that's right. Go with them …' Max spotted the face in the crowd. Piggy, well-fed. A snub nose and a glowing blue light in his ear. Max remembered his promise to Felix's grandmother. 'Hang on,' said Max. 'Rosie – I'll be –'

Then Max broke away, dodged through the crowd. The blue light disappeared through the bronze revolving door of the deep-bellied purple Londonskaya hotel. The door rotated. Max followed. Passed the uniformed attendants. Up the grand fading staircase to the second floor. Down the long high-ceilinged hallway. The old wooden floorboards creaked in protest under his feet. At the end of the hall-way, he used his credit card to pry open the plastic door. Made his way across a glassed-in elevated walkway. Down the stairs. A woman in yoga pants was passing on the other side of the cloudy plastic win-dow. He knocked, and she opened the door for him. Max speed-walked through the columns of Odesa's most exclusive fitness club, past the girls who worked there – they were all wearing tight black leather skirts – and through the front door. This let him out behind the opera house.

Max looked around. A glowing blue light. Going up the steps, towards the opera. Max hung back, now. Saw Felix turn onto De-ribasivka Street. The pedestrian way was more crowded than ever. Max followed at a distance. Past the horses with hearts shaved into their pelts. Past the horses with leopard spots shaved into their pelts. Three donkeys dressed up as sparkling butterflies. *Vyshyvan-kas* everywhere. Max looked down at his own sweaty dress shirt. Slipped one of the *vyshyvankas* over it. Hoped it did the trick; kept the devil out. Then he ducked. Tried to stay out of sight.

Past the city garden and an abandoned building with griffons. Past a cluster of silver and gold 'living statues'. Past a fountain that lit up in every colour of the rainbow. Now it was clear where Felix was heading.

The Passage. Of course.

Max followed, slowly. The place exuded a feeling of calm after the hectic, tacky pedestrian street. Beneath the glass-paned ceiling, female nudes raised their arms to the heavens as if to protect him; a handful of tourists posed for pictures by the long, mottled mirrors built into the plaster walls.

Behind an old piano, Max ducked into a Soviet-style tourist shop. Past the Lomonosov porcelain from St Petersburg. Past a seller of thick, handmade woollen gloves and socks. Past the flowered Rus-sian scarves – black and green and blue and purple. Here he found a spot at the window. Watched Felix enter Café Delicious.

Once Felix was safely inside, Max followed. He stood just outside the café's open door.

Max heard something murmured. 'What?' said the voice. 'Why?'

'The client wants her there. She's on board already.' That was Felix, thought Max. Rodion spoke next.

'But, why? What does Sima have to do with this?'

'Look, Rodik. We just have to do what he says. Otherwise Sima –'
Even from outside the café door, Max could hear the fear in Felix's voice.

'Otherwise Sima – what?' Rodion's voice was dangerous now.

'It's going to be ok,' said Felix. 'I'll take care of everything. After tonight, everything will change. We'll get a real lab, with real funding. Rodik –' Now Max thought he heard something heartfelt in Felix's voice. 'This technology will change the world. Make it a better place.'

Max heard some more arguing. Then he stepped back, behind a narrow pink column. As he pretended to be studying a handsome, hand-embroidered red tablecloth with matching napkins, Felix's grandmother's words came back to him. 'The King likes redheads.' And then, Fimka Fishman's innocent, handwritten notes: *Patient X recently learned about the existence of an adult daughter. Wants advice for how best to make contact.*

*

After Felix had gone, Max entered the café. It was empty. He locked the door behind him. Slowly opened the door to the back room. Rodion was making a phone call. No answer. He hung up. He turned, still frowning, and said, 'I'm sorry sir, we're closing now – oh, hi, Max! Sorry, we're –'

'Sima's in trouble,' Max said.

Rodion's blue eyes opened wide.

*

'It all started,' said Rodion, 'when Felix found the papers in the archive.' The two men were sitting at one of the café tables. Outside beyond the plate-glass window, the evening stole over the Passage slowly, almost artificially. Pink light merged with the pink of the arcades.

Rodion slumped against the dusky-rose wall. Reached out, picked a daisy out of a vase. Plucked a tender white petal. 'Felix showed me the papers,' Rodion said. 'I'm a biologist by training. Well, right away I could tell there was something special there. I told him I'd work on it. But we needed a lab, we needed equipment. Nothing fancy. Well, Felix – he's good at fundraising. We made the video, with Sima's eyeballs. That got things rolling. This American investor, he sent us $5,000. That's when Felix had his brainwave.' The petals were falling fast now. *She loves me, she loves me not*, thought Max.

'Felix came to me, right here in the café. He said, "Rodik! Who's the most famous person in Odesa?" "Grisha," I said. "Exactly," said Felix. "Grisha."' Rodion stopped plucking for a moment. He sighed a deep sigh of existential regret. Then he continued: 'And you know how Grisha's always shaking hands, and his hand is so distinctive, too? "Simple marketing," Felix said – "sure, a hand will sell. But Grisha's hand? That's a brand-name! A body part recognised throughout the world. God's Dolce and Gabbana," that's what he said to me.' Rodion shook his head. 'And, of course, he's right.'

'Yes,' said Max. 'Of course.'

'So,' said Rodion, miserably. 'We just went to one of the meet-and-greets. Where Grisha sits down for three hours and listens to a bunch of *babushkas*. It was really easy to get his DNA.'

There were only two daisy petals left. *She loves me? She loves me not?*

'It worked,' Rodion went on. 'That's the thing that's crazy. It really worked. And when the hand was ready, Felix took it away. Said he had to send the customer the goods. I didn't ask – I don't know what he did. But it seemed to work. Because next thing I know, we've got another $5,000, and I'm growing three, four different body parts. But Felix, he starts acting strange. Cagey. Then like he's scared to death. And now … now somehow Sima's involved.'

The daisy petals lay on the table. Only the sunny centre was left. 'I don't like it,' said Rodion, shaking his head. 'I don't like it one bit.'

'You shouldn't,' said Max.

Rodion looked up then. Straight at Max, with those clear blue eyes. 'What does he want with Sima, this "investor"?'

Max frowned as the words ran through his head, again. 'The King likes redheads.' *Patient X recently learned about the existence of an adult daughter.* Yes, thought Max. For a man like the King, kidnapping probably constituted a valid 'getting to know you' strategy.

'Do you still have the hand?' Max said. 'That's our ace in the hole. With that, we have leverage.'

Rodion shook his head. 'I went to the lab this morning before work, to feed the axolotls. And the hand –' Rodion was almost crying. 'The hand was gone.'

'You're a good man,' said Max. 'Don't worry, I'll look out for her.' He looked down at the second *vyshyvanka*. What had he been thinking? It was much too big for Rose. Not her style at all. Max tossed it on the table. 'For you,' he said. Rodion shrugged. Max looked at the petals strewn on the table. Remembered Sima's violet eyes when she talked about her friend. 'And it's none of my business,' Max said. 'But – I think she loves you.'

\*

Back outside, Max crossed Deribasovskaya to the City Garden. He took a seat on a bench, next to a teenage couple entwined in one another. On the other side of them sat an elderly pair, holding hands. A juggler stood in front of them. In the background, the lights of the fountain were constantly changing colour. The background noise – running water – was steady. A good place to make a phone call.

Max checked his watch. Then he dialled.

'Sandy Jones,' said a voice.

'Hiya Sandy,' said Max. 'Jim Dunkirk here. I've got kind of a – funny question.'

'Shoot, pardner,' said the scientist. 'Here in the salamander community, we like to say there's no funny questions.'

'Ok,' said Max. 'So, have I got this right? The idea is, if you could crack the code – the "axolotl gene" – you could figure out how to regenerate human body parts?'

'Yeah, in a nutshell. But we're a long way from that, still.'

'So, there's no chance that somebody's already cracked the code? Like, say, in the 1930s?'

'Well, no,' said the scientist. 'We're doin' genome sequencing. That's only existed for a coupla years.'

'Gotcha,' said Max. 'Does "Mexican nuns" say anything to you?'

'I mean, sure, there are stories,' said the scientist. 'That one in Mexico, that's one of 'em. And you're right, that legend, it started in the 30s. Round about.'

'Humour me,' said Max.

'Sure, pardner. So, there's this lake, oh in the middle of nowhere, Mexico. And in the centre of this lake, there was a little community of nuns.'

'Ok,' said Max.

'Supposedly, these nuns had discovered a way to grow back simple digits: fingers and toes. And at some point in the 1950s, a bunch of American pharmaceutical companies sent their representatives down there to get the recipe.'

'Any truth to it?' said Max.

'Nah,' said the scientist. 'They never found anything. If they had – the world'd be a real diff'rent place.'

'Gotcha,' said Max. He hesitated. 'So, basically, what you're saying is that it's impossible? That there's no way those nuns figured out how to grow body parts?'

There was a long pause on the other end of the line. Finally, the other man spoke. 'To tell you the truth, Mr Dunkirk, as a scientist – heck, as a man – I would say, nothin', and I do mean nothin', in this world is impossible.'

*

After Max hung up, he stared at the fountain for a while. Pink-green-blue-yellow-pink, in the deepening twilight. A fancy pigeon breeder wandered by. Tried to get Max to pose with a white bird with an enormous, frilled tail. Max shook him off. Then he slipped a new SIM card into his phone and dialled.

# 69

The Darth Vader statue was truly impressive in the gathering darkness: looming, solid, iron, black. Standing at its foot, dwarfed by the Dark Lord of the Sith, was Joe Homily. His white socks glowed a little, bright spots in the night.

The two men shook hands. Then they turned, looked up at the statue. 'Used to be Lenin,' said Homily. 'But when the Bonbon Baron called for the de-Sovietisation of public symbols, one of our local oligarchs bought the statue and had it melted down.'

Max shook his head. Homily shrugged; he went on in a lower voice, one more suited to the gloom of the evening. 'Guy's a typical Ukrainian success story – made millions with internet credit-card fraud.'

Homily and Max had been walking slowly away from the statue. In the cool, humid night, the city felt different. Lonelier, sadder. Like summer was over, and it was never coming back. Finally, Homily spoke. 'Max,' he said. His eyes held a kind of appeal, an importunity that Max didn't understand. 'Are you really sure you want to do this?'

Max nodded.

'The Vodka Option – I mean, if it's really him – he'll kill you if you lose.'

Max looked into Homily's eyes. 'Joe,' he said. 'I'm sure.'

Homily sighed deeply. 'Ok, then. The wife gave me a phone number. Let's go back to the statue, log onto the dark net, and I'll call.'

'You know what to say?' said Max.

'You've got important information about his child,' said Homily. 'And you want Grisha's hand.'

'Right,' said Max.

Homily looked at him, then, and the light of the distant streetlamps seemed to pool in his dark hazel eyes so that Max could see into them, like he was fishing.

'Max,' said Homily. 'What the hell is this? It really sounds bizarre. Even for you –'

Max looked for another moment into those two dark pools. Then he shook his head. 'Joe,' he said. 'It's better if you don't know.'

The two men reached the base of the statue. In the shadows, they could just make out young people perched all around, like giant pigeons. Checking iPhones, iPads, laptops. God only knew what they were up to, thought Max. Ukraine, after all, was the land of the dark net. Max glanced down at Homily's screen. 'DO YOU WANT TO JOIN THE DARK SIDE YES/NO', read the phone. 'YES,' chose Joe Homily.

'Wait –' said Max, before Homily dialled. 'Are you sure you want to do this for me? I don't want to get you in trouble.'

Homily nodded. Dialled. Walked a few feet away. Nodded. Spoke. Nodded. Hung up.

After that, it was done. Everything was planned. Tonight, Max would slip out of the conference's Farewell Dinner Dance in the Volga Room of the 'Intriguing Inna'. Then he would meet the King downstairs in the *Inna*'s Boomerang Room. Where – if Max survived the Vodka Option – the King was prepared to grant him an audience.

As they parted, Joe held Max's hand in his own sweaty palm just a little longer than necessary. Max wondered why.

\*

After he said goodbye to Homily, Max had just one more call to make. He ducked into the crumbling entryway of a house covered in caryatids. It was quiet, here. Out of sight. He had the nagging sensation, again, of being watched. Here, though, he was sheltered.

Then Max dialled a local number. Heard the phone being picked up. Pictured Inspector Krook cradling the large old-fashioned receiver on one shoulder while he poured himself a drink. 'He's on the *Inna*,' said Max. Then, in the most laconic terms possible, he outlined the plan for the evening: The Vodka Option, Max told Krook, was scheduled for ten thirty. Max heard a sharp intake of air on the other end of the line.

'Rushmore, you sure you know what you're doing?' Krook said, finally. 'The Vodka Option … you'll probably lose. And then – if it's really the King – if anything goes wrong at our end – and it's summer, it's vacation, it's going to be hard to get a decent team together at such short notice, it'll probably be me and a bunch of fools. Max, what you're doing. It's dangerous.'

'I've made up my mind,' said Max. 'Tell me: Who owns the *Inna*?'

Krook sighed on the other end of the line. 'Officially, it belongs to a couple of weapons dealers. *Legal* weapons dealers. Nice guys.'

'I see,' said Max. 'There's no way *legal* weapons dealers could afford to gold-plate a boat that big.'

'Exactly,' said Krook. 'We don't know who really owns it. But there's a rumour … it's an oligarch who served in the Soviet navy. Stationed on the *Maxim Gorky*.'

Max caught his breath. Krook continued: '… hated every minute of it. So when he made his money, and saw the *Gorky* was up for sale … he bought it. Plated it in gold. Made it his luxury yacht.'

'Who rents the suites out? The weapons dealers?'

'Yeah,' said Krook. 'They're in charge, it seems. Trying to make a buck. Kind of a floating hotel. Doing pretty well, too. There are shipments of fresh fruit and caviar going out to the *Inna* every day. Your ambassador, McClellen, he held a big to-do out there just last month.'

'Ok, Krook,' said Max. 'See you tonight.' He thought back to his conversation with Sandy Jones, axolotl researcher, and added: 'I don't want to get your hopes up. But this could be pretty earth-shattering.'

'Whatever you say, Rushmore. Just try not to get yourself killed.'

\*

Oh, Mr Smiley did not like this! The little supplies launch rocked back and forth in the dark. Black night, black sea; back and forth, and back and back and forth. Oh, no. The cat almost hissed as an invisible spray of Black Sea water washed up over the deck. He had never been out on the open sea before. Well, it was important to challenge yourself, especially with advancing years. Some cats did Sudoku. But a sea voyage! It was probably very good for the brain synapses, for keeping young.

But it was unpleasant. There was salt everywhere! Matting his fur. Mr Smiley shuddered. To distract himself, he thought about bats. A bat! Now that was a fine animal. Radar! Absolutely ingenuous. Yes, if – God forbid – Mr Smiley couldn't be a cat, he wouldn't mind being a bat ...

The launch rocked hard. Stopped. He heard footsteps and human grunting. Someone seemed to be tying the supplies launch to the yacht. Finally. Boots was a good lieutenant – he had scouted every part of the boat, already. At the last minute, Mr Smiley told his son, Vladislav, to send a message to Miss Kitty. An extra precaution. This was the first time he had entrusted Vlad with such a big responsibility.

The launch rocked again as it pulled up to the yacht. Mr Smiley crouched, ready to spring from his hiding place beneath the fresh fruits and vegetables. Then, if a cat can grin, Mr Smiley did: after all, he had taken careful note of where the caviar shipment was. When they got on board, he would refresh himself in style. After that, he would get to work.

# 70

Max made it to the dock just in time to catch the last transport to the *Inna*. Overhead, the night seemed to grow darker. As if a storm was approaching. Out of the corner of his eye, Max caught a glimpse of white. Fluttering, then disappearing into the shadows. Strange, he thought. But before he could investigate, it was time to board. He stood shoulder to shoulder with the other men in grey suits, as the little boat rocked up and down over the choppy sea.

They disembarked. Climbed up a set of broad stairs under the incredible crystal chandelier from the magazine photo. In real life, it looked tawdry. A spill of sequins.

Upstairs, the Volga ballroom had been redecorated recently, in tactful blue-grey. A sign at the entrance, by the buffet, announced that the special guest tonight was the legendary band The Time Travelers, visiting from St Petersburg. Max was distracted from his plan for a moment – long enough to be impressed. The Time Travelers were one of the seminal underground rock bands in Leningrad, philosopher poets who, some said, wrote lyrics so powerful they helped bring down the Communist regime. Max had always wanted to see them live ... back to business, Maxiboy!

He scanned the room. Grey suits and more grey suits. Blue-grey tables, blue-grey floral arrangements. Where was Rose? Max checked his watch. The timing was good. Just enough time, not too much. He breathed deeply. Remember Trilby's advice: 'You have to really *feel* your body.'

Onstage, the band was warming up. Max wandered over as they struck up their first song. They were greying, of course. But spritely, still. Now they were in danger again, thanks to their non-conformist texts. The current Russian regime was persecuting them, this time.

Another glimpse of white caught Max's eye. Long blond ponytail, a familiar white shirt. Where did he go? Max scanned the room. Saw that all the servers were wearing traditional Ukrainian *vyshyvankas*. Max took a glass of water from one of the trays.

Just then the lead singer launched into one of The Time Travelers' biggest hits of the 70s, 'Time is a Field You Can Walk Across'. Max watched, fascinated. What a song! As the legend sang, Max noticed that there was something familiar about him. As if Max had met his older brother, or an uncle of his …

As the song ended, Max looked around. None of the grey men had so much as glanced up from their dull conversations. Cretins. The next song was a cover of another underground band's smash hit from the 80s. 'Gertrude.' The singer put his mouth to the microphone, and crooned:

> Don't drink the wine, Gertrude!
> Don't drink the wine!

All of a sudden Max had a brainwave. 'Don't drink the wine.' Of course! This was the missing piece. His half-cocked plan suddenly seemed as if it might work. But first, he had to find Trilby.

Max looked around. Grey men. Grey suits. Where was Alan Trilby? Cocktails, cocktails, cocktails. Max moved through the room, searching. 'It's a little funny,' he heard a local say, 'to hold an anti-corruption conference's final dinner in a place like this …'

'We never come here,' added his friend. 'It's basically the most oligarch-y place in the whole city …'

In the corner. Rose, in a low-cut summer dress. Deep in conversation with an elderly man with a face like a dead animal. She was smiling, nodding. 'Uh've been in Donetsk training some of these fine boys,' the man was saying.

Oh God, thought Max. Poor Rose. He should save her … but there was no time …

Just then, Mark Hope glided over and stood behind the military man. Rolled his eyes. Rose smiled with relief. Introduced Mark

Hope to the military man, who nodded then went on talking as if Mark Hope wasn't there. 'Uh kin tell you,' he said, leaning in conspiratorially, 'you have got to be on the ground to be makin' decisions about, say, providin' weapons.'

Max moved off, searching the round tables. Laden with fish, mayonnaise, slices of beef. Blue-grey candles. Where was Trilby?

'Max!' – it was Rose.

'Hi sweetie, look, I ...'

'Yeah, yeah, I know,' her eyes narrowed. 'You're working.'

'I really am ...'

'Sure. I just wanted to tell you before I forgot – the doctor called before I left. Your results got mixed up with somebody else's. You're not allergic to cats.'

'Hey, that's great!' – Just then, Max spotted Trilby. 'Look sweetie ...'

Max made a beeline for Trilby, deep in conversation with the ambassador from one of the EU's olive-oil nations, who was still sporting a red silk bowtie. '*Casablanca* was the most excellent propaganda. We need Hollywood to help us again! We should not allow a crazy man in a cave in Afghanistan to exercise more soft power than we do ...' Max pulled Trilby aside. Ten minutes to go until the meeting with the King.

'Alan,' he said. 'I need you.'

'My dear Maxwell, you know I can't get you a position at Chatterley House. You simply have to go through channels.'

'No –' said Max.

But Trilby spoke right over him. 'Your lovely wife already asked me if I could help with your – situation. But my dear man, my hands are ...'

A quick wave of chagrin washed over Max. Rose was trying to get him a job? Followed by a wave of pleasure – Rose was trying to get him a job! Then the urgency of the situation blocked everything else out. 'Listen to me,' said Max. 'I need you. Now. It's a drinking contest, and the stakes – I'll explain later – they're high. You're the only one who can help me.'

Trilby paused. Smiled under his felt hat. 'Maxwell Rushmore, are you saying what I think you're saying?'

'Come on! I'll tell you about it in the hallway. In private.'

'My dear man,' said Trilby, 'Are you admitting, after all these years, that I can out-drink you?'

Max stared at him. 'Alan!' he said, finally. 'There was never any question. You're the best! You were always the best. For God's sakes, come on!'

Trilby smiled for a moment. Then he pulled his hat down a little further over his head and followed Max out of the room.

They passed Rose on the way. The military man had attached himself to her. 'Don't get me wrong, I love women,' the military man was saying. Leaning in too close, with his dead animal face. Max should really step in. 'If I had a wife like you at home, I'd be on the ground, worshippin' ...' As Max watched, Mark Hope ducked around the general's elbow to stand sentry, close to Rose.

In the doorway, Max motioned Mark Hope over. 'Mark – take care of Rose. Make sure she gets home alright. In fact – sleep in the room with her. Not with her – but on the floor. Please.'

Mark nodded. 'Aye aye, captain,' he said. He leaned in conspiratorially. 'I think the singer from the band was hitting on her,' he said. 'He kept asking her if she liked wearing diamonds. But I pretended to be her husband, and he backed off!'

'Uh, good,' said Max. 'I guess.'

# 71

'Gold-plating your yacht!' Trilby was saying as the men concluded their tête-a-tête in a niche outside the Volga Room. Max had explained everything as quickly as possible. Trilby seemed positively titillated by the impending Vodka Option. 'Really very bold, the gold-plating. Though perhaps not in the absolute best of taste.'

'Good luck, Alan,' said Max.

'Oh,' said Trilby. 'Luck has nothing to do with it.'

The other man stuck an unlit pipe between his lips and set off down the hall. Towards the Boomerang Room.

Max turned back towards the music. Something had occurred to him. Now, he needed to find the blond ponytail in the *vyshyvanka* …

\*

… but the blond ponytail in the *vyshyvanka* was heading straight for him.

'Rodion! What the hell are you doing here?'

The younger man grinned. 'My buddy is in charge of the catering,' he said. 'He told me when to catch the last transport out here.'

'Yeah,' said Max. 'Now what I am supposed to do with you?'

'That's easy,' said Rodion. 'You're going to take me with you. And I'm going to make sure we save Sima.'

Max looked into those resolute blue eyes and made a decision. 'Fine,' he said. 'Come with me.'

Then, instead of following the path taken by Trilby, Max led them down a service hall. In the middle of the gangway, he stopped. Felt with his fingers. Took out a wine opener he had nicked from the buffet. Slit the wallpaper, in the shape of a door. Then he searched for the button that opened the door. The door popped open. It would lead, he knew, to the kitchenette at the back of the Boomerang Room.

Because, while Max had never been on the 'Intriguing Inna' before tonight, in 1996 he had spent six weeks working as a cabin boy on the *Maxim Gorky*.

## 72

Trilby – as he recounted later – was met by an armed guard and led to the Boomerang Room, formerly the captain's cabins, which had been untouched since the *Maxim Gorky*'s virgin launch in 1969. 'Think, oh, I don't know, *Octopussy*, and you've got a pretty good idea of the décor,' Trilby liked to boast afterwards.

There, in a swirling red-and-brown-carpeted lounge, he was confronted by 'a little old man'. 'Well,' he would say, 'not little, per se. But dried out. Sucked in. Smaller than he was – if you know what I mean.' Trilby's listeners always ate it up. They were always the same: a pack of young men who hadn't yet realised that there was no future in this relatively glamorous career, that they should go and work for Wall Street or as government lobbyists if they wanted any kind of steady job. To a one, these men were too young to have seen *Octopussy*. Nonetheless, as Trilby told this story in years to come, they listened, glasses poised, breathless: 'And as I entered, this "little old man" rolled up his shirtsleeve. Slowly – very slowly. And …' Trilby would pause here. 'What did I see?'

Here, Trilby always stopped talking to make eye contact. Whether the hotel lobby was in Minsk or in Devonshire, he went around the circle of young men, once. Looking them each in the eye before saying: 'A tattoo. Blue – prison-made, of course. Shoe polish and a hot needle. An evil eye. Worn only by the highest rank of criminal. And so,' Trilby always continued, 'I proceeded with caution.'

*

Alan Trilby was all he had ever claimed to be. And more. When he sat down at that table, Trilby was ready. A lifetime of practice. A certain *je ne sais quoi*. The King threw back a shot. Trilby matched him. A man approached, all in black. Brought a new bottle. The King drank. Alan Trilby followed suit. And so – the night went on.

*

Meanwhile, Max and Rodion crouched side by side in the kitchenette. Waiting.

In the next room, the clink of glass on glass continued unabated. Until finally, there was a soft thud. Max's heart jumped.

'My dear sir!' – it was Trilby's voice. Max breathed a sigh of relief.

'Yes, Mr Rushmore?'

'I regret to point this out, but your cranium touched the table. Have you decided to forfeit?'

A gravelly voice. 'As you can see, I have recovered myself. I am not as young as I was. But it doesn't matter. Let us continue.'

They drank to Russia.

They drank to Odesa.

They drank to Ukraine.

They drank to brotherhood.

They drank to Count Tolstoy.

They drank to war.

They drank to peace.

They drank to *War and Peace*.

Then Max heard Trilby's voice. Calm. Right on time. 'Mr King,' he began, 'if I may call you that. I understand that you wish to create a – how shall we say – disruption. Tomorrow, after the football game.'

There was no answer except for the clink of glasses. Max held his breath. This was exactly what he had instructed Trilby to do. But now that it was happening, the degree of risk seemed unconscionably high. 'I understand,' Trilby's voice again, 'that this is an attractive idea for a man like you. Ruined by Grisha. Cast out of Georgia. Your businesses destroyed. A riot – a civil war – the Russians marching in – well, it would be the end of Grisha, wouldn't it.'

The silence was deafening. Max felt Rodion tense beside him. Then Max almost jumped out of his skin: there, sitting at his side, a cat had appeared. A fat, dirty cat. With mottled grey fur and a terrible-looking scar running across his face. He, too, seemed to be straining to hear what was going on in the next room.

Suddenly there was a loud crash. Several sets of feet. Oh, no. This was bad. This was very bad. Max signalled to Rodion to stay where he was. Max ducked beneath the kitchenette's counter, emerging at the far end of the Boomerang Room. Crouched beneath a velour love seat. It was very dark in here, he saw. The only illumination came from the large window, which looked out over the city lights. Twinkling in the distance.

The guard with the Kalashnikov had returned, trailed by three figures. The first was well-fed, with a piggy look and a blue light that glowed from his ear. Next came a pretty strawberry blonde, wearing a short pink skirt and tennis shoes. Sima. Then – Max swallowed hard. A big, blowsy man. In a faded polo shirt and Tevas. Disaster.

The gravelly voice thought so, too: 'Mr Rushmore,' it said. 'As you see, you have been betrayed. Of course, I thought you were a spy when you relayed to me that you were a sex tourist. Thankfully, Joe Homily is married to the daughter of the brother of an old associate of mine. He explained that you're a mercenary. That the CIA isn't behind you. That you know a lot – too much – and that there's no one to protect you. No one even knows you are here! That's why I thought it was a good idea to bring you to the ship tonight. You haven't got the whole story, which means you haven't sold it yet. And that means that after this little exercise – which I must say you are acquitting with far more aptitude than I would have given you credit for – my people can shoot you and drop you over the side of the boat. If there are any fish left in the Black Sea – which is doubtful – they will eat you.' The gravelly voice paused. 'A man like Joe Homily, there's not much he won't do for money.'

Max felt his stomach leave his body. Homily was going to say, 'That's not Max Rushmore.' And then they were all as good as dead, right now. No time to think of a Plan B. But to Max's surprise, Homily didn't betray Trilby. Instead, he turned to Alan Trilby and said, 'Hi, Max.'

'Well, hello, Joe,' said Trilby.

'I'm – real sorry,' said Homily.

'I understand,' said Trilby. 'Perfectly.'

Sima's voice interrupted. 'Felix! What's going on here?'

Max heard the sound of velour seats moving. The gravelly voice again. Somehow very frightening now. 'Mr Rushmore, I thought you and I would be finished by now. I underestimated your stamina.'

Trilby lowered his head modestly.

'You're a dead man. So it doesn't really matter what you hear now.' The gravelly voice. 'Now, let us take some time for the sweeter side of life. Sima, my darling girl, we can finally be together!'

'What are you talking about?' said the young woman. In the distance, Max thought he heard footsteps. Krook? The sound died. No Krook. Where was he? It couldn't be long, now. Max looked over. Rodion had crept silently to his side. Shit. Max prayed that Rodion would sit still, not do anything stupid. Then Max decided he couldn't risk it: Rodion was a hot-blooded type, and there was no knowing when he might decide to take matters into his own hands. Quietly, Max reached up and pressed the young man's neck. A look of surprise showed in his eyes, then he slumped to the floor. Max mouthed a silent apology. Still, no harm done – the kid would be right as rain in ten, fifteen minutes. By then, Krook and his men would be here and everything would be over.

Max just had to make sure nothing happened before Krook arrived. No shooting, no fighting, no killing. The gravelly voice was still speaking … 'you see, my dear, I am your father.'

A scream sounded through the carpeted room. 'Liar!' shouted Sima. Poor Sima, thought Max. There was a scuffle, and when Max looked up from behind the velour chair again, he saw that the guard with the Kalashnikov had twisted both the girl's arms behind her back. Brute.

'Come here,' said the gravelly voice. 'My dear, come closer.'

Max heard the sound of another scuffle. He took advantage of the noise to creep behind another velour chair. Now he could see: The guard had pulled Sima closer to the King. The King, meanwhile, had lifted his leather eye patch. The scent of breath mints filled the lounge.

'What?' said Sima.

'That's right,' said the King. 'I have the exact same birthmark as you do. A black heart, beneath my left eye. Believe me now?'

Sima stood, unmoving. Shock.

The old man turned to Trilby. 'Of course, Mr Rushmore, you are completely right. I have a rather wonderful idea for how to ruin Grisha. It is so wonderful, you will not believe it – and it is so wonderful that if you were going to survive the evening, well! Every country in the world would want you working for them, if you could report to them what you are about to see here.'

'I doubt that's true,' muttered Trilby.

The King turned to Felix, barked: 'Give me the hand.'

Max slowly crept a little bit further forward. He hadn't told Trilby about the hand, of course. It would have sounded incredible. Now, as Max watched, Felix passed a plastic bag to the King. The King reached inside. Max saw Alan Trilby's eyes open wide, then just a little bit wider, as the King pulled out a fully-formed man's hand. Marked by a distinct wine-red stain, shaped like the state of Florida.

'You know,' said the King, placing the hand on the table, then looking up at the assembled group. Trilby removed his hat, wiped his brow, rubbed his eyes. 'This is fate. You see, my father was the one who invented this technology, for regenerating body parts. He was going to save mankind, starting with the Soviets. In thanks, the Soviets shot him. I was just a boy. Before he left, he told me to hide the papers if the soldiers came. So I did. In the old book of my mother's, in the synagogue. Later, after the occupation ended, I tried to find them again. But by then the Soviets had turned the building into the archives. And my father's papers, they were somewhere in there, lost. A needle in a haystack.'

There was silence. 'It doesn't matter that you didn't bring the papers, Felix,' said the old man. 'I know where you've stored them. In your lab, in Pearl Number 4. I'll get them in the morning. In the meantime, there is something just as important that I must do. Sima, darling.'

'My father died at sea!' she said.

'Angelina was always a pretty little liar,' said the King. 'Your mother kept your existence secret from me. But I won't punish her. After all, I suppose she did think I was dead! Still, before you and I sail away, I just have one piece of unfinished business, here in Odesa.'

He looked at the hand on the table.

Now Trilby spoke. 'What are you going to do with that?'

'Very simple,' said the King. 'Tomorrow, after the soccer game, when the pro-Ukrainians and the pro-Russians start to fight, I will throw Grisha's hand into the crowd. That should start a stampede. And he will lose control of the city. Perhaps there will even be a civil war. Grisha will be humiliated. It will be the end of everything for him. By then,' he turned to Sima, 'we will be far away.'

'I'm not going anywhere with you,' said Sima.

'Oh, but you are, my dear. You see, I lost my only child, my son. But now I have you.'

Max felt all the muscles of his body contract: the grey cat was sitting next to him again. What was this cat doing here? It didn't matter: Max knew what he had to do. But before he could put it into action, he heard Trilby's voice.

'Dear Mr Lerner,' said Trilby. In a split second, Max reconstructed what he had just seen: Trilby had reached inside the felt hat lying upside down on the table. Now, he was brandishing a tiny pistol, no bigger than Mark Hope's unlined palm, at the old man's head. A miniature Colt. Built in 1873 as a gift for Wyatt Earp. So Trilby hadn't been able to resist nicking it … 'Thank you so much for the explanation. In just a few moments, the Odesan police will be boarding. As I understand it, they've been watching you for some time. Now, if we can all simply remain calm, everything will soon be settled.'

Just then, a second guard stepped from the velour curtains behind Trilby. He brought the butt of his rifle down over Trilby's hat. Max's colleague stood for a moment. Swaying. Then he crumpled.

Max was about to step forward, when a high-pitched scream, like a banshee, sounded through the lounge. A crash, as a tall, very pretty redhead wearing a spangled red skirt strode into the room. Her legs were even longer in real life, Max noted, than they had looked on the cover of the *Odesa Preview*'s special BOATING! issue. 'Vanya!' she screamed. 'Who is that girl? What is she doing here? Do you think I'm stupid? Do you think I won't find out when you bring my replacement on board?' Max heard the sound of glass breaking. 'Anyway, you bed-wetting old man! I'm leaving you!'

The King stood. Swayed slightly. Steadied himself. Then he rolled up his sleeve. Max caught a glimpse, now, of the evil eye. Jesus Christ, Krook! Where are you?

'Kill me if you want!' screamed the girl.

'Oh, Inna,' said the gravelly voice. He was holding a pistol now. A regular-sized one. He lifted it. Oh no, thought Max. This is bad. This is very bad. Where are you, Krook? From the corner came a sudden flurry of movement. A flash of red necktie. Max couldn't believe his eyes: it was Felix! Felix, mustering all his courage! He lunged at the old man. He was going for the gun. He had it! Was Felix going to save the day? No! The guard was too fast. He got the gun and hit Felix on the head. The young man crumpled to the ground. The guard returned the gun to the King. He looked down at Felix, the way you'd look at a buzzing fly. Then, he reached down, took hold of that red necktie …

Max remembered his pledge to Felix's grandmother. This was his moment. He just needed to keep the King distracted long enough for the police to come. He stepped out of the shadows. 'Stop!' he said. He pulled the paper from the orphanage from his pocket. 'You think you've found your only child,' said Max. He had to speak quickly but clearly to make the King listen. 'Your daughter. That may be! But you also killed your only living son,' said Max. 'Yesterday.'

The King froze. His face turned grey. Max stepped forward. The guard lifted his Kalashnikov, but with his eyes, the King made him lower it.

Max walked to the table, stepping over Trilby. Homily hung his head. Max held out the papers from the orphanage. With a trembling hand, the King took the paper. Read it. Looked around the lounge with an expression of utter despair. Just then, the lights of the city flickered, through the window. Once. Then they went out entirely.

There was only blackness, all around. Footsteps pounded over-head. The King grabbed Sima. Before Max could follow, something hit him over the head. As he looked up, he noticed two things. The first was a good-looking young man in a black police uniform. As this young man brought his baton down on Max's head for a second blow, he smiled. A nice smile, prominent dimples ... Max slipped from consciousness into darkness ...

*

... The Odesite with one eye had taken Sima by the arm, twisted it behind her back. Bastard! Now, in the darkness, he was dragging her to the ship's hold. Mr Smiley thanked God that he had overcome his hatred of water and had sneaked on board this monster ship. Events were even more serious than he'd imagined!

Now, on his silent paws, he followed the man and his captive – the lovely Sima! Mr Smiley's one and only! – down to the inflatable life rafts. The Odesite with one eye climbed in. Dragged Sima along. Oh, that man didn't care if he lived or died. That was dangerous, very dangerous! Now or never, thought Mr Smiley. Now or never. The cat gathered all his love and courage into a great big bright ball. Then he jumped.

He landed in the inflated raft just as the Odesite unhooked it from the monster boat. Rain was pouring down, the waves were washing over the side; the Odesite had pushed Sima into a corner with one arm and was guiding the boat into the open waters with the other. In the distance, the city lights flickered back on. For just one moment. Then the lights went back off, and all of Odesa disappeared. As if it were the end of the world.

Mr Smiley had to act fast. Sima was a good swimmer. Mr Smiley unsheathed a claw – his most powerful claw, the one that had mur-dered Cheeky B – and he plunged it into the plastic raft.

Rain fell harder, pounding down, blinding. They were sinking, fast. Death by water. The worst thing that can happen to a cat. The King slipped, fell. Went under. Then the cat could not see the King anymore. But through the rain and the water and the darkness, Mr Smiley watched Sima realise what was happening. Saw her slip out of her shoes.

Swim, my girl! thought Mr Smiley, concentrating all his energies. Swim! Swim to safety! Swim! Swim!

# Epilogue

You know what, Pan Sholem Aleichem?
Let's talk about something more cheerful.
Have you heard any news of the cholera in Odessa?

Sholem Aleichem, *Hodl*

## 73

'So, Max,' began the young man with the hangdog eyes, as he leaned forward in his chair. For some reason, you had to take your shoes off in the Couples Therapy waiting room and put on a pair of plaid slippers. There was a mountain of plaid slippers, in every size. Rose crossed her legs. She was wearing plaid slippers. Max was wearing plaid slippers. The therapist – Matt, that was his name – was also wearing plaid slippers. It was the plaid slippers Max hated the most. 'Rose says she feels like you don't listen to her. Rose remembers that, on the – the – uh, stairs –'

'The Potemkin Steps,' said Max.

'Thank you, Max, that's very helpful. The Podunkin Steps. Rose remembers that she tried to talk to you about adoption, and you – you "ran away". Literally, Rose says. I imagine …' Here the couples therapist ducked all the way forward to catch Max's eye, which was trained on his own left plaid slipper. It was a little too big. He wondered if it would fall off when he walked out. If the session ever ended, that is. '... What I imagine, Max, is that you felt uncomfortable. That, adoption, it's something that's hard to talk about.'

'Uh, yeah,' said Max. 'Plus, a work thing came up.'

The therapist smiled. 'Work is a very common refuge for men – women too, but more often for us men – when we're uncomfortable.'

'Yeah,' said Max. His mind wandered back to that night on the *Inna*. The total collapse of Pearl Number 4 into the catacombs had shut down the city's electrical grid. The accident struck at just the right moment: the sudden darkness provided the perfect cover for Krook and his men. Of course, Max only learned about the collapse and the electric outage – it was the biggest disaster of its kind, ever – when he woke up with a big lump on his head on a cot in Inspector Krook's office, the following afternoon. To his surprise, a sheepish Fishman was there, looking dishevelled. He performed a cursory examination, pronounced Max healthy enough, and went on his way.

Krook shook his head. Then he told Max that Fishman had stormed into the police station the night before, raving; there was a crook in the police, and Max was going to die. The doctor had refused to say where he'd got this information. Finally, they stuck him in the drunk tank. In the morning, when he heard Max was alive and well, Fishman calmed down. Insisted on seeing for himself – he was a medical doctor, after all – that Max was unharmed. 'That's why we were late to the boat, last night,' Krook had said, shaking his head. 'These artistic types!'

The raid had been a failure, all things considered: Lerner, if it really was him, had disappeared. Probably drowned. They would see in the next weeks if a body washed to shore. Then they'd know more. They didn't find a hand.

As for Felix, when he came to he started crying and took all the blame for the bombing of Angelina's restaurant. Further questioning made it clear, however, that he was just a pawn. It was Luddy 'the Lion' Shturman who had planned the attack, to keep Sima from displaying the eyeballs where the King might see them.

Sima was safe: Rodion was just regaining consciousness, as the King dragged her to the life raft. He had followed, groggily. Roused the crew of the supplies launch. Together, they picked up Sima as she swam to shore. Pulled her out of the water. Along with a cat, apparently.

By the time Max woke up, the soccer game had come and gone. There was the usual fighting, but nothing dramatic. Max gave Krook the diary to give to Sima. Then the two of them drank vodka and toasted fate.

When Max got back to the hotel, Natasha called. He had left his number at the Gagarin, just in case. She was back early from the dacha. Did they want a ride to the airport?

Max said, sure. Rose wasn't speaking to him, and he thought maybe the presence of a third person would force her hand. Natasha picked them up in her little French car. She and her fiancé had taken a trip to a sanatorium in the east. It was supposed to be healthy! But then her fiancé overdosed on berries and mineral water, and his face puffed up! Twice its normal size! 'Really?' said Rose. 'Yes,' said Natasha. From then on, the two of them got along like a house on fire. They even started joking about how Max had booked a room in a brothel by accident. They both rolled their eyes.

'And did you hear,' Natasha had said as the airport building came into view, 'that Grisha and Mephisto gave a joint press conference this morning?'

'No,' said Max.

'Yeah,' she said, 'apparently they're teaming up. To try to get Eurovision to be held in Odesa next year. Even though it's already been decided it'll be in Kyiv.' But that was nothing, she said, compared to the other latest rumour that the Bonbon Baron's most serious challenger in the upcoming election was the star of a hit TV series about a regular guy who accidentally becomes president of Ukraine. 'What a country!' she said, with that tinkling laugh …

'Max,' said Rose.

'Huh?' said Max.

'I don't feel like you're really trying.'

'Now, Rose,' said the therapist.

\*

'A-a-a-a-a-asshole!'

'A-a-a-a-a-asshole!'

A dim screech penetrated Mr Smiley's mid-afternoon nap. He rolled over, stretched, yawned. 'A-a-a-a-a-asshole, A-a-a-a-a-asshole, A-a-a-a-a-asshole,' echoed like a lullaby. He hummed along. 'A-a-a-a-A-a-a-a-A-a-a-a.' Then the noise stopped and there was quiet. Just the sounds of the kitchen: spoons and bowls and whisks and chopping blocks, as Angelina prepared the day's *forshmak*. Mr Smiley's belly rumbled. Should he get up and wander in? Make sure the *forshmak* was up to snuff today?

He heard the sound of water sluicing, and he shuddered. Sima came out, petted him. 'Neptune, Neptune, don't shake. It's just a little water. Stop shaking, little kitty-cat.' Mr Smiley felt the tremors ease under Sima's soft hands. Ever since that night, water was anathema to him. It was a miracle he'd survived. He didn't know he could swim – another of his astounding qualities, apparently. He was choking on seawater. He was sinking. He paddled with his paws. He gulped air with his mouth. He used his tail as a rudder. A piece of wood had been his salvation. He clung to it.

Then that Rodion, the man with the green lizard back, came by in the little launch, the one that smelled of caviar. Sima was in it. Safe and sound. She spotted Mr Smiley. Pulled him out of the water. Clung to him! Said he was coming home with her. (In spite of the water, it was one of the happiest moments of Mr Smiley's life).

That night, Sima blow-dried his fur. Then she and Angelina nursed him back to health, with cream and *forshmak*. Now, this was his home.

The truth was, he had no other. It was one of the night cats who told him. One of the loyal ones, eyes matted with bugs and gunk. Mr Smiley's back-up plan had been his undoing: Vlad had a dinner date, so he sent an underling – a veritable kitten! – to warn Miss

Kitty. Of course the kitten garbled the message for Fishman. Which delayed the police. Which landed Mr Smiley in the water!

Then came Vlad's real treachery. While the old cat was recovering, that son of his, Vladislav, staged a coup! Now Vlad was in charge of the port. Cheeky B? He had been innocent. Mr Smiley rolled over in the sunshine. When a cat makes mistakes like that, he thought, that cat no longer deserves to be the cat boss.

Should he go in? wondered Mr Smiley. He heard another, masculine voice. Rodion. Well, Mr Smiley could understand Sima's choice. Rodion was young and strong and human. Simochka's laughter came wafting through the kitchen window. 'Yo hablo espanol,' she said. 'Yo tambien,' said her mate. This strange language was a new thing; Mr Smiley didn't quite know what to make of it.

The cat decided he wasn't quite hungry yet. He rolled over. Sometimes he dreamed about eating Jacques. He leaned over the grey bird, who was bound and trussed – but still alive – with a silver knife and a silver fork, like a human, and set about dinner.

Ah, how nice that would be. Putting an end to this racket. Once and for all …

From the restaurant's dining room, the cries began again:

'A-a-a-a-a-asshole!'

'A-a-a-a-a-asshole!'

Mr Smiley's tail twitched. Articulated a long lazy arc, like one half of the heavens held on the shoulders of Atlas, across the street.

'A-a-a-a-a-asshole!' cried Jacques.

But the cat had fallen asleep.